Cry for the Devil, Book 1

written and illustrated by Piper Sweeney

This book is dedicated to my Youtube subscribers. Thank you for believing in a piece of shit like me; otherwise, this book would still be in a 3 ring binder propping up my television and you'd be reading something else.

Xoxo,

Piper

Table of Contents

Tuesday, February 24, 2015
Philadelphia, Pennsylvania

Gasoline, dirty shoes, truckers who haven't showered in days. Can you think of a workplace filthier than a gas station? I'm not saying I have the *right* to complain. I knew it would be like this before I walked into this dump asking for a job application. Much to my dismay, I got the job last week. I committed almost every resume crime I could think of, including sloppy handwriting and no references, and they still hired me.

As usual, things didn't go as planned. All I wanted was to put in enough job applications to qualify for unemployment until I could find a tolerable bartending opening, but no. I just *had* to apply to the only business in town that has a harder time keeping nightshift employees than I have keeping a job: a gas station that had to change its name to "Wayspeed" for legal reasons. I would quit, but I can't count on getting anything better in time to pay the rent. That's what I get for taking my ex-roomie's advice and trying to cheat the system. Why did I think that would be a good idea? He's in *jail*. At this rate, I'm going to have to move back in with my parents in Allentown, and I'm 25 years old.

This job in particular is the worst I could've gotten, and now I wish I hadn't filled out my other job applications equally as badly. Maybe then I would've gotten the second-to-worst job possible. I like to consider myself a man who is strong of mind, but working here is giving me a germ phobia. Would it be unreasonable for me to start crying? I used to be an average guy. Now I'm an average guy who's been stricken with the obsessive need to scrub down everything in sight. The floor tiles? Dirty. The door handles? Dirty. The toilets? Dirty. The water? Also dirty. But nobody ever notices because they're distracted by the out of season Christmas decorations that are faded from years of sunlight.

There are even fewer customers here than I'm used to seeing on night shift, since the weather is below freezing and the streets are sheeted in ice. Tonight's consumers have consisted only of brave pedestrians and reckless drivers who think they're invincible. The most interesting my job ever gets is people-watching, which I'm technically supposed to do to catch shoplifters, so I'm pleased that the three people who *did* manage to make it here within the past few hours are on the unusual side. There are two teenagers, possibly stoned, looking through all the food like it's gold. The closest thing to a normal person here is a *definitely* drunk woman dancing through the aisles.

She's too adorable to be in a gas station called Wayspeed, or to be within fifty feet of me, but she's a peculiar girl in general. She's dressed head to toe in black, wearing a poofy dress under her frilly coat. Her long hair is black too, with pointed bangs that taper down in the center. She acts too peppy to have gotten back from a funeral, so I assume either A, she hated whomever it was that died, or B, she always dresses like this.

My daze is broken by the two teenagers, who, upon closer observation, are not baked. High on hormones, but 0% stoned. They dump a wide assortment of junk food onto the counter.

"Wow," one of them says. "Wayspeed. So fast. Much doge. Very gas station."

They cackle and high five. I have no idea what he's talking about, and I admit I'm uncomfortable. Are they making fun of me, or my workplace? Is that the same thing in retail?

After checking them out, I pump some hand sanitizer into my palms and rub my hands vigorously. Money has more germs than a household toilet, you know. I hear it can carry a flu virus for over two weeks, and I don't want to find out if that's true.

Two 1950's Christmas hits later, the drunk woman finally finds whatever she was looking for and pirouettes to the checkout counter. She'd be about 5'8" without her heels, but something about her is small and delicate; it must be her wispy figure. She's just as cute up close; she looks like a Victorian porcelain doll, with her pale skin, big eyes, and little nose. But her light gray irises give her this alert, natural look of surprise that makes her come off as kooky or empty-headed.

I know women love cute shoes, (my older sister is especially shoe-crazy) but heels aren't meant for drunk-dancing. She finishes her dance with a nasty fall to the floor. It isn't a graceful fall, but she takes it in stride. I walk around the counter and help her up, trying not to think of where in this store her hands have been. As if it isn't bad enough for her to touch that filthy, industrial floor tile. The gray dirt stands out against her black attire.

"Are you a cosplayer?" I ask. "The way you're dressed kind of reminds me of the dark Chii from *Chobits*."

Okay, in retrospect, that was an annoying question. I wouldn't *dare* compare a sober woman to a cartoon character, and what's worse is that I just implied I watch anime. Looking like a baby-faced fourteen-year-old and coming off as a socially awkward nerd gives me the luxury of usually being in line as long as I'm sincere, if only because I'm instantly ruled out as a potential threat. I'm horrible at flirting, and asking dorky questions like this is the closest I ever come. My most impressive skill is mimicking a cat meow, a useless talent I've been honing since I was five.

"Nope, mate," she slurs, wagging her index finger. "*Goood* taste in anime though."

If my comment bothers her, she doesn't point it out. She says something about Misa Amane from *Death Note*, but slurs too much for me to understand whatever it is; maybe something along the lines of "Misa Misa is my anime idol."

She brushes a strand of hair away from her face and tosses it over her shoulder. She smiles and drops a three-count package of condoms onto the checkout counter, ending my internal debate on whether it's morally correct (or even logical) to ask a drunk girl for her number.

I ring up her order in silence, trying not to look at her. It's difficult because her protruding eyes are burning a hole into my forehead. There isn't anything particularly interesting about me, so I'm not used to being stared at.

"Four o' five," I say.

Deep in thought, she tilts her head a few degrees to the left. "Past four o'clock already?"

"The price, ma'am," I say. "Not the time."

"Oh, okay! Gotcha, sailor!" She salutes me US Marine-style, and digs through her coffin-shaped purse. She reveals a wallet that was stuffed to the limit with cash. "Uh oh! I'm out of small bills. Do you have change for a hundred dollar bill?"

"No," I say, wondering what a rich, white girl is doing at the trashiest gas station in West Philadelphia. "We don't keep a lot of money in the register after eight."

"Oh..." She glances at her feet before handing me a crisp, new one hundred dollar bill. "Just pocket the change."

"What?" I say. "Are you sure? That's a lot of money."

"Nah. I'll just consider it my good deed for the day." Great, I'm charity.

She mutters something under her breath that sounds like *it's not like it's really my money anyway*. Unsettling, but when I rub the counterfeit detector marker over the bill, nothing happens. All is good, and if a 100 is the smallest bill in that fat wallet, she's not going to miss it in the morning.

"Do you want a bag?" I ask.

"Yeah, thanks."

Satisfied that it's real, I accept the money, making a mental note to put $4.17 from my own, worn out wallet into the cash register when she leaves. Any other day I would cling to my pride and refuse the money, but my electric bill is late. I don't want to sit in the dark eating uncooked Ramen blocks all week until pay day.

Once I hand her the bag, which she almost drops, she looks the receipt over. She holds it closer to her face and runs her finger across the top.

"Your name is William?"

"Yeah."

"That's strange," she says. "I could've sworn I knew your face from somewhere, but I don't recognize the name. Maybe you know mine? I'm Arete Konstantinou. It isn't a common name. I'm Greek."

The way she rambles and slurs, it's difficult to understand her. It's hard to trust her too, since she's drunk and doesn't look Mediterranean. Her skin has an alabaster quality I'd expect from a Swedish or Irish person, for example. I'd bet my $95.83 on her being Northern European. Then again, nobody would look at me and say "I bet that pale kid with the golden blond hair is half Mexican," so I decide not to question it any further. After all, being pastier than most Latinos comes with its own set of issues. I've been accused of faking it for oppression points, whatever that means. My jealous cousin tells me I'm not a real Latino because I have "white privilege." Back in high school, some girl who didn't know me called me racist for wearing a sombrero during my class presentation, and even though my classmates heckled her beyond belief for her mistake, I felt embarrassed for weeks.

My older sister got through it by giving everyone the finger and reminding everyone in fluent Spanish that she was born in Mexico, but I didn't have any of that going for me so I handled it the coward's way. I flipped my mother's and father's surnames around just because of the mixed reactions I got when I said my last name was Quiñones. It's not that I identify as white now; I'm not sure if I even believe white is a real thing because of how often the definition changes or varies from person to person. I just prefer not to identify myself to others. Brown sounds more legit and I don't have to give my life-story to everyone who sees my ID. I feel a slight pang of guilt for doing to her what so many others have done to me. Arete could be lying, but it's there in her name. Not that being rude was ever an option since I'm at work.

I shake my head. "No, ma'am. Doesn't ring a bell."

"AIR·EH·TEE," she says, as if speaking louder is going to make me remember something that never happened.

"Nope, sorry."

"Are you sure, mate? Is it Pitt Street... or is it Christmas?" Arete laughs at her own... joke? I'll spend the rest of my life wondering what she's talking about.

"Yeah, uh... You know, I have some pretty average features, maybe I just look like someone you went to middle school with."

"Oh... I guess I'll be on my way then."

She looks so disappointed. Even though there's nothing I can do about it, and she's probably just a delusional party girl, I feel like I did something wrong. I wish I could help her figure it out. Actually, I should've pretended I knew her from somewhere because then maybe I could've had the chance to see her again when she was sober.

I stick the $100 bill in my sock like a schoolboy. It feels awkward, but my uniform-approved, discount khakis don't have pockets and my coat is hanging up in the "employee lounge." (An area in the stock room with a couch and a vending machine.) I'm too poor to complain about the inconvenience of a $95.83 tip, even if it makes me feel like a charity case. $95.83 is more than I'll earn for the night.

"Be safe!" I call out to her as she leaves. A few minutes after she makes it beyond the automatic doors, I feel a pang of guilt. Any excuse for a man would have done something to ensure her safety; it can't be more than 2° F outside, she's three sheets to the wind, and the sidewalk is probably coated in ice. It's dangerous for any woman to be walking alone at night in this part of Philadelphia. I should have made sure she got into a cab or something.

"Hey, Kristi!" I call out to my only present coworker.

Kristi pretends she can't hear me and continues to stock the clearance shelves with mayonnaise we failed to sell. I shout her name again, louder this time. Knowing I won't stop until she turns around, Kristi reluctantly pulls herself away from her task like it's a crying baby and walks briskly toward me.

"What do you want, *William*?" The way she addresses me sounds like she's swearing on my name. That said, I generally avoid talking to her. Unfortunately, she's the assistant manager, so it's unavoidable.

"I need to take a break to... smoke."

"You don't smoke."

I pick up a random pack of cigarettes from behind the counter. "I'm starting in five minutes."

"Fine, put that back where you got it and get lost. I was thinking about closing anyway on account of the weather. It's late and it's not like we have customers."

I want to say something smart-assy, like "then what do you call the three weirdos who were just in here?" but this is a blessing. If the manager hadn't called in (fake) sick, Kristi wouldn't be here; and the woman who hates this job the most just happens to be our favorite supervisor.

"So I can go home?" I ask.

"Yes, *William*," she says more firmly than usual. "You're a grown man. You can even go to Atlantis if it's open. See a real live tit for the first time in your life."

I got what I wanted, so why do I feel like I lost?

The frozen air nips at my hands the instant I crack the door open. Bracing myself, I rush out into the cold to make sure AIR·EH·TEE isn't in trouble. I shiver, but not because of the subzero temperatures. It's the foreboding feeling that I can't quite place. Pushing the weather out of my mind, I look around, wondering which direction she went. Embedded in the snow are fresh prints that looked like they may have been left by one particular pair of heels with bows on them. Footprints. That's one good thing about snow—the only good thing about snow.

I follow the trail of what is definitely Arete's heels, which leads me two blocks to my right before it's joined by a second trail of footprints, side by side at a leisurely pace. The second pair is large, maybe about a size 13. She isn't alone after all, but whoever she's with could be dangerous. I continue to follow both in the direction of an alleyway between Wayspeed and a condemned building.

Just as a streetlight flickers out, I catch a shadow sidestepping around the corner. I stop dead in my tracks. I know I need to be brave, not stupid. But I hear a shrill scream. I don't have time to think or hesitate anymore. I can't let this girl suffer when I could have done something. Instead of jumping in to the rescue, I rush in shouting "Hey!" So much for not being stupid.

As Arete cowers in the corner, two men turn their heads at me. It's too dark to see them clearly. A stocky man in a black trench coat is being pinned up against the wall by the forearm of a tall man with broad shoulders, probably the owner of the huge footprints. While the shorter man is distracted by my idiocy, the other grasps an enormous icicle hanging from the gutter overhead. He snaps it off and deftly plunges it into stocky man's throat. This buys him time to slam the stocky man's head against the brick wall. He slides down the wall and plummets.

Unable to see well with the street light out, I hesitate trying to figure out which direction to run. This brief moment of confusion leads me to trip and slide over the ice and into the alley. I'm stopped when my back hits something—no—*someone*. And I knock him over. I check over my shoulder. The streetlight flickers on, and I see red. I scramble backward, my hands raw against the snow, but do a double-take.

If he's not dead yet, he will be in a minute. There's a foot-long icicle lodged in his throat. It slowly starts to slowly slide out, gradually melting from his fleeting body heat, and blood spurts out from the artery. I squeeze my eyes shut to keep myself from passing out. My mother called me up last winter just to warn me that 15 people in the US die from icicles every year, and I was so annoyed I hung up on her. I googled it, and it turned out to be true. The number in Russia was 100, making icicles more dangerous than sharks globally, but I never thought it would happen like this. This *is* happening right? Should I open my eyes again? I cringe and turn away, but look again when I hear crunch of snow under someone's feet.

Arete is walking in my direction. She looks different from this angle. The street light flickers on and casts eerie shadows over her face. There's more makeup smudged on her cheeks than on her eyes. She sniffles, her runny nose raw at the nostrils, and coughs to clear the phlegm from her throat.

She's not coming for me though. She runs straight to the tall man and wraps her arms around him.

He puts his arm on her shoulder. I avoid looking at him directly, but I notice his eyes are on me. His thousand-yard stare is colder than this alley. He's probably determining whether or not I'm a threat and if it would be easier to just kill me too. I cover my eyes, trying to become invisible. I won't bother trying to defend myself because I don't stand a chance. He's obviously strong, deadly, and maybe even fast enough to outrun a cheetah for all I know. I would have assumed he was just trying to rescue his girlfriend, but the way he's acting and the fact that he looked like he knew exactly what he was doing when he killed that guy makes me doubt his intentions. I can only assume the worst of myself. I am screwed. I am completely screwed.

I should've taken my $95.83 tip and gone home like a good boy, but *nooo*, I had to tail a cute girl and witness a murder instead. I can't hope to be found by "that one guy who's out tonight by coincidence and witnesses a crime" because I *am* that guy. I *am* the one person who the murderer hopes isn't out that night, and I'm going to pay for it. It's dark. It's icy. No one else is around to hear me cry for help. Even if someone notices me and calls the police, the odds of them battling the inclement weather and arriving in time to rescue me are not in my favor. I can't fight my way out of this situation because my spaghetti arms don't just repel women.

There is no scenario imaginable that ends with my survival. It would take a miracle of epic proportions.

"Are you okay, Arete?" he asks.

"Y-yes," she says.

"You're lying." He says this firmly, almost like he's scolding her.

"Th-thank you. You saved my life." Arete's voice, already smothered by alcohol, cracks a little as she stutters.

I peek, reminding myself I should've learned before my first birthday that other people don't disappear when I can't see them. Her pallor makes her look more corpse-like than the man that I'm trying to forget is crumpled up less than a foot away from me. She flashes him a smile of gratitude.

"You're welcome," says the man next to her, almost devoid of emotion.

Not the nurturing type, I assume. I mean, if a smile like that didn't make his day, his heart must be made of coal. He must be one of those obsessive, jealous men who stalk their girlfriends and have to pre-approve every bathroom break. What does she see in him? Sure, she probably feels safe with him, but there's only one reasonable explanation for a girl putting up with someone that scary in her sober life.

His sole redeeming quality must be his appearance. It's hard to tell since he's wearing a coat, but judging by the broad shoulders and strength in combat, he's muscular. Men everywhere are probably jealous of his defined cheekbones, olive skin, and thick, dark hair. He could have any woman he wanted, you know, until they find out that he's *evil reincarnate*. Hell, he's so Hollywood perfect that even *I'm* questioning whether or not I'm attracted to him. Actually, I'm pretty sure I am—not. I meant to say I am *not*. Not even in an aesthetic way. But is that a chin dimple? Stop.

Stop, stop, stop, stop, stop, stop, stop. It doesn't make sense to be thinking about these things to begin with, especially not right now.

He turns toward me again, this time capturing eye contact that chills me to the core. "Now, what to do with *this one...*" he says.

I hold my breath. He's got to be at least a foot taller than me, which isn't saying much since I'm five foot four. I'm going to be just as dead as—no. *Stop thinking about it.*

"Ah, there it is," he says, relieved. At first I don't know what he's talking about, but then I notice a knife lying in the snow near my feet. He must have lost it in the struggle. I have the urge to grab it before he does, but I can't will myself to move and he beats me to it.

"Whoa, wait," Arete shouts and points at me. "I know why you looked so familiar! You're Nathan Faust!" Her demeanor changes entirely, and she once again resembles the excitable drunkard I met earlier, if not ecstatic. "I have so many questions for you!"

There are tons of questions I would have liked to ask her too, since I'm never addressed by that name. Also, right next to me—*Stop thinking about it!*

The man I presume is her boyfriend is, finally, more confused than me. "Who the fuck is Nathan Frost?"

She stomps her left foot. "It's *Faust*!" I'm glad she corrected him, because my compulsion to do so would have gotten me killed, just like the man—*Stop thinking about it, for fuck's sake, William. Do you* want *to toss your cookies at Death's feet?*

"Nathan Faust, huh?" He glares at me. "Who are you, and how do you know my girl?"

Great—he really is the jealous type. I'm too scared to respond. Arete, who is apparently quite the inappropriate chatterbox when she's drunk, speaks for me.

"He's one of my favorite authors *ever*!"

Well, that's something I never expected to hear in my entire life. I'm about to die, but at least I get to live every writer's dream first, if only for a few moments. I force my shaky legs to stand up so I can go down with a little dignity. I brush snow off of my pants. The big, wet patch near my crotch is *snow* right? Please tell me it's snow.

"Favorite author?" I ask. "I wrote, like, one book and it tanked. My agent told me to never speak to her again."

Arete's boyfriend has the most annoying smirk on his face. Being a loser may just save my life. But then she shakes her head, bends over, and laughs. "They just don't appreciate your genius!"

Please don't speak so highly of me, number one-and-only fan. Sasquatch will crush me. Now that I've spoken a few words, now is the best opportunity I'll ever get to diffuse the situation.

"So, you know I won't say anything about this? As far as I know you were defending Arete. And I mean, who would believe me, right? Icicle. Heh..." I hold my breath.

"I know," says the most intimidating man alive. "You're not going to say a word."

"Well, then. I guess I'll be going now. Nice meeting—"

Sasquatch pins me against the wall like the thug earlier—and when I feel the blunt end of a knife pressed up against my throat, I wonder if anyone will remember to hold a funeral for me.

His face is a mere two inches away from my nose. "You were afraid of that little icicle, huh? Do you want to see what I can do with a knife?"

Is that bourbon that I smell on his breath? Great. I'm going to be murdered by a drunk man and all I got was a $95.87 tip. Well, a buzzed man. I'm actually kind of impressed by his coordination. The real question is... is this really happening to me right now, oh my god, my life is over and I'm not even thirty yet, please don't let me die a virgin, God, I'll be good from now on, I'll go to church and get a real job.

"Stop!" Arete says.

He keeps the knife's pressure against my throat consistent and doesn't give me any room to move, but turns head away enough to give her his full attention. "Honey, if I just let him go, we're going to be knee deep in shit."

"Not the throat!" she slurs. "If you kill him, he won't be able to write more books!"

Seriously? My miracle of epic proportions is a drunk woman liking my crappy book?

He looks up and exhales in frustration before pulling the knife away, not leaving a single scratch on my tender throat. He slips it into the pocket of his pea coat with care. That knife must be precious to him, but I guarantee it doesn't mean as much to him as my throat means to me.

As he turns his head a tad further away from me, he mouths the words "trust me" to her; I wasn't supposed to notice, so I don't acknowledge it. I feel at least 7% safer now, maybe 7.01%.

He lets go of my shirt collar and pushes me back a little. "Don't run off," he says. "And don't start trouble. Got it?"

I nod, feeling like the luckiest man on earth. A man dying in front of her isn't significant to Arete, but my piece of shit novella is. As of its 2010 publication, I have sold 97 copies. The rest are in cardboard boxes that line the walls of my home, a constant reminder of my failure. I have an average rating of 3 on Goodreads, but my reviews are in the single digits. I can only vaguely remember what my agent titled it. Fiery Night? Night Campfire? Angel Fire? It doesn't matter. I haven't written another book ever since. I haven't even *read* a book since then.

"Well," says my would-be killer, "what are we supposed to do with him?"

Arete shrugs. "I don't know... but anyway, I have *tons* of questions about *Night in the Fire*."

Hey, I was close.

"Oh, I got it," she says. "We'll just take him with us!"

Now I wish I was the guy with an icicle lodged in—*Stop thinking about it already!*

Her boyfriend looks at her like she's an idiot, (and she must be to like my novella) to which she says, "What, are you going to make me blow in the bag now?"

He grunts. "This guy doesn't look like he's changed his haircut since the mid 90's." He gestures at me by throwing out his palm. "Hell, look at that get up he's wearing. He *is* the mid 90's."

For this brief moment, he reminds me of a teenage girl—a frightening teenage girl who could snap my femur in half with his bare hands. That considered, I decide not to make fun of his TRESemmé, wavy locks. He's sparing me, and I don't want to change his mind.

"Oh, please." Arete rolls her big, gray eyes. This expression actually has a more creepy feel to it than that of annoyance. "Yeah, so he looks like the main cast of *Boy Meets World* thrown into a blender. But, hey, at least he's still a master of the pen."

Ouch. Is that her idea of a compliment? Also, is she including Topanga? With every passing moment, her boyfriend's jealousy of me is more and more unwarranted. If I was tempted to steal a psychopathic gothic lolita from a homicidal beast, I wouldn't have gotten very far to begin with. All I want is to go home, watch Netflix, and sob into my pillow like a grown man.

"We could cuff him," Arete says.

"To what?" he asks. "Our magic snowmobile? We walked here."

"To one of us, then. I have those handcuffs in my purse, remember?"

"Not *those*! We didn't even get to use them yet!"

As if he couldn't get more unlikable, he has a whiny side. I almost understand why he doesn't want to put me out of my misery, but what's so special about a pair of handcuffs?

Arete unzips her purse and pulls out a plastic shopping bag. Unfortunately for me, she has enough coordination to undo the packaging and pull out a pair of handcuffs that was meant for restraint in a different context. They're decorated with rhinestones, and the cuffs themselves are wrapped in a fuzzy, pink fabric. If a policeman walks by, I'll be too humiliated to cry for help. At least they'll be comfortable.

"All right, Elijah," she says. "Which hand do you want it on?"

His name is Elijah? As far as biblical names go, I think "Lucifer" is more fitting.

"No thank you," he says, squinting. "I think the person who came up with the idea should be the one who has to do it."

Arete groans and looks away. "No way in Hell." She pauses for a few seconds, presumably thinking of an excuse to get out of it. "I'm tiny and fragile. What if he knocks me down and gets away?" Drunk logic. Gotta love it. The bitch is half a foot taller than me in those heels.

Elijah laughs. "This shorty probably hasn't ran more than ten feet since high school. Besides, you're the one who wanted to keep him. I'm sure you have plenty of questions about Nigh—... *Night Firefly* or whatever it's called."

"But aren't you jealous?" Arete makes her best pouty face, which proves ineffective.

"You said it yourself—he's *Boy Meets World*, and I'm going to have a lot to do tonight."

Arete can't think of a good counterargument, not that her impaired logical skills would have allowed her one. Besides, It's clear he made this decision as part of a silent plea to prove to Arete (and himself) that he isn't jealous of me. I would find Hollywood Perfect's insecurities hilarious under different circumstances. *Safer* circumstances.

"Faust," Elijah says. "Slowly lift your hand and wave at me."

I hesitate for a few seconds before honoring the strange request. What the hell is he doing? Well, I'm sure it makes sense in the drunk world.

Elijah motions for me to put my hand down. "Okay, Arete. He's right-handed, so put it on your left and his right."

Oh.

Arete struggles, but manages to lock one cuff on her left wrist, and the other on my right as Elijah holds my arm in a forceful grip. I'm now short of my dominant hand. Why he still thinks I might be dumb enough to flee the scene is beyond me. By now he should realize such precautions are beyond unnecessary. During my three years as a bartender, I learned how drunks operate. There's no point in asking them to let me go, but if they did, I guarantee that I would never mention a word of this to *anyone*. I don't even want to remember it, let alone relive it.

After he double locks the cuffs and feels confident that I'm secured, I'm on the receiving end of a quick, unwelcome pat down by Hollywood Perfect. In the time he spends frisking me, all he discovers is my thrift store wallet and a Nokia 3310. He fumbles around until he can pull the case off the back and remove the battery entirely; he returns the phone to me, but pockets the battery. No phone calls for me. Upon opening my wallet, he finds less than seven dollars in change and my ID. "William Arthur Brown," he says. I catch a disapproving look in his eyes when he looks it over, like he both pities and despises me. It's a good thing I didn't have to put my full name on there. My middle names are almost as embarrassing as my ID photo.

After he pockets my belongings, they set off with me in tow. Arete falls to her knees twice to vomit along the way, jerking my arm down both times. At this rate, she'll end up tearing it off.

"Eli," Arete whines. "I'm so tired. Can you carry me?"

"Sure, Kit Kat. This dope wouldn't be able to catch you if you fell anyway. It wouldn't surprise me one bit if he slipped on the ice and dragged you down with him."

I'm offended, even though he's right. Walking is almost impossible. As if it isn't hard enough to balance oneself when being dragged along in unpredictable directions, steadying myself as I walk on ice is nearly impossible. When Elijah takes a sharp, unexpected turn around a street corner, I slip and fall. When my stumble jerks her arm, Arete yells out melodramatically, like I've plucked it out of its socket. Needless to say, I get a swift kick in the ass for that one— literally. "If it happens again," Elijah warns, "I'll lower my honor and aim for the groin." I will spare the details, but I would like to confirm that yes, it happens again.

Due in part to my low pain tolerance, I waddle like a maimed duck as I'm led to a nearby sleaze motel. This is starting to sound like the plot to a bad porno. Although I don't frequent the area, seeing the familiar landmark reminds me that we aren't actually that far from my workplace. Time flies when you're having fun, and it slows down drastically when you're being kidnapped by drunkards. Don't get me wrong; my fear isn't easing up because they're drunk. I just can't seem to process that this is real.

When I first realized our destination was a sleaze motel, I had hoped that Elijah would go by the office to rent a room so I had a 0.01% chance of getting help. Much to my dismay, he walks past the office and orders me to pull a key from his back pocket and unlock the door to room three. I understand that he doesn't want to disturb the princess, who somehow managed to either fall asleep or pass out at some point on the way here, but he's condemning both of us to an awkward situation.

Since my right arm is, well... *occupied*, I thank my genetics for being just flexible enough to take the keys out of Elijah's back pocket without accidentally groping his firm ass *too* much. Bad porno, strike two. Of all the places in the world, I don't want to be murdered in a filthy motel.

When we enter, I pull back the blankets as instructed, and Elijah gently lays Arete down on the left side of a double bed, thus forcing me to occupy the floor. I assume that means I'll be uncomfortably chained there while Mr. & Mrs. Satan sleep soundly, dreaming of robbing blind people and drowning puppies. Instead, after he tucks her in like a baby and kisses her on the cheek, Elijah opens the door to leave— but not before glaring at me, nonverbally communicating that I'll be dead if I try to bolt; or maybe it's more about waking his adorable "Kit Kat" up in the middle of the night. Again, he shouldn't bother.

*

Instead of sleeping, I desperately try to slip my hand out of the love cuffs. You'd think with wrists as bony as mine, I'd be able to slide them right through, but no. Meanwhile, I can't stop raking my mind with questions. Where did he go? How long am I going to be held prisoner? What are they going to do with me in the end? Who was the man Elijah murdered and why? Elijah clearly had combat experience, so why not knock him out as opposed to killing him? Is he just a sadist? Was this really just a typical mugger who paid for it with his life, or was Arete a planned target? Most importantly, if Elijah didn't do anything wrong, why not just call the police like a normal person? He has two witnesses who can testify that it was in his girlfriend's defense. There's got to be something else going on here.

I also wonder when the few people in my life will notice I'm missing. I have the tendency to be a loner if not flaky. I haven't visited or talked to my family since Christmas because I find it too draining. It wasn't rare for me to go weeks without talking to anyone at all outside of wherever I worked at any given time. Speaking of work, Kristi will just assume that I quit without notice like I did at McDonald's last year, something I was sure to write on my application. Realizing the first people to notice my absence will be bill collectors saddens me. Maybe it wouldn't be such a big deal if I died after all. No one would miss me, and I don't have a future to look forward to. As much as I hate to admit it, this was the most interesting thing that's ever happened to me. All I have to go back to is an ugly rental home.

The best way to make use of my time, honestly, would be to brainstorm some ideas for a sequel to *Night in the Fire*. It turns out that I'm not in a porno, so I must be in a Stephen King novel. I could see myself being locked in my only fan's house, forced to write stories until I either die of old age, or until she gets bored. How did that book end again? I was too much of a coward to finish reading it.

I don't know how much time has passed when the box springs in the mattress creak and my petite captor rolls over on her side. She opens her eyes slowly, and mutters.

"Eli?" she asks.

"Uh... He left," I say. "I don't know where he went."

I don't understand how something so cute can be so dangerous. Even with smudged makeup and a crooked rat's nest that I now realize is a wig, Arete looks like a supermodel. If nothing else, and there really is *nothing* else to look forward to, at least I get to look at her. In any other situation, she would be my dream girl. But my worst nightmare comes true.

"Nathan... I have to pee."

Kill me. As if being in danger isn't enough, this has to be awkward too?

"Is it an emergency?" I ask.

It's too dark for me to make out her face, but she sounds impatient. "What do you think, dag? I had half a bottle of Kentucky bourbon!" How is that even possible for a woman her size? When I don't respond, she adds, "And *the worst* hangover!"

"You won't be able to get any privacy though," I say, desperately looking for an excuse to go free. "And I'm a guy, so..."

She turns on the lamp on the table behind me and unscrews the cap off a bottle of bourbon. She's evidently a fan of the "hair of the dog" treatment, because she unceremoniously downs another ounce or two. "So what? I don't care! I have to pee, now stand up."

Maybe I can turn this around if I use the right words. "I'm sure Elijah would be upset if a man went into the restroom with you. Maybe you should cuff me to the door instead."

She closes her eyes tightly and puts her right fingertips to her forehead. "I'm hungover, not completely *stupid*. You'll just do the Harold."

I have no idea what that means, but as long as she doesn't barf on me, I don't care. She steps out of bed, and begins walking toward the bathroom. Naturally, I have no choice but to follow, what with the restraints and all... but what if Elijah comes back while we're in there? I'll be toast. Before she closes the bathroom door behind her, she pauses for a moment.

"Well, it's your lucky day. The toilet's next to the door, you can wait around the corner."

Thank god. I still have to listen, but at least I don't have to watch. I close my eyes anyway and keep them sealed tightly, trying to imagine a fountain in a nice garden. After the park maintenance shut off the fountain and drained the water—a fantasy that doesn't quite drown out reality—I hear a peppy shout.

"Your turn!"

I shudder, partially at how quickly her attitude can change. If she's this unpredictable, I may as well be chained to a nitrogen bomb. "My turn?"

"Well, we may as well get it all done at once. Besides, you might need to get used to it."

"What do you mean, *get used to it*?" I want to tell her she's crazy, but something tells me that's not the best idea. I doubt she knows how badly she needs a psychiatrist.

"Just get it over with," she says, exasperated.

"I... have a certain aversion to motel toilets."

She laughs; I cry.

"No, really!" I say. "Think about how many asses have been on that thing—and don't even tell me you 'warmed it up for me,' or something."

She raises her eyebrows and smiles. "What, like a teenage boy?" After hearing her speak smoothly without slurring or raving, I notice a light Australian accent. Or maybe it's a normal Australian accent, and not everyone sounds like Steve Irwin. I can't place Elijah's accent either; it's kind of a strange mix of Philly and something else. I almost never venture outside of Pennsylvania, let alone outside the United States. I went to Mexico every summer until my abuela died, and that was when I was nine.

"You look a little lost," she says. "Look, I'm not going to make fun of you. Eli might, but I wouldn't."

"Did you wash your hands?" I ask, knowing she didn't. "Because the sink's on the outside of the bathroom for some reason, and I kind of have to be there in order for you to—"

"No, silly! Of course not, we'll do that part together. There's a second sink in the bathroom, by the way. The one on the outside is for girls to do up their makeup and such without hogging the dunny. No—don't groan, I hate it when men do that. Sorry about earlier, by the way. I'm always in a bad mood when I have to pee."

Apology not accepted. That was too much information, and if anything, I'd rather receive an apology for the whole kidnapping thing. I just nod, tell her it's okay, and take care of my business, fearing we'll be having this conversation again.

Princess Arete complains as we wash our hands. First the water is too hot, then it's too cold. I use too much soap and I scrub too hard. If I get the fur on the handcuffs wet, it'll be uncomfortable against her skin. I've been washing too long. She might cure me of my chronic hand washing compulsion; they never did decide how long I was going to be chained to her. Surely when they sober up, they'll realize this isn't ideal... right? I mean, how are we going to change clothes?

"I'm going to lie down and watch the telly," she says. "You'll have to lie next to me though, the right side of the room gives me a better view."

I shudder visibly, not from the idea of sharing a bed with a crazy woman, not the idea of getting scalped by Hollywood Perfect for sharing a bed with his ultra-hot girlfriend, but from the nastiness of motels. Motels are disgusting.

"The dirtiest surface in a motel room is the remote," I say. "It's true, I saw it on a documentary. They did tests and—"

Before I can finish my tirade about how poorly motel rooms are cleaned, she's already picked up the remote and is flipping through the channels. "Well, Faust, I hope you don't mind *Law & Order*, 'cause that's all that's on. It's one of my favorites anyway."

She hops onto the bed and yanks my arm until I reluctantly join her. Crawling over her is awkward enough without cringing over the fact that she grabbed me with the same hand she touched the remote with. And to think, we just washed our hands.

"Please, call me William," I say. I don't want to be reminded of my garbage book every time she calls me by name.

"Sure thing."

I find it uncanny that a felon would thoroughly enjoy *Law & Order*, particularly since she's rooting for the police. Something tells me that she won't do that in real life. Does she even *have* a moral compass? It's tough to tell for sure, since I've only met her drunk side. I ponder sober Arete. Sober Arete is still irrational, I can only imagine, since she's dating *that thing*. They're like an episode of *Fatal Attraction*. And do Australians use a lot of weird slang in general, or is Arete just over-doing it for attention?

She sits cross-legged on the bed, hugging a pillow and leaning forward slightly, oblivious to my discomfort. In the short time I've known her, she hasn't shown any signs of maturity. Her attention span isn't finely tuned either. She spends a lot of time looking around the room instead of watching the "telly," as she calls it. I politely wait for her to speak to me (for fear of finding out what she's like when she's pissed off) before asking any of my burning questions. I get my wish during the first commercial break, when she asks me to pass her what was left of the bourbon.

"Would you like some?" she asks.

No matter how unbearable this is, there's nothing I want *less* than to put my mouth on that germ-ridden bottle, so I come up with my best excuse. "No, there's only one shot left. You should have it. Hair of the dog, you know."

"All right." Judging by how relieved she looks, she was only asking to be nice.

I take a deep breath. "So... I don't want to start anything, but when will Elijah be back? Like, what is he doing?" Passed out somewhere dying of hypothermia, I hope.

Arete shrugs. "Probably disposing of that wanker back there. He can't leave his body out there, can he? That icicle isn't going to melt in this weather, ya' know. No body, no murder weapon, no crime."

Those words give me the impression that this wasn't his first murder, nor was it the first that Arete witnessed. Maybe I'm just paranoid. I mean, if she likes something as ancient as *Law & Order*, I'm sure she's a crime show junkie. To be honest, other than the fact that I'm being held captive, this isn't much different from what I would usually do on a weeknight. Or, well, any night. All I do is watch TV; it's sad, really.

"It'll probably take him quite a while," she says. "He's got to make sure no evidence was left behind—he's a thorough person in general, so I'm sure everything will be all right."

That's *just* what I wanted to hear. She knows that nothing about that benefits *me*, right? She must be trying to reassure herself. It was a hard night for her too, I guess. I had forgotten someone just tried to murder her a few hours ago.

Two or three episodes of justice later, Satan returns. I'm ready to retreat the instant I hear keys rattling at the door, but Mrs. Satan pulls me back down. How *dare* I put my survival before her telly time? Elijah doesn't look at me on his way in. He slams the door behind himself and walks straight to the sink on the counter outside of the bathroom. On his way there, he tosses a plastic bag from a convenience store onto the other bed.

"Damn, it's cold!" He shouts with frustration and throws his gloves onto the floor.

"How long were you out there?" Arete asks. "You could've frozen solid."

"Too long." He kisses her on the forehead. "But the cold was nothing compared to being without you for so long."

Gross.

"So everything's going to be okay?" she asks.

"You don't need to worry anymore, Kit Kat. The job's squared away."

She opens her eyes as wide as they could naturally go without strain and smiles. "Ohhh, do I get the gory details? Please?" She's either a sadist, or still drunk. Maybe both. That bourbon was 120 proof and she can't possibly weigh more than that in pounds. One shot of that shit could kill me.

"No, not with *him* around." Elijah shoots me a quick glare before returning his attention to Arete. Did I just get the stink eye from a grown man? He never said it out loud, but he probably *is* upset that I'm sitting next to her on the same bed, as if I have a choice. Arete has too much faith in his ability to stay cool and collected. If his trust issues are this bad, I actually feel kind of sorry for her.

Elijah sits at the edge of the bed. "Then again, I have something to tell you two, because it's extremely important that *both* of you understand this thoroughly... Earth to Arete!"

"Huh?" She snaps out of whatever haze she was in. "What did you say?"

"I'm not going to tell either of you where or how I hid the body for obvious reasons. But I did leave some DNA evidence behind."

"What? Why?" Arete asks.

Feeling up to the risk of crossing boundaries, I ask him, "Are you going to go back and fix it then?"

"It wasn't an accident," he says.

"I'm so confused," Arete says. "Can't you just... Come out and say it? Really, stop rattling me, I'm tired!"

Elijah, who is probably just as tired, turns to face me. "Well, kid. One of your cutesy, Eric Matthews-ish hairs landed on his shoulder when you slid into him. I'm sure someone will testify that you left work around the right time to murder him. Also, I covered Arete's footprints and my own. Yours though? Why would I bother?"

I have to give Elijah some credit for that one—he's good. He's an evil genius. He just ruined my entire life in one night at a time when I didn't know I had anything to lose. There's no television in prison cells.

"I know what I'm doing," he says, "and there's nothing to link it to me or Arete. But it doesn't look good for you, now does it?"

Once again afraid to speak, I settle with nodding.

"Here's how it's going to work," he says. "If you rat on us, I will see to it that the rest of your days are spent in agony. Understood?"

"Yes," I say. I don't question that he'll actually do it; I mean, I just saw him kill someone for her. And after seeing the way he looks at her, I almost understand why he's putting so much effort into scarring me for life. But she isn't in on his plans. I glance at her, and she's definitely hearing this for the first time. She doesn't object. Regardless, it's not smart to start trouble when you don't understand the situation, so I don't ask any questions about John Doe Dead Man.

"William, please, look at me," Arete says. I obey as if it's an order, half expecting Elijah to kill me for not turning around fast enough.

"You don't have anything to worry about," she says. "Just do as I say, and no one is going to get hurt. I promise." Her smile is so angelic that I almost believe I misjudged her.

Once again, I respond with a nod. I don't know what to make of this, but it looks like she's sobered up enough for some degree of intelligent conversation.

"Stop nodding," she says. "I am *not* going to be friends with someone who never speaks. Always say what's on your mind, even if it's something that will make Eli grouchy." (I don't want to know what kind of face Elijah is making right now.) "You will address me informally and casually. Do you understand?"

"Yes, Arete. I understand."

"Always act naturally toward us. You know what..." She places her hand on my right shoulder and looks into my eyes. "Think of us as your best mates."

"Best mates?" Yeah, she's definitely from Australia. And delusional.

She laughs out of pure glee, without any trace of sarcasm or contempt. "I already think of you as a friend, Na— William. I really connected with your book."

At first I think she's patronizing me, but then I realize she's serious. And since my book is about a teenage girl who was stalked and bullied, I almost feel like *I'm* the asshole here for assuming she's a monster. How old is she? I bet she was a teenager when it came out. That doesn't give me a lot to go on, but tomorrow will go one of two ways. She could always be like this, thinking kidnapping people and asking them to be your friend is perfectly reasonable, and we'll be "BFFs." If not, *man* is she is going to be embarrassed in the morning.

"Oh, did you get the stuff?" she asks Elijah, a little too cheerfully.

I'm not sure when she had the time to send him a text message. I must have been glued to the screen; *Law and Order* is pretty intense. Elijah mutters an especially grouchy *"yes"* under his breath and takes a container of disinfectant wipes from a plastic shopping bag.

"Toss 'em here," she says.

He tosses them in her general direction, but the container hits me square in the nose instead.

"Oops, my bad," he says. His voice is deadpan, but he's smirking. "Don't judge my aim based on this. I still have a buzz."

I don't think he expected me to conclude that a man who could stake someone with an icicle in just the right spot could miss while tossing a shopping bag to his girlfriend three feet away. If Arete notices, she doesn't say anything. Or maybe she doesn't care.

"Wait, did you drink more without me?" Arete asks.

"Sorry," he says. "But I got you vitamin water."

"Boo! Fine."

Yeah, she doesn't care. She leans over and moves her chained hand to drag my own over the wipes. Great; it went from feeling like we share a hand, to her having three.

"They're for you!" she says.

She does a fist pump with her right hand, and forcefully raises both of "her" left hands, nearly yanking my arm out of its socket. I'm not sure how to respond.

"Oh, nice..." That's the best I can manage. "Thank you, Arete... and... Elijah?" Am I supposed to thank a man who was only doing this for me because his girlfriend was ordering him around?

Arete is overjoyed, probably seeing this as a sign of true friendship, and responds with an overly enthusiastic "You're super welcome!"

Elijah looks away. "She said you have a serious case of OCD."

I rub the back of my neck with my only hand. "No, I just... yes." Close enough. Before I know it, I'm thoroughly cleaning the remote, removing 99.9% of common bacteria from its surface. Wait... was this Mr. & Mrs. Satan's plan all along? To make me like them so much that I'll overlook what is, at the absolute best, being the victim of their drunk decisions? If so, I'm ashamed to admit that it had been working pretty well until she shouts, "Let's do nicknames!"

I guess this isn't an appropriate time to bring up that I already gave them nicknames.

Elijah groans. "Can we not?"

Arete speaks sternly this time. "We're doing nicknames. Friends give each other nicknames. That's how it works."

I haven't made many friends throughout my lifetime, and most of them only still speak to me every now and then because they feel sorry for me or are concerned that I'll die alone. I'm not good at making friends, but I'm pretty sure this *isn't* how it works.

"All right!" Elijah gives a single, frustrated clap. "Nicknames... I like *Boy Meets World* for that pussy over there."

"No, Elijah," I say, matching his cynical tone. "We're *best mates* now, remember? Our nicknames have to be friendly."

At this point, I'm begging for them to kill me. I can't go on after this; it's getting too complicated and the rest of my life is just going to be one big panic attack from here on out. Unfortunately, he and I share a mutual perspective, so my snarking doesn't bother him. He actually cracks a smile, and it deeply grieves me that I made him feel better. I'm halfway to asking him to drag me to the police station so I can confess to impaling a man in the neck with an icicle. I'll plead insanity. Nothing can be worse than this tug-of-war between friendship and fear.

"That's right," Arete says. "Best mates. *Forever.*"

Forever?

"Now, Arete, honey," Elijah says, pleading. "Forever is a *really* long time."

"*Forever.*" She says it more firmly this time. "You two are absolutely incompetent." Being lumped together in the same category as Elijah makes me want to barf, but it causes him to spiral down into shame. "You two don't even *deserve* nicknames," she says.

Her lover is left in inappropriate dismay. "What? All of the pet names I come up with for you on a daily basis and I don't deserve a nickname other than *Eli*?"

"That's different!" she says. "I'm talking about, like, special monikers. Just for us three!"

They then start bickering. I can't take it anymore. Arete and Elijah are driving me insane. Soon I'll be just as crazy as they are. While they're busy arguing about something petty, I come up with three scenarios where I actually *could* make it out alive. Maybe.

One: I could tell them to nickname me *Patsy* and tell the police they apprehended me after killing John Doe. I would spend the rest of my youth in a jail cell for premeditated icicle murder.

Two: I could nickname them Bonnie and Clyde, wait for Bonnie's friendship with me to become contagious, and convince Clyde that friendship means freedom.

Three: I could provoke them to argue amongst themselves until they finally murder each other in cold blood. But if I'm not strong enough to drag Arete to the door, that would leave me to die slowly of starvation while I smell their rotting flesh.

You know what... Never mind. They're some combination of drunk and hungover, so I risk changing the subject to the one and only thing I'm sure we can all agree on.

I clear my throat to get their attention. "Is anyone else hungry?"

The two stop to stare at me, and an awkward silence ensues. For some reason, I didn't think they would actually pay attention to me, and despite having made zero attempts to humanize myself in their eyes, I'm embarrassed.

Arete responds by whining like a four-year-old. "I am too. Can we go to Waffle House? Please?"

Elijah buries his face in his hands for a moment, then removes them and takes a deep breath. "I walked by Waffle House. It was closed."

"Liar!" Arete says. "You just hate Waffle House!"

"I didn't say when," Elijah says.

"I hate it when you do that," Arete says.

Elijah stands up and faces the wall. He takes the deepest breath a man has ever taken before answering.

"Put on your shoes, hon. We're going... to Waffle House."

*

I don't know whether or not to consider this a small victory. On the one hand, I'm not cooped up in a sleaze motel awaiting my fate anymore. On the other hand, I hate Waffle House and every other breakfast-for-dinner restaurant. Something about eating pancakes at 5:00 AM bothers me almost as much as being the third wheel on a date with two felons. Or being the third wheel period. Maybe I should've taken Arete up on that bourbon offer before it was empty. A clear head doesn't help much when you're weak and stupid.

It's been eleven years since I last ate at Waffle House, but it's every bit as tacky as I remembered it, and as desolate as I expected it to be. It stinks heavily of maple syrup and doesn't look very clean. To my luck, I spot a lone police officer drinking coffee in a booth near the entrance. This is the only chance I might get. I have to cry for help now, unless I want to spend the rest of my life handcuffed to Mrs. Satan.

Before I can get a single word out of my mouth, Elijah says, "Hey, Mark! Still an Awful Waffle regular?"

No. They know each other?

"Elijah Walker!" Mark says, cheerful but surprised. "I never thought I'd see you here again. How's law school going?"

Elijah smiles. "It's pretty rough, but that's the price you pay for an education."

"That's great. Patrolling hasn't been the same without you, Walker. My new partner is kind of dry. All she talks about are her cats and daytime soaps," he says with disdain.

"Oh man, now you're making me feel bad for leaving again."

Cop buddies. They're cop buddies. Elijah was a policeman. Life absolutely *cannot* get worse. There's just no way.

"Nah, I understand," Mark says. "I guess you would've left anyway, since you were offered that promotion."

"Detective sounded good, don't get me wrong," Elijah says, a little defensive. "I wasn't aching to leave or anything, I just wanted to be a lawyer."

"It's fine. This may be hard for you to believe, but crimes will get solved without you." Mark chuckles. "So, if you don't mind me asking, what is that little noodle doing chained to that *beautiful* young woman?" He winks.

Arete blushes and smiles, as if a girl like her isn't used to being called beautiful. For all I knew, she could be a supermodel. Elijah looks like he can't wait to spin my story. "This is Arete, my girlfriend."

She curtsies and gives him a cute smile. "Pleased to meet you."

"And *this*," Elijah says, gesturing to me, "is William Brown, a local author. Getting fake kidnapped could inspire a crime drama, and you know writers. They always want inspiration."

Oh, how wonderful and clever. I get what's going on here. He always tells half-truths instead of lying directly. I want to throttle that self-righteous bastard, but I don't even have what it takes to finish off a dying chicken.

"A novel, you say?" Mark asks.

Elijah looks at me through the corner of his eye, and I swear he's suppressing a supervillain laugh. I wish he would just slip up and let it loose. Surely then the cop would realize that his former partner is the human incarnation of the Devil. Can you arrest people for being the Devil? That's got to be some kind of crime, right?

Mark *hmms* and nods after careful consideration of his words. "In that case," he says, "let me know when you're done with it. I love crime dramas."

"Sure," I say, all my hopes and dreams deflating. "A friend of Elijah's is a friend of mine."

Now that I'm being framed for murder and found out Elijah is probably friends with every cop in Philly, I consider asking Arete to drop the formalities of kidnapping and remove the handcuffs so we don't look like bondage freaks. It doesn't make sense for them to continue to keep tabs on me when I made my surrender clear from the beginning. They're slowly sobering up. Arete still thinks we're going to be the best of friends, but Elijah is just being overly cautious. Maybe it's actually a small consolation that he's a former police officer. He knows what to do, and if he burns, we all burn together... because he's an asshole who just framed me for murder. Never mind.

"So, Arete is it?" Mark asks.

"Yep, that's me."

"How long have you been together?"

Arete taps her foot as she ponders. "Well, we started dating on Valentine's Day, so... About ten days, then."

Ten *days*? I'm being framed for murder by a crooked ex-cop over his girlfriend of ten *days*? Now I'm mad.

After Elijah and Mark are done catching up, Mark leaves to return to his patrol and we're seated at a booth. Elijah sits with a stiff back, his feet at a 45 degree angle and his heels together. Arete slouches over the table and kicks her legs back and forth. Even when she accidentally kicks Elijah and apologizes profusely, he doesn't move a muscle. I lean back against the booth, wishing I was anywhere else right now.

Arete charms the waitress into letting her order off the kid's menu, and she chooses grilled cheese and hot chocolate. And to think, people call *me* a twelve-year-old. Just thinking of that combination makes me gag. Elijah evidently hates Waffle House as much as I do, because he has a sour expression just looking through the menu. He settles on, and I quote, "Just the hash browns, only the hash browns, no I would not like anything else." He jokingly adds, "Except maybe a beer." The waitress doesn't laugh, but Arete does just to humor him. He ends up ordering water, (or "wood-er," as native Philadelphians tend to say) furthering my assumption that he's dreading his hangover.

I'm about to order a Texas cheesesteak when Elijah speaks for me.

"He's kidding," Elijah says with a sense of urgency. "He'll take hash browns too. Like I said. Just the hash browns, only the hash browns."

"And he wants hot chocolate too!" Arete says.

I just want something that isn't breakfast for dinner and can be eaten with only my left hand. Hash browns don't exactly meet the criteria, but I'm too nervous to complain about something so small. As frustrated as I am, I still have to admit that free food isn't so bad compared to being locked in a basement or left to be eaten alive by pigs.

The waitress walks away, but Elijah doesn't bother to wait until she's out of earshot before he says, "I just saved your life, Boy Meets World."

"By ordering me hash browns?" I don't hide the skepticism in my voice.

"Don't say I never gave you anything." With an inappropriately serious tone, he says, "The hash browns are soft and golden. Everything else..." He narrows his eyes. "*Is toxic!*"

"No way," Arete says. "You didn't try the pecan waffles."

He starts origami folding a napkin. "What if I'm allergic to pecans?"

"Bullocks," Arete says. "You ate chocolate turtles yesterday."

"And I vomited."

Arete crosses her arms, dragging my hand dangerously close to her breasts. "You're probably lactose intolerant!" she says. "Like half of Greeks are. Have you tried taking a pill?"

"It's a secret." He's halfway through folding a jumping frog. "And I don't need to know what something tastes like to know I don't like it."

"You're talking like a bloody six-year-old!"

"Oh, this coming from the grown-ass woman who ordered off the kids' menu."

Arete throws her arms in the air, causing my hand to brush her breasts. Awkward. "So what?" she says.

Personally, I think Elijah has a point, but I'm not about to get involved in a lover's quarrel between the people who ruined my life. Nobody in their right mind would expect me to defend a man who thinks ordering me hash browns makes up for kidnapping me and framing me for murder. And actually, now that I think of it, he *did* steal my wallet. No telling if I'll get that back.

They don't say another word to each other, but the argument is clearly still ongoing. Rather than paying any attention to the waitress when she brings out our drinks, they exchange bitter looks. Arete doesn't take her scornful eyes off her boyfriend for more than a second, even when she leans over to blow the steaming surface of her hot chocolate. Elijah, on the other hand, tries to communicate disinterest by occupying himself with his napkin origami. He takes my napkin to create a paper crane, but occasionally glances in our general direction to let us both know he's still annoyed. I check my watch; 5:48 AM. I didn't check the time before I left Wayspeed, but I'm pretty sure it's been about seven hours or so.

I yawn and slump over in my seat. I want to go home and sleep on my own lumpy, box spring mattress. It isn't comfortable, but at least it's home. Why did I have to follow a cute girl into that dark alley? I've seen enough horror movies to know better than that. But if I was going to use "what if" statements, what if I didn't go to work? What if I never applied to work there to begin with? I definitely wouldn't be sitting here pressing my fork into stray hash brown pieces with my left hand because it's the only way I can get my food to stay on the fork. And why did I worry that a girl who bought a pack of condoms would be walking alone that night? Going after her was a serious lapse of judgment. What if I followed those footprints to... well... you know. Screaming in another context. Help. The mental image of Elijah and Arete getting it on won't leave my head.

"God no."

I don't realize I spoke out loud until Arete jumps, spilling a little bit of hot chocolate on her dress. "You are *so* lucky I'm wearing black."

"You always wear black," Elijah says. "It washes you out."

Wonderful, I've started them up again. Just kill me now so I don't have to listen to any more of this. They've been together ten days, yet they argue like it's been ten years.

"Excuse me," she says, "I have a gothic ambiance going on. My alabaster skin only adds to my look, which, I might add, you have complemented on multiple occasions."

"Haven't you ever wondered why you're so pasty if you're Greek? Whitey," Elijah says, strangely bitter.

"My mum was pale," Arete says. "What kind of question is that anyway? What, you think you're... *better* than me? Just because you're Greek on both sides?"

"No," he says. "I'm just more Greek than you."

"Then why is your last name Walker?"

He exhales sharply. "My parents were both Greek expats, my dad was a lying asshole, my mom abandoned me, I got tired of everyone tripping over Papadópoulos, and I thought Walker sounded cool. Can we not talk about this?"

I see the sympathy in Arete's eyes. She didn't mean to hit a soft spot... so naturally, she's going to show her sentiment by not taking any responsibility for her actions.

"You started it!" she says. "Ηλίας Ιάκωβος Παπαδόπουλος!"

"Σκάσε!" Elijah says.

No. Please tell me they aren't going to do what I think they are.

"Σε μισώ!" Arete says.

Elijah raises his voice. "Σε αγαπώ περισσότερο από όσο με μισείς!"

Arete's cheeks flush. "Σκάσε μαλάκα!" she shouts, matching his volume.

"Μαλάκα;" Elijah asks, pretending to be offended. "Μόλις σου είπα πως σ' αγαπώ!"

Whatever he said, Arete isn't buying it. "Αυτό σημαίνει καβγά!"

Elijah bats his eyes and holds his hand over his heart. "Σε αγαπώ ακόμα περισσότερο τώρα!"

Arete throws out her arms, bumping mine on the table. "Γιατί είσαι τόσο σαρκαστικός, γαμώτο:"

"Επειδή σ' αγαπώ," Elijah says with a seemingly-genuine smile.

Arete maintains her scowl in spite of her reddening cheeks. "Δεν θέλω να ακούσω αυτό τώρα!"

God help me. I'm not even sure what language this is. I guess Greek because they both said they were Greek. Maybe I should've trusted Arete on her ethnicity from the beginning instead of being an ass about it, not that I'm the one who owes anyone an apology. The waitress comes out with our food, and I make a mental note to never ask Elijah about his family. The first thing Arete does is pull out her iPhone.

"Τι κάνεις;" Elijah asks.

"Βγάζω φωτογραφία," she says.

Elijah squints. "Γιατί;"

"Για το Instagram." Arete holds her phone level with my food and snaps a picture. "Θα το επισημάνω ως «hashtag hashbrowns». Είναι αστείο."

"You're posting my food on Instagram?" I ask. "After saying you aren't a white girl?"

Arete's eyes widen, embarrassed. "You can speak Greek?"

"No," I say. "That one was just kind of obvious."

Arete lets it drop, probably out of embarrassment, and the three of us eat in silence. Arete's table manners are childish, but it's Elijah's dining habits that strike me as odd. He rests his left hand on his knee, and eats only with his right hand. If he can eat hash browns with only one hand, so can I. Granted, I have to use my left hand, so it doesn't quite work out that way.

As glad as I am that they've stopped trying to out-Greek each other, their staring match to the death is worse. At least the hash browns are as good as Elijah said they are. They're nothing like the ones I tried at McDonald's when I worked there. Not that anything they had was good, and it smelled horrible there. I did like my coworkers, though. Alice was always nice to me.

"Ah! *Alice!*" I whisper to myself. I was supposed to meet her for lunch tomorrow, but it looks like that isn't going to happen. Arete and Elijah are my best mates forever now. I don't get the chance to choose my friends.

"Alice?" Elijah asks, confused.

"She's just some girl I used to work with," I say like I'm hiding a secret best mate, which is probably like cheating on them or something. "She wanted to get coffee with me tomorrow at noon. I don't really like Starbucks that much anyway. It's just overpriced coffee you can get anywhere."

"Sounds like a date," Elijah says.

"Nah, she just wants to catch up," I say. "We didn't talk a whole lot outside of work."

That's close enough. The unfiltered truth is that it can't possibly be a date because she just broke up with a guy who looks like James Dean and embodies a Lana Del Rey song. Nobody downgrades from a modern James Dean to the personification of taco filling dripping onto your lap.

Arete grabs my shoulder. "She was *asking you out*, you drongo."

"Asking *me* out?"

"You're totally dense," Arete says.

I put my hand to my forehead. She's right, I don't know anything about women, and I'm a fool for ever thinking I did. Alice wasn't exactly a crush of mine except in the sense that I fall in crush too easily, and she was only a friend in the sense that we always got along at work. Still, it's sad to think about a cute girl in distress wondering why even a scrawny nerd stood her up.

"I'm missing a date that I didn't even know I had," I say. "She's going to think I stood her up."

"Give me the rest of your phone," Elijah says. "I'll text her and cancel for you." By this time, he had already finished his food, while Arete and I aren't even halfway done. Damn. Then again, we're at a free hand disadvantage. I'm especially behind, dripping food onto the counter and missing my mouth with the fork.

She frowns. "Aww. This is so sad. Eli, we have to let him see her."

Arete and Elijah re-bonded over how stupid I am, and now they're probably going to start fighting again over whether or not I should be allowed to go on a date. What have I done?

"I don't necessarily *have* to go," I say.

"Arete, I don't trust him," Elijah says in a hushed tone. "We haven't even had time to get our story straight yet."

"We have a story?" I lower my voice to a whisper. "I thought the story was that I murdered a man with an icicle, and that you're a cop so nothing I do would ever get you in trouble."

Elijah smirks. "I wouldn't say nothing."

"It doesn't really matter anyway," I say. "I'll just call and tell her I have ebola, and I'm probably going to die soon."

"Oh, no you won't," Arete says. "Eli, how do you feel about double dates?"

"I hate them because I hate sharing," he says.

Arete shields her mouth with her right hand. "That was rhetorical," she says through a mouth full of grilled cheese.

"Thanks," I say, "but isn't she going to think it's weird that I'm handcuffed to another girl?" It may have been an obvious way of bringing up my imprisonment, but it's still a legitimate question.

Elijah pulls a small key out of his pocket and slides it across the table. "Well, we've come to an understanding that bad things will happen if you try anything funny," he says. "And I'm kind of tired of you being chained to my girlfriend. How many times have you *accidentally* touched her boob now?"

Hallelujah. Jealousy has set me free. I should've known he was the one with the key all along, though. And to think, I was wasting my time pleading to Arete all night.

"Does that mean I've found the inspiration for my crime drama then?" I ask.

Arete unlocks the handcuffs.

Elijah reaches into his coat pocket and returns my wallet. "You're free-ish, if that's what you mean. But we're still going to keep tabs on you; we don't want you changing your mind in the morning and burning yourself out of panic."

That's where I draw the line. "No. You are *not* staying with me, there is no way in Hell. Don't you have a place of your own? What were you doing at a sleaze motel anyway?"

"I just wanted to drop you off at your place." Elijah sighs. "I meant we'd stop by in the morning..." he checks his watch. "Okay, the afternoon. And do you really want to know what we were doing at a sleaze motel?"

Arete laughs.

"No," I say. "I guess not."

"So, what's the plan?" Arete asks. "We drop him off at his house, then go back to the motel? Or are we just going to go back to Penn?"

"College dorms?" I ask. Now that I'm "free-ish" and we're in public, it's a lot easier to talk to them. "Excuse me for asking, but I know that you're loaded, and Elijah just looks a little old for a dorm." *I should not have said that. Curse my mouth.* I tap my foot. "What are you, uh..." *Should I say 22? No, too many creases to be believable. 30? Too risky.* "About..." I take a deep breath. "25?"

"31," Elijah says. "But thanks for lowballing."

I grimace.

Arete takes a sip of her hot cocoa. "I'm from Oz. And cut me a break, I'm only twenty-one."

Let's see... There are ten years between them. Half of Elijah's age plus seven is 23, rounding up. He's a bit of a cradle robber then, isn't he?

Elijah crosses his arms and leans back. "As for me, I wanted to start over, so I went to law school. I live in an apartment with a married couple. It's not exactly a great place to bring a girl."

I test my hot chocolate; it's now lukewarm, just how I like it. "Oh. That makes sense, I guess."

"What about you, Boy Meets World?" he asks. "What did you do with your life?"

That isn't a question I want to answer, but since we're "best mates," I feel obligated to. Other than witnessing murder, I spend my time working minimum wage jobs, lounging around the house watching television, and thinking up novels that I know I'll never finish... or start.

"Uh, my life is pretty boring," I say. "I couldn't afford college. My grades weren't good enough for scholarships, and the National Guard said I didn't weigh enough to get in. I work at a gas station and live in a rental home. My roommate got caught with a pound of marijuana last year, so I don't know how I'm going to keep paying rent."

"Mitchell Bane?" Elijah asks.

"Yeah. How'd you know?"

"I made that arrest," he says.

"Oh." The same man who kidnapped me arrested my roommate. He ruined my life before I even knew he existed. Figures. "So, we're pretty far from my house right now."

"No problem," he says. "I know where you live. I'll drive you."

I don't want a ride from him, but I also don't want hypothermia. "You can get your car out of the driveway now?"

"It has four-wheel drive," Elijah says. "Arete just wanted to do a midnight stroll. She likes the cold." That's obvious, since she's dating a coldblooded killer. "Besides," he says, "I take drunk driving seriously, especially when there's ice on the roads. But I'm okay to drive now, and we've teased you enough for the night, I'll take you home now."

Teased. *Teased*. Teased is not the word I would use. I don't know to what extent I'm free, but if anything is certain it's this: My life is about to get *interesting*.

Wednesday, February 25, 2015

After what happened today, I will never go to Starbucks again; I had completely misunderstood, thanks to my new "best mates." Alice had recently applied for a job there, and lied during the interview process by saying she was a regular. To cover her tracks, she became an actual regular so she would run into the manager more often. She brought me along to make herself look more sociable. She wasn't exactly impressed by my new "friends" either, not that I expected her to be. To sum it up, we spent twenty minutes attempting idle chitchat while Elijah stared out the window and Arete rambled about how her croissants are "way better than anything she's ever had at a café." Believe it or not, Alice wasn't the one who left early—it was me. I couldn't handle it after Elijah nicknamed her "Alice in Wonderland" and told her to "stop daydreaming and directly talk to the fucking manager if you want a job so badly instead of using Boy Meets World to make you look like a friendly team member." I was secretly relieved to have an excuse to leave, but I'd never tell him that; it's not like he did it for me. He wanted out of there just as badly as I did.

Now Elijah is driving me home, all the while trying not to laugh as I sulk in the back seat, wallowing in humiliation.

"Cut that out," I say. "That was embarrassing. It's not bad enough that my DNA is on a dead body?"

"If it makes you feel any better," Arete says, "if we had a choice, he wouldn't have done that. And we're both grateful that you were worried enough to come out and make sure I was getting home safe."

"Even though it was really stupid," Elijah says.

Arete is about to elbow him, but then looks at his hands on the steering wheel and keeps her limbs to herself. Thank god she has *some* sense, because Elijah is a terrible driver. Quite possibly the worst. It has little to do with skill, and everything to do with patience. The man has some serious anger management issues when it comes to traffic. He drops more F-bombs than a fighter aircraft, and the angrier he gets, the Greeker he gets. I almost ask Arete what "γαμήσου" means since I hear it a lot, but decide I'd be better off zoning out.

When we arrive at my house, Arete hops out of his blue Dodge 4x4. "Let's hang out for a while. We can get your mind off things."

"That's okay," I say in quick defense of my alone time. "You don't have to do that."

Elijah takes the key out of the ignition and steps out of the truck. "Nice house. It looks even better in the daylight."

Note to self: Elijah disconnects his lie detector for obvious sarcasm. I don't need anyone else to tell me that my rental is a dilapidated eyesore; that's the only reason I can afford a decent-sized place in the city since I can't find another roommate. That, and I've been gradually hawking off

Mitchell's stuff. I'll apologize to him when he gets out of prison, which is probably never. Mitchell hired a painter two years ago to paint the house yellow of all colors, and the shutters are this hideous shade of red. I'm almost grateful that the paint is chipping off, because that gives me an excuse to paint it another color if someone buys his vintage Air Jordans off eBay.

I ignore Elijah and unlock the front door. I really don't want any guests to see the disaster that is my house, even if it's just Arete.

"I really don't understand what makes you want to visit me," I say.

"I won't lie," Arete says as she walks through the door. "I was always curious about what Nathan Faust's life was like. Your book was so dark, so I must say the decor surprises me a little."

She's just saying that to be nice. There's no way anyone with taste would consider my house decorated. All of the walls are the standard white, and the whole house has the same gray carpeting. Or, at least it used to be gray. So many things have been spilled on that carpet over the years that I don't even worry about staining it. There's no hope of getting my damage deposit back. Even my couch has a huge orange juice stain on it. It's weird how germs bother me anywhere else, but in my own house all I do is sanitize all the surfaces, wash the linens once a week, keep track of the expiry dates in the fridge, and clean the toilet, sinks, and showers every night before I go to sleep.

"I'm not staying," Elijah says. "Professor Hicks hates me, and I don't want to be late for class."

I feel you, Professor Hicks. I feel you.

Arete gives Elijah a long hug. "I'm going to miss you."

"It's only for a little while," he says. "I'll be back in about... two hours, maybe less."

"I hope it's less."

Barf. I'm tempted to tell them go get a room when they start making out, but I find it's generally better to ignore them. Arete loses her excess energy when Elijah leaves. She looks lonely. I guess I'm no substitute for Hollywood Perfect.

"Well, what do you want to do?" I ask. "I don't have much."

"It's your house," she says. "Elijah told me to keep an eye on you, but if you really want to be alone after what happened, I understand. You must be a little mad at me for convincing you it was a date."

I put my hands in my pockets. The "date" isn't why I'm "a little mad."

"No, no. It's okay," I say. "Getting rejected sucks, but you're right. I don't want to stay here alone and mope over it." Wait... that sincerity in my voice... What's wrong with me?

Arete sits down on my juice-stained couch. "And I wanted to stay behind so I could apologize about last night. I am *so* embarrassed, I almost can't believe this is all real. It was a drunk decision, and Eli takes everything I say so seriously, and I thought he was going to kill you or something. But then I sobered up and realized he was just trying to scare you so you wouldn't report it."

Her story sounds legit, but I feel like I'm missing part of the picture. Maybe I can catch her in a lie. She's sweet enough, but I don't trust her any more than I trust her boyfriend. I sit down on the other end of the couch, leaving a chastity cushion between us.

"No, it's okay," I say. "It isn't your fault that you were attacked in an alley."

"It may as well have been," she says. "I should have had Eli come in with me. But he was embarrassed about buying condoms, and he waited in that alley next to the broken street light so no one would see him. Men."

Yeah, that's complete bullshit, but Arete isn't such a bad person. She was excited to meet a writer she liked, and I wasn't used to that attention. I want Elijah, however, to stay the hell away from me. Unfortunately for me, they came packaged together.

Like she can read my mind, she adds, "Eli will come around. He likes you, he's just nervous about trusting you."

Sure.

"So why didn't you go to the police?" I ask. "I mean, if he was trying to defend you, why would he get in trouble with the law?"

"I did ask him that," Arete says. "He's pretty paranoid. He said something about 'malice aforethought.' He said he could've restrained the guy, but he apparently 'chose' to kill him. That's how he saw it in the heat of the moment, anyway."

"But doesn't he have the cop brotherhood on his side?" I ask.

She shrugs. "He wasn't a detective. I'm not sure how it works, but I think he was a traffic cop mostly. But he's talked about arrests he's made too. You'll have to ask him."

A traffic cop? Really? He tailgated a red Sedan for five blocks because the driver was going "too slow," AKA, the speed limit. The more I hear about this guy, the more I hate him.

"I guess that makes sense," I say. "I'm not going to tell though. Especially not with that little detail of my DNA being on a dead body."

"I know," she says, "It was wrong of him to do that. But he's totally *freaking out*. We ended up going back to the motel instead of campus, and the *second* we were alone he started pacing and going nuts. It scared me... I'm still scared."

"I guess I can understand that," I say.

I don't want to admit it, but now that she's explained what was going on in his head, the situation isn't as far-fetched. Well, other than the icicle part. That I'm still trying to wrap my head around. It was quick thinking after he was disarmed, and I at least respect that. Well, at least he doesn't have to worry about a murder weapon, since it's part of the water cycle now.

"Please try," Arete says. "I really do want to be friends."

"After that, we're already friends, aren't we?" I try to turn on the television to stop this uncomfortable conversation, but it shorts out. "That's weird... Well, there's another TV upstairs. It's smaller, but it's connected to Netflix."

"Let's go then," Arete says. "Want my HBO password?"

"Yes!" Curse my enthusiasm. Am I so easily bought?

*

We're a few minutes into the third episode of *Game of Thrones* when I smell something burning.

"Do you smell that?" Arete asks.

"It smells like smoke." I get up. My eyes start to water. "Maybe I forgot to turn my stove off after we made the ramen. Some of the noodles probably fell into the burner again."

I open my bedroom door and realize too late that I can't remember the last time I changed the batteries in my smoke alarm. Smoke is crawling up the stairs, and the kitchen is already engulfed in fire. My phone, where is my phone... shit. Elijah never returned my phone battery. I'm dead.

"Arete!" I say. "We need to call the fire department!"

She digs through her purse. "I can't find it... crap!" She turns her purse inside out and dumps the contents onto my bed. "Awh, bullocks!"

I cough, and the smell of smoke stings my nose. This incident may beat yesterday for the Worst Day of my Life title. All we can do for now is open both the windows and beg that this isn't also the *last* day of my life. Okay. Someone will call the fire department. The neighbors, maybe, if they're home. If they don't, it'll spread to their houses in a few minutes.

"Look," Arete says. "It's Eli's truck!" She sticks her head out the closest window and calls out to him like a damsel in distress. I guess we're both damsels in distress, or else I wouldn't be happy to see *him* of all people.

Elijah doesn't even bother to cut the ignition before jumping out and rushing to the front door. Personally, I think it would've been smarter to call 911, but that's just me—me and probably everyone else ever. Elijah is overconfident. For the first time, I'm glad that my front door has a weak lock, and I couldn't be happier that Elijah has the strength to kill me six times without blinking. He kicks open the door, and rushes inside. Like a moron. A moron that I am grateful for, but a moron nonetheless.

When he makes it up the stairs, he grabs Arete and tosses her over his shoulder like she's as light as a rag doll. "Cover your nose and shut your eyes!" he says. "Pool Noodle, open that window and wait there!"

I don't understand what he's doing and I don't like being called *Pool Noodle*, but it's better than *Boy Meets World* and I'm not going to pick this moment to question him. It's hotter than Mexico in July and impossible to breathe. By the time my pathetic ass manages to open the window, I see him setting Arete down outside. I wish I was that fast. It would have been useful last night.

"Okay, jump!" he shouts.

Jump?

"I am *not* going to jump out the window!" I yell. Did he plan all of this so I would fall to my death? Better not risk it.

"A beam fell at the base of the stairs, I can't get in there anymore!"

With a fire raging behind me, I don't have a choice. I have to jump out the window and trust him to catch me. I look straight down to gauge the distance. It's a sickening, dizzying feeling. I take a deep breath of tainted air and cough. I have to trust Elijah, or I'm not going to make it.

Come on, William. It's just like a cannonball at the pool. Except there's fire everywhere and a homicidal traffic cop is waiting for you at the bottom. And you were never a good diver, and you haven't been to a swimming pool since you were eleven.

"On the count of three!" Elijah shouts.

I crawl out headfirst, as ready to drive as I'll ever be. I try to be graceful, but I scream like a girl as I fall before he even starts counting.

I cough and wheeze, but I'm alive. He caught me. I expect him to drop me like a sack of potatoes, but he helps me come to a stand.

"See, Boy Meets World?" he says. "I'm not going to let you die."

"You better not think we're even now," I say.

He chuckles and pats me on the head. Bastard.

The fire department arrives at the scene a few minutes later. I might have been fine if I waited up there instead of trusting Mr. Satan with my life, but I'm so glad to be out of that oven that I don't even care. I look over my shoulder and see Elijah comforting his girlfriend. She's crying and having a panic attack, but otherwise fine, so I divert my attention to what's left of my home. Two hoses are pointed at my house, and a firefighter asks Elijah (Not me? Really?) if there's anyone else in my house. By the time the fire is out, it's clear no one is going to live in that house again.

I speak to one of the firefighters after she comes out, asking her how it happened. I'm worried it was my fault.

"Not sure, but I'm pretty sure it's an electrical fire," she says. "Something downstairs in the kitchen shorted out, and your smoke alarm didn't sound. There were no batteries in it."

I nod slowly, having a hard time taking it in. How did I mess up this badly? I may be lazy, but I'm not scatterbrained. I change them every year on daylight saving's time, that's how I remember. Did I get distracted halfway through?

"It was the neighbor who called 911, by the way," the firefighter says. "You're lucky that Officer Walker got there at the right time, or else you two could have been toast... Say, why did he quit the police after he saved that kid?"

"What?" I ask.

"You know," she says. "This past summer, when he took a bullet for that kid. He didn't tweet about it or anything, he just quit."

"I'm not sure, I just met him yesterday." Officer Walker? Local hero? Twitter user? This guy has all sorts of surprises. Sacrificing himself for a little boy is impressive, but for it to endure this long it's got to be hot people privilege or a niche fangirl coincidence. Maybe both. I'm sure a lot of them came from dating Arete, AKA "@battybabyx," who was boasting about all her Instagram fans earlier. She was paid $5,000 just to wear a dress. I wonder if I could convince her to give my book a shout out so I can make enough sales to get a new place when renter's insurance inevitably screws me over. "We knew he was coming around now," I say. "But yeah, we got lucky."

The firefighter frowns and nods. "We'll see what we can salvage. I hope you didn't have anything too important downstairs."

"Not really," I say.

Most of the notes for a novel I was planning were downstairs, but I probably would have used them to tinder my fireplace if I had one. That and the unsold copies of my novella... but it looks like my book has finally ascended to its rightful place. *Night in the Fire...* was literally on fire.

"Well, at least there's that," she says. "I talked to Walker, and he said he's going to take you and that girl to the emergency room now. You're *so* lucky to be friends with him! Like, you have no idea."

"Yeah... He's a good friend to have." He may have framed me for murder, but if it was really an electrical fire, it would have happened eventually. I hate admitting it, but she's right. Thanks to my blunder with the smoke alarm, I could have died of smoke inhalation if none of this ever happened. That doesn't mean I forgive or trust him, just that I hate him less. Or maybe more, since he obviously has more fans than I ever will.

Soon after, news vans park in front of my house. The main attraction is Hollywood Perfect, two-time hero, and the star of the local news' next fluff story. He tries to get out of it, but they're annoyingly persistent. His modest sense of duty makes him likable, and Arete pulls herself together for her public image. Behold, Channel 4's cutest couple. I slip unnoticed into Elijah's truck to hide and, of course, turn off the ignition. It was really bothering me.

*

After our release from the hospital, Arete returns to her dorm and I find myself at Elijah's apartment to crash on his couch. His apartment is nice for the budget of a former police officer, nice being a bit of an understatement. For the life of me, I can't understand how a traffic cop can afford a medium-size, two bedroom apartment with a study, let alone the way he furnishes it. While it isn't over the top, it's nothing to sneeze at either. Most of the furniture looks new, as does the flat screen TV that I'm shamelessly drooling over. Unfortunately, the couch I get to sleep on isn't as soft as it looks. I'm going to wake up with a terrible cramp in my neck. After giving me a quick tour, he motions for me to follow him to his bedroom, which is right across from the front door.

Like the rest of the apartment, it's tidy but not in an anal way where it looks like no one lives here. It's still nice, but it's objectively the least stylish room in the apartment. Whereas the rest of the apartment looks like something out of an interior design magazine, this room is sparsely decorated. The colors, mostly grays and muted shades of blue, are harmonious but aren't tied together as well. The bathroom, for example, looks like everything was planned out and arranged like a work of art. This bedroom looks like it was put together slowly over time by a lonely guy who just really likes blue.

The way he makes his bed is the weirdest part. It's a nice queen size bed, but there's no comforter or anything like that. The blanket is stuffed under the mattress and folded diagonally at the corners like a hospital bed. A second blanket is folded and draped over two pillows, one on each side. It's the saddest bed I've ever seen. I never made my bed, but even it had two fuzzy blankets and sheets with puppies on them. Of course, they're probably smoke damaged. Maybe I should just start over.

"Thanks again for catching me," I say. If I have to live with this guy indefinitely, it's best to be polite and submissive.

"Uh..." Elijah stretches and looks away. "I'd have done it for almost anyone. Don't mention it."

I like how he says "almost." There's that technicality mode again. At least I never have to worry about him lying to me; but what happens if one of us gets caught for that murder? Is he going to say, "Yeah I took an icicle and staked that guy like a vampire, sorry, if I plead guilty can I get off with ten years?" I don't want to think about that right now, so I change the subject.

"The firefighter I talked to said you took a bullet for a kid once," I say.

"Oh, yeah," Elijah says, voice flat. "Want to see the scar?"

"Not really."

"Good." Elijah turns around and starts rummaging through boxes in his closet. "Frankly, I'm kind of tired of hearing about it. I was just doing my job, I didn't want it to end up on the front page. But still, I don't want that kid to grow up and hear that Officer Walker killed a man in cold blood for his girlfriend of not even two weeks. Especially not with an icicle. I mean, it was a smart move, but it's savage. I don't think anyone would understand."

I can't believe I'm hearing this. Is this even the same guy as this morning? Does he have a twin? "I'm sure everyone would have understood," I say. "The saving Arete part, I mean. Not stabbing a man with an icicle."

"It's too late now anyway," he says. "And nobody would ever understand it."

"Why not?" I ask. "It seems pretty clear to me. You don't want to watch innocent people die."

Elijah pushes a box aside and starts digging through another one. "I saw plenty of people die when I was in the Marines. Saving civilians is my duty. Or at least it was. You're not special, and there's no need to thank me."

A vet. Now that he mentions it, that explains a lot about his character.

"I didn't mean to offend you," I say.

"Then do me a favor and pretend none of this ever happened."

"Why?" I ask. "You're actually pretty nice."

"Hereee it is!" Elijah pulls a red t-shirt out of the box and hands it to me. "I hung onto some old souvenir shirts from when I was twelve," he says. "They should fit you."

"Is that a short joke?" I ask.

"It's an observation. Since you look like the mid-90's anyway, I figure they're right up your alley. There's even a Mickey Mouse Club sweater in here. Merry Christmas, kid."

Note to self: Do *not* call Elijah "nice."

Thursday, February 26, 2015

The gaudy, out of season Christmas decorations are nothing compared to the pile of ash that used to be my home. Considering what happened yesterday, I love my job. No matter what happens, at least I can escape to work. If today is busy enough, I can even forget that I'm the homeless victim of a kidnapping who's being framed for murder.

My manager greets me with a fake smile. "Oh, Will. I need to talk to you."

"Hey, Kristi," I say. "My shift starts in five minutes."

"Why didn't you answer my calls?" she asks.

"My phone was... stolen." I don't want to get into it.

Kristi tilts her head toward the back room, prompting me to follow. The second I get there, she scurries to shut the door behind me.

Kristi shakes her head. "This is nothing against you personally, but professionally, your behavior was out of line."

My heart sinks. "What behavior?"

Kristi takes a remote off the table and unpauses the television. "You were caught on tape."

A security tape shows Arete drunkenly handing me a hundred dollar bill and me bagging her condoms. It's unsettling seeing myself on a security tape.

"Yeah, I checked her out. It's my job. So?"

"Keep watching."

I see myself checking the change drawer, and then slipping the hundred dollar bill into my sock. "Oops."

She holds her fingertips to her forehead and shakes her head in frustration. "There's no *oops* about it. This is serious."

"I know," I say. I open up my wallet (which Elijah finally returned to me) and make change. "She tipped me, and there wasn't enough change in the register. So I was going to take the money from my wallet, but then we closed and I got distracted because I was worried about her walking alone."

"I don't think you understand," Kristi says.

She cups her hands together and I drop $4.17 into her hands; mostly change. I can't tell if she feels sorry for me or just thinks I'm stupid. She's hard to read.

"*William*, you technically shoplifted condoms from the store, and as the manager, I can't let this slide. Also, that Nickelodeon Studios shirt violates dress code."

"What are you saying?" I ask.

She sets the change on the table behind her and leans forward. "I'm saying that you need to find another job."

"But you can't just fire me!" I say. "How about a warning, I swear I'll be the perfect employee from now on."

"*William*," she says. "I appreciate your honesty, and I'm glad you gave the money back. I'll give you a good reference, I'll even lie and say you worked here longer than you did if that helps you get a new job, but we can't keep you here."

There's no point in fighting it. I consider playing the "but my house burned down yesterday!" card, but it wouldn't change her mind. It would just make her feel sorry for me. I swallow and take a deep breath. "I understand."

*

I find myself on Elijah's couch, my face buried in my hands. How could I be so stupid? It wasn't my dream job, but it was still my job. How am I going to find another one? It's my fault, but I still blame my new "best mates." If Arete never walked in there that night, none of this would have ever happened. My life would be boring, and boring in a good way.

I miss the days when my biggest problems were poverty and disappointing others. I refused to so much as go to technical school because I was so dead set on being a writer. I'll never forget the look on my mother's face when I told her. She offered to get a second job to help pay my tuition, but I wouldn't let her. I could work at the post office like my father. That sounds boring enough.

I'll never forget the look on my father's face when *Night in the Fire* was published. He was even happier than I was. It took me years of rejection to get a novel published, and my parents were genuinely proud of me for the first time as opposed to pretending. When it tanked, my mom and I stopped talking and I couldn't face my dad either. It's just as well, because if they knew everything I had gotten into in the past few days, they'd give up on me all over again. Even if my cell phone wasn't melted, I still wouldn't want to talk to anyone.

My thoughts are interrupted by the voice of one of Elijah's roommates. His name is Tommy, I think; my face is in my palms so I can't see who it is, but I recognize the voice. He has a light country accent, but I can't place the region.

"Hangover?" he asks.

"No," I say without moving. "I got fired for technically shoplifting condoms for Elijah's girlfriend."

Tommy sits down on the other side of the loveseat. I feel the cushions flex as he leans back. "Man, that is *all kinds* of fucked up. But... Technically?"

"Long story short," I say, "I couldn't make change for her $100 bill and she just told me to keep it, and I decided to stick it in my sock and deal with it later. Except I forgot. So now I have no house *and* no job."

"Tough break... Want a beer?"

I pulled my hands out of my face and look him in the eyes. "It's ten in the morning."

"Ten fifty-six, actually. And it's five o'clock somewhere."

I sit up and stare out the window. The morning sun is high in the sky, but it's obscured by winter clouds. Snow is melting on the ground, turned dirty by the filth of Philadelphia traffic. We live in a sad, gloomy world.

I take a deep breath. "You know what... Make it vodka."

Tommy stands up and smiles. "We're out of vodka, but we have, like, six bottles of Kentucky bourbon."

If my memory serves me right, the bourbon in question is 120 proof, and the bottle is bigger than my head. I'm a 5'4" "pool noodle" who rarely drinks. A single shot could screw me up for hours.

"Even better," I say.

I can hear his voice from around the corner in the kitchen as he rummages through the cabinets. "Oh, wait, five bottles. Whatever. How do you want it?"

I don't spend a lot of time contemplating. "On the rocks. I'll pay you back."

"Nah, don't bother," Tommy says. He comes back into the room with a Brooklyn Lager for himself and a bottle of bourbon for me. "I get more than I want. My dad owns a brewery in Kentucky, and he sends me free booze. I'm too ashamed to admit that I hate the shit. I only drink beer and fruity cocktails."

"You're from Kentucky?" I ask. "But you don't sound Southern."

"Dude, fuck the Mason Dixon line," Tommy says. "That was made because of some 1700's border dispute. Kentucky is totally not Southern. At all. Period." He crosses his arms and spills a little bit of beer on the couch. "Hell, even West Virginia is under it, and they're practically in the ass crack of Canada. It's right next to Pennsylvania. And I'm not even just talking politics. Kentucky is in the middle of a blizzard so sick that they can't even get out of their driveways. A waterline broke and cars got frozen to the ground. They put out an arrest warrant for Queen Elsa last week—no joke. Or, well, maybe it was a joke. I didn't read the article, just the headline. They had a picture and it looked weirdly legit."

"Sorry," I say, hoping he doesn't continue to ramble about this. "Didn't mean to... offend you?"

"Nah, I'm not offended. I'm specializing in real estate law," he says, as if that explains something. He continues to ramble. "I just think Appalachia and the Deep South are too culturally different to be lumped together. Appalachia is pretty isolated. Not to mention the fact that Kentucky ended up siding with the North in the civil war, and they're on the top half of the map. I mean, it should be pretty obvious." At this point, Tommy finally notices I'm barely listening. "But I'll save that for another day. It looks like we'll be living together for a while. But there's something I've been wondering about you since I met you last night. Just curious."

"Sure," I say, hoping this topic never comes up again.

"How long have you known Elijah?" Tommy asks. "I've only been rooming with him since November, but he's never talked about you before."

Jackpot! With the unwitting help of a drunk roommate, I'll finally get something straight about Elijah. I've been thinking, and I don't exactly trust Officer Walker, local hero. I got caught up in the moment yesterday, but I was a typical average Joe before he showed up. Now I lost my job, my house, and my freedom all within 48 hours. I stop believing in coincidences as of today. This marks the last time William Donatello Julio Romeo Arthur Brown Quiñones takes shit from any bitch! I will win this!

"We just met that day, actually," I say. "I went after Arete to make sure she wasn't walking alone at night, and she recognized me. I'm a local author. Then the three of us hung out at Waffle House."

"But Elijah *hates* Waffle House," Tommy says.

I wipe bourbon off my chin. Thank *god* he didn't ask about my sorry excuse for a book. "Arete chose the place," I say. "He didn't look too happy about it."

Wait, wasn't I supposed to be the one asking the questions... Wait... What was I going to ask? Oh well.

Tommy laughs. "Dude, you totally cock-blocked him."

"Him?" I ask. "Don't you mean *them*? I mean, Arete bought the condoms."

Tommy tries to regain his composure. "Elijah's too obsessed with her to just hang out with a stranger on a date night. He seems to like you, but he probably wishes Arete bumped into you some other day."

Elijah likes me? That's news. At least Elijah and I agree on one thing; I sincerely wish I had bumped into Arete on some other day. Or never. Never sounds good.

"Obsessed with her?" I ask.

Tommy groans, no doubt reminiscing bygone days. "The second he saw her for the first time, he would *not*. *Shut*.

Up about her, but he was too afraid to talk to her for some reason." Tommy leans back, spreads out his legs, and downs a huge gulp of the lager. "And that was back in September. But I shouldn't complain."

"Why not?" I ask.

"It's just kind of douchey," he says. "He paid the entire year's rent for the apartment ahead of time in full, and when he heard I couldn't afford to get a place with my husband on our last year of school, he just let us move in with him. No questions asked. I pay the utilities, and bam." Tommy laughs. "Way better than a married couple living together in a dorm."

"Wowww!" I say. Somebody clearly isn't suffering from the curse of Elijah's presence. "He never told me th-tha-the thing... But how did he afford that? He was a traffic cop, right?"

Tommy nods. "I'm no Elijah Walker expert, but here's what Keyon and I have managed to get out of him since moving in: His parents were Greek expats. They split up when he was young, like, eleven-ish. His mom wasn't in the picture for some reason, so he had to stay with his grandparents in Greece after his father disowned him. Maternal grandparents, probably. He came back to America to take care of his mother when she was sick or something. He didn't elaborate on what was wrong with her, so Keyon thinks she had a nervous breakdown or something. At some point, he joined the Marines. Then his mother went missing, and he got discharged somehow and decided to become a detective so he could find her. But by the time he worked his way up through the ranks, his dad died and he was like 'fuck it,' and used his inheritance on law school. I'm not sure what he did for a living, but I think it involved Greek food. When Keyon asked him if his grandparents were still alive, all he said was 'I hope not,' so it looks like he's a lone wolf."

"That's *all* you got out of him after living with him for three months?" I ask.

"Yeah," he says. "And believe me, it wasn't for lack of trying. I guess some people just don't talk about themselves much, and he's one of 'em.'"

A pang of guilt strikes me for a moment. Elijah isn't that bad of a guy after all. He's an honorable officer of the law who saved a little boy's life, helped out a nice gay couple, and framed me for murder... No. He is a bad, *bad* guy. Something doesn't add up. He may save people, but he still disposed of a body instead of calling the police, and his obsession with his girlfriend is off the charts. I mean, sure, Arete is super-gorgeous in a quirky way, but they haven't even been together for two weeks, I think. Okay, February 14th. That's Valentine's Day. And we met on two days ago. The 24th? So fourteen, fifteen, eighteen... wait, no. I can't math.

"How long has he known Arete?" I ask. "Like, not just crushing on her, but really *known* her? Because when I first met them, I was under the impression they'd been dating for years. But it's only been at least ten days?"

"Uh..." Tommy squints. "Like... a month?"

"A MONTH?"

"I know, right?" he says. "It took him forever to introduce himself, give or take a week."

That's the last time I ask anything about their relationship ever again. This is just creepy and weird. They fight like a married couple; I was banking on at least a few months of close friendship.

He asks me to "report back" if I learn anything "interesting" about Elijah. I consider contributing a warning, but instead the next few hours are filled with unintelligible banter between the two of us. I thought getting drunk would make Elijah's secrets pour out, forgetting that I've always been the tipsy talker. Tommy just rambles on and on about anything that came to his head, and I follow along. At one point, I don't know if we're talking about the same thing, but he laughs a lot. I'm not sure what at.

The Devil himself comes home a few hours early to the drunken mess that was my life—or, more rather, the mess that was his living room. The throw pillows are on the floor next to an empty bag of Doritos. Tommy had knocked over a pile of DVDs looking for *Ferris Beuller's Day Off*, which we never found, and my coat and shoes are in the middle of the floor. To complete the picture, my feet are resting on his coffee table and four empty beer bottles lie down at Tommy's feet.

"I see you two have... bonded," Elijah says.

I look at him with terror in my eyes, but Tommy just gives him a thumbs up before collapsing into the couch.

"Drinking before lunch time?" Elijah asks.

"Maybe," Tommy says. "The kid just lost his job, give him a break."

Elijah rubs his temples. "Whatever. Just... Clean up when the buzz clears, okay? Arete's coming over tonight, and this place is disgusting." I doubt Tommy's claims that he 'seems to like me.' "Never mind," he says. "I'll do it."

"Sorry, bro," Tommy says. "Say, Keyon and I are leaving for Kentucky tonight instead of in the morning. That way the kid can sleep in our bed instead of this hard ass couch, and you won't have to get a sleaze motel. I mean, if William can tune out your love-making."

Those are bold words, even for a drunk man. Does he not know he's talking to the Devil? Even so, Elijah just shrugs and accepts it. Not long after, Keyon (Tommy's husband) comes back from work. Tommy tells me he's a professional interior designer, which is why the apartment looks so gay. He says hi, but scurries off to help Tommy pack. It looks like it's just me and Hollywood Perfect now.

Having nothing better to do and feeling like a bad guest, I help Elijah clean up my mess. Or, should I say, I try. The second I manage to place every movie back on his shelf, I stumble over it, piles of DVDs raining down on me. I direct a timid glance at Elijah, ready to feel his wrath. Instead, he takes it in good humor.

"Maybe you should go lie down," he says. "It doesn't look like you can hold your liquor."

"Yes I can!" I say. "Everyone in my family has the iron liver. I'm not even that drunk right now. I could do summersaults."

Elijah shakes his head; his eyes are shut tight and his fingertips are placed at his brow. He's trying his hardest to stay reserved, but instead has fallen victim to that silent laughter that looks like crying. I don't think I've ever seen him laugh like this before—a friendly laugh, not a condescending snicker.

"What? Can *you* do summersaults?" I ask.

"I did them when I was a kid," he says when he manages to calm down. "So, other than summersaults, what are your life goals?"

Life goals? What kind of friend would ask me a cruel question like that? I don't know what I'm doing, and I never have. There are times I thought I had a grasp on life, but I'm always brutally proven wrong.

"Are you okay?" he asks. "You look like you've just taken the SATs."

I hold up my index finger. "I'll have to take your word for it on that one. I barely graduated high school at nineteen after the summer classes. I was almost twenty, so I know I was the family loser. Then I got a job at Walmart. All I ever wanted was to write amazing books, but writing was harder than... hard stuff. Like the ACT. I got a 13." I reach for the bourbon, but I change my mind; the floor is just so comfortable. This rug must be made of cotton candy, but it smells like cheese powder.

Elijah tosses the emptied bag of Doritos into a trash bag and then proceeds to toss each fallen chip fragment into it one by one. Why he's taking his time is beyond me. He could be done, why is he stalling? It's not like he needs an excuse to talk to me. I'm trapped here.

"So you've only written that one book?" he asks.

I nod. "Yeah."

"Why?"

Not again. I hate that question. "After it tanked, I just can't bring myself to finish anything. Everything that came close, I just gave up and threw away. Everything else was set on fire yesterday. My career was over before it began."

Elijah pats me on the shoulder. "There is nothing to writing. All you do is sit down at a typewriter and bleed."

I stare off into space. "Whoa... you're deep."

"No. That's Hemingway." He frowns. "It gets better, kid. You just have to keep working at it."

"I just don't know what to do with myself," I say, hugging my knees. "You know. Life is hard, adulthood sucks, blah blah blah."

Elijah, having finally picked up every corn chip, looks me in the eye. "It is not life that's complicated, it's the struggle to guide and control life."

I hiccup. "Hemingway again?"

"Fitzgerald," he says. "I tend to give bad advice, so I use quotes from my favorite authors instead."

"Well, whatever works," I say. If he can count Hemingway and Fitzgerald among his favorite authors, I'm guessing he hasn't actually read a novel since high school. Not that I can judge; he's still smarter than me, not that that says much.

Elijah is tying off the garbage bag as the doorbell rings. It's kind of pathetic how his face lights up because he knows it's his girlfriend, like he doesn't see her every single day. The rest of the evening is so boring that I almost think I have my old life back. Elijah orders Chinese. I barf half a bag of Doritos and a quart of lo mein. Elijah turns down my offer to do the dishes. Arete brings over a cult classic called *Repo! The Genetic Opera*, and Elijah pours me a glass of water out of fear that I'll puke on his floor in the middle of the night.

When Arete is out of earshot, he says to me, "For the record, I do feel bad. Almost, anyway. I don't usually act like that, but a stranger witnessing me kill a man kind of set me on edge. I wanted to think I didn't have a choice, but I did... And I'm sorry about what I did to you yesterday, but it's too late to go back now."

"Yesterday?" I ask. "That happened Tuesday."

His response is to wave his hand dismissively.

"Fine," I say. "I accept your... apology?"

That *was* an apology, right? It's the best apology I'm going to get, at least. In the back of my mind, I still think he's only being nice to me in case I'm stupid enough to rat him out.

"And you don't have to sleep in their room if you don't want. It smells weird in there, and god knows what they've done in that bed. Or that uncomfortable couch."

"Thanks for the mental images," I say. I did sleep on that couch last night, after all.

"There's a fainting couch in my room that doesn't smell like beer and cat piss. Arete suggested it earlier. If you don't mind being in the same room as us."

I make a sour face. "I'll take the closet."

"Hey," he says, "It's cushier than the couch, and I think you're short enough for it. I'd push it out in the hallway, but last time I tried to get it through the door I almost broke the leg off. It's an antique—belonged to my mother." He pauses. "Besides, if you throw up in the middle of the night it'll eat away the lacquer on the hardwood floor and I won't get my damage deposit back."

Ah, the truth comes out. The thought of sleeping in the same room as him and his girlfriend isn't pleasant, but it could always be worse.

"Are you sure you're okay with that?" I ask with feigned politeness.

Elijah stares into his bedroom. "I *do* have a moral code, it's just rather... eclectic." That's an interesting word for it. "I take care of my guests. I'll buy a blow up mattress tomorrow and set it up in the study until you find a place of your own. For now, just think of it as... a slumber party that neither of us want."

"Sounds good to me," I say. It doesn't actually, but it's either that or sleep on the floor. Though I'd be lying if I said I wasn't thinking about it.

"Good," he says. "And I'll take you shopping tomorrow so you can get what you need."

"I can go on my own," I say.

He scoffs. "With what money?"

He has a point, but I opt to scowl rather than admit it. He must not know about the $100 Arete gave me the other day, and it's unlikely she remembers giving it to me. I'd bet the full amount that she'll never notice it's missing. I'm better off saving it for an emergency. Homelessness is starting to sound like a better option, though I can't quite put my finger on exactly why I want out of here so badly; I'm starting to feel like Elijah's actually a pretty reasonable guy.

Elijah lines the fainting couch with spare sheets and tosses me a few pillows and blankets. I test it out. I guess it could be worse; like he said, it's way more comfortable than the couch. I'll have to sleep in a t-shirt and boxer shorts, of course. I wonder if I even own any pajamas, since I haven't sorted through the wreckage yet.

When Elijah leaves to use the restroom, or "latrine," as he calls it, I seize the opportunity to really take a look around his room without it being so awkward. I was too nervous to give it a good look yesterday, but I'm curious about his life; after all, he dragged me into it.

There's a framed photograph on his nightstand. He and Arete are in an outdoor ice skating rink, covered in snow. He has his arm around her and she's smiling, but she also looks like she's a little shy about it. It was probably their first date. I hate to admit it, but they actually do look cute together.

Despite his irritability and modesty whenever his heroism is brought up, he has mementos related to the police and Marine Corps on display. I can only guess why. I doubt it's pride. His dog tags are draped over a portrait on the night stand, which shows a younger Elijah in his military uniform standing next to a middle-aged woman. He and the woman, probably his mother, were laughing as he saluted her. She was a petite woman who had the same dark hair and caramel eyes as Elijah. He must resemble his late father, though nothing in the room acknowledges his existence. He may not like talking about those days, but he won't let go of them anytime soon. I suppose no veteran ever does.

What captures my eye the most is a framed medal, hung on the center of the wall so it's the first thing you see when you come in. A simple, bronze star hangs from a red ribbon with a blue and white stripe down the center. It's framed with a certificate.

THE UNITED STATES OF AMERICA

to all who shall see these presents, greeting: this is to certify
that the president of the United States of America authorized
by executive order, 24 August 1962 has awarded
THE BRONZE STAR MEDAL
To
Sergeant Elijah J. Walker, United States Marines
FOR
HEROISM IN COMBAT AGAINST HOSTILE FORCES
In Iraq from 1 October 2006 to 1 August 2009

I don't know what that means, but it sounds like a big deal. I find myself perplexed by another medal, hung in a display box. There's no certificate with it, but there's a small embossed plaque on the box that said something in Greek. (Ηλίας Λεωνίδας Παπαδόπουλος.) A circular cross dangles from a blue and white stripped ribbon. The cross is formed by the blades of two swords, with a Greek word on each leg. Did he serve in Greece? I'm so confused.

"It was my uncle's."

I jump. He's standing behind me. Is it okay to turn around?

When I don't, Elijah walks up to my side. "1974, Elijah Leonidas Papadópoulos," he says. "I was named after him. He died before I was born, but he was important to my mom, so I hung it up."

"Oh…" To steer myself away from dangerous territory by asking about Elijah's family, I ask, "What about the bronze star?"

He huffs and looks away. "All I did was almost kill myself and diffuse…" The rest of his words trail off into incoherent mumbles.

"If you're not proud of it, why hang it up?" I ask.

He smirks and whispers. "I hung it up last week to impress my girlfriend, duh."

"*That's* your reason?" I whisper back.

"What, can you think of a better one?"

"Uh, yeah," I say. "Because you probably saved a lot of lives that are worth remembering?"

He flips the light switch. "Good night."

"But I'm not ready for—"

"*Good night.*"

"Arete isn't ready yet," I say in protest. "I'll just wake up when she comes in."

He leaves the room. As much as I want to be obstinate, I really am tired, so I decide to go ahead and give in. I've had a long two days.

*

There's a scream. I'm jolted awake, and see Arete sitting up, breathing heavily. Elijah turns on the lamp on the night stand and surveys the room as she backs up against the headboard. Covered in cold sweat and not fully aware that she's in the waking world now, she backs into the headboard. The last time I heard her scream and rushed to her side, I was kidnapped with a sex toy, so I decide against helping her get over a nightmare. It's Elijah's burden to cradle her in his arms and rock her back and forth as she cries, not mine.

When she's not looking, he pulls a retainer out of his mouth, and a line of drool drips out of the corner of his lips. He covers his mouth and frantically glances in my direction to see if I'm awake. I shut my eyes as fast as I can, but I'm not sure if he buys it or not. I now know Elijah has a nerd side, and he will never live it down. I wish I wasn't too tired to laugh. When I peek, he's wiping the drool onto the pillow. As far as he knows, this is a secret between him and his retainer.

"*Shhhh,*" he says. "It'll all be okay."

I close my eyes again and roll over in attempt to go back to sleep, but their voices cut through the night. It'd be easier to sleep through tornado sirens.

"I had the dream again," Arete says, her voice loud and cracking.

"What dream?" Elijah asks, much more quietly than Arete.

Arete sniffs. I cringe thinking of snot running down her throat. "For as long as I can remember, I've had this recurring dream. It slowed down when I was thirteen, but it started up again last semester. Not every night, but enough to make me not want to sleep. That's why I tend to be up all night, but I was just so tired."

"Do you want to talk about it in the morning?" he whispers.

"I'm sorry, I don't think it can wait another second," she says. "William is sleeping like a log anyway."

Puta.

Elijah groans, probably more tired than me. "Okay."

"It's the same every time," she says. "It's not so much the stuff that happens in it; it's mostly emotions. I'm in my old house, you know, that one on Philly's Main Line, playing with my stuffed bunny, Hoppy. No matter how old I am, I'm always playing with Hoppy. Then I see a shadow creeping up the wall in front of me and something wraps its hands around my neck. And then I drop Hoppy and try to pull the hands away, but I can't get free. And I try to scream, but I can't breathe. I kick and cry, but the dream never ends until I black out. I can never wake myself up before that."

Would it be mean for me to tell her to shut her mouth? I can't help but take a peek, and I'm rewarded with the image of Elijah looking more distraught than I thought possible. He looks so human; it's bizarre. I want to laugh, both at the lame dream and his dramatic reaction to it, but I'm too tired. They kidnapped me and now they won't let me sleep. Assholes.

"I'm so sorry," he whispers.

"I'll be okay." Arete says. "It's not your fault."

He doesn't answer her. He just continues to cradle her in his arms and brush teardrops from her delicate cheeks. It looks like she'll quiet down and cry herself to sleep, so I don't storm off to sleep on the uncomfortable couch. But just as I'm finally starting to drift off to sleep, Arete explodes into tears.

"I did something bad!" she says.

I'll say, loudmouth.

"No, you didn't," Elijah says.

"I kept having the dreams and I had to stop them," she says. "I thought I had to do it."

"Do what?"

Arete sniffs. "Hoppy was my favorite toy, but I couldn't take it anymore. I was eight years old and having that dream every night. Hugging her at night didn't give me comfort at all, she never protected me. One night, I ran downstairs in my pajamas without thinking twice and... and I tossed her into the fireplace! Eli, I burned Hoppy alive, and the dreams didn't even stop!"

"No, no! Kit Kat, you didn't do anything wrong," Elijah says. "Stuffed animals aren't alive, okay?"

"Hoppy was alive to me," Arete says. "I betrayed her, and I knew it. I tried to pull her out of the fire, but the flames were so hot. The next thing I remember was Mum holding me and Dad throwing a rug on the fire."

"I'm so sorry," Elijah says again. "Do you want to tell me what happened after that?"

"You'd think setting stuffed animals on fire would make a parent think their child was off their rocker, but they weren't even angry. They didn't punish me, they pulled me out of school the middle of the next day to take me on an impromptu trip to Disney Land. It was like... they knew something I didn't."

"Maybe they knew you were just trying to stop the dream," Elijah says.

Arete takes a deep breath. "That's the weird part. I never told them that Hoppy was in my dream."

Elijah's eyes are open wide, and he takes her hands. It's an overreaction, if you ask me, just like everything else he does. I just want to them to shut up and go back to sleep. I should have told her to be quiet while I still had the chance. I don't want them to know I've been listening to this, albeit against my will.

"Mum wouldn't let me see, but she said Hoppy was fire retardant," Arete says. "Dad offered to have her fixed, but I didn't want to see Hoppy ever again after what I did. He never did tell me what he did with her, and I regret it now. Before Mum died, I asked her where Hoppy was and she wouldn't tell me. I searched that house up and down, but I never found her anywhere."

Elijah promptly kisses her, probably because he doesn't know what to say to that and he thinks swapping spit is the only solution. I close my eyes; I can't sleep if I'm gagging on their passion.

Friday, February 27, 2015

"Wheel. Of. Fortune!"

Obnoxious clapping and cheering fills my ears, and I look toward Elijah's bed. Nobody's there, and the bed is made. The clock on his end table reads 12:02 PM. In a zombie like state, I drag myself to the living room and find Arete typing on her laptop, with *Wheel of Fortune* in the background. It's painful to watch—not just the show, but Arete herself. She types with her index and middle fingers, hunt and peck style. The frantic girl's uncombed hair peeks out of the hood of her UPenn hoodie, and she isn't wearing pants; just a pair of full butt panties. It's what she slept in, I think. School papers, notes, and textbooks are strewn across the floor and coffee table, but I have a feeling that, unlike Tommy and me, Arete won't get a lecture from Hollywood Nerd.

Arete lets out a frustrated cry and throws her notebook at the TV. "Why is this so hard?"

"Why is what hard?" I ask.

She jumps. "Oh! Will," she says. "You scared me."

"Sorry."

"It's this stupid paper I'm writing," she says. "Or, well, I'm supposed to be writing it. But I'm no good at difficult books."

"Do you need help with it?" I ask. "I can proofread."

Arete purses her lips and shakes her head. "I can't," she says, throwing up her arms in defeat. "There's no time, I'm stupid, and I have dyslexia."

She switches windows on her laptop. I hover over her shoulder and see her Google the words *William Shakespeare Romeo and Juliet History Report College Level*.

"That is *not* a good idea," I say. "You could get in serious trouble for that."

"I have to get straight A's this semester, or I can't get out of academic probation."

I don't know what's less surprising—the fact that she's on academic probation, or the fact that she's trying to cheat her way out of it. Unlike Elijah, Arete is simple and easy enough to figure out in three days.

"Trust me on this one," I say. "Don't do it."

Arete snorts. "I'm not taking advice from someone whose eyes are all puffy and crusty. You slept in 'til noon, and you *still* look like shit."

"Whatever."

I consider telling her she looks infinitely worse, but instead I pick the eye crust out of my tear ducts and walk to the kitchen. Normally I would be too socially awkward about living with someone I just met to eat his Raisin Bran, but the man ruined my life. Apology or not, he ruined my life. He owes me more than cereal.

When I return, bowl of cereal in hand, Arete is texting someone. That phone could have been helpful when my house burned down.

"You found it?" I ask.

"Nope," Arete says. "Eli did. It was in his truck all along. Oh, and he has something for you."

I don't want anything else from Elijah. Is it not bad enough I'm stuck wearing the man's underwear? It doesn't even fit right.

"Relax," she says. "He went to your house this morning and found some stuff you could salvage."

"He must *really* feel sorry for me."

"Of course he does," she says, not registering my heavy sarcasm. "And guess what still works!"

"Nothing at all?"

"Your Nokia!" She opens her purse and presents my Nokia. "It's true! They really are indestructible!"

"Wow…" I hold the power button and it turns on. A true miracle.

"He put his number in it for you, and I added mine too."

"Thanks?"

Arete prints something out, no doubt 'her' paper on Romeo and Juliet. "Don't worry about the bill, he put you on his family plan."

"Family plan?" I ask.

"Yeah. We'll be spending a lot of time together." Arete carelessly staples the paper several inches from the corner and stuffs it in her backpack, which she slings over her shoulder as she runs out the door. "See ya, mate!"

"Wait," I say. "Are you really going to leave the house like that?"

Arete skids to a halt, and looks down at what she's wearing—or, more rather, what she's not wearing. "I'm such a basket case!" Without taking time to close the door all the way, she runs to Elijah's bedroom and slides yesterday's pants up her slender legs. "I can't *believe* you saw me in my underwear and didn't say anything until now!"

I blush; she's making me feel like a pervert. "Well, I thought maybe you just weren't shy about it."

"Is there *any* way I can get you not to tell anyone about this?" she asks, clapping her hands together like she's praying.

"Yeah." I contemplate for a moment. "I want to hear you say *crikey*."

On her way out the door, she looks at me like I'm a bag of trash. I couldn't care less how she looks at me now, because if everything goes as I planned it, this will be the last time she'll see me at all.

I only have $17.38 in the bank, but I still have that hundred dollar bill stashed in my only pair of socks. I doubt Arete remembers giving it to me, so I figured if I left it there, they wouldn't find it if Elijah took my wallet again. It's not a lot, but I don't need a lot. I head to the study to write a note for Elijah.

Dear Elijah,

Thanks for getting my phone!

I'm heading out to look for a job, and I'll bring some applications home later. I hope it's okay for me to use your home address until I save up enough to get out on my own. I'll probably be out all day, so don't expect me back for a while... I'll stop by red box on my way home.

Your best mate forever,

William

Masterpiece. This should buy me some time. Now all I have to do is take a cab to the 30th Street Station and catch a train to Maryland. Actually, no—it's close enough that I can walk. Sorry, Arete, but you'll have to kidnap someone else to be your best mate. I know this won't be easy and my DNA is on a dead body, but I think it's worth the risk. I haven't seen my sister in a while, but I know she works as a marine biologist at a lab in Baltimore. I don't know which one, but if I show up there and look around, I'm sure I'll find Sherry eventually. If not, well... anywhere is better than here.

*

The 30th Street Station is beautiful on the ground floor, where everyone goes to pick up family members and wait on their (probably late) train. It's actually beautiful, and was the first piece of Philadelphia I ever saw when I moved here from Allentown five years ago. It's a huge, art deco intermodal transit station in Philadelphia's University City. There are these beautiful columns that are several stories high, and an enormous bronze statue of an angel holding a dying man. There's also a Dunkin Donuts, but I don't have time for that right now.

Once you get under the surface and down to the loading zone, it's like being in a concrete cave. The thing I hate most is the huge gap between the loading zone and the tracks; I'm always afraid I'll fall in. Except today. Today, I hop on that train like it's the bridge to freedom. After I go through the awkward tasks of boarding and take my seat, there's only more social nightmare to endure: making a phone call. I scroll through my contacts looking for my sister, Sherry, and find... Arete, China Kitchen, Don't answer, don't answer, don't answer, DOn't answer, don't answer, dont anwser [sic], don't answer, DON'T ANSWER, Elijah, and Pizza.

I know "DON'T ANSWER" is Alice, because I changed her name before we even *left* Starbucks. But one of the other seven is my mother. This is like minesweeper. Anyone, and I do mean *anyone* is better. I'd rather accidentally call Elijah than my mother. I can hear it now.

See, I told you Philadelphia was dangerous! And now you want to stay with your sister in Baltimore? You'll get murdered this time. Get off at the next stop. I'll pick you up and take you to Allentown, what kind of sandwich should I pack, do you want me to cut off the crust, I changed the sheets for you, is birria still your favorite?

I'm going to have to find a library so I can reverse search these numbers. But I'll worry about that later. When the train stops, I don't hesitate to leave. Not because I'm still terrified for my life, but because I really have to pee; the train was delayed for hours. And when I open the bathroom door with my elbows, I almost wet myself.

"I figured this would be the first place you'd go," Elijah says.

"Wha—but—how?"

"A train toilet?" Elijah asks. "You'd rather hold it for three hours or so. But a public restroom? I could see you going in one of these if you're desperate enough."

"No, I mean, how did you..."

There's no point in pretending I came all the way to Maryland for job applications. He caught me. I'm toast.

"Please come home," he says. "Don't tell her I told you, but Arete bought you some fuzzy socks and new underwear. And she's making bouillabaisse for dinner, and I have no idea what that is, but it sounds good. I was planning a family movie night."

I take a deep breath. He's good. Too good. Am I really going to fall for this?

"How did you pull this off?" I ask.

"I was going 70 to beat the train and I had to talk my way out of a speeding ticket. I told him my γιαγιά was dying in the hospital," he says.

I remember how he never lies and I almost feel sad. Mostly awkward. "Oh... I'm sorry..."

He shrugs. "Don't be, that was over twenty years ago."

"Just tell me how you caught me," I snap.

Elijah lowers his voice. "I installed a tracker in your phone. That note you left was so fake it's not even funny, so I checked your GPS location. Oh, and you forgot to sign out of your email, so I found the tickets. Trains are notoriously tardy, so I figured I'd take a chance and see if I could beat it."

"You put a tracker on my phone?"

He hushes me. "We're in public," he says. "And yeah, I thought about it, and I'd prefer you not leave. I wanted to keep tabs on you in case you did something stupid, like run away and take a train to Baltimore alone and with no money. And it's for your own good anyway."

"My own good?" I ask. "I don't understand how you're justifying this."

"Because that attack on Arete wasn't just some random thing," he says. "He had a knife out and was going straight for her throat. Muggers, rapists, opportunistic serial killers, doesn't matter—they *all* prefer women who are walking alone. Arete wasn't alone. She was with me. No one would dare. I have reason to believe this was a hired hit."

"How do you know all that?"

"I was a cop," he says.

"Yeah, a traffic cop."

"Θα αυτοκτονήσω, γαμώτο," he mutters under his breath. "Look, I'm not the one who gave you the tracker without telling you first. That was Arete. I'm trying to help you, here."

"How is this helping though?" I ask. "I have nothing to do with you people."

"You were there that night and you can't guarantee nobody saw you. So, would you rather me cover you or not?"

I back up a little. "You're... offering me *protection*?"

"Yes," he says. "Is it really that hard to believe?"

"Yeah. Why not Arete, if she was the target?"

"She has an anxiety disorder," he says. "If I put a tracker on her, I have to explain why so I don't look like a creepy control freak. And if I tell her someone wants to kill her, the rest of her life will be nothing but a series of panic attacks."

Anxiety? Arete has anxiety? What does she have to be anxious about; which black wig she's going to wear? How she's going to fit all her shopping bags into the taxi cab? Someone saying something mean to her on Instagram?

Do not argue with him, William. Do not come between them. You will die.

"That makes sense," I lie.

"So, are you in or out?"

I groan. "In."

"Good. Now, I have some terms and conditions."

"Seriously?"

"Disobedience voids the conceptual contract," he says, "and if anything happens to you then, you're on your own to become a hobo in Baltimore, or whatever your plan was."

"Fine," I say. "What do I have to do?"

"Just do what I say and keep the tracker on you at all times, easy."

"I know how you are with loopholes," I say. "If I get my head blown off, I'm going to haunt you and your ancestors for three generations."

"Very well." He takes a moment to think. "I will offer you protection from this day forward, within a reasonable margin of error, from physical harm, in exchange for certain freedoms that would endanger Arete, me, or less importantly, you. From now until further notice, said exchanged freedoms

are as follows: ratting us out, venturing out of bounds
unattended by a custodian of my approval, removing the
tracker from your phone or leaving it behind. Disobedience
will void the contract. These terms and conditions are subject
to change, but you can opt out at any time."

Law students.

So, in other words, I'm thirteen again. Do I have to be
home by seven o'clock? Still, it sounds pretty solid for an air
contract. He's smarter than I give him credit for, but I don't
want to jump into this blindly. I never did get a good
explanation for why he didn't just call the police the night it
happened.

"What does 'out of bounds' mean?" I ask.

He gestures broadly toward the station. "Doing
something crazy like this."

"And what about psychological harm?"

He cracks a smile. "It's a little late for that, don't you
think?"

"Fine." I take a deep breath. I can't believe I'm making
a deal with the Devil. "I have read and agree to the above
terms and conditions."

"Good," he says. "If I go to prison because of you, I'll
kill you."

"How will you do that from jail?" I ask.

"You'll be my cell mate."

Oh, of course. If he gets arrested, I'm *definitely*
screwed. But I doubt we would ever be cell mates. My DNA

being found on a dead body equals jail time for the ugly, little Chicano, and a plea deal for the Mediterranean sex god with the wavy hair. When I think of it that way, running away was kind of stupid. They hit the jackpot finding a patsy like me. Elijah's being nicer than Sherry ever is anyway, which says more about her than Elijah. There is a 100% chance she would make fun of me for this, and she would do it in Spanish knowing I wouldn't be able to understand her. Maybe this is for the best.

"Let's head home now," he said. "You'll be glad you made this choice. I think. At least you're less likely to get shot hanging out with me than you are in Baltimore, that's what I'm trying to say."

My choice... Yeah. I did get to choose, didn't I? This isn't going to be so bad. The hard part's already over. As long as I don't snitch or run off, I have nothing to worry about. It's not like I'm an adventurous person. Give me a TV and I'm happy.

Saturday, February 28, 2015

After taking a pre-approved, mid-afternoon walk to get some distance from my current living arrangements (about one block; not because I'm not allowed to go further, but because it's cold), I come "home" to find Arete in tears on the couch. Elijah is trying to calm her down, but she's like a human water faucet with a broken valve. When I ask her what happened, she buries her head in Elijah's chest and cries harder. He runs his fingers through his girlfriend's hair to calm her down, but keeps hitting knotted up snags. He gives up and strokes her shoulder with his thumb instead.

"She was suspended," Elijah says.

"Really? What for?" I ask like I don't already know the answer.

"She got caught on that paper she plagiarized," Elijah says.

Through her sobbing, she says something incoherent. Whatever it was, Elijah understood.

"Why?" he asks.

She says something. I'm able to make out the words "you warned me" and "trusted."

He shushes her. "You don't need to apologize to me. You know what... your uncle's a Penn alumni and he makes annual donations, maybe he can get them to change their minds. I'll talk to him for you if you're too afraid."

It takes a moment, but she finally slows down enough to speak. "I guess... But I'm so ashamed."

"Don't be," Elijah says. "You were stressed. It's not like you set off fireworks in the cafeteria or something, you just plagiarized a paper. I'll help you with the next one."

Just plagiarized an entire paper? That doesn't sound like a minor offense to me. I'm surprised they didn't expel her. I don't know how things work at UPenn, but I bet her name is the only reason she wasn't.

"Thanks." She sniffs. "But... How did you know my uncle was an alumni? I never told you that."

"How else would I know?" Elijah asks.

"I guess I must have," Arete says. "I'm just stupid."

"You're not stupid," he says. (Ha!) "You just need to take a break after everything that's been going on. You had a lot going on at school, someone attacked you in an alley, you got caught in a fire..."

Arete closes her eyes. "Suspension is a *punishment*. I don't deserve to treat it like a break."

"Sure you do," Elijah says. "Don't you think she deserves a break, Boy Meets World?"

I automatically say, "Yeah, of course," but I know daddy's money and her uncle's good word can get her out of this situation in a heartbeat. She probably hasn't worked a day in her life, and now she's learning that her actions have consequences. It's good for her.

"Why do all these things keep happening to me?" Arete asks.

I get up and start to walk out of the room, leaving them to their own world, only to be called back by Elijah.

"Where do you think you're going?"

"The bathroom?"

He motions me to come back and says, "I set up a blow-up bed for you in the study, like I promised."

"Okay," I say, grateful that he isn't dragging me into Arete's problems. My unsympathetic input wouldn't help, and he could probably tell from the slight edge in my voice earlier that I think she deserves it. That doesn't stop her, though.

The drama queen slumps over in her chair. "The last day of February. The last day of my *life*."

"Maybe it would help to get off campus for a while," Elijah says. "Want to stay here with me?"

"I guess," Arete says. "Can we talk about this later?"

"Okay then," Elijah says. "I'm calling for a family meeting tonight."

"Family meeting?" I ask. "Since when are we a family?"

He ignores me. "I'm sure Whitney will be okay with having the dorm all to herself for a while. Tommy and Keyon are still in Kentucky, but they won't mind. As a matter of fact, I'm sure they'd love to have you here."

Arete answers with a weak "okay." She doesn't believe him.

*

When Elijah suggests we go out for dinner, I brace myself for Arete to pick Waffle House again. Thankfully, she says she'd rather just stay in for the night and order food. Elijah suggests pizza and she's glad he understands. I frown at her choice of toppings: pineapple, red peppers, and black olives—no meat. She's apparently a vegetarian, which makes me stifle a laugh. You don't bat an eye when your boyfriend murders someone in front of you, but the idea of killing an animal is too hard to stomach? I feel like rebelling, so I ask for chicken instead of pizza. Elijah just rolls with it, but Arete looks at me like I broke some sort of cosmic carryout law *and* slaughtered an innocent farm animal. It's funny what something as simple as ordering food can tell you about your friends.

After the meal, Arete points out that Elijah looks a little sick.

"Are you *positive* you're not lactose intolerant?" she asks.

"Yes. I am *positive* I'm not lactose intolerant." Elijah goes to the bathroom, locks the door behind himself, and wretches.

Arete shakes her head. "He really is the most stubborn man on earth. I know lactose intolerance when I see it. My mum had it."

"Ah, really?"

"Yeah," she says. "Actually, wait. I bet he planned this. Pizza was his idea. He's using it to avoid talking about our relationship."

She has a point. Despite being the one to call the meeting, not once did Elijah bring up what happened. He continues to procrastinate when he returns from the bathroom with bloodshot eyes. But even though Arete blames him, she's enabling him by conversing about lighthearted topics in a heavyhearted tone. Elijah wants to go easy on her, but I don't want to sit here all night waiting for her to decide whether or not she wants to move in with her boyfriend of two weeks. Based on his reactions, he's expecting her to reject him.

"So..." I fidget awkwardly. "Are you moving in?"

Please say no. I'll never get any alone time if they're living together.

Arete sighs. "I've made up my mind. I'm sorry, Eli, but my mum was right. America sucks. I'm going back to Australia."

"Australia?" Elijah asks. "You're leaving me for kangaroo meat and giant spiders?"

Boo hoo. Your girlfriend of two weeks wants to go back to the vegemite hell she came from. Is it really that big of a deal? Elijah apparently thinks so, because every crease in his forehead deepens when he lifts his brows and whines like she's dumping him. I can tell he's overreacting, because Arete wouldn't just dump him in front of me while she and I are trying to eat dinner.

"Arete," he says, "you're the best thing that ever happened to me. You can't just leave now, our life is just getting started."

"Yes, I can," she says. "I'm sorry, but I can't take it anymore. I'll just take roles in indie films and work my way up to the top the hard way. There's nothing for me in this country other than a DUI and... well... you."

No. They *are* breaking up in front of me. As if being third wheel on their dates wasn't bad enough, I have to third wheel their breakup?

I clear my throat loudly. "So, I'm going to bed."

Thankfully, they ignore me leaving the room, but I can still hear their voices clearly through the study's thin walls. It's hard not to listen in.

"Why can't you just stay here with me?" Elijah asks. "I don't understand. You can act in Philadelphia, and you practically live here anyway."

"Key word *practically*," Arete says. "I'm not usually big on statistics but couples who live together before getting married usually break up once they do. And there's just no point in staying abroad for a temporary relationship, I'm sorry."

"So then you just want to get married?"

"No... Well, maybe someday. I don't know!"

"What about your house in Philly?" Elijah asks. "There'd be plenty of space between us there. We could have separate bedrooms. And I can tutor you in math."

Arete softens her voice. "Well... It is a pretty big house. I'll consider it."

"*Please* do," he says. "Come on, let's get to bed. Maybe you'll feel better in the morning."

"I'm going back to my dorm tonight. I have to talk things over with Whitney. Is that okay?"

"Sure," Elijah says, in a way that implies *nothing* is okay. "I'll drive you back."

I hear their footsteps approaching a few minutes later, but they pass the study and go out the door. Whoever closes it slams the door behind them. It looks like I'm alone for the first time since I met them. I want to lie here and bask in my alone time, but being tired wasn't just an excuse for dodging my potential role as breakup referee. I'm physically and emotionally exhausted. The mattress is already made and firmly inflated and the sheets are really nice, so it's time for bed. I'll sleep more soundly tonight than I have in a long time.

Monday, March 2, 2015

I'm in the study enjoying alone time when I hear what sounds like knocking. It's so quiet that, at first, I think I'm imagining it. Then I realize the sound is coming from the front door. Since no one else is home to answer, I consider ignoring it. Who would come here looking for me, after all? But the knocks are so timid and persistent that I sense Arete's depression sucking me in. Sure enough, I open the door to her back as she's walking away.

She turns around. "Elijah?"

"Sorry, it's me," I say.

She takes a deep breath and tries to smile. "Are you his butler now?"

I open the door wider to let her inside. "No, it's just me today."

She looks around as she gingerly steps inside, and I notice the morose look on her face. I don't mean morose in a goth chick way, I mean she looks unintentionally dead. Her skin is white as snow against her black coat, and there's a flushed ring around her lips and under her eyes. I notice her makeup is slightly smudged around the inner corners, and realize the cold isn't why her nose is stuffed and sniffling.

"Did he say when he'd be back?" she asks.

"I haven't heard from him all day," I say. "Did you call him?"

"Only a hundred times," she says. "Him and my roommate, everyone is rejecting my calls. You too."

"My phone is on vibrate," I say.

She gets out her phone and dials; I assume she's calling Elijah again, when the default AT&T ringtone comes from my butt. She glares at me.

"Sorry," I say. "It's just been awkward since you dumped him."

"What are you talking about?" she asks. "I never dumped him. We went out just yesterday."

"Then why does he mope around like he's dead inside?" I ask. "The closest he came to talking to me was when he asked how long I'd be in the shower because he had to throw up, like, a shit load of ice cream."

Arete scoffs.

"No, really," I say. "He refuses to admit he's lactose intolerant."

"I'm not doubting you," she says. "I'm just annoyed. You're seeing a *completely* different side of him. He was up my arse all weekend, wouldn't give me a break, but then I need him for something and *poof*! Gone."

"Maybe he just has it turned off," I say. "It is a Monday. He could be studying or in class or something. I mean, just because he doesn't have a job doesn't mean he's not busy—"

"Maybe he'll answer for you," she says before I can give him any more excuses.

I relent and dial his number, only to hear a loud vibration coming from my right. I turn to see a phone vibrating on the coffee table. Looks like no one is getting through to Elijah today. Our favorite veteran has gone AWOL.

"Wow," she says, sarcastic. "So much for 'whenever you need me I'll be there for you.'"

I have my doubts those were his exact words, not because of his feelings but because of his technical nature. I do understand the sentiment though.

I expect Arete to storm out, but instead of leaving, she removes her coat, tosses it onto the back of the couch, and sits cross-legged at the coffee table. She digs through her purse and takes out a white candle, a framed photograph, and the most expensive looking cigarette lighter I've ever seen. It's patent black with genuine silver octopus tentacles wrapping themselves around the casing. She doesn't smoke, so she probably just bought it because it looks cool.

"Will you join me for a candlelight vigil?" she asks.

"Really?" I ask. "I'm not catholic. Or Elijah."

"I'm agnostic." Arete pats the space next to her on the carpet. "And fuck Elijah."

I don't particularly want to sit next to her in case the man of the hour comes home and pulverizes me, but I could never say no to pretty girl. I lack the strength.

I sit with her and look at the photo next to the candle. Arete is posed linking arms with a girl who doesn't look much older than her. They look similar too; most notably, they have the same wide, protruding eyes and alert brows, though the other girl's eyes are light blue and her hair is red. I wonder if Arete is a natural redhead too under all the wigs and pitch black hair dye. The other girl's face is more mature than Arete's in general, less doll-like and more adult. Her face is longer, her lips are fuller, and her nose isn't as perky.

"Is this your sister?" I ask.

The corner of her mouth twitches. "That's my mum."

"Oh! Well... she looks, I mean *looked*..."

"Young?" Arete hands me the photo for a closer look. "She was only seventeen when she married my father. She told me eighteen, but she was lying."

"What?" I ask. "Seventeen? How old was your dad?"

"40-something." Arete rolls her eyes. "Let's not talk about it."

So her father is a sex offender. That has to sting. I take another look at the portrait; she looked happy, but it's hard for me to believe that a teenager would be happy married to an old man.

"She was pretty," I say. It's actually an understatement; she was stunning, and I can see how she bagged a billionaire. Saying that would be tacky, though. "What's her name?"

"Simone," she says. "That's the last picture we took before she died... in an... *accident* a few days later... She died this day last year."

"I'm sorry."

"I want to say 'it's okay,'" she says, "but it's not. Or I'm not. I mean, she's been dead for a year now and I don't miss her any less. She always knew exactly what to do. I'm not half as competent as she is, and she came from nothing." Arete looks at her hands in her lap, shaking and grasping the hem of her sweater. "I'm *nothing* like her at all. She was brave, I have anxiety. She was smart, and my GPA is a 1.31. She was strong, and I can't run, like, ten feet before I'm out of breath. After she died, I couldn't handle anything at all, but my psychiatrist wouldn't give me a higher dose of Xanax because I can't even be responsible with my own medication. I'm no good at all."

"I'm sure you're capable of more than you think," I say.

"Doubt it. I was a goddamn diseased preemie." Her eyes widen and she covers her mouth for a moment before looking at the ceiling. "I'm sorry, God!"

I can't help but smile. It's pretty easy to see what Elijah sees in her. As for what she sees in cold, moody Elijah, that's still a mystery. It has to be the butt. Keyon told me he has some complicated, optimized exercise regimen based on science and never misses a workout, even if he's tired or sick. As for how Elijah has abs when he drinks the way he does, Keyon's only theory was that he has really good genetics. He's preoccupied with his appearance in a way most men aren't and puts a lot of effort into maintaining an image his girlfriend likes. It's a wonder he doesn't strategically go goth. I imagine him in all black with eyeliner and leather pants and choke back a laugh.

"I think God understands," I say. "So how do you hold a vigil?"

"Nothing complicated," she says. "I'm just going to light a candle for her and remember her."

"But I didn't know her."

"Neither did Elijah, who was, regrettably, my first choice," she says. "I just wanted someone to listen while I remember my mum and blab about my future ex-boyfriend."

Whatever it is Arete sees in Elijah, I have to remind her of that. Otherwise, I'll lose my buffer to Australia and I'll be stuck here in Philadelphia with Hollywood Nerd for the rest of my life. Tommy and Keyon will move out this fall, leaving me alone to bear the weight of Elijah's sobbing for the rest of eternity. I know I don't have much of a future, I never have, but that's not the one I want.

"Did he know about all this... goth nonsense?" I ask. "The vigil, I mean."

"No... are you saying I'm being unreasonable?"

"Of course not," I say. "I was only going to think it."

She smiles sheepishly and elbows me.

"Seriously though," I say. "He really does care about you. Otherwise he'd just let you leave without a fight."

"But he's not doing it for me." Arete tries to light the candle. "It would be different if he thought me staying in Philly was in my best interest, but he's not even pretending. He's just shamelessly obsessed with me, and it's actually getting kind of annoying. Don't tell him any of this, okay?"

"I won't as long as you don't tell him I told you he ate and barfed a whole pint of ice cream." I want to keep my head, thanks. "But wouldn't it be worse if he pretended otherwise?"

"I guess." She rubs her thumb raw trying to turn on the lighter. By the time she succeeds, her thumb is indented and red.

"Talk about whatever you want," I say. "But hear me out... Melbourne—"

"Hold on," she says. "My nails look good today." With her left hand, Arete holds the lighter even with the candle, but doesn't light it. With her right, she holds up her phone camera and snaps a picture for Instagram. "Okay, now we're good."

"Melbourne isn't going anywhere," I say. "You can go back home any time. Stay with your family, visit your father, wh—"

"My father's gone too," she says. "I inherited everything."

"Oh... I'm sorry."

"No, It's okay. You're right. I... I guess I'm just running away because Penn wasn't the fresh start I wanted."

I nod to buy myself a few extra seconds to decide what to say next. "Elijah isn't... perfect. I mean, he really gets on my nerves. But the perfect man... there's no such thing. I'm sure he'll get less annoying in a few months when honeymoon fever clears up, but in the meantime, at least you found someone who's wholly devoted to you. Most girls never find someone like that."

No answer. What was it... what... what can I add... oh, yeah.

"And he saved your life," I say. "Twice."

"Right," she says. "You're right. I'm just being emotional."

Arete has got to be the most flexible girl on the planet. This talk was supposed to be a lot harder. Maybe if I strike now...

"So what do you say, then?" I ask. "Should I pack all my worldly possessions into a grocery bag and get ready for the Main Line?"

"Yeah, I guess."

SCORE! Precarious victory achieved!

"Anyway, are you ready to help me pray for my mother's soul?" she asks. "Because if Hell is real, she's gonna need it."

"Oh, so you think she's in limbo?"

"No." Arete ignites the wick. "She's *definitely* in Hell."

I can't tell if she's kidding, but I guess her morbid sense of humor had to come from somewhere. So we pray to a god we're not sure we believe in, for a soul who is allegedly burning in Hell, and reminisce about a woman I'll never meet as long as I live.

Simone Hope Konstantinou, you beautiful train wreck, may you live on through your equally disturbed daughter.

Although your soul is probably lost forever, at least take comfort in the fact that you will never have to meet her boyfriend.

Wednesday, March 4, 2015

When I see Arete's house for the first time, I'm too awestruck to fully process that I'm going to be living here. I can't imagine why she would rather stay in a tiny dorm than live here. I expected a large house because only a woman with deep pockets would hand me a hundred dollar bill without noticing it's missing, but that was a gross underestimation. We're pulling into the driveway of a 1920's old money estate straight out of The Great Gatsby. The Main Line is so extravagant and beautiful in a way that it doesn't even feel like we're still in Philadelphia. Now I understand why Elijah was pressuring her to make this move. I thought his apartment was nice, but this is a major upgrade.

All of my remaining worldly possessions (including the souvenir shirts Elijah gave me) were shoved into one of his old gym bags, which I held on my lap as he drove me here. When I get out of the truck, the first thing I see is Arete sitting in a black, patent leather swivel chair, watching other people unload her things while she sips at her hard lemonade from a bendy straw. I look closer and notice the purple bendy straw is formed in the shape of a bat, and her cooler is plastered with stickers of Goth band logos and cult films. I'm sure her fans and hate-stalkers would be pleased to know that her real life looks just like one of her Instagram posts, with even the most mundane objects getting the Gothic touch.

She spins around to wave at us—no, sorry, to wave at Elijah—but does not otherwise budge from her throne. Elijah rushes to embrace her as if he hasn't seen her in years, and she humors him even though it's been eight hours at most. For a woman who complains about how he's always "up her arse," she basks in his attention like she needs it to survive. Then again, she is an Instagram girl, so it's not a stretch to guess that attention is her sole source of serotonin. I stand by the truck awkwardly as I wait for them to finish; I don't have much to unpack myself and, to be blunt, I don't want to fill my idle time chatting with Elijah or helping him move his overstuffed boxes. I've had enough of him this week, and the first thing I'm going to do in that house is find a quiet place where I can tune him out.

When Elijah's done with his PDA, she resumes talking to one of the movers. The life slowly drains out of his eyes as she drones on and on about god knows what. When Arete finally shuts her mouth, he nods in response and promptly turns around to accost one of his fellow movers for not carrying her stuff carefully enough. I can't believe she ordered the poor guy to yell at someone because she couldn't be bothered to do it herself. Another mover brings her a new hard lemonade and a plate of cheese and crackers, and she points him in my direction. He comes over and asks me, exhausted, if I want any "oar durbs." I turn down the alcohol but accept the food, feeling somewhat guilty and wondering how much he's being paid to put up with the bratty wannabe monarch stretching the limits of his job description. He's been told to come fetch me, apparently.

Meanwhile, Elijah paid movers to take his stuff over as well, only to end up helping them load and unload the van anyway. The movers assume he's being considerate, but I'm convinced he's only helping because he can't surrender any control. He should be occupied with that for a while, so I accept the invitation to sit on a cooler next to Arete while she eye-fucks Elijah's biceps and runs me through a limited history of the Konstantinou Manor.

According to Arete, the house is actually a lot newer than the Great Gatsby vibes were letting on, and was commissioned by her father (Georgios Konstantinou) in the late 80's after the booming success of his business, Konstantinou Enterprises. Her family left Australia "more or less kind of permanently and stuff in, like, 2001, I think." Before that, they went back and forth a lot. Arete's parents constantly fought over whether they should stay in their much larger mansion in Australia, which was best for "Arete" (actually Simone), or if they should stay in Georgios' dream mansion. Eventually, Simone won, I assume through the same soul-sucking chastisement that Arete is torturing the movers with. She had to have learned this from someone.

Even after they moved in "like, 2001," her father still stayed here on business for half of the year, since "the family business" was founded in Philadelphia alongside his brother, 49% owner Antonis Konstantinou. Her family would stay here during the summer, when it was cold in Melbourne, until Georgios was on his deathbed. Now he's buried alongside his wife in Australia, but this house is almost like a monument to his memory in a way. Most men don't ever achieve the dream of designing their own space from the ground up with a team of elite architects, but Georgios Konstantinou did, and his imagination rests here. Perhaps that's why Arete wanted to avoid living here, but I don't ask because I don't want to sound rude. I don't know if I can hide how excited I am to live here from this woman who is so unsure about it. The idea of living here is almost worth the anxiety of having my DNA on a dead body... No. Never mind. It comes close though.

Arete is waiting for her maternal grandparents to ship the rest her things from the other side of the world. My renter's insurance money has yet to come in as the investigation is still ongoing, but Arete at some point slipped a $100,000 check in my bag without me noticing. The memo says "housewarming gift." I'm not going to cash it. No amount of cash can make up for being kidnapped and famed for murder, and I don't want her to think we're even. We can be friends, but we can never be even.

By around three o'clock, the movers are finally finished. Though originally anxious, Arete is starting to get excited about the move—she takes Elijah and me on an hour-long tour of the entire estate. It's all disgustingly lavish— there's a six-car garage, seven bedrooms, ornate bathrooms, a kitchen as big as Elijah's whole apartment, a dining room with a crystal chandelier... It makes me dizzy in a way to know that people live like this. I spent my life poor, and all the while people lived in places like these. And now I'm one of them in the blink of an eye. Without a frame of reference, I have no way to guess if I'll be able to fit in here or if I'll easily adjust to living in luxury. Because of that, this move is more nerve-wracking than it should be.

"My only wish is that we had an indoor pool," Arete says when we make it to the back deck, overlooking the barren gardens. "I love snow, but I'm *so* sick of waiting till June just to swim without getting hypothermia. I can't believe you wouldn't let me go back to Oz."

Elijah laughs and hugs her from behind. "Well, Kit Kat, you're doing just fine in America right now." He whispers in her ear, and she giggles. *"At least there's a hot tub."* I know I wasn't supposed to hear it, but he wasn't quiet enough to spare my nausea. I just pretend not to notice, and Arete shows me to my room in the west wing of the house. Like every other bedroom, it has its own bathroom, which is nice.

"This used to be my room when I was a little girl," she says. She lets out a quiet, nervous laugh. "I'll give you a better one later, but it's been so long since we've lived here that the water beds in all the guest rooms were drained. Or would you like a new mattress? Memory foam? I personally never liked either, but..."

"Whatever's convenient," I say. Again, I don't want to take advantage of these living arrangements because I don't want her to feel like they can mask all the things they've done to me behind a veil of dead presidents and Tempurpedic mattresses.

"Well," she says, "you already know where everything is. So I'll just leave you alone."

Arete's childhood bedroom, where she's dropped me off, is on the west wing. To my left at the end of the hall is the master bedroom Georgios stayed in, and to the right is the room I'll be moved to, which was a guest bedroom. Across from that room is a room that's always locked. Arete doesn't know what's in there; only that it scared her as a kid and she never went near it. Simone locked it and threw away the key, assuring Arete that the monsters wouldn't get her, which is actually kind of cute. Arete still has "bad vibes" and avoids it to this very day.

Luckily, Arete and Elijah will each have bedrooms on the east wing. Even though they'll have separate bedrooms, they'll probably go back and forth sleeping together in rotation, and I'm more than happy to not have to hear them having sex. The layout somewhat mirrors the west wing, but with noticeably fewer doors. Both Arete's room from when she was a teenager (which she is moving back into) and Simone's "bedrooms" are on the east wing.

When discussing a separation, Simone apparently moved out of Georgios' room into a guest bedroom, decided that bedroom was not big enough for her, knocked out a wall between two bedrooms, turned a third adjacent bedroom into a private office, and walled up all the hall doors. Arete doesn't show me inside either of the master bedrooms, but if I'm doing the math correctly, that means Simone had at least three closets and three bathrooms by the time she was done remodeling, unless she knocked those out too. After spending some time apart, her parents decided to stay married after all but continued keeping their living quarters separate. It turned out what Simone really needed was space. Lots and lots of space. I wonder why Arete didn't do the same and place Elijah in the west wing with me since the whole point of moving here was that they could move in with each other without feeling like they were stuck with each other.

I'm not going to admit I want Elijah on this side of the house, but between the creepiness of a mysterious, off-limits room, being in a foreign house, and the room I'm staying in, I'll have nightmares all night. It's not that the pink wallpaper is threatening my already questionable masculinity or anything like that, but all the dolls are creepy. My weary brain is already cooking up images of the dolls watching me lie awake all night, waiting for the opportunity to drag me to uncanny valley as I sleep.

"It's okay," I say. "Thanks."

*

It's around noon, and Arete and Elijah are already taking a break from packing. Arete somehow conned me into helping her unpack and hang up her clothes while she was getting ready to go. For some reason, the outfit she had on this morning just wasn't good enough. An hour later, she's still getting ready, or as she calls it, "gothing up." She's taking her sweet time, dancing to an industrial goth band called Angelspit and talking to me about her life problems like I'm her gay best friend. I don't know why nobody believes me when I say I'm not gay, but being gay wouldn't help me tolerate her babbling on about how hard it is to find a good foundation in her skin tone and the challenge of mixing different shades of black. She thinks my silence means that I'm a good listener. Out of all the clothes she brought from her dorm, only one dress was a color—red. Everything else was black, and I wonder how she manages to find anything. Her goth aesthetic didn't creep throughout the rest of the house at any point as far as I've noticed, but her own room is somewhere between grunge revival and vampire night club.

Elijah taps on the door and peeks through when it creaks open. He gives Arete a geeky smile and invites himself in. Last time I checked, he was downstairs organizing his school supplies in the study. I never doubted he was smart, but it's impressive that he's learned how to navigate this place so quickly.

"Are you ready to go?" he asks.

"Sure thing," Arete says. "Wait, hold on, I want to change into some heels. And I think I'll touch up my makeup, just to be safe. Uh... Give me five minutes."

"All right," he says, but he gives me a look and I know what he's thinking. *I'll give you another hour, Kit Kat. But if we're late, I'm going to be pissed.*

The sooner the better for me. They planned a trip to some aquarium in New Jersey for a date, and the drive alone will buy me enough time to investigate. I don't believe in consequences any more than I believe in chupacabras, and I'm convinced that something is off about Elijah. I saw him lift a floor safe into the moving van earlier, and I have high hopes that he doesn't have all of his belongings settled yet.

After I watch them pull out of the driveway over an hour later, I walk into Elijah's room and try to crack the key to his safe. It doesn't take long; for such a smart man, his code is surprisingly easy. Or, should I say, surprisingly dumb. 27383 is the set of numbers that corresponds to ARETE on a phone keypad. It was my first guess.

Once I'm in, I open a shoe box to reveal stacks of photographs, mostly of Arete and her family. There were pictures of her in her high school uniform, and even senior portraits. It's a weird thing to keep in a safe, but nothing incriminating. I mean, it *is* his girlfriend. Truthfully, I think nothing of it until I find a file containing a stack of papers. When I open it up, there's a photocopy of Arete's birth certificate.

Pennsylvania Hospital
Arete Renee Konstantinou, March 20, 1993, 1:13 PM

Born to Mother Simone Konstantinou (Wagner)
Melbourne, Australia
And Georgios Konstantinou, Athens, Greece

Snore. The next page is a photocopy of a 1992 newspaper article with the headline *Gang Rape Behind a Saint Joseph's University Sorority House*.

Saint Joseph's is a nearby private Catholic college that I used to drive by on my way to the pub I worked at. You know, back when I had a job... and a car. I'm about to pass up the article until I notice fine-tipped red ink in the margins. Written in small, messy handwriting is *Simone*.

I compare the article to the birth certificate; the rape took place not quite a year before Arete was born. The next document is a photocopy of Simone and Georgios' wedding certificate. It's dated around three months after the assault, and five months before Arete was born. I can't breathe. Arete isn't a preemie—she isn't even a Konstantinou by blood.

I don't understand how he got access to these documents, but that's not what concerns me. What does it all mean, and why is Elijah collecting all these files on his girlfriend? Could it have something to do with the man who tried to murder her in an alleyway on a particularly cold February?

The next page is Arete's criminal record, but I don't get a chance to read it. I hear a thump, and summarily put everything back where it belongs in fear of getting caught. It turns out just to be a "house noise," like a pipe or something, but I'm too nervous to dive back in after what I discovered. The coward in me wishes I never looked. My curious side really wishes I didn't pass up the chance to look at Arete's criminal record.

VI

THE LOVERS.

Thursday, March 5, 2015

The Konstantinou Manor isn't the largest house in America, but it's the largest I've ever been inside. I'm not sure I'll ever learn to navigate it, no matter how long I'll end up staying there. After a long trek through the overlarge house, I find Arete sitting on the deck in the backyard.

"Hey, Mate," Arete says when she notices me. She's reclining on a deck chair, curled up in a lace-trimmed wool shawl; I don't understand how she can tolerate the cold so easily. She tears her raccoon eyes away from her e-reader and smiles at me. "What's up?"

"You said you wanted to be the first to see the next thing I've written." I hand Arete a printed copy of the short story I had been working on, *Beautiful City*. Ever since moving here and seeing their gigantic private library, which Arete told me was an uncreative but very expensive romantic gesture to Simone, I've been reading and writing a lot more. My productivity has never been higher.

She's ecstatic. "Wow, you churned this one out fast!"

What can I say? She's my #1 fan. Actually, she's my only fan. She's also the only person in this house whom I've consistently *not* hated lately, including myself and the maid I caught sweeping dust under the rug. (Gross.) Elijah has been pretty happy since we moved here, and he's somehow worse when he's happy. He was bragging to me about how great his relationship is, and how Arete is the one. I asked him why he was being weird, and he responded with a quote. "Love is the most common miracle. John Green." I didn't peg him for a John Green fan, but for all I know, he read it in a listicle titled *25 Quotes That Will Impress Your Girlfriend*.

"It's just the first draft," I say. "And it's only seven pages long, but I want your opinion on it before I get too far."

"That's fine," Arete says. "What's it about?"

"It was inspired by your nightmare, sort of," I say. "It's kind of stupid when I try to explain it. The main character is having a recurring nightmare, and he spends it trying to escape to this city, but every night something different is keeping him from getting in. So he decides to try to turn the nightmare into a dream."

She smiles to hide her nerves. "I knew you overheard that."

"It was kind of hard not to." I rub the back of my neck. I didn't want to make her nervous. Maybe I shouldn't have told her how I got the idea. I was trying to make it *less* awkward.

"It's fine," she says.

I hover over her as she reads. I try to follow along as she reads so I can guess which lines make her laugh and which made her frown, but she turns out to be a much faster reader than me. I shouldn't be surprised; every time I see her, she's either reading, hanging out with Elijah, or hanging out with Elijah while ignoring him for a book. Dyslexia must not work the way I thought it did.

"This is wicked awesome, mate!" she says when she's finished. "When it's done, I think it might be better than *Night in the Fire*."

"Really?" I thought it was hard for anything I wrote to be *worse* than *Night in the Fire*, but I'm not trying to outdo myself. I was doing it for her. She may be a spoiled brat, but this is the first time anyone's ever believed in me and my trash.

She hands the story back to me. "It just wasn't long enough. You should—"

Whatever Arete was about to say, she forgets all about it when she sees Elijah coming around the corner of the house.

"I'm home." Elijah steps onto the deck holding up a lumpy object wrapped up in baby shower-themed wrapping paper. "And I have a surprise for you!"

"Another one?" Arete asks as he hands her the present. "What is it?"

Elijah is more excited than I've ever seen him. "Open it and find out!"

Arete carefully lifts the tape off the wrapping paper, throwing Elijah into a fit of suspense. She pulls the paper back six inches before she screams and drops it.

"What's wrong?" Elijah asks when Arete backs away. "I thought you wanted to see Hoppy again."

Devastated, Arete tears up and throws her arms around me, and sets her head on my shoulder. I'm afraid to return her hug with Elijah burning a jealousy hole into my forehead, so I give her an awkward pat on the back. He picks the present up and pulls off the rest of the paper to reveal the 18" tall, white rabbit that I overheard so much about. But it isn't burnt at all. It looks brand new.

"What kind of *drongo* do you think I am?" Arete asks. "I don't need a replacement!"

"No, I promise it's the real deal!" Elijah says. "I just took it to the stuffed animal hospital!"

"I'm not three anymore! There's no hospital for toys!"

"Would I ever lie to you?"

"Apparently, yes!" Arete says.

Elijah is about to grab her shoulder, but thinks better of it. "No, baby, please, look at the tag!"

"Stop yelling at me," she says between sobs. "You wanker!"

"Dammit, woman, do you think they still make these?" Elijah says, losing his temper. "*Look* at the *fucking tag!*"

She turns her back on him and crosses her arms. Why are they having a blowout fight over something this stupid? I hate being the mediator, but I don't have a choice. Right now she trusts me more than her boyfriend for reasons I can't figure out, so I cautiously approach him so I can see the tag. I read out loud to her.

"Manufactured and distributed by Stuffie Friends, Inc. Copyright 1993. San Francisco, California. Plush fiber and wool stuffing. All new materials... I can't read it, but there are faded, pink letters on it. ARK? Like Noah's ark?"

"Arete Rene Konstantinou." She turns around. "It's my initials."

Elijah unceremoniously shoves Hoppy into her chest. He isn't trying to use force, but having forgotten his own strength, it's enough to push Arete back a few steps as she takes hold of the rabbit. The two say nothing, but Arete looks terrified. He crosses his arms and watches her run her fingers over the tag. The most expansive backyard I've ever seen is starting to feel small, so I decide to slip out.

"Where do you think you're going?" Elijah asks without looking at me. Either his eyes are like a fly's, or he has some sort of bat sonar. I wonder if he's always been like that, or if it's a skill he was taught in the military.

"I just thought you two would rather be alone," I say. Just when I think I've gotten used to Elijah, he always manages to come back full circle and scare the living hell out of me.

Elijah pulls a set of car keys out of his pocket. "No." He points at me with the key. "*You* stay here with Arete. I have things to do."

"No, wait!" Arete says. "Please don't go! I'm really sorry!"

She sniffs and her lips quiver as he stomps off. Something about the sight of Arete standing there sobbing while holding Hoppy disgusts Elijah. He probably rehearsed this moment in his head while he searched for Hoppy, the whole time he was waiting for Hoppy to be fixed, and up until the second he came home with a lumpy package. But when I hear a car door slamming in the distance, I'm reminded of his foul temper.

"Is this my fault?" Arete asks, wiping away her own tears with her free hand.

"He's just disappointed. He needs some time to cool off," I say. "He'll be back soon."

She sniffles and wipes the snot from the tip of her nose onto her sleeve. *Eww.*

"That's not the question I asked," she says.

I take a deep breath. I was never good at comforting people. "No. This isn't your fault, it's his. He's a stupid asshole. I'd freak out too if someone brought back a stuffed animal that I set on fire. Not that it was a bad thing or anything. I mean, you had your reasons."

"How do you think he found her?" Arete asks.

"What do you mean?"

Arete cradles her stuffed animal like a baby. "I looked everywhere for Hoppy. I knew all of Dad's best hiding places, or at least I thought I did. So if I couldn't, then how did Eli find her so quickly? I mean, we've only been here for two days. And stuffed animal repair can't happen overnight."

"Good point," I say.

Maybe I shouldn't have. A few years ago, my mom mailed one of my old baby toys to a stuffed animal hospital to be repaired, and it took two weeks. There was no way Elijah found the rabbit, sent it to a stuffed animal hospital, and brought it home in three days. I change my answer to the only thing that makes sense, not because I believe it, but because I can't stand to see her upset.

"Maybe your dad hid it in plain sight, and Elijah found it by accident while we were moving in. He was out for a while Tuesday, he could have visited a toymaker in person and payed extra to finish it as soon as possible. Or maybe he knows someone."

Arete doesn't spend a lot of time contemplating my words. "Yeah, you must be right. Nothing else makes sense. He didn't even know where my house was until the other day."

"I wouldn't worry about it," I say. "Are you still going with him to Melbourne to see that concert?" *Please say no.*

"Of course I am."

Shit.

"Are you sure?" I ask. "I mean, you saw how he just blew up over a stuffed animal."

"Obviously, you have no idea how obsessed I am with Die Antwoord," she says. "Eli was just... disappointed. He'll be cooled off in an hour, if I know him at all."

She's probably right; he never stays mad for long. It's like he concentrates all of his anger into brief but intense bursts and then magically gets over it. Still, something is off, and I have this foreboding feeling that something terrible is about to happen to her.

"I'll have to take your word for it," I say. "Just, please, *please* be careful."

"Oh, Willbaby," she says, teasing me to cover up her nerves. "I'll be fine."

Sunday, March 8, 2015

Omniscient View

Melbourne, Victoria

It's 4:00 AM in America, and William Brown Quiñones is sound asleep. In Melbourne, however, it's 7:00 PM and time for the Die Antwoord concert Arete begged Elijah to take her to. That's not to say that he isn't fond of Die Antwoord. He simply isn't obsessed with them like Arete is. He doesn't get the hype and thinks they crossed the line on a few of their music videos. Sure, their music is good and the lead girl is cute, but Arete eclipses every woman on earth.

All in all, it was as successful a night as Elijah hoped it would be. He's been scheming something for weeks, and tonight is the night he will finally set it in motion. There's no better time to bring his ideas to catharsis. The concert was exciting, dinner at Vue de Monde was perfectly romantic, and now he's taking her out on a two person yacht he rented for the evening. Arete would be susceptible to his will, which was absolutely crucial.

The couple boards and sets out to sea, sailing so far into the distance that they can barely see a sliver of Australia. Arete can't help but be impressed that Elijah can drive a yacht; then again, he is a US marine vet, a retired police officer, and generally talented. She's certain he knows all sorts of things she has yet to see or imagine. That poor, fascinated girl wants to learn everything about him.

"How did you afford all this, though?" Arete asks. "Not that I'm complaining."

"Don't worry about that," Elijah says. "We have things to do."

The stars twinkle behind the clouds, and the full moon hangs over them like a bad omen. No one else is around for miles, and no one will be. Our captain leads Arete to the deck and guides her to the nose of the yacht. It's easy to fall into a false security when everything is so quiet. Elijah puts his hands on Arete's hips, and takes her a step backward. The guard railing is cold against the backs of her ankles.

"Thrilling," Arete says, trying to pass her nerves off as an adrenaline rush. "But aren't we a little close to the edge? I don't want to fall into the ocean."

Elijah smirks, slides his hands up to her waist, and spins her around to face the ocean. "What was that thing Jack did with Rose again?"

Arete holds her arms out to the sides and laughs. "How did you know I liked *Titanic*?"

He rubs the back of his neck. Why did she have to ask that question? "I found the disc in your DVD player when we first moved in."

He searched her room when she was gone to find out what stuff she liked? That's a little on the creepy side, but it's his honesty that endears him to her. And besides, she has plans of her own.

He leans forward and kisses her on the back of her neck, his hands trailing up toward her breasts. His touch is electric, and she has no intention of resisting tonight. She turns around to kiss him on the lips.

Elijah steps forward once more, pushing Arete to the very edge. His girlfriend lets out the littlest gasp he ever heard as her torso bends backwards over the railing. He extends his hand and catches her. She releases a grateful breath, but her heart still cries out as her head leans back toward the ocean. True relief is when Elijah pulls her back into his arms, and as she buries her head in his chest, she feels justified in her choice to place all of her trust in this man over all the others.

He whispers in her ear. "How do you feel about a home mixed mojito by yours truly?"

"That didn't sound as sexy as you wanted it to," Arete says, repressing her cringe with an unnatural giggle. "But, yes. That sounds nice. Will you show me how to make one, or is it a secret recipe?"

"Oh, honey," he says. "Of course I'll let you watch. All you ever have to do is ask me, and I'll always tell you the truth."

But never the *whole* truth. If the *whole* truth was offered, she would learn that there is no secret mojito recipe. As a matter of fact, Elijah's never mixed a mojito in his life, not that it matters in the grand scheme of things. He texted Boy Meets World that morning asking for instructions (to save cellular data, of course) and finally got a reply twenty minutes ago. Sometimes he swears that kid does nothing but sleep at odd hours of the day and clean things that are already clean. It is the afternoon in Philadelphia, after all, but so long as it doesn't interfere with his plans, it is of little consequence.

Elijah takes her by the hand and leads her into the yacht's kitchen. It's actually a tiny yacht compared to what she's used to, but Arete doesn't dare point it out, assuming Elijah must have taken out loans just to afford one night on a small luxury liner. On top of that, she hasn't yet gotten the opportunity to sleep with him. Something had always interrupted them before, and it was usually William, but tonight is the night. She doesn't dare let the conversation go down such a trivial path.

While Elijah is digging through the cabinets, she seats herself on the barstool, crosses her legs, and hikes her skirt up a few more inches. Bored if not impatient, she watches Elijah hunt for the necessary ingredients. One by one, he sets out sugar, a lime, club soda, fresh mint leaves, and rum. Arete rolls her eyes and slides her hands into her bra, adjusting her small breasts for maximum cleavage. She stares at him, thinking *notice me, dammit. Notice me.*

Finally, Elijah turns around. "You don't have any food allergies, do you?"

Arete leans on bar's surface and pouts. "And with that question, my lady boner is officially *gone.*"

The blade of a knife screeches as Elijah withdraws it from the cutlery holder. "I wouldn't worry about *that* if I were you."

"Why?" Arete asks with her best seductive smile—after all, her leaning over gives him the best view. "What are you going to do to me?"

Elijah holds up the kitchen knife, takes careful aim, and uses all his might to strike the cutting board. He's good at a lot of things, but mincing mint leaves is not one of them. Arete wants to huff, but holds it in. This is going to waste the whole night if she doesn't intervene.

"Want me to help you mince that?" Arete asks. "I may not look like it, but I'm actually pretty good at that part."

Elijah takes a glimpse at Arete's reflection in the blade of his knife. She's so beautiful and sincere, innocent without a doubt. It's how those round, dollbaby eyes make her look both quirky and cute, and her small, perky ti—...uh, *nose*. Women like her are such a rarity, and the innocent never last long in such a cruel world. He knows what he must do. He's rehearsed his plan in his head all night, and has fully excused his actions ahead of time.

"Sure." Elijah points his knife forward and deals a powerful blow to the lime, splitting it in half. "Sorry. I just had to do that first. There's something deeply satisfying about whacking a vegetable in half."

"Fruit," Arete says, though she has a feeling he was aware of this.

She can always tell when Elijah is downplaying his intelligence so she won't feel intimidated. He means well, but it's rather insulting that he doesn't think she could handle him at his true intellect, whatever that may be. All she knows is that he's sharper than most, and definitely sharper than her. But she always felt that she has one trait he lacks: common sense.

Elijah sets the knife down, bows, and gestures toward the cutting board. "It's all yours, Kit Kat."

Arete bunches the mint leaves into a tight pile. "The trick is to push them all together, so you can chop them more easily," she says.

Elijah stands behind her and presses his body against hers. "And to think, I thought I was the one teaching you."

"I'm hoping you'll teach me lots of things tonight," Arete says.

"I love the way you think."

Once they've finished mixing the mojitos, Arete has to use the bathroom, leaving her drink unattended. Unbeknownst to her boyfriend, she's actually excused herself to "freshen up." Meanwhile, Elijah has his pick of toxic fluids at his disposal. Carpet cleaner, dish soap, bleach, rat poison, and so many other possibilities exist if you use your imagination. Elijah, being the clever man he is, makes sure Arete isn't around to see and slips a few more mint leaves into their drinks. According to William's recipe, she didn't put in enough to properly bring out the flavor, and he needed to amend the error in secret so she wouldn't be offended. Luckily, she doesn't notice upon her return.

The two lovers head to the yacht's deck to relax on the lounge chairs and enjoy their drinks in the night. Arete desperately wants to lose her virginity, but Elijah has something else in mind. He's nervous as well, but it's all he's thought about for weeks. He has to do it tonight. This could be his last chance for a long time and it's too late to go back now. She's lying on the chair, exposed and vulnerable. He wonders if she notices her skirt is riding up, allowing him to be tempted by a peek of her lacy lingerie.

"Are you comfortable?" he asks.

"Of course," Arete says.

"Are you sure?" he asks, approaching her. "You look tense."

Elijah stands over her, the distant light from the kitchen windows casting his imposing shadow over her pale body. She sets her drink down and slides her feet toward her rear as she spreads her legs, exposing the crotchless intimates she bought for the occasion. She closes her eyes and waits for him, but he instead goes straight for her delicate neck. He puts one hand at either side, his fingertips gliding over her trachia, and gives her a massage. Strangely enough, she was not disappointed in the slightest. If anything, she was more excited than before.

"That feels nice," she says. "Where did you learn how to do that?"

Elijah takes pause to lovingly twirl a strand of Arete's hair around his finger and lets the coil slide away as he gracefully returns his hand to its station. "I picked up a lot of completely irrelevant skills while I was in the military."

She considers asking where he learned the art of neck massages in the Marine Corps of all places, but she keeps her mouth shut. That's not where she wants the conversation to go. She doesn't want conversation at all, unlike her boyfriend, who has prepared a small speech for this moment.

"So there's something I've been meaning to do all night," Elijah says. "And only just now have I managed to work up the nerve. And before I start, I want you to know that I genuinely do love you and always will. And if I'm allowed some creative license, it's not just because you're the only beautiful thing on this otherwise dank planet, but because you're the most authentic friend I've had."

It wasn't what she had in mind, but she opens her eyes and grins in spite of herself. His little speech got the better of her libido and touched her heart.

She sits up. "But you must think I'm a total drongo," she says. "You risked your life to save me, twice... And you didn't judge me even a little bit when I was suspended from Penn, even though it was my fault. I don't deserve someone as perfect as you."

Perfect? Unfortunately not, for Elijah has a dark mind. The man slides his right hand into his coat pocket, careful to make slow movements and maintain constant keep eye contact to keep Arete from noticing. He withdraws his late father's knife from his pocket and hides it behind his back.

"You're not a drongo," Elijah says. "You're the most wonderful woman I've ever met. I know it's only been three weeks, but they were the most beautiful three weeks of my life. And with everything we've fought through already, I don't want to have to fight this too. Tragedy brings people closer, and we're no exception. Arete Konstantinou..." He bends down on one knee and opens a compartment at the butt of the knife handle, shaking out a diamond ring. "Will you marry me?"

Also Sunday, March 8, 2015
William Brown Quiñones
Philadelphia, Pennsylvania

For the first time in years, my life is starting to look up. *Beautiful City*, the first thing I've written in ten months, is finally finished in short story form, though I've decided to expand it into a novelette. I have Arete to thank for that, I realize. The work is mine, but not only did the inspiration came from her, but living in the large and quiet Konstantinou Manor provided me the perfect work environment. I decide to wait to tell her the good news in person. I haven't heard from her since she left, but Elijah texted me a few hours ago.

Elijah:
Hey how do u mix a mojito??
Plz ur my only bartender friend
Hey
Wakeup shithead

I eventually respond while half asleep.

Lazy way:1 1/2oz rum, mint leaves, club soda, 1oz lime juice 2tsp sugar. Mince mint leaves and muddle them with lime in the bottom of collins glass fill with ice pour in rum

then club soda stir with straw

Thanks ur my 2nd favorite person

Oh and fuck you

Me being Elijah's "2nd favorite person" as of now doesn't change the fact that I don't trust him. Now that they're gone, I have a week to dedicate to uncovering his secrets. His bedroom door is already cracked open, so I push it aside and look around. He didn't leave behind any messes when he packed to leave for the week. Everything was right where he left it, except his dog tags. He must have taken those with him. The only thing he moved drastically was the floor safe, which he had pushed inside his closet. I crouch down and enter the safe combination.

2... 7... 3... 8... 3!

I grab the handle and pull with all my strength, but the door doesn't budge. He didn't just move the safe, he changed the combination. Before he left, he must have realized that ARETE is the dumbest passcode conceived.

I retrieve a pencil and some notebook paper from my room, and proceed to spend the night testing every combination of numbers that I can work out. It's frustrating, and my neck hurts from crouching over the notebook on the floor. Still, I won't give up, and I only take a few short breaks to eat and use the bathroom. I can't rest until I find out exactly who I'm living with. As the hours pass by through my work, the sun starts to rise. By the time I manage to crack the code, the birds are chirping.

When the safe finally clicks open, I'm so tired that I can I hardly believe it. What used to be a shoe box has been replaced by a lock box—which, of course, is locked. I lean over and notice a sticky note adhered to the top.

Checkmate, Veronica Mars.

That's definitely Elijah's shitty handwriting. Did he figure out I was digging through his things? How could he? Surely this was just an extra precaution to unnerve anyone who might open it, unless he wired security cameras all over the house when no one was watching. Otherwise he would have written *Boy Meets World*, right? I leave the safe open and retire to my room for the... morning. I'll find the key tomorrow.

Monday, March 9, 2015

The key to the lock box was hidden somewhere clever, where Elijah knew nobody would ever look—the only messy drawer in his dresser, next to a fingerprint dusting kit and under a Mensa International t-shirt. I'm almost disappointed after my five hour expedition. I wasted time searching for secret compartments in his binoculars and turned his mattress over. I expected more from him, especially now that I know he's a member of a high IQ society. You have to score a 130 to enter. Then again, breaking into his safe became a two day project, so he isn't doing too badly.

The things in his lock box are in the same order as they were in his shoe box, so he most likely didn't go through any of the papers when he moved the safe. I breathe a sigh of relief; he must not know I was digging through the contents. I find a thick, manila folder that's stuffed with documents Elijah shouldn't have access to.

I already know that Arete isn't a Konstantinou by blood, but I have to know why this is so important to Elijah that he keeps a secret file on his girlfriend. I also can't figure out how he got all this to begin with, since he turned in his badge and gun to attend UPenn, which is where he *met* Arete. How did he gain access to full police records of Arete's mother, both from Philadelphia *and* Melbourne? I do a quick scan; Simone was convicted of nothing more than a speeding ticket, making me wonder what she did that warranted Arete and me praying her out of Hell.

Elijah researched Arete's late mother and the gang rape in great detail. Simone Wagner was sixteen when nothing short of determination and hard work allowed her to graduate high school early, near the top of her class. Papers show she left Melbourne to study abroad at St. Joseph's college in the spring semester. It sounds like she was the capable woman Arete made her out to be, but that's not all Elijah has on her. He's compiled all her available phone records, credit and debit purchases, and even her *will*. (Which can be summarized by "I leave everything to my daughter.")

I check her death certificate. Simone died in her home on March 2, 2014; the cause of death was not given. In red marker, Elijah wrote "redaction ordered by Arete?" in the margin. Wait, why is there an old burner phone in a plastic baggy? Focus. I divert my attention to the 1992 assault Elijah is obsessed with.

I look through the criminal records for each of the seven men accused of raping and brutalizing the teenage exchange student from Australia. None of them faced jail time for their crime against Simone, though a few of them were arrested for other violent crimes later on in life.

Elijah kept a death certificate for each of the seven men as well, and all of them died in a short time window. From November 2009 to February 2012, six of them went down in miscellaneous accidents, from drug overdoses to suicide. The only exception is the seventh and final rapist. According to a police report, he was tortured, murdered and dismembered in January, 2014, a mere day after he was released from prison. His body was found in his mother's home, beaten to a pulp and murdered in a way that was so graphic, not even a slasher movie could compete. I don't want to go in detail, but it involved castration.

I close the envelope when I see a flash of the crime scene photos. I choke back some vomit. Sweet mother of baby Jesus, I know he deserved it, but whoever did this was depraved. Even with the others, the time frame was too suspicious for karma alone. The "accidents" started around the time Elijah left the marines. Elijah had something to do with it, he must have. He's killed before, and effortlessly at that. He demonstrated that when he staked a guy with an *icicle*. I'm pretty sure the Marines didn't teach him that move. Who's to say he isn't capable of premeditated murder? All that's missing is the motive. What connection could Elijah have possibly had with Simone? She died before he and Arete met.

But I can't exactly call Simone up and ask her anything. I compare the photos of the rapists to the photos of Arete. One of those men was her father, and she doesn't know it. How would that conversation go?

Hey, Arete. I just found out that your father isn't your real father. No, sorry. Your real father is dead too. Also, he's raped at least one person, and you're actually pretty lucky that you've never met him. By the way, you might be dating a serial killer. I have no hard proof, but he has this creepy, secret file on you, so he's probably guilty.

I'm going to do the smart thing and not tell her, but I'm going to have a hard time letting this one go. The more I know, the harder living here will be, and I don't exactly have a way out. Even if I remove my cell phone from my pocket, Elijah will be suspicious if the tracker says that I haven't changed position the whole time he left for vacation, and he'll eventually catch up with me. I can't look through this anymore. There are just some things I'm better off not knowing, and I have a feeling whatever he's researching is one of those things. I put the files back in the proper order, put everything back the way it was, and close the safe. I'm never opening that thing again.

Tuesday, March 10, 2015

I'm watching TV in my room, trying not to think about Elijah, when I hear a car door slam. *Speak of the Devil.* I look through the window and see Arete's Ferrari pull into the driveway. Who would exit the driver's side of the vehicle other than Elijah Walker—my favorite jerk, stalker, and probably serial killer.

Putting his head down and not looking back, Elijah walks straight through the front door. I walk to the staircase to greet him in whatever way I can muster.

"Hey, man," I say, trying to sound casual. "I didn't think you'd be back until Thursday."

Elijah doesn't take his eyes away from the ground as he walks past me and heads up the stairs without saying a word. In the distance, I hear his bedroom door slam.

So where is Arete?

Worried, I run outside to make sure she made it back in one piece. She never did text or call me when I checked in on her, and after finding out Elijah may have an ulterior motive to dating her, it's hard not to fear the worst.

Thankfully, Arete is okay. At least, she's *physically* okay. She bears a humorless expression and greets me with a half-hearted wave rather than the usual "G'day, mate!" Well, okay, she never actually says "G'day, mate!" That's just how I see it in my head.

"Hey," I say again, still failing to sound casual. "You've... So, you're back early."

She rolls her eyes. "Shame it didn't end sooner. Good to see ya, mate."

"So..." I stick my hands in my pockets. "What's Elijah's problem? He just went straight to his room and locked himself in. Didn't even say hi."

"He's been like that all day," Arete says. "Literally, over 24 hours, I swear."

"Not a single word?" I ask.

Arete opens the trunk and lifts out a Skelanimals carryon bag. "Only when he had to. He usually communicated by nodding and shrugging. He actually used *sign language* once. Like... I can't speak sign language. He knows that."

"I'm afraid to ask, but what happened?"

"In Melbourne?" Arete pulls the bag up over her shoulder and reaches for small suitcase. "He proposed."

"WHAT?"

"Yep," she says, humorless. "I'll tell you all about it if you help me carry these in."

"Sure," I say. "So, I'm guessing you said *no* then?"

"Of course I said no!" Arete pulls up the handle of a rolling suitcase. "He basically just said that three weeks was long enough because we've, quote unquote, *fought through so much already*, but I told him I needed more time. I mean, maybe a year from now, or a few months even, but three weeks?" She crosses her arms. "I feel bad because he saved my life twice and spent all that money on me, but... I was just... It's too soon."

I try to heave a large suitcase out of the back of the trunk, and my arms are nearly pulled out of their sockets. "What is *in* here?"

"That's Elijah's gym crap," she says. "His barbells or whatever they're called are probably in it. Just leave it. He'll be back for them, I'm sure."

"I called you a few times," I say.

"I noticed once I got off the plane," she says, "but I wouldn't have been in the mood for talking either, what with Elijah in a chronic meltdown. He sobbed for hours, it was obnoxious. I wanted to scream. I did scream."

"Oh. Wow."

Elijah cried? I wish I could've seen that. She continues to vent about everything from his extreme moodiness to his taste for pop music. It was a little surprising to find out he's on fire for Lady Gaga—I always imagined him as more of a classic rock kind of guy. I think about the MENSA shirt I found earlier, and look for a way to slide it into the conversation.

"You think he'd be smarter than to call a lime a vegetable," I say. "His IQ is how high exactly?"

"You're still caught up on that one?" She pouts. "I don't know anything about IQ tests, I barely passed Psych 101. I feel so *stupid* around him sometimes, and I think he's dumbing himself down for me. Reason number three hundred *billion* that I can't marry him."

"Well, it's only been a few weeks," I say. "Maybe you'll change your mind. Eventually."

She scoffs and shakes her head, but smiles. "You always see the best in everyone, don't you?"

"Usually, yeah. But he's creepy."

"He wouldn't make a very good husband," Arete says. "I used to like sensitive men, but this is just too much!"

Elijah is... sensitive?

"I'm never going to live this down," Arete says. "Whitney—that's my Penn roomie—totally warned me there was something off about him... I *cannot* let her find out about this."

"You don't have to make a decision about Elijah today," I say. "Just stay at home, hide out, and chill. Elijah sounds like he'll steer clear, and that girl is only still your roommate on paper. She won't know you're back from vacation early unless you tell her."

She looks down at her feet. "I suppose you're right. I'll do that."

Thursday, March 12, 2015

I'm awoken by a phone call around eight o'clock in the morning. I groan and burrow deeper under the covers, only answering when I realize the phone won't stop ringing. "Who is it?"

"It's your old landlord."

"Why?"

Of all the things I could say, that's what tumbles out of my mouth. *Why*.

"The fire," he says. "Sorry I didn't call at night, I know how you nocturnal writer types are, but this is important."

"The fire?" I ask. "What happened?"

"The insurance company just finished their investigation, and it was, oh... what was the word she used..." He pauses. "Inconclusive. They said it was most likely an accident, because any money you'd get from renter's insurance would never cover your losses, but they want me to check in."

I'm too tired to think about this, but I knew it was inevitable. I just didn't expect so much skepticism. I thought it was an electrical fire and I'd get money to cover what little I had, bam, wham, and done.

"Check in how? I'm okay, if that's what you mean. I'm living with some... friends."

"That's good, but an agent from the insurance company asked me if there's anyone who has a grudge against you," he says. "It could have been an accident, but some details looked deliberate. I told them you were a friendly recluse—no offense—and I didn't know of anyone who would want to hurt you, but they advise you to call the police if there's someone who would want to kill you."

"Someone who would want to kill me..." I say.

"That's right. Or scare you, get revenge, anything like that."

"Nope... Nobody."

Who would target me? This must be about Arete, who is generally more trouble than she's worth. I hate jumping to conclusions, but what if what Elijah said was true, and someone is after her? I could get caught in the crossfire. Again.

"Okay then," the landlord says. "I'll tell them. I hope things work out at your new place."

"Thanks," I say.

We say our goodbyes and he's the first to hang up. When I set my phone down, I notice black ink covering the pad of my thumb. Weird. I have no idea how it got there, but I'm too tired to care. I sleep the rest of the day.

Friday, March 13, 2015

I'm settled in my home in the beautiful city when there's a knock at my door. I don't want to answer it, especially not when I hear the voice on the other side.

"Hey, sleepyhead! It's your best mate forever, Elijah!"

Absolutely not. I, a bestselling author, am enjoying a cup of white tea and am almost done with my 40th novel. I'm a bigger money maker than James Patterson. If I miss my deadline, my editor will be horrified.

The knocking gets louder. "Rise and shine, kid!"

That's when I wake up.

"Fine!" I say through a yawn. "Come in."

Elijah bursts through the door the second I give him the okay, and he flips the light switch. I groan. When he draws the blinds, I resort to pulling the blankets over my face to block the light.

"I've been waiting for you to wake up since yesterday," he says. "Do you always sleep in this late? It's been like 15 hours, and that's kind of sad, even for you."

What's "kind of sad" is the fact that he's been waiting for me to wake up. Knowing he won't give up, I rise and wipe the crust from my eyes.

"No, just most of the time. Why are you here, anyway?"

"What do you mean?" Elijah turns around, and I see that he's already dressed. "Can't a man stop by and visit his friend?"

"Someone else? Maybe. You? No." I want to say *we're not friends*, but the sad thing is, at this point, we may as well be. He evidently sees it that way, and I'd rather not piss him off by rejecting him.

"Oh, so you hate me too," Elijah says. He had been hiding in his room for the past three days and I made no real attempt to talk to him unless you count being Arete's messenger boy, so maybe a little bit.

I busy myself with making the bed, as if direct eye contact would provoke him. Or maybe I just don't want to look at him.

"Arete doesn't hate you," I say. "She just thinks you're pathetic. That khaki button down shirt you're wearing, though—that she *does* hate."

"Somebody's grouchy in the morning," he says, far too cheerful.

Please die.

"*I'm* the one acting off?" I say. "You've been holed up in your room all week. If I didn't hear occasional footsteps, I'd think you moved back in with Tommy and Keyon."

"Well, get dressed," he says. "We're going to hang out."

He's starting to sound like Arete did when we first met that fateful night in February. But as long as we aren't going to be handcuffed together, it might be worth it just to get him out of the house. I can't concentrate on my writing with him around, but not because he interrupts me or makes too much noise. It's the negative energy that creeps out from under the cracks of his bedroom door and flows through the halls like carbon monoxide.

But at the same time, I know what it's like to be lonely in a house full of people; that sums up my teenage years. I barely spoke to my parents, not because I hated them, but because my mother was overbearing and naggy, and my father had the tendency to travel with his job. As for Sherry, I pleaded no contest to a sibling rivalry. She and Mom would often talk to each other in Spanish, and I felt excluded. I hid in my room and rarely came out. Even now, I still don't speak to them. I show up on the holidays, but I just eat and leave so I can dodge questions about how badly I'm failing life. I'm okay with this system because I'm a loner by nature, but Elijah can only stay alone for an hour at a time before he has a meltdown from social deprivation. Back when I was crashing at his apartment, he was almost never home. Even then, he had someone to talk to. That's probably why he asked Tommy and Keyon to move in with him. Sure, they *think* he did it to help them, but he surely needed them more than they needed him. He can't even watch TV alone; he once made me sit through this weird foreign film even though I can't speak French.

"Fine, I'll go," I say. "But only so you'll stop hiding in your room like a butt-hurt little bitch."

"I like this side of you, Boy Meets World."

With that, Elijah leaves the room. I throw on jeans and a t-shirt, like always. I may live in a mansion, but I'm still a simple man at heart, and now a starving artist. No handouts. Living here and eating their food is compensation for my house being burned down. If I never met them, my house would have *never* burned down. I'm convinced it's somehow their fault. The timing is just too perfect, and somebody is out to kill that girl.

Speaking of Arete, I recall her saying something about retail therapy. Now I understand why Elijah picked this moment to come out of his dungeon. It's a good thing he did, because Arete was talking about going back to her dorm and kicking him out if he didn't show himself tonight. I don't know what would happen to me, and safety concerns aside, it's easy to get used to a billionaire's amenities.

It doesn't occur to me that I don't know where we're going until we make it to Elijah's blue 4x4. I'm about to ask when we make it to the truck, but he immediately starts small talk. Surely he has plenty of friends down at the station that he could talk to, right? Why me?

Elijah starts the truck. "So, what have you been up to?"

"I'm doing freelance writing," I say.

He already knows that; he's probably just procrastinating all of the questions he thinks I'm going to ask him about Arete. In reality, I don't want to know anything, hence why I'm never touching that safe again.

"What about you?" I ask. "I haven't seen you leave in days. Are you even still a law student?"

"It's called spring break," Elijah says. "Haven't you ever heard of it? Grad students take breaks too, I have to go back Monday."

"You okay, man?" My concern for him is *almost* genuine. Mostly, I just want him to go back to normal. I'm catching his crazy like the flu, and honestly, this is kind of depressing.

Elijah pulls out of the driveway. "I don't know. Hasn't Arete told you anything? I know you two are in some sort of book cult."

I sigh. Cult? "Whatever. Where are we going?"

"We're getting some... fresh air," Elijah says. "And I left a note on the fridge telling Arete we were going fishing. That way I don't have to talk to her in person."

What was it about that girl that brings out the worst in him, and why do I have to be dragged in the middle of it?

"Okay..." I say. "I don't know how to fish."

"I don't either," Elijah says.

"Then where are we going?" I ask.

"The lake."

"But you just said you didn't know how to fish?"

Elijah turns up his chin. "Yeah. I'm driving *into* the lake."

"Wait, what?"

"I'm going to drive into the lake and kill us both," he says.

I frantically grab the door handle and pull, but no matter how hard I jerk it, the handle won't open and the lock won't disengage. I can't let my life end because of Elijah's suicidal tendencies. Should I grab the wheel? Break the window and jump out?

"I'm kidding," Elijah says. "It was just a joke."

My chest heaves. "But... But you said it with such a straight face."

"Calm your tits, we're going to Paddy Whacks."

Paddy Whacks is an Irish sports pub that's close to UPenn. "You're still kidding right? For breakfast?"

Elijah shakes his head. "It's a quarter 'til three. We're going there for a late lunch. You brought your license, right?"

"Yeah."

"Good. I'm going to need a designated driver."

"Oh, come on," I say. "You're dragging me there to watch you drink and cry because your girlfriend of three weeks wouldn't marry you?"

"Eh," Elijah says. "Pretty much. Where else would we go?"

"You said fresh air. I mean, we live five minutes away from a park."

"We're also near a golf club, but that doesn't make it a good idea."

"And isn't you saying we're going fishing an outright lie?" I ask. "Because I thought you didn't do that."

"We *are* going fishing, but I didn't say when. We just have to make sure to go fishing someday, just you and me, my favorite pool noodle." He playfully punches me on the arm, proving my every suspicion that he's gone mad.

There's no point in further arguing, so I concede defeat. "Fine. Paddy Whacks for breakfast."

"We're going to have fun, kid. Don't worry."

"I *am* worried," I say. "Seriously, you're not going to kill yourself, right?"

"Eh."

"That's it? Eh? All you're going to say is *eh*?"

Elijah jerks the steering wheel, swerving in the direction of another car. I cover my eyes and brace myself for a fatal impact, but all I hear is a car honking at us. I look up and realize he just did it to scare me.

"Gotcha!" he says.

I huff and look out the window to confirm that he's back to driving in the lines. "Elijah, I'm not kidding. I think you need a therapist or something."

"No, I need a day out with friends," he says. "Well... A day out with *friend*. Singular. A day with my favorite pool noodle, my best mate forever."

Today is the first day I remember Elijah calling me his friend at all, let alone several times within one hour, and it's actually disturbing. He turned cabin fever into an art form.

Elijah slams the brakes, crushes the horn, and yells so loudly that it brutalizes my ears. "Dammit, Missouri! Can't you go a little faster? Put your useless feet on the fucking pedal, you dickweed, or get your ugly ass Nissan Cube out of my fucking state!"

All the way to Paddy Whacks, Elijah throws fits about the slow Nissan that he has to follow all the way there, the white Subaru that cuts him off, and the banged-up Oldsmobile that rides his bumper. He orders me to reach into his glove box for a small notebook and record the plates of a Toyota that has a broken tail light, and a Chevrolet with expired plates. There's no point to it, so it must just make him feel better. He then proceeds to preach about road safety. Hypocrite.

*

Paddy Whacks is a dimly lit sports bar with an Irish pub theme. When the staff greets Elijah like they expected him, I realize he's a regular. He's not a sports person, so it's safe to assume he either likes the food or the atmosphere. He's not much of a foodie either, though. On top of being extremely picky, he usually eats bland, unseasoned things like baked chicken, steamed vegetables, and plain Greek yogurt. That leaves the atmosphere.

A casual lunch with Elijah isn't as awkward as being the third wheel at Waffle House while in handcuffs, but it doesn't feel normal, either. He waits until another couple is done dining because he's insistent on choosing the table in the corner by the windows, since he can't bear to sit with his back facing people and needs to have a view of all the exits. He says he always chooses this table every time he goes.

Elijah knows exactly what he wants to order the second we're seated: medium spicy wings and fries. He didn't steer me wrong at Waffle House and I feel awkward ordering, so I ask for roughly the same thing. I have my wings mild and my fries cheesey. Maybe by ordering his plain, he's finally accepting his lactose intolerance. I want a Heineken to calm my nerves, but the second he orders a hard cider, I know he was serious about me being designated driver. I assume that's the only reason he brought me along, but then realize he has plenty of money to call a Lyft or something. It's hard to believe he just wants me here as a friend, but I can't think of any other reason unless everyone else is either busy or mad at him.

We were actually having a decent conversation about how people reacted to Luke Skywalker and Princess Leia kissing in *Star Wars* until we're almost done eating (we finished at roughly the same time, but only because he ate way more than me) and he's graduated from Angry Orchard hard cider to Jameson whiskey. After he returns from the longest bathroom break known to man, all his questions start pouring out.

"So, what do you think about Arete and me? Be honest."

"I don't completely understand the question," I say. "Can you be more direct?"

There's no way in hell I'm going to tell the truth, but he's welcome to try. I have to analyze everything he says because It took me a while to learn about the ways he lies. Now I've had over two weeks to figure it out, and I'm going to beat him at his own game just to spite him. This is what I've got down:

Hollywood Perfect's Rules of Honesty:
1. Everything I say must be true.
2. Misleading isn't the same as lying.
3. Omission isn't the same as lying.
4. I can be sarcastic or hyperbolic if the intent is clear.
5. Jokes aren't lies as long as I clarify myself.
6. No wonder I want to be a lawyer.
7. But I'm not going to do this in the courtroom. *
8. * Strike that from the record, Your Honor. I haven't decided yet.

"I mean our relationship," he says.

"Do I absolutely *have* to answer that?" I ask.

Okay, I admit it. Elijah's game is actually pretty hard. Then again, I'm not a MENSA kid. I looked it up last night after I dug through his safe, and you have to score in the 98th percentile on an IQ test in order to get in. Let's just say I'm at a disadvantage.

"Please," Elijah says. "You're my only friend who hates me enough to tell me the truth."

Fair enough. "I think you're creepily obsessed with her and you need to stop."

Shit. Can I just rewind and unsay that?

I'm about to forfeit the lie detector game until he says, "That was blunt. Why?"

Uh... "I was blunt because I can't decide if I hate you or not."

"No," he says. He's frustrated now; he must know I'm playing his game. "Do you mean I need to stop *dating* Arete, or that I need to stop *obsessing* over Arete? And give me every single reason why you gave the answer you did. And just in case you try to pull a fast one, I am referring specifically to Arete Rene Konstantinou, my hopefully-still-girlfriend, not a Greek word meaning moral virtue or excellence of any kind."

His game is all about asking the right questions, isn't it?

"Fine," I say. "You need to stop both dating *and* obsessing over 'Arete Rene Konstantinou,' and I'm not going to tell you why, because you're a grown ass man and it should be obvious that this relationship is just unhealthy and *wrong*."

I expect him to be angry, to get defensive, to yell at me, or even to just get up and leave me stranded here. But he doesn't. He actually looks... anxious. I should go easier on him; he cares about this woman.

"Look," I say. "I'm not going to tell you what to do, and I'm not going to get in your business. But you need to think about what your end goal is—love, money, sex, career, one of those couples that has dogs instead of kids, whatever. Ask yourself what you what you *really* want in life, and think about whether or not you need to marry Arete this week to get it."

"I don't know how to answer that." He hiccups and takes a moment to ponder. "Did I ever tell you the story of how we met?"

"No, and I really don't want to know."

"I was at the theater watching what was the worst production of Romeo & Juliet that I'd ever seen. I knew twenty minutes in that I wanted to leave. And then I saw her: the most beautiful angel who ever lived." (Barf) "I found the play script on my phone so I would know when Arete's appearances were."

"You can stop now," I say.

"Unfortunately, her role as the nurse was in the whole damn thing, so I had to sit through two more agonizing hours of that play. The second it ended, I stole flowers from the vase in the women's restroom—"

"YOU WENT IN THE LADIES' ROOM?"

"—and brought them backstage, acting like she was my girlfriend. The door guy fell for it and let me in. After that—"

"But how did you know there were flowers in the ladies' room?"

"—I looked for her backstage, gave her the flowers, and I ended up asking her out for Valentine's day. She said 'no' because she never met me before, but I just kept asking until she gave up and said yes. It was the most magical moment of my life."

Once again, he's misleading me by trying to get me to conclude that he didn't know about Arete until that day, even though I know very well he's at least known about her since August, recalling my conversation with Tommy. He's probably known *of* her for a while now. Judging by her social media presence, he may have even known who she was for several years. But I'm not going to address that. I go with the flow and act like I'm taking the bait.

"And you're surprised that she didn't accept your marriage proposal on your three weekaversary?" I ask.

"Yeah." Elijah leaves a $20 tip and throws his coat on. "I thought tragedy brought us closer together, and she may be young, but I'm turning 32 this summer. I don't have as much time to waste as she does. I want to settle down."

"Okay," I say. "In other words, you want kids and a picket fence?"

"Kids, yes," Elijah says. "But no, I don't want a picket fence. I like it at the Konstantinou mansion. And don't even ask about Australia, I hate it there."

"How can you be sure you hate it if you've only been there once?"

"Oh, no. I've been there many times before. It's worse than Iraq. I'd rather go back to war for the rest of my sorry life than have a free vacation in Melbourne."

Wow. Talk about strong feelings. He's too emotional to function; I can hardly believe there was a time when I was afraid of this guy. I can't even completely hate him despite knowing he's a psycho stalker who gets away with everything by flashing a charming smile. I can't fathom how much better my life would be if I were that hot.

"Let's get going," I say. "Arete will probably know that we're not really fishing, so it's probably better to get back before she does. It's time for you to face her like a man anyway, before she kicks you out. Because she's talking about kicking you out."

"What if I stay anyway?" he asks.

"She'd fucking kill you," I say.

He smirks. "She can't kill me if I kill myself first."

"And if you come home talking like that, she'll just think you're pathetic."

"You're right," Elijah says. "Let's go."

He tosses me the keys, which I almost drop, when we make it out the door. I notice how well he handles his liquor. He talks more about personal things, too much, actually, but his coordination is fine. He could probably drive if he wanted to, but "Officer Walker" has serious issues with drunk driving... and yet he proposed marriage to someone with two speeding tickets, three parking tickets, and a middle tier DUI that got her license suspended for an entire year. Being a terrible driver got her 48 hours in jail; how many people can say *that*? (I couldn't help but look through Arete's criminal record too; the temptation was too strong.)

Something about being behind the wheel of Elijah's truck is nerve-wracking, and it's not just because I haven't driven in a while. Part of me is afraid he'll snap my neck if I put a single scratch on it, so I'm sure to drive more carefully than he does, and especially better than Arete.

After he scolds me for pulling out of the parking lot without buckling my seatbelt first, he says, "Kid, there's something I need to come clean about. I've never told anyone this before, and it's driving me crazy. But you can't tell Arete, no matter what. Are you okay with that?"

"Of course," I say to be polite. How bad can it really be?

Elijah leans up against the window and watches downtown Philadelphia traffic zoom by. "Without her, I feel so alone. My mom went missing in 2009, and my father died of ALS in 2014. I didn't get the fortune of spending a lot of time with either of my parents after they split up when I was ten, but both losses were hard to deal with. I'm still working through it."

Oh, great. Another tale of sorrow from Hollywood Perfect.

"I was forced to move in with my maternal grandparents after my mom lost custody, and they were... I hate to say it so flatly, but abusive. And most of my father's side are long dead by now because his parents were so old. The ones who are alive should go eat shit and die. Figuratively."

"I know what you meant," I say.

"Just checking," he says. "In the last days of his life I patched things up with my father. But when he had my uncle pass my inheritance to me under the table, I eventually had to accept that even in death he didn't fully accept me as his son. None of my cousins are old enough to know I exist, I don't have a shred of the family business, and I only have a small fraction of the money because he didn't want anyone else to notice. But it was enough for me to go to law school, and whether or not I wanted to admit it, there was no one left in my life to tell me who I could and couldn't talk to. I was free…ish."

He pauses, so I nod to let him know I'm still listening. But really, half of the stuff he's saying just registers as loose rambling about disconnected events.

"I decided to go to Penn Law, my uncle's alma mater— my father went to Wharton—and reconnect with my family. Except with the second bit, I kind of chickened out. One of my cousins and my stepsibling attend Penn, so I thought I'd bump into them eventually. But the fact that they don't even know I exist threw me off, so I just kind of… watched them."

"Oh, that's not creepy at all," I say.

"Shut up, I'm spilling my guts all over the floor here."

"Sorry," I say. "Don't feel obligated to continue."

"Well, I eventually approached my stepsister. She didn't even know my dad adopted her and she was raised to think he was her father. So Dad lied to her too, and that made things awkward. It doesn't help that she's hot either, since I have to either act like she's my biological half-sister, or tell her she's adopted—"

"Stop!" I say. I turn around and look Elijah straight in the eye. "Stop right there! Did you just call your stepsister hot? One, that's disgusting. Two, what about your girlfriend?"

He looks out the window again. "Well, my stepsister *is* my girlfriend, so..."

I see something approaching from the corner of my eye and slam my foot on the breaks. In what feels like an instant, metal collides with metal. I'm thrown to the side, but something hard hits my face. After a flash of black, I look around. The windows are cracked and there's a mist of smoke around me. I cough as my lungs are filled with the pungent cloud of chemicals and gas. The whiplash in my neck is unpleasant, but the real pain is from the high-pitched sirens assaulting my ears. It's a good thing "Officer Walker" reminded me to buckle my seatbelt, or I'd be toast.

Wait... Elijah!

Friday, August 14th, 1992

Omniscient View

Philadelphia, Pennsylvania

Georgios Konstantinou leaned back in his swivel chair and stretched. It was a long day at work, but in two hours the day would be done and he could spend some quality time with his son. Every Friday after work, Georgios would pick him up and they would spend the evening together at Chuck E. Cheese. It wasn't his idea of a good time, but his son was the #1 light of his world. He couldn't easily say no; since he was the 51% owner of a conglomerate company, he hardly got to see him. Elijah was a good boy. He always understood making a living came first, and he still wanted to be just like Daddy.

The phone on his desk rang, and he checked the caller ID—Simone Wagner, his other favorite person. He happily answered.

"Hey, babe," he whispered.

She wasn't supposed to call him at the office, but he never scolded her. If she were just a sugar baby, it would be different, but this one was special. This one came dangerously close to giving him the courage to forsake the mother of his child. The little girl made him feel young again, and her lips tasted like freedom. She was his Aussie princess with the long legs and the big attitude. That's why it devastated him when her greeting was rendered nearly incoherent by her sobbing.

"Georgios... I need to see you now."

"I have to see my son soon, you know that," he said. "Can it wait until tonight?"

"No," Simone cried. "It's an emergency. Right now."

Georgios slumped over his desk. He had no clue what to do when a woman was crying, especially not his particularly sour "Tangerine" who never shed a tear.

"Honey, I'm at work," he said. "You know I can't just leave."

But still, she insisted that it was a "level ten emergency" and he had to come "right now." He didn't have a choice; Simone never used words like *emergency*, nor was she the type to show weakness. She could pull off "power bitch" from a hospital bed, and the only one who could see through her was Georgios himself. But this?

"Where are you?" he asked.

"Exton."

"Exton? I won't be able to get back in time."

"Please," she said. "You know I don't call you unless it's important, and you promised me that you'd always come if it was an emergency."

He covered the mouthpiece so she couldn't hear him exhale in frustration at a promise he almost regretted. He had to choose which promise to break. His son, or his mistress. "Okay, Tangerine. Where are you?"

"I'm at the servo on the intersection of route 38 and Hartford road."

"Okay, I'll be there." He hesitated. "What's a servo?"

"Service station."

He had been bracing himself for a fiery edge to her voice, and was disappointed by her passive answer. Georgios had no idea why Simone would be all the way out in Exton at a "servo," but he recalled a time when she said she liked to run away when she was upset. He told himself he had no choice but to cancel on his son and lie to him, and Simone was a wreck. He reluctantly called Elijah to break the news to him. His girlfriend of fourteen years, the mother of his son, answered.

"Hello?"

"Hey, Tansy."

"Oh. It's *you*." Tansy was spiteful as always, no doubt still angry that he hired someone to paint the kitchen without her consent. Or maybe it was something from last week. He stopped caring years ago. Of course, she didn't bother to ask why he called. It was for the better. Every time he talked to her lately, she made him wish she had stayed in Greece. From the other end of the line, he heard her pounding on his bedroom door. *Elijah! Phone!... It's your dad!* And then there were the excited cries of his son.

"Daddy!"

"Hey, squirt!"

"What's up?"

Georgios twitched his leg and tried to think of a good lie. His son wasn't wise to his tricks yet, so he went with the usual exuse. "Your uncle has an important meeting with a business partner, and he's insisting I come along."

"Why?" Elijah whimpered.

"I don't know, but I have to reschedule."

"But—"

"We'll go to Chuck E. Cheese's tomorrow, I promise."

"Okay," Elijah said, defeated. "I'll wait."

What a patient kid he raised. When Georgios hung up, he was left with a bitter taste in his mouth. Did he just put his mistress before his son? No. Simone was more than a mistress...but still less than his son. Elijah wanted to be just like daddy; he always said so. So how could Georgios dare be a bad role model? He swore to himself that he would never lie to his son again. But a part of him knew that it was a lie.

*

Exton, Pennsylvania

Simone was standing outside a gas station waiting as she was pelted with raindrops. She wore a casual, yellow sundress that brought out the red tones in her strawberry blond hair. The sixteen-year-old girl was always attractive and well put together, but today she was nothing short of pitiful. Her large, blue eyes were swollen with tears, and her long, slender legs were shaking.

Georgios pulled into a parking spot across from Simone. When she opened the door and crawled into the passenger seat, the smell of heavy rains and diesel made him cough. He hated "servos."

She didn't greet him. The first thing out of her mouth was, "Do you have a tissue?" Her voice was usually deep and alluring, but her normally compelling Melbourne accent showed signs of increasing anxiety that day.

Georgios turned up the heater so she wouldn't die of hypothermia. "Check the glove compartment."

Simone opened the glove compartment and held the tissue to her nose. In spite of it all, she attempted to be a quiet, proper lady about it, but Georgios still winced and looked away. He always thought nose blowing was disgusting, but now wasn't the time to bring that up. Like any good businessman, he knew how people worked and what made them tick. Knowing how his mistress worked was no different.

"Tangerine, what happened?" he asked. "You've been distant these past few weeks. I can feel it, and it worries me."

"I don't know how to say this, so I'm just going to get it over with."

Georgios wiped her tears away with his handkerchief. "Go on."

"I went to that party... Did you hear about the gang rape behind the sorority house?"

Georgios took her hand. "Please say it wasn't you."

Unable to get the words out, Simone clenched her right fist around the hem of her dress and bent over with sobs.

"Θεέ μου... Simone, I'm so sorry."

"That's not even the worst part," she said.

The rape wasn't the worst part? What could possibly be worse than being violated that way, and at a party no less?

Simone couldn't look Georgios in the eye. "I called my parents, and I didn't know how they'd react. So I just asked if they read about it, and you know what they said?"

"What did they say?"

She blew her nose like it was her last tissue. "That that girl... That I was a *slut*. My parents think I'm a slut, and if they find out they'll just tell me that I'm going to hell. I can't even show my face at St. Joseph's anymore, and now my own parents think I was asking for it? Or just making it all up? I can't say anything."

"Did you call the police?"

"No, a witness did," Simone said. "But that doesn't matter, it's all too late now."

"No..." Georgios said. There had to be some way to comfort her. "Your parents should be ashamed of themselves to feel that way."

"That's not what I mean!" Simone said. "It's really too late!"

Georgios jumped back. He had never heard Simone yell before. "Why? What's too late?"

Simone was silenced, choking on whatever sounds she tried to make were drowned out by the rain beating down on Georgios's Cadillac. She didn't want to look at him, so she watched the raindrops flow down the sides of the windows, only to be pushed away by the squeaking windshield wipers.

"Honey, please," Georgios said. "Answer me."

His tangerine pulled her hands away from him and covered her eyes. "I'm pregnant!"

Georgios' mouth dropped. What was he supposed to say? "How do you feel about abortion?"

Not that, Georgios. That is absolutely not what you were supposed to say.

"I already tried!" she said. "I took a ton of pills, but the stupid thing is *desperate* to live, and my family will disown me either way. Abortion? I'm a murderer. Raped? Slut. Raped *and* pregnant? Super slutty slut."

He assumed correctly that the pills were the reason she was in the hospital. He tried his best to stay calm. "It'll be okay," he said.

"Oh yeah. It'll totally be fine... *Not!*"

Georgios often forgot that she was a teenager, but her façade of adulthood cracked at the most inopportune moments. But, legally speaking, she was emancipated, set free into the adult world. She wasn't still considered a teenager since she was emancipated, right? There was *nothing* wrong with her dating a man thirty years her senior. So long as he wasn't bedding her before her eighteenth birthday, there was no crime. But there might have been a way, he thought, that he could fix both of their problems, all of them—and most importantly, his Tangerine could blossom again.

"There's always a way out," he said.

"Like *what*? My parents will *never* talk to me again when they find out I'm up the duff."

"What if you married a billionaire?"

"...what?"

"I said..." This wasn't a bad idea, right? How could it be? Simone's life was ruined otherwise, and he felt like it was his duty to save her. She asked for him. He couldn't let her down. "I said, you're the most wonderful woman I've ever met, and I can't bear to see you hurting like this. The few months we've spent together have been the best few months of my life. I want to help you fight your battles, to let tragedy bring us closer instead of distancing us like it has been. Simone Wagner... Will you marry me?"

"I..." Simone wiped the tears from her eyes. Uncertain, but fearing he would retract the offer if she hesitated any longer, she quickly said, "Y-yes. Yes, I will!"

Georgios fished a PO box key out of the glove compartment and removed the key ring. Simone held out her hand and smiled as he slipped it onto her finger. It wasn't conventional, but it couldn't be more beautiful. Even so, she was still concerned.

"Don't worry," Georgios said. "We'll pick out real rings first thing in the morning," he said.

"No," Simone said. "That's not it. It's just... What about Tansy?"

She wanted to slap herself for reminding him. Her five months was nothing compared to Tansy's fourteen years, and a mere hour ago, Georgios' daydreams of leaving the mother of his child had no signs of coming to fruition. She believed herself to be a fling, no matter how much he insisted otherwise.

"Things were over between Tansy and I years ago," he said. "She just won't admit it. And I'm sick of her 'I hate you, don't leave me' act."

"But won't she be upset that you lived together all those years and never married, but now you're marrying a teenager?"

Why oh why did she have to bring that up? It answered his question from earlier and almost made him feel disgusting. He refused to dwell on it. Simone being emancipated meant she didn't need parental permission to marry an older man, and statutory rape laws didn't apply to married couples. It wasn't doing anything wrong on paper, and as a businessman who had a lawyer for a brother, paper was the only thing he worried about. There was no expiration date on true love. And really, he was doing her a favor. It was mutually beneficial. And besides, it would be typical, almost expected for a rich man like him to trade in his life partner for someone younger and prettier. He didn't just deserve better than Tansy, he deserved the absolute best. He's seen larger age differences in his business partners' relationships. What difference would it make if he waited for Simone to turn eighteen, right? It's just a few months. And she was the one who lied about her age, so he was the real victim here—not that there *was* a victim in their dynamic, since Simone was so mature.

"Tansy doesn't believe in marriage," he said. "That's why her last name is still Papadópoulos."

"Oh…" Simone noticed the bitter note in his voice. She always felt guilty about the affair, or at least she pretended to be, and knowing that there was a time Georgios wanted to marry Tansy sickened her. But that was a long time ago, before Simone was even in Kindergarten. But Georgios was a smart man, and he knew it would take more than an impulsive promise of a future together to feel wanted.

"Simone," he said. He loved saying her name. "You may think your body is tainted and that no one will want you after that, but that's not true. I want you."

More than anything, he wanted her—and oh, how the anticipation was killing him, and the suppression of rage that those savage college boys would rob the innocence that he found so seductive in her. It was supposed to be him taking her innocence. He deserved it. He was the one who was in love with her. He was going to take her virginity on her eighteenth birthday, and the anticipation of that day excited him. To know it wasn't going to happen that way enraged him, but he had to act strong for her sake. No matter how disappointed he was, she was going through something far harder.

"But there were seven men," Simone said. "I can't be a virgin bride."

"Real men don't attack women, and virginity is a state of mind," he said, partially to reassure himself. "And I wouldn't care if you were a prostitute. I'd still marry you. You and me... and that little boy or girl inside of you, we can all be a family. You'll see."

"What about your son?" she said. "I've never even met him."

"He'll get over it," Georgios said.

"Are you sure?" she asked, ignoring how cold that sounded. It wasn't like she knew the kid.

"He's smart," Georgios said. "By now he knows I'm kicking Tansy out. And she keeps doing these little things to piss me off, like opening chip bags upside down and turning all the picture frames so they're crooked on the wall. She's killing me."

Simone laughed. It was a weak laugh, but a laugh nonetheless, and a sign that she might be okay. Georgios found a twinkle in her smile and brushed away a strand of hair that was stuck to her lips. When she didn't flinch, he leaned in to kiss her on the lips. Even after all the times they had kissed, it was still just as good as the first time if not better. Tansy was just a waste of time. Simone was his true love.

Saturday, March 14, 2015

William Brown Quiñones

Philadelphia, Pennsylvania

Here's a list of things I hate more than anything else, in no particular order: hospitals, interrogations, and Coldplay. Who knew I'd be in a scenario that would involve all three?

"Turn it off!" I say, trying to jerk the headphones out of Arete's iPod.

She snatches it away, steps back, and turns the volume up even higher. "I'll make you listen to 'Fix You' every day for the rest of your life until you tell me what happened."

"Why do you have Coldplay on your iPod? You don't even like Coldplay!"

"I went through a phase," she says. "And it's a phase I no longer regret. Tell me what happened."

"I hit a semi!"

Arete doesn't point out how vague my comment was, but she has this condescending look on her face that speaks volumes. Telling her I temporarily lost control of the vehicle because I was distracted by a disturbing revelation would be a huge mistake, so I pull something Elijah-ish out of my ass.

"Elijah was lonely, so he took me out to lunch. He got drunk and started talking about all this sad shit. Anyway, then we left, he passed me the keys because he was too drunk to drive, and, well… I guess it wasn't until that semi blew a stoplight that I realized I wasn't used to driving stick."

"And what's this about lunch?" she asks. "I thought you were going fishing."

I don't want to cover up that lie either, but I'm just glad she didn't question the stick shift. I just needed an excuse other than "he blew my mind and I wasn't paying attention to the road." Elijah's truck is an automatic. Or, should I say, it *was* an automatic. Now it's a hunk of scrap metal.

"We were about to," I say. "But we stopped for food on the way to the fishing… place. Then I wrecked. Haven't you talked to Elijah yet?"

"Of course not," she says. "Why would I be in here asking you if I was even remotely interested in talking to him? Have you?"

"Yes," I say. I'm lying, of course. I can't bring myself to face him, since this is 100% my fault and I'm the worst "best mate" ever. Also, I haven't been formally discharged yet, and we haven't been in the same room.

"So… how is he then?" She tries to keep her tone neutral, but her voice cracks a little. Whatever her last words to him were, she must regret them, since she seems to think he's dying and doesn't want to face him either.

I repeat what the nurse told me, even though a lot could have changed since yesterday. "His air bag failed and he hit his head on the window pretty hard. He was out cold for a while, but he's feeling better. No permanent memory loss, internal bleeding, or any of that, just whiplash and some deep cuts." I decide not to mention the herniated disc or broken rib.

"He might be able to leave tomorrow morning, they just want to keep him one more night."

She turns off the Coldplay song. Whoever is watching over me: *bless you.*

"Before you take me home, can I visit Elijah?" I ask.

"Oh, I'm not taking you home," she says. "I have a DUI, duh. I had to cab here thanks to the damn booze bus."

Nice to see that she takes responsibility for her mistakes. She hands me a $50 bill and calls it "cab fare condolences." I accept it since it's clearly not a "sorry we framed you for murder" bribe.

"So, um…" She sets two tote bags on the table. "I brought you and Elijah a fresh change of clothes for when you leave," she says. "Can you make sure Elijah gets his? Because I can't do it. I just can't go in there."

I take a deep breath. "Sure."

"Thanks… and good luck," she says on her way out.

*

I peek inside Elijah's room, half-hoping he'll be asleep. Not only is he awake, but he notices my presence immediately. He looks away, pretending he didn't, but I know about his military sonar. He's looking a little less like his Hollywood Perfect self right now; rotting in the hospital never really flattered anyone, and it looks like he's in worse condition than I am. All I got was whiplash and what turned out to be a bruise from the seatbelt, not a broken rib. There's an IV connected to his inner elbow, and a blood-stained bandage covers his forehead.

He doesn't look at me directly until I approach him and set a gift shop present on the table next to him; it's a brown teddy bear holding a foil "Get Well Soon" balloon. It doesn't take $50 to take a cab across town; what kind of ignorant world do the 1% live in?

Elijah raises his eyebrows at the gift. "You know I'm not dying, right?"

I rub the back of my neck. "But I figured I owe you *something* at least."

He chuckles. "That's a nice gesture though. Thank you."

The guilt is squeezing my lungs. "How are you not completely pissed at me?" I ask. "I acted like a dick to you all day, totaled your truck, and almost killed you! And I am so, *so sorry!*"

"Meh. I admit, I was angry at first," he says. "But then I remembered I was looking for an excuse to buy a Benz anyway. Now I can do that and still look like a responsible adult."

Somehow, his smile makes me feel about a thousand times worse. He's not supposed to be happy to see me, he's supposed to scream at me and make me serve a life sentence locked in the basement.

"So... How are you feeling?" I ask.

"It's nothing serious," he says. "I woke up here with whiplash, herniated disc, head wound, concussion, bla bla bla. I could technically leave right now, but they want me to stay longer in case something changes. I really want to go on a run, but if I stay *here*, that's one more day to stall before I have to face Arete and admit I fucked up. How is she, by the way?"

"How is *Arete*?" I ask in disbelief. "I put you in the hospital, and the first thing you ask about is Arete? You're the one who got carried off in a stretcher because of me. *She's fine.*"

"I'm still worried about her," he says. "It was my fault anyway. I thought you already knew she was my stepsister, and I didn't think it would throw you for a loop."

I squint. "How would I know that?"

Then it hits me. He knew. He knew I was in his safe all along, and he spent yesterday scattering hints, trying to figure out how much I found out. I'd bet everything I have that he's already figured out exactly what I do and don't know. I should be upset that he played me, but I don't think everything that happened yesterday was all an act. I mean, there isn't really a way to dodge calling me his friend over and over again. If he was going to get back at me for invading his personal business, he wouldn't have taken me out for lunch and tried to explain himself. He would've stabbed me in the neck with an icicle for knowing too much. Also, I almost killed him, and that's pretty sobering.

"You know what?" I say. "Go for it. Date your stepsister, you have my blessing."

"Thanks?" he says like it's a question.

"But you should probably tell her now," I say. "The longer you wait, the worse it'll get when she finds out you're a Konstantinou and thinks you're her legit brother."

He wrinkles his nose. "That would kind of suck."

"Kind of?" I say. "How hard did you get hit?" I'm still trying to process that he's been knowingly sleeping with his stepsister from the beginning. Gross.

"Don't call me a Konstantinou, Sass Queen," he says. "I'm a Walker for a reason. My dad completely cut me off for his mistress. Last time I saw Arete, she was two. Now it's like she's suddenly become a woman and my brain just can't connect her to that little girl who chewed on her toes and spat out everything I tried to feed her. I mean, if we were raised together, I swear on *every Greek god* that I would *never* sleep with her."

Still gross.

"The Roman ones too?" I ask.

He tilts his head up and looks genuinely upset. "Look, I get it. It's weird. Her mother had really strong abdominal muscles or something and she didn't start showing for twenty weeks. And when everyone saw that tiny baby, no one questioned her being a preemie, and she thinks my dad is hers. It's not complicated, just sucks for me."

I close my eyes and hold out the palm of my hand. "Okay, that's enough, I don't want to know anything else."

"Fine," he says. "Just promise me you won't say anything to her, and I'll try to avoid bringing it up again unless I tell her about it first."

I have two options here. One, I could forfeit all questions about all the police reports and photographs I found and live in blissful ignorance. Two, I could spend the rest of my life listening to Elijah whine about how hard it is to date his stepsister. It's not worth it.

"I'm okay with that, but can I ask one question first?"

He waves his hand. "Fire away."

"How did you know there was a vase of flowers in the ladies' room?"

He laughs. Looks like I'll never know.

Sunday, March 15, 2015

Arete and Elijah sit on separate couches that face each other in the family room. Arete's eyes dart around the room and she hugs her knees together. Elijah, who decided to come home after all (but not before buying a shiny new Benz,) forces himself to maintain a bored expression. Closer observation shows that he's nervous; his feet are twitching, and his thumbs are tucked into his belt. To be fair, I'd be nervous too. I mean, the last time he confessed to dating his stepsister, he got hit by a semi. With timing like that, it was like God himself came down from heaven just to kick him in the balls.

"One of you has to speak," I say.

They don't respond, but they exchange clueless, sidelong glances and turn to me like I know what to do.

"Are you two still together?" I ask. "It's pretty hard to tell when you're acting like this."

They still say nothing. I'm not cut out for couple counseling. I'm not exactly fond of their relationship to begin with, but as painful as it is, I have to admit that I'm better off if they stay together. I have nowhere else to go; Arete will never stay here without Elijahpoo, and he's not staying if his Kit Kat dumps him. Then where will I end up? A blowup mattress in Elijah's study, that's where. That's what inspired me to print out a list of questions that marriage counselors use and just wing it.

"Okay then," I say. "I'll tell you. You're still together, because you love each other."

"No we don't," Elijah says. He crosses his arms and points his nose toward the ceiling. In Lie Detector Mode, that probably translates to something along the lines of "technically *we* don't love each other because *she* doesn't love me." I'm not in the mood to play that game today.

"*Elijah*," I say in my best warning tone. "Tell her how you really feel."

"I don't know how to describe how I feel."

"Try it. How do you feel about that?" Gag. Did I just say those words?

Elijah sits up straight and clears his throat. "Arete. I once had a coworker named Stacy. Every quality I *hate* in a person, she had it. She was rude, always late, lazy, arrogant, et cetera, et cetera. She smelled like a litter box sprayed with vanilla perfume, and she looked like the Crypt Keeper. Not even Jesus would love her."

"Why are you telling me this?" Arete asks.

"Because right now, I would rather be handcuffed to Stacy for the rest of my life than be in the same room as you."

Arete rolls her eyes. "And yet, here we are."

This is going nowhere, and I don't appreciate the accidental reminder that I had to be chained to Arete while she was on the toilet. That's where it all began. I have to say something to get them on the right track, but I don't know what. Is there even a right track to get on when their relationship is just so wrong?

"I know you two care about each other, or you wouldn't be here," I say. "So. Arete... How about you tell Elijah how you feel?"

Arete may be ten years younger, but she's a bit more mature than Elijah when it comes to relationships. Maybe I should have reached out to her first.

"Sure, mate," Arete says. "Elijah Walker. I hate you even more than you hate me." She sticks out her tongue, proving me wrong.

"I don't think that's possible," Elijah says. "Because I hate you like Cain hated Abel—"

"*Okay*, let me ask a slightly different question," I say, thumbing through the list. This is not the ideal time for Arete to find out they share a father. Actually, I hope Elijah changes his mind about bringing it up at all. Does Arete really *need* to know she's the product of a rape? "Name one thing about each other that you like," I say. When it becomes apparent that neither of them are going to participate, I add, "And if you don't take this seriously, I'm going to stop writing. Forever."

That elicits a response from Arete. "I like your hair."

"I like your tits," Elijah says without hesitation.

It's a start? Whatever that was supposed to be, it isn't good enough. Elijah is too sore to admit he loves her, and Arete can tell. It's a cycle. No—it's a cyclone, and I'm caught in the middle of it.

"Okay, listen up." I toss the list aside; it's useless on these two. "You're pretending that I'm forcing you two to sit and talk, but you're sitting here because you want to be. I'm not a relationship guru, I'm your all-purpose patsy. Elijah. Why are *you* here?"

He takes a deep breath. "Because I want this relationship to work." He's being more forthcoming now, but he still has a sour expression that reminds me of a six-year-old whose mom forced him to apologize to a girl for yanking her ponytail.

Arete isn't sunshine and rainbows either, but she manages to say "I do too."

"Good," I say. "Now you're on the right track. Arete, do you trust Elijah?"

"With my life. I mean, he saved it twice." She holds her hand to her chest. "I'll never forget it."

"And you trust Arete?"

"Ye—" Elijah hesitates. "Mostly."

Arete frowns with that weepy, puppy-dog look. Great job, Elijah. This is the absolute worst time to be honest. I think back to some of the things he told me in on our way back from Paddy Whacks.

"Elijah... Why did you want to marry Arete so badly?"

"That's not how I would word it." Deep in thought, Elijah bows his head and swallows. Finally, he faces his girlfriend and looks her in the eyes for the first time in a week. "I *still* want to marry you. I knew you were the one on our first date, maybe even before that. I'm not a patient man, but I'll wait as long as I have to."

Arete moves and sits next to him. She doesn't speak, but at least they're then on the same couch now. Hallelujah! A sign of progress.

"I sincerely apologize for my reaction," Elijah says. "I shouldn't have acted like that when you turned me down. There was nothing wrong with your logic, and I know you weren't doing it to hurt me. I was just afraid of losing you."

Arete's face softens. "Why?"

"My father kicked me out and abandoned me when I was twelve. My mother went missing after years of neglect, and I'll never find her. I was just afraid you were going to leave too. Arete, I don't think I could live without you."

I actually feel sorry for him. This is pitiful.

"And I'm sorry too then," Arete says. "I was just surprised. And then you got mad and ignored me, so then I got mad. But I can't really see myself with anyone else after all you've done for me, and I don't want this to end."

Great. I'm supervising the most embarrassingly sappy make-up conversation, and there's no way out because it was my idea. How do I get myself into these messes?

Elijah scoots next to Arete and puts his hand on her knee. "So... You're saying it wasn't too far-fetched? Getting married, I mean."

Arete leans her head on his shoulder. "Maybe someday, but we'll talk about that later. I think we need to spend some time together. Alone."

They both glance at me, and I've never been happier to be dismissed.

On my way up the stairs, I hear Arete shout, "Let's throw a party!"

I desperately hope for Elijah to shoot that one down. I can see it now. *Sorry, not all of us were suspended. I'm a busy law student, and an uptight asshole. And besides, that came out of nowhere. Will you marry me?*

"I'm awfully busy right now," he says. *Yes!* "But I'm not in the position to say no to you." *No!* I stop halfway up the stairs to listen.

"Great... My birthday is Friday."

"Really?" Elijah says, feigning surprise. Of course he knows when his baby stepsister's birthday is; he has a photocopy of her birth certificate locked in a safe. "Well, I'm going to make sure it's the best birthday you've ever had."

Best birthday she's ever had? I don't want to know what that means.

*

Elijah is out buying a new suit for a law school mock trial, paving the route to a better future. Arete is happy for him, but her suspension is wearing her down. Lately, I'm starting to feel bad for her, and after taking my advice to do something constructive, she calls me to the kitchen and declares her intent to cook dinner. She's come prepared by dressing herself like a morbid 1950's housewife, complete with frilly, black apron.

It's easily the most impressive kitchen I've ever seen in my life, not just in size but in tools and design. The wooden floors are so polished that I can see the reflection of my feet. I think it's coated in some kind of shiny lacquer that keeps spills from staining the floor, a must for kitchens with hardwood floors. I haven't been in a house this lavish before, but I find it fascinating that the microwave is in the overhead cabinets (but also unfortunate, since I can't reach it without a chair) and a steamer is built into the quartz countertop. There are things in here that I never heard of, like pasta arms, modular cooktops, and indoor compost bins. I may not know the first thing about cooking, but if I were a chef, this kitchen would be my wet dream.

"I know you're a great cook, but I didn't know you could bake too," I say as I fish a bag of flour out of the walnut cabinetry. "And from scratch."

Arete sets a mixing bowl on the counter and grins, reminding me of a pin-up girl. "Well, mate, it's only been, like what, a month? You can't possibly know everything about me."

"That's true." I know more about her than she thinks, but that's only because I was digging through Elijah's safe.

Thanks to that move, not only will I forever wonder what he's hiding, but I'm now doomed to an internal argument about whether I should see him as her boyfriend or stepbrother. Maybe now that Georgios is dead, it doesn't matter anymore. Yeah. Let's go with that. They are *ex*-stepsiblings. No. Never mind. Still gross.

"I don't know a lot about you either, really," Arete says. "But you're pretty easy to read."

"I've been told that before," I say. "There's just nothing about me that really stands out. Anything else I should know about you?"

"Well, I used to collect dolls when I was a kid," she says as she measures two cups of flour. She's precise, using a knife to level the flour perfectly with the top of the cup, like it's a delicate science. "That's why there are dolls all over the house. I didn't want to just keep them in my room to myself—I wanted everyone else to see them too. They made the cleaning lady wet her trousers."

I force myself to laugh, but her housekeeper isn't the only one who wet her trousers. Something about dolls sends me straight to uncanny valley territory. I think it's something about those dead, expressionless eyes that can't see. The worst kinds of dolls are the ones that can talk. Lucky me, she bought me a new mattress while I was with Elijah in the hospital. No more Hello Kitty bedsheets, no more creepy dolls. I have my own room.

"Pass me the baking soda," she says.

"All right!"

Arete holds the container and takes a closer look. "That's baking *powder*."

"Is there a difference?" I ask. "I thought they were the same thing."

"I swear to god," she says. "You're about as useful in the kitchen as an arsehole on your elbow."

"Sorry. I don't know how to cook."

She cracks a smile. "It's all right, I should've known. Can you open the fridge and pass me a Guiness Stout?"

"Drunk cooking doesn't sound like the best idea." I hunt through the cabinets for the baking soda. "Once I tried to reheat some chicken when I was drunk, and I burned myself because I tried to pull it out of the oven with my bare hands instead of using a rag."

Arete cringes at my story while she pours half a bottle of Guinness into mixing bowl. Apparently, it's a cupcake ingredient in her world. "No! And you use a rag instead of oven mitts? Really?"

"Well, hey," I say. "I'm a bachelor. I lived alone."

Arete hands me the rest of the Guinness, implying that I shouldn't let it go to waste. Even though it's a horrible idea, especially considering that I'm such a lightweight, I start drinking anyway. She did insist.

"Well, I'm glad you're here now," she says. "Elijah's going to be flat out like a lizard drinking now that uni is back in, and I'm going to be *so* lonely. But don't think I'm cracking onto you or anything."

Lizard drinking? Cracking on? I know the official language of "Oz" is slang, but her Australiaisms are making me dizzy, and yet I still haven't gotten to hear her say 'crikey.' That doesn't stop me from trying. I think I've earned the right to tease her a little. "I don't know what any of that means, but great!"

She laughs and started mixing the dry ingredients with a whisk. "I just said he's going to be busy, but I'm not flirting, just lonely."

"Ah," I say. I feel guilty that I'm just watching her do all the work, but I don't want to ruin the cupcakes either. She does let me mix the beer and melted butter, but I'm sure I'm somehow messing that up too. "I didn't think you were. Hey, what's in that bag?"

She looks around. "What? Oh, that?" She points at a plastic shopping bag on the counter. "I got tired of Elijah barfing so I bought him some lactose pills. Maybe when these cupcakes don't make him sick, he'll finally admit that I'm right and he's wrong."

I don't want to get into this. "So, why don't you sound like Steve Irwin?" I ask. *Please say 'crikey.'*

She groans. "Why don't you sound like George Clooney? I'm from Melbourne, like Emilie de Ravin. You know, Belle in *Once Upon a Time*. She also played Claire in *Lost*. Steve Irwin was a Queenslander."

"Okay," I say, surprised she's taking me seriously. "So... Who's George Clooney?" *Please say 'crikey.'*

She drops the mixing spoon in the bowl and leans over, her palms on the edge of the counter. "*O Brother, Where Art Thou? The Ides of March? Gravity?*"

"Nope." *Please say 'crikey.'*

"Forget it," she says in defeat. "You're killing me. He's only one of the hottest blokes alive!"

"What about Elijah?" I ask—joking, of course.

Arete reaches into the cabinet and pulls out two bottles of liquor, in spite of my warnings about drunk cooking. It would be hypocritical to stop her now, especially since I just had half of a beer, albeit out of peer pressure.

She shrugs. "Well, I'm obligated to say that Eli's at the top of my list. Ugh, I'm so tired of *waiting* though! Why is he being such a gentleman?"

"Gentleman?" I ask.

"Can you believe it?" She sets the liquor bottles on the countertop and opens the cabinet to retrieve two souvenir shot glasses; one is from Sea World, and the other depicts a kangaroo. Arete has to be the most obnoxiously Australian woman to ever emigrate to the US, and sometimes I swear she's acting more Australian than usual for attention. Maybe she's just homesick. "Anyway, Jameson or cream liquor for the frosting?"

"We're getting drunk off the frosting too?" I ask.

"By the time these are done," Arete says, "we're going to be in the hospital. Now, drink your shots."

Going to the hospital (again) doesn't sound terribly appealing and I'm not a fan of whiskey, but I don't want to be rude. Before I even put the whiskey to my lips, the vapors burn my nose. I turn my head away so she doesn't see me scrunching up my face. You'd think I'd get used to the fumes of alcohol after working in a bar for so many years, but no.

"Let's go with this Irish cream liquor stuff," I say.

"Alrighty," she says.

"I've got to ask, what's wrong with being a gentleman? I mean, I thought women liked the chivalry thing; I try to do it. Is it anti-feminist or something?"

"Nah," she says. "I'm talking about in the sheets."

"In the sheets?... You two *haven't* been sleeping together?"

You're not screwing your stepbrother? Thank god.

"I'm a virgin," she says. "Why does everyone think I'm such a cum bucket?"

"I got fired over the condoms you bought, and now you're telling me you didn't even use them?"

"We were interrupted," she says. "Would you have liked it if we started going at it while you were handcuffed to me?"

Back then I'm sure I would've been scarred for life, but it wouldn't be so bad now. Oh, great. If I'm thinking along those lines, I must already be drunk enough to die in a hospital bed. Arete is a *horrible* influence.

"Not really," I say.

Arete purses her lips and shakes her head as she combines all the ingredients for the batter. "And then he was so sweet that night in Melbourne, but then I rejected his proposal and he just stood there on the dock like his brain shut down. He didn't even join me in bed. And when I woke up, I found him *sleeping on the kitchen floor*, with a huge bottle of rum tipped over next to him. I thought he was *dead*."

"Do you regret it?" I ask.

She shakes her head. "A little. Will you stir this? My wrist hurts."

"Sure thing."

"I feel slutty for feeling this way. Am I slutty?"

"No, I understand," I say. "I've never had the desire to sleep with a man before, but if I had to choose, it would be Elijah."

I can't believe I just said that. Did I really just say that? Please tell me I didn't just say that.

Arete just shrugs it off, clearly not surprised. "I know *exactly* what you mean. His arse is so perfect, it's the best one I've ever seen. Forget George Clooney."

"I agree on that one," I say, betraying myself again. "George Clooney *is* pretty hot though. I mean for a man. But I'm not gay."

"Wait a minute," she says. "I thought you said you didn't know who he is?"

I stop mixing the batter. I hate myself when I'm drunk. "I lied. I was just trying to surprise you so you'd say *crikey*."

Arete groans. "Crikey."

"That wasn't as satisfying as I thought it would be," I say. "Will you say it in a Steve Irwin voice?"

Arete puts those little, ridged paper cup jawns in the cupcake pan. "Did I ever tell you the story about how Elijah and I first met?"

"Yes!" I shout. "Yes, and I don't want to hear it again!"

She hums. "No, I don't think I did."

"Please don't—"

"It was after my first showing of Romeo & Juliet. I wasn't even out of my maid costume yet when some random stranger approached me with a bouquet of flowers. I was going to tell him to go away, but one, he was really hot, and two, it made me feel like a famous celebrity."

"I already heard—"

"He started rambling about how pretty I was and how he saw me around campus but was too afraid to approach me. And then he asked me out before he even got my name—"

"Elijah told me this—"

"—I said no because I had no clue who he was, also he was wearing a shirt with one of those hideous patterns that's so tight that it burns your eyes. But I didn't tell him that part. I just said I was busy and he gave me his number. It was kind of annoying, but I still—"

"I really don't care—"

"—accepted it because I felt rude. I waited four days to text him, and he replied IMMEDIATELY. I thought it was desperate, but when he admitted he was the secret admirer who left me this bracelet before Christmas," she flashes her wrist, "I decided I at least owed him a social lunch. But we didn't start officially dating until Valentine's Day."

"It took that long?" I ask. Elijah sees it through rose-colored glasses, I guess. I like Arete's version more, but god only knows who's telling the truth. The whole truth, I mean.

She scoffs. "Of course, whacka. Why would I get in the car with a stranger?"

"I thought you said yes the same day he..." I hiccup. "Because bathroom flowers."

She furrows her brow in confusion. "Bathroom flowers?"

"N-never mind."

"Oh!" Arete says at the sound of a knock on the front door. "Eli's home! Will, can you go let him in while I finish up?"

"Of course."

After that call with my landlord, I started to wonder if the fire was really an accident. As much as I want to forget most of what I've learned, one thing has been bugging me lately. If someone burned my house down to kill Arete, it would have to be planned very precisely ahead of time. And the only person who knew she would be there is the last person on earth who would harm her: Elijah. I rethought Elijah's apology from the day I got fired; he talked about the night we met, but he didn't explicitly say what he was apologizing for, and he said "yesterday," not "the day before yesterday." It wasn't about kidnapping me, it was about burning my house down! Why didn't I see it? I don't have a motive, but now that Elijah is out of his pity-party coma, this is my chance. The best way to find out is to pretend to know more than I already do. It was my mother's signature move for finding out what I was doing out so late, since, and I quote, "it's not like you have any friends." Angst aside, maybe it'll work for me too. Growing up, I always spewed everything the moment my mother gave me her death stare, but things will be different with Elijah. He has too much nerve to give up. He'll lie, most likely by omission.

"Hey," I say when I open the front door. I trip over my own feet, but manage to step away without falling down. "Arete's in the kitchen."

Elijah raises his eyebrows. "Are you *drunk*, Boy Meets World?"

"No," I say.

"Okay," he says, skeptical. He starts to walk past me.

"Wait! One more thing." I try my best to channel my mother, keeping my voice strong and my eyes stern. "Why did you burn down my house?"

This was supposed to catch him off guard, but his eyes don't widen. He doesn't tense up. He doesn't so much as twitch.

Instead, he says, "None of your business."

"Wait, what?" Part of me didn't actually think he did it. I had to rule it out so I could move on with my life.

He crosses his arms. "You heard me."

"Um, if it's anyone's business, it's mine," I say. "It was *my* house!"

"You were renting it."

"For five years!" Not only am I right, but he doesn't think it's a big deal? How twisted is the logic he's using to justify this?

"Hear me out first," he says. "There are certain things you're better off not knowing."

"Why can't you just give me an answer? Were you just trying to keep an eye on me? Kill me?"

"If I wanted you dead, I wouldn't have caught you when you jumped," he says. "I'm sorry, you running off was a risk we couldn't take. It's a lot easier than kidnapping you forcibly, or convincing you to stay with us for no reason. Besides, you could have stayed with your parents after your house burned down, but you didn't. You asked if you could stay with me. Why?"

A valid point. I wasn't always bound to a GPS Nokia. I had full autonomy at that point.

"My parents wouldn't exactly be happy to see me on their couch again," I say.

"See, Boy Meets World?" he says. "We're more alike than you think. If it's any consolation, and I'm not going to confess to anything... but hypothetically, it was supposed to blow up while you were at work."

"That is *not* helping!" I got fired that day. If it had gone off when I was supposed to be at work, I would have been toast.

"Why do you care about that crap shack anyway?" He gestures around the room. "*This* is the kind of place a man dreams about. You've got free room and board, plenty of room to stretch your legs, and a nice cleaning lady that picks up after you every day."

I facepalm and catch the top of the couch to steady myself. "Don't pretend you did this to help me."

"And don't forget, we're opening up the pool in June."

I glare at him. Does he really think he can buy me with his girlfriend's pool?

"And I do feel bad. I apologized, remember?" Elijah sits on the edge of the couch and turns on the Tiffany table lamp that sits on the night stand. The soft glow of light through the stained glass brings out the warm tones in his hair. "I'm just saying, you could have had it a lot worse. I know you think I'm a psycho murderer, but just because I was trained to kill doesn't mean I like doing it. And believe me, I've met enough killers to know the difference."

He has a point. If he enjoyed murder, I would have been dead a long time ago, whether Arete vouched for me or not. Even so, three words stuck in my head: *trained to kill*. It never crossed my mind before, but Elijah was formally trained to kill other human beings. He wasn't trained to disarm or restrain someone with a deadly weapon. He was trained to dehumanize, point, and shoot.

He opens the end table drawer and pulls out a rectangular notebook and a black pen. "I can help you out though." He writes something.

"Hush money?" I say in disbelief.

He looks at me with pity. "Kid, this is an address book."

"Oh..."

"I was copying down the number and address of a magazine I used to work for when I was a teenager," he says. "They need an editor, and you still need work, right?"

"Yeah..."

"How do you make it through life so paranoid?" Elijah carefully rips out one of the pages and hands it to me. He should be used to making people feel paranoid.

"Thanks," I say.

Before I can return to the kitchen, Elijah stops me. "One more thing."

"Yeah?"

"I can tell you didn't really know I was the one who burned your house down," he says.

I stop dead in my tracks and stare at him.

"You were trying too hard," he says as he stands up. "So what's for dinner?"

"Beer cupcakes..."

Once again, I find myself feeling like a moron. He could have played dumb and I would have believed him, but he chose to tell me the truth. Every questionable detail I ever brought up in the past, he was able to explain away in under ten seconds. I'll never decode it and I don't want to know, so why do I bother? Why can't I just drop it? He promised me safety, so why can't I just accept what my life has become and sit tight? Why does something always feel off about Elijah?

"Beer cupcakes? Hmm." Elijah tilts his head to the right and turns a corner of his mouth down, not from disappointment but from slight surprise. "I didn't know you could do that. Clever."

Arete baking cupcakes with beer for dinner surprised him more than a confrontation about burning down my house. Of course. Maybe I really am as predictable as everyone says. Maybe I should take up something unexpected, like hang gliding, tap dancing, or getting a *real* job. Or a girlfriend, assuming I'm allowed to have one of those.

"I have to go to the bathroom," I say. "Bye."

I wasn't exactly lying, but I have to hide somewhere and reflect for a while before I run out there and spew any more drunk talk out in front of them. I've humiliated myself enough for one day. When I make it to the toilet, I remember an old saying my mother taught me between tequila shots on my 21st birthday. *Beer before liquor, never been sicker. Liquor before beer, you're in the clear.* Well, I'm not in the clear. Thanks a lot, Arete.

This sounds like a weird thing to say, but this isn't a bad room to toss my cookies in. The white marble flooring compliments the porcelain throne I'm kneeling to, and the little blue and gold accents around the room create a soothing atmosphere. Above me, a quartz crystal candelabra hangs from the ceiling, which is painted to depict bare-chested angel ladies. This is truly the classiest barf I've ever had. From now on, I am marking this territory as my favorite place to puke.

As I lose my breakfast, I have an epiphany. I'm judging Elijah for keeping secrets from Arete, but what am I doing now? Lying to her and keeping secrets, that's what. And they're not hurting me, they're helping me. I started writing again, I live rent free in a fangirl's mansion, and Elijah pointed my career in the direction I always hoped for. There's always hot water in the showers, they have century old wine, and the toilets are fitted with seat warmers. HD TV has me so spoiled that I never want to move out. I finally admit it. I'm happy here. This may be the happiest I've ever been because I finally have real friends.

There's just one loose end I don't understand. Elijah and Arete's uncle is the co-CEO of Konstantinou Enterprises; he founded it with their late father. Does he not know that his nephew showed up again to bone (or to be a "gentleman" to) his niece? Maybe he's okay with it. But Georgios must have had some reason for keeping his own flesh and blood child a secret from his stepdaughter. Even *I* know that.

After crouching over the toilet for a good twenty minutes, I realize that I'm pushing the limit of how long a man can hide in the bathroom. When I return to the kitchen, I find Satan's #1 couple grinning like a stock photo, when this morning they hated each other.

Arete looks like she's about to burst. "Guess what!"

"You're kind of freaking me out," I say.

Arete shows me back of her hand, and the two simultaneously chorus, "We're engaged!"

I don't know what to say, so I just stare at Arete's left hand. However much money Elijah inherited, it was nothing to sneeze at, but he's definitely broke now. This doesn't match Arete's description of the "pathetic" ring he proposed with in Australia. She's wearing an engagement ring that costs more than a house, and I'm not talking about a charming suburban cottage. I don't know much about jewelry, but the band looks like white gold, and it has two hands holding up a *huge* heart-shaped, black diamond. The gem is topped with a white diamond crown that screams, "Arete, *you will* marry me."

The man doesn't have a dime left to his name, I can see it in his eyes. Goodbye, inheritance. I want to say she just said yes because he bought her a more expensive ring, or that she feels sorry for him for giving up everything he had for her, but neither of those things quite fit. You see, the truth is that *neither of them has any common sense at all.*

"What's with the frown?" Arete asks me. "Can't you ever be happy?"

"I'm just a little... surprised, that's all," I say. "You said no a week ago."

I decide against reminding them they've only been together for a month. Arete's still drunk, right? She had a beer, so the engagement is void. You can't marry a man you just met. Didn't she watch *Frozen*?

"I know," Arete says. "But when he proposed, he wasn't wearing this suit." She traces her finger along the seam of his jacket, and I gag. The mock trial is real, but he was just using it as an excuse to buy a suit that would make Arete soil her panties and to give him a time window to pick up a ring. He's good. Too good.

Arete skips away to the stove when the kitchen timer goes off, and I pull Elijah out of the kitchen.

"What changed since this morning?" I ask, keeping my voice low. "A few days ago she told me she wanted to rip your guts out."

"I bought her a Claddagh ring that was similar to something she pinned on her Pinterest account but better," Elijah says. "Oh, and this." He pulls back the hair fringe that swoops over his forehead, revealing stitches from the car crash. The cut extends from his hairline to the tip of his eyebrow. "This helped a lot too."

"Stop it, you're making me feel bad! I already said I was sorry!"

"And I can't forgive you because there's nothing to apologize for," he says. "You fixed my relationship and gave me a cool scar. I already promised Mark he could be my best man if I ever got married, but if you're nice, Arete might let you be a bridesmaid."

"What an honor," I say, deadpan.

"What? Jealous?" He laughs.

"What's so funny?" Please tell me he doesn't know I have a small crush on Arete. Do I have a crush on Arete? No, I'm still drunk. Arete is poison, no matter what the cream liquor is trying to tell me. "Jealous of what?"

"Well," Elijah says, trying to keep a straight face. "You *did* say you wanted to sleep with me."

I could throw up all over again from the humiliation. Pass me another shot. May I forget today or die before tomorrow begins.

"Oh, stop teasing him," Arete says from the doorway, toting a bowl of frosting. "We have to ice the cupcakes!"

Before I can say anything, she returns to the counter. Meanwhile, Elijah leans over and whispers in my ear. "You might want to stay away from the hot tub tonight."

It looks like each of them is finally getting what they wanted. Elijah is in such a good mood, he doesn't even throw a fit when Arete makes him take a dairy digestion pill, although he's clearly not happy about it. Even after he doesn't get sick, he still refuses to admit he's lactose intolerant, but submits and says he'll keep taking the pills "to humor her."

This is a pretty big deal in Elijah Land, so Arete takes it as a victory, and I do to. It's nice to see him slowly relent and stop being so stubborn. At this point, I'm willing to set aside the step-sibling thing if this is really what it takes to calm him down. After all, if I'm going to be stuck with him for the rest of my life, I'd rather be stuck with Agreeable Elijah.

Thursday, March 19, 2015

Part of me is disgusted that one woman alone could have all of this property to herself without working a day in her life, but Arete isn't Scroogey with it. She's a girl who's eager to share with people; I think back to the $100 bill she gave me the night we met. At the time, I thought it was a gesture of drunken laziness. Now I realize she's a kindhearted idiot *and* lazy. I don't know why she doesn't have more friends, or at least people who want to take advantage of her. Everything in the Konstantinou mansion is state of the art; at first, I treated it like a museum and didn't want to touch anything, but now I feel at home. Extravagance is easy to get used to. I'm with her right now, staying up all night watching the telly (as she's gotten me in the habit of calling it) in the "theater room." That's right, they have a theater in their house. This place is amazing.

We had been watching *Law & Order*, which I've learned to love, when the eleven o'clock news starts. I'm close to dozing off on the couch, meanwhile, Arete has her laptop in her face, looking at wedding decorations.

"What about your birthday party tomorrow?" I ask.

"Everything's taken care of," she says. "Should I go with a *Phantom of the Opera* theme, or *Sleepy Hollow*?"

"Both are kind of morbid for a wedding, don't you think?"

She laughs. "This coming from the person who suggested we add *Home Sweet Homicide* to the play list?"

"Good point, but aren't weddings supposed to be white? I just think you're going overboard with the goth thing."

"First of all, they're very romantic movies," she says. "Secondly, my aesthetic is spooky-perfect. And it's for the engagement party in April."

I hold out my palms at chest level. "Okay, okay. I get it. Your goth wedding, not mine."

Arete stifles a snort-laugh. "Besides, only *virgins* wear white."

"Wow, um... Congrats?" Elijah wasn't kidding about the hot tub, I guess.

We're distracted by a newscaster with the stereotypical long bob cut and socio-apathetic voice.

"During the search for missing person Audrey Chang last night, a body turned up off the coast of Delaware—but it wasn't the missing seventeen-year-old. The body has been identified as Hoyt Galligan, an alleged contract killer from Maryland."

At first, I'm mostly paying attention to the lipstick on her teeth. Then Galligan's face appears on the screen. Where have I seen him before...

Where...

Arete covers up her mouth as she gasps. Her eyes are wider than I've ever seen them. I turn up the volume.

"The body was found in pieces, chopped up into garbage bags," the newscaster says. "Police officials say the body was washed downstream after being dumped in the Delaware River."

"There was no missing persons report filed for Galligan," says a sheriff who's being interviewed, "but we can't say we're surprised."

Well, it was surprising enough for us. Arete trembles as she hugs her knees to her chest, panting like she's just climbed a mountain. I stay frozen and listen to the broadcast.

"Galligan's home was searched this morning, where police found classified evidence that he was a *contract killer*. He is believed to have killed several missing persons whose names have not yet been released."

Unable to handle another word, I run to the study and call for Elijah, who greets me with a disgruntled, "This better be important." He likes to have all of his homework finished before the weekend, but this *is* a little more important. The second the jumbled words "They found the body and Arete's down in the theater curled in the fetal position and we're all screwed" fly out of my mouth, he's in the theater. I return to find Elijah trying to comfort Arete, who is crying and screaming something incoherent. He rewinds the television to watch the news report; his jaw hardens, but he doesn't react otherwise. He has the dead gaze of a sociopath, even when he scoops Arete up into his arms to comfort her. He doesn't show many outward signs of panic, which is understandable. I'm the one who's going to jail.

"She's having an anxiety attack," he says. "Turn it off, she needs quiet."

"But we need to find out what's going on!" I say.

"I said I'd take care of it," he says.

There's a slight edge in his voice, spurring Arete to cry even harder. I turn off the television, not because Elijah told me to, but because the newscaster's story on Galligan has devolved into sensationalized dribble. The whole story will be on the Internet soon, and I can read about it to my heart's discontent.

"Are you dense?" Elijah asks in a whisper, as if Arete can't hear him.

"No," I say. "I'm going to *jail*, and it's *your* fault!"

"A hitman tried to *kill* her, and meanwhile you're worried about *jail*?"

What I want to say is: *Oh, I get it. Someone hired a hit man and they're trying to kill her. Oh, Elijah, I'm so stupid. I wonder why I didn't think about it that way before. I mean, it's so easy to think once you find out you're downgrading from a king size bed to a jail cot. But I'm so sorry you're anxious, Arete. Here, let me get you a $100 bill from your purse so you can blow your nose on it.*

Unfortunately for me, I'm the spineless fall guy. I don't have the guts to lay on the sarcasm, so I settle with faking sincerity.

"Sorry, Arete," I say.

Elijah ignores me and clings to his girlfriend. That's when I finally understand. It wasn't about me being rude to her; it was never about me period. I'm not part of this. I've been nothing but a nuisance from the beginning. It makes me wonder if I was right that night, and "best mates forever" was just a bad, drunk decision. It wasn't my decision to make, so how much can I really matter?

After Elijah manages to get Arete to sleep, which I'm 100% positive involved him slipping something into her tea, I'm invited to the balcony to have a "rational" talk. It's not my place of choice seeing as how it's dark and cold, but Elijah wants to stay as close to his Kit Kat as he can without waking her up. So, down the hallway and into the cold night we go. I may as well practice being uncomfortable, since prison isn't warm and cozy either.

The first thing that flies out of my mouth is "Man, we *have* to tell the police."

"Are you crazy?" he says.

"No, think about it," I say. "This guy is a hitman. Self-defense is completely valid now. Arete can get police protection. They'll find out who did it, and we can just relax."

"You're so naive," Elijah says. "What? You think that because I'm a former officer, they'll just ignore the fact that I chopped a body up into pieces and dumped it into the river?"

At first I think he's angry, but there's a barely noticeable shake in his voice.

"I'll say we panicked," I say in attempt to appear cool and logical. I'm trying to convince him to do the right thing, or at least the safe thing, and I'm not going to accomplish that by freaking out. A fake-calm conversation is better than screaming at each other, but he doesn't take my lead.

"And then the three of us will go straight to jail," he says. "Want me to guess what will happen?" I don't appreciate his harsh tone or the fact that he's scolding me with knife hands like a drill sergeant, but I keep as firm a grip on pacifism as I do on the railing.

"Not particularly."

"First thing, you'll be beaten to death in prison," he says. "Arete will be convicted of being an accessory after the fact and go to a women's correctional facility for the mentally ill, because she will *never* be okay again. And me? I'll take a plea deal for naming you as my accomplice, just to piss you off, and I'll spend the next ten years of my life trying to make peace with the people *THAT I FUCKING ARRESTED*!"

I probably have the best deal out of the three of us. "So how many friends do you think you'll make there?"

He crosses his arms. "Not many."

"Okay, fine," I say. "I won't tell."

"Good, because I was about to throw you off this balcony."

I jump. "What?"

"Kidding," he says. "Only kidding."

"That doesn't make me feel much better."

"It didn't make me feel better either," he says, his grumpiness now with a dash of disappointment. Looks like snarking doesn't fix everything. "I'm going to try to study," he says as calmly as he can. "Good night, kid."

By "study," he wants me to think he's going to act like nothing happened, he's not worried, and everything is going to be okay. The *whole* truth is that he's going to be trudging through his textbooks to help build a proper defense for Walker and Brown vs. The State of Pennsylvania.

"Wait," I say. "Before you go..."

"Yeah?"

I swallow. "Why did you bring me here with you? You framed me for murder and planted a tracker on my phone, so what good is it to keep me around?"

He looks confused. "What are you talking about?"

"I just mean you don't have a real reason to hold me hostage."

"You consider this a hostage situation?" he asks. "You crashed at my apartment and I like having you around. Do I need another reason?"

I try to look away before he can see me smile. I guess he only snapped at me because of the stress. Best Mates Forever fight sometimes. It's life.

Friday, March 20, 2015

Elijah didn't consult his new fiancée before calling up her party guests and informing them of a last minute change of venue. The poor girl was dead set on canceling her own birthday, (not just the party, but the whole day) and asked him to warn her friends and family. Instead, he saw it as the perfect opportunity for a surprise party, where Arete would be able to enjoy both the safety of her own parlor and the birthday girl spotlight. Granted, his idea of a surprise party is to warn her ahead of time so she doesn't come down in her pajamas and have a panic attack over people seeing her without makeup.

And so, for what is probably the first time in her life, her party will have cheesy "Happy Birthday" banners and cheap balloons. We didn't have anything planned, other than the catering and the fancy cake that she ordered ahead of time. Just bouquets of roses, dinnerware and cutlery that Elijah said were untouched wedding gifts for Simone, and fancy tablecloths and candles we found in the kitchen.

Going off her previous mention of a *Phantom of the Opera* theme, I found the soundtrack from the 2004 movie and played it in the background. I'm not a fan of musicals, but it's Arete's party, not mine. In spite of myself, I know I'll be humming the tune of *Masquerade* all night after the party ends. Elijah took it a bit too far by wearing a white mask that covers the left side of his face, like the Phantom. I don't know where he found that thing, but Arete thought it was hilarious. At least she's happy enough to forget her life is at risk. I'm glad he took it off before the party began, because it was giving me secondhand embarrassment.

And it all lead up to this one moment, where a seemingly oblivious Arete walks down the stairs, as we all wait around the corner.

"Elijah?" she shouts. "Where are you?"

And then, as planned, she turns on the lights and looks up just as everyone shouts "happy birthday!" Her face lights up and she gasps as we all clap in honor of her 22nd birthday. She laughs, thanks everyone, and integrates herself into the party, not like an effortless social butterfly, but like a girl who is shocked her birthday wasn't canceled after all. Even I believe she's surprised. She's just that good.

The only sign she knew it wasn't a surprise is the fact she was dressed up, and even with that she was careful and avoided wearing whatever #BirthdayDress she said she posted on Instagram. It was just a cute, but casual dress paired with long gloves to hide her engagement ring—none of those fluffy things she sometimes wears under her skirts, or impractically tall shoes.

Arete has way more college friends than I expected. And I can tell they're her actual friends because they make conversation other than "what is your major" and "so I heard you got suspended." Not a single one asks to mooch off her, and everyone in the group I'm standing in now has already met Elijah. I actually walk away because I feel suffocated by the *I miss you*'s and the *we never hang out anymore*'s. All this time I thought she was a hermit and I was her only friend. Man, am I an idiot. I don't know this girl at all.

I may not know Elijah either since he avidly collects rocks, and I am apparently the only person who did not know this, despite the fact that he can't remember any of the girls' names if he ever knew them. My search of his room must have been a joke. In consolation, I remind myself that no one else knows the nerd wears a retainer to bed, owns vintage clubmaster glasses, and has read *The Hobbit* eighteen times. Even Arete doesn't know he wears a retainer, because he always takes it out before she can see. How he managed to get engaged to a girl without her finding out he's a closet geek is beyond me—oh, wait. That's right. It's because he almost died, thanks to me.

Family-wise, few people show up; the Konstantinou family must be cursed. None of Arete's family from Australia took a flight to visit her, and it seems all that's left of Elijah's side is their uncle, who comes in toting a small present for his... stepniece. (Is that a thing?) I've heard him come up in conversation before, but this is my first time seeing him. I recall he's the one who co-founded Konstantinou Enterprises with Georgios. He makes annual donations to UPenn, and has at least two children, one of which studies at UPenn. Neither attend the party, nor does his wife. As far as things go with his nephew, it appears he's in on Elijah's secrets and even approves of their relationship; he introduces himself to Elijah as "Antonis Konstantinou, Arete's uncle," as Arete stands by Elijah's side, arms linked.

Antonis looks like an older, more approachable Elijah. They're not an exact match; Antonis is a lanky man who has his brother's eyes and softer brows. His mouth has a smiley curve to it that fits his clownish reputation. It helps that his hair is dirty blonde, probably dyed the color it was when he was younger, but the family resemblance is unmistakable. Looking between the two of them standing together and Georgios and Simone's memorial portrait, Elijah looks like his father's clone. I know Arete is oblivious, but how stupid do you have to be not to notice something like that? Elijah is standing *right in front* of his father's portrait. Turn around, woman!

I compare their faces and play a quick game of spot the differences: eyes, age, and hair. The end. Elijah's eyes aren't so big, but they're wider and brighter than his father's. They're also slightly downturned, while his father's eyes are straight, but narrower. Elijah's eyes are an inviting shade of dark caramel, whereas Georgios' are nearly black. In addition to Elijah's hair being longer, I think it's a darker shade of brown, but it's hard to tell from a painting. And even though I know eyes are the most distinguishing feature a person has, I can't believe Arete hasn't even questioned it. She must be one of those people who can't recognize someone after they change their hair, but did she just rarely see her father? I know the man pictured in that portrait is at least sixty years old, but still.

Elijah separates from Arete to talk to his uncle in his native language. I want to say they're trying to hide what they're talking about, but Arete is at least somewhat fluent in Greek. They should have probably waited until she was more than ten feet away before talking—or, better yet, twenty. I'm starting to take the "Greeks are loud" stereotype as gospel.

"Ηλίας!" Antonis shouts. "Τι κάνεις;"

"Καλά είμαι," Elijah says. "Κι εσύ;"

Why am I eavesdropping? I can't understand a word they were saying, but something about a foreign tongue always sounded pleasant. Their body language suggests that this isn't the first time in twenty years that they've seen each other, but that they don't get together often.

"Πρέπει να πάς και να συστηθείς," Elijah says.

Antonis looks quizzical. "Σε αυτόν;"

"Τον φωνάζω Boy Meets World. Ξέρεις όπως την αμερικανική τηλεοπτική σειρά. Μοιάζει λες και βγήκε από κωμωδία του 90'."

Did I just hear my name? For the first time in my life, I find myself wishing I took Greek in college. But that would require finishing college.

Antonis laughs. "Για τη πινέζα μιλάς;"

"Μίλα όμορφα! Είναι ο κολλητός μου." I can't tell if Elijah is slightly aggrivated, or if he just speaks louder in Greek than he does in English. Maybe both.

Shortly after, Antonis approaches me at the refreshment stand, and we exchange pleasantries and conservative small talk. A change of subject is overdue the second he stars talking about the stock market.

"Arete grew up here, right?" I ask.

I pour some apple cider from a crystal pitcher into a champagne glass. Almost everyone else is drinking, but after what happened last time, I'm swearing off alcohol for the rest of forever. Nothing quite like saying if I had to sleep with a man, it would be Elijah, only for Arete to pass it on to him as soon as she could. I bet it's the first thing that flew out of her mouth when she saw him.

"Mostly," Antonis says, just as loudly as when speaking his native tongue. "When she was about, oh, five or so, they moved to Melbourne. I was kind of upset about it, but they still came to visit on school breaks, and Georgios made frequent business trips in and out of the country."

"I'm sure you missed them," I say.

"No, that's not it," he says. Ouch. "Georgios still wanted 51% control of the business, but he wasn't around half of the year. See the problem?"

I don't know what to say, so I just nod.

"I'm sorry," Antonis says. "I shouldn't gossip about my late brother, especially not at his little girl's birthday party. My μαμά would be rolling in her grave."

"That's okay."

"I still feel like I should apologize, Mr. Brown."

I never want to talk to anyone who calls me Mr. Brown. Even with that aside, my first impression of Antonis isn't exactly positive, especially not with the ease at which he could lie to his stepniece (or whatever their relationship is,) but he doesn't seem like a particularly horrible man. Suspicious? Yes. Horrible? No. Rather than continue to talk to him, I decide to excuse myself.

Other than him, the party is mostly populated by Arete's aforementioned college friends and Elijah's police crew he talked into coming, just to fill up space from the people who didn't show up. I could either find the drunkest officer in the room and ask him questions about Galligan, or I could chat up Arete's cute friends. Both options would probably end in failure, so it doesn't really matter.

Arete stands in front of the dining table with Elijah by her side, and clashes a fork against a champagne glass to get everyone's attention.

"Everyone!" She says. "I have an announcement to make!" The chatter dies down, and Arete begins her "improvised" birthday speech. "On this day twenty-two years ago, I was born. So it only makes sense that, while you're all here, this would be the day I announce the very next chapter of my life. If you haven't already, I would like you all to meet Elijah Walker, my boyfriend. And as of Sunday..." Arete pulls off her right glove. "My fiancé!"

Everyone claps, including me. Arete is good with the theatrics and speeches, no matter how big or how small. She isn't over learning about Galligan last night, but you wouldn't know it by looking at her. She's a natural; if she were graded solely on performance, she'd be valedictorian. For all her friends know, she lives in paradise.

But there's one, and only one, person whose clap is less than enthusiastic. From the corner of my eye, I see Antonis look both ways before slipping out the French doors to go outside. Normally I wouldn't care, but when someone is acting *that* shady at a birthday party of all places, I can't help but follow and eavesdrop on his end of the conversation. I exit through a side door and take cover behind the deck. I trip over a rock, but he doesn't hear the thud over the volume of his own phone voice.

"She's sensitive, if she thinks you hate her, you'll never get it." ... "See! This is *exactly why* you'll never inherit the company. Not because you're not in line, but because you don't even try." ... "Because she's getting married. Yeah, I just found out myself." ... "Well, see? Maybe you don't know her as well as you thought." ... "I've got to go back in, but we're not done yet! Αντίο, χαζέ γιέ μου!" ... "Dammit, Mikhail, just learn Greek! If your dipshit cousin can do it, why can't you?"

Antonis mashes the cancel button so hard I think his phone is going to crack in half. Since it's an iPhone, it's entirely possible. He looks in my direction, forcing me to duck.

When I hear his footsteps approaching, I crawl under the deck, trying not to think about what bugs and rodents are under here. No. I can't not think about this. It's like being held underwater, unable to breathe, except I'm drowning in bacteria instead of chlorine pee water.

To my right, I can barely make out a pair of shiny shoes stomping through the light snow that powders the ground. I do what any grown man would do. I constrict my vocal chords and meow.

Antonis grumbles. "Damn cats."

What? How can someone not like cats?

Long after the cat-hater's footsteps fade into the distance, I go inside through the side door and search for Elijah. The second I find him, I grab him by the arm and drag him away from the party; physically, this isn't something I can do, but he follows along after initially resisting so he could give Arete a goodbye kiss. (How dare I pry him away from his princess for five whole minutes?) Before I can tell him my concerns, he figures out the tone of what's going on and suggests we go into the study where nobody can interrupt us. He shuts the door to the soundproofed room and locks it.

"Did you hear anything?" Elijah fixes his hair in the mirror. Yes, there was once a time I was terrified of this man. His hair obsession is on par with a girl's.

"Who is Mikhail?" I ask.

"My first cousin," he says. "I've never met him, but I talked to him on the phone when I was planning the party. He refused to come when he found out his ex-girlfriend was invited, but he's Uncle Antonis' firstborn son. About nineteen years old. Why?"

"I overheard him on the phone saying he wants him to inherit the business, but Georgios didn't put him next in line or something?"

"That's right," Elijah says. "Arete owns 51% of the company, and he's been sore about it ever since Dad died. I mean, I love her to death, you know I do, but she doesn't have any business instinct. She had good judgment when she appointed a CEO though, so I'm not too worried about the company's future."

He has too much faith in that girl. I know nothing about business and I've only known Arete for a month, but I guarantee she would run Konstantinou Enterprises into the ground faster than Elijah could say "Kit Kat, don't make that investment." I bite my tongue because any attempt to warn him would just piss him off.

"Okay," I say. "But what if something happens to her? Who gets KE? You?"

"Me?" Elijah scoffs. "I *wish*. No, Dad wiped me from the will. Antonis would get it all."

"You don't think her own uncle..."

I can't finish my sentence. It's hard to imagine the root of Arete's problems being family, especially since she has so little of it left. But if blood wasn't enough for Georgios to keep Elijah, how would fake blood be enough for Antonis to stay loyal to Arete?

"No!" Elijah explodes, blind to my train of thought. "I can't believe you would even go there! Uncle Antonis was the only one who stayed in contact with me when the rest of the Konstantinous kicked me out to stay with my γιαγιά and παππούς in Athens while my mother was strapped to a bed in a mental hospital. If it wasn't for my dad, Uncle Antonis would have definitely taken me in, he told me so. He always made it a point to visit me when I lived in Greece and he helped me move back to America, and when I got here my mom didn't even want me anymore. Uncle Antonis may be a little greedy sometimes, but he's a good man, and he would *never* kill *anyone*!"

Hair obsession or no, my fear of him returns. I should've known better than to accuse the man's only family member of trying to murder his fiancée, but there's no turning back now.

"Are you sure?" I ask. "Because he didn't have a single good thing to say about Arete since he got here."

Elijah says nothing. He just keeps glaring at me as my heart rapidly fires blood into my cheeks. This is the worst mix of awkwardness and fear imaginable, and I really wish I never brought it up. I didn't think he'd be this angry. I'm about to apologize when he interrupts me.

"What did he say about her?"

I'm caught off guard by his sudden receptiveness. "Uh, well, he complained that they moved away, and when I said he must have missed her, he corrected me and said he was mad Georgios was never around to run KE in person. And he said it in a way like he was shading her. Oh, and then he called her a dipshit. And on the phone he was complaining that you're engaged. Well, I think more that *she's* getting married."

He exhales and looks to the side. "There's a chance she'll pass it on to me, and any children we have will be shareholders and eventually inherit the company. He knows I want kids."

"So, what you're—"

"Drop it," he says.

"Okay." I switch topics, moving on to the other thing that I don't want to talk about. "Did you ask any of your drunk-ass cop friends about... the case?"

"Yeah," Elijah says. "That's the real reason I invited them... They're telling the public that they're cracking down on the case, but they actually don't give a shit who killed him. It could be anyone. They're more interested in who's hired him in the past and who he's killed so they can close more cases. All they're coming up with are dead ends. Either way, it looks like we're safe. For now, at least."

I breathe a sigh of relief. "At least something is working out."

"Don't worry," he says, pulling me into a death grip hug. "If anyone wants to take down you or Arete, they have to get through me first."

It's amazing how quickly he can change his attitude. I can't tell if he's forgiven me, or if he's just suppressing his emotions. Then again, this hug is extra-tight, so I'm betting he'll never forgive me. This is a hate hug.

"You're... squashing me!"

He releases me. "Sorry. I couldn't resist."

"If you don't mind me asking... Why did your father disown you?" As an afterthought, I quickly add, "You don't have to tell me. I just don't get why a man would abandon his own kid. It's pretty gross."

"Let's get back to the party, Boy Meets World. Arete's going to be missing me."

"Yeah." I overstepped my boundaries; I'm lucky he's not still yelling at me. "Wait... What were you guys saying about me in Greek?"

"You mean me and Uncle Antonis? I was telling him to introduce himself," Elijah says. "As for what he called you... You don't want to know."

"Seriously?"

"Trust me on this one."

The rest of the evening is relatively uneventful. We return to the party, where Arete eagerly introduces me to her friends and engages in polite networking and idle chitchat. I'm still surprised she has an actual circle of friends. She's never mentioned any of them in detail, so I thought these were all just acquaintances and people who came for free food and booze. I'll never remember any of their names, but that doesn't stop her from insisting that I meet each and every one of them. She introduces me to at least eight women—Whitney DiPietro and a bunch of people she's never referred to by name before—but I don't ask for anyone's number. I never do. What's the point? I know I'm worthless.

I run into officer Mark again later, and he asks me if my crime novel is done yet. I tell him it's "in progress" and will be finished "eventually."

How sad is it that the fanciest shindig I've ever gone to is a last minute "surprise" party? Something about the Konstantinou Manor makes it seem more polished than it really is, and the party runs late into the night. It's also the fanciest thing I've ever had to clean up after. Some of Arete's college friends are disgustingly messy. After my favorite couple goes to bed, I brace myself, put on a pair of gloves, and start with the vomit on the floor. I could accuse Elijah of being lazy for not helping, but he's probably making good on his promise to "make sure it's the best birthday Arete's ever had."

Saturday, March 21, 2015

The Konstantinou Manor's tearoom is relatively cozy in size, and rows of tall windows illuminate it with afternoon sunlight. There's thin, stained glass paneling trimming the tops that casts colorful patterns on the walls when light passes through. It's an odd, but pleasant feature that's well-suited to this dainty tearoom. Whoever decorated it favored blue and yellow accents, but no two pieces of furniture match each other as a set. The antique tea cups are also mismatched, as are the floor tiles. It doesn't meet Arete's "aesthetic," but she spends a lot of time here with books and dolls. I recall her saying this was Simone's favorite room in the house. Being here probably makes her feel closer to her. This is my first time here other than the other night, when Elijah dragged me through on the way to the connected balcony. There are plenty more rooms left for me to discover, but this is the most charming thing I've seen so far.

In the corner of the room, there's a small stove and a cabinet stocked with a wide assortment of tea bags. I peek through the cabinet and see the usual blends like English breakfast, and peppermint, to obscure blends I've never heard of. Jamaican butter rum black and organic chocolate orange herbal sound too pretentious for my tastes. I choose Earl Grey because I fancy myself a boring man.

I sit across from Arete and pour tea for her, myself, and one of her dolls. I've seen it before; it's a 24" tall ball-jointed doll (apparently called a super dollfie) that Arete named Zanna. Zanna enjoys literature, classical music, and above all, a good tea party. She and Arete are wearing matching loligoth outfits. In a way, Arete looks more doll-like than Zanna does, with her huge eyes, porcelain skin, and button nose. Zanna looks like a polymer anime girl.

"Thank you for joining us for high tea," Arete says. "And for the birthday party. I can't believe you blokes two managed to throw it together last minute."

"It wasn't that hard," I say. "But for such a quick party, it left one hell of a mess. It took me hours to clean."

Arete raises her eyebrows and her mouth droops slightly. "You… cleaned that?"

"Yeah," I say. "I had to. It was disgusting."

"William, I have a maid that comes in daily."

"Oh." I wasted hours of my life, but I did so knowing I prevented a googolplex of germs from swallowing my "family."

She tries not to laugh. "I'm sure the maid really appreciates it." She drops two sugar cubes into her cup. "Do you remember Whitney? From last night."

"That sorority girl who vomited on the floor?" I ask.

"No. That's Kayla Bradshaw; she wasn't invited. Nobody ever invites her, she just shows up. I'm talking about the brunette in the LBD."

"LBD? Your Australian slang is killing me."

Arete stares at me like I'm a lost cause. "LBD. Little black dress. Anyway, she told me she liked you. I totally knew she would. Do you mind if I give her your number?"

"I have a lot on my mind right now, with... you know what." I reconsider. I'm a stir-crazy writer, and I'm passing up the chance to feel a boob and get a life outside of Arete and Elijah? What is wrong with me? "Actually, yes."

"Good," Arete says. "Because I already gave it to her."

"Oh my god." I pray that Whitney is the shy type rather than the desperate type. "Wait, she *actually* likes me, right? This isn't like Alice all over again?"

"Nah," Arete says. "We go way back, I wouldn't lie about something like that. Anyway, I think it would be nice if you invited her out."

"Someone was looking at me?" I ask.

It's a dream come true, almost. It would have been better if she talked to me, but now I'm getting that chance. It's a miracle anyone was looking at me at all when Hollywood Perfect was around. Hell, even I was looking at him. But I can't let myself get distracted. I have an ulterior motive for this friendly tea party, and I have no intention of backing down this time.

"Today might not be the best time," I say. "There's something we need to discuss."

Arete puts her elbows on the table and hides her downcast face into her palms. "Hoyt Galligan. I know."

"Elijah told you what's going on, right?" I say.

"Of course not!" she says. "He just told me to stop thinking about it, so I didn't bother asking. Can you tell me? Please?"

I blow the steam off my tea, thinking that a long sip will buy me enough time to come up with an Elijah-approved answer. All I get for my efforts is a scorched tongue.

She bats her eyes. *"Pleeease?"*

"Fine," I say. "Elijah asked one of his cop friends. They don't care who killed Galligan, they're more interested in convicting the people who hired him and closing the unsolved murders."

She lets out a sigh of relief. "Thank god."

"Don't relax yet," I say. "They found no evidence. None whatsoever."

Arete swallows hard. "That's... that's great!"

"None at all," I say. "It's funny, because after I had time to calm down and think about it, I remembered my DNA being on his body. Do you remember that?"

Arete says nothing, keeping a stern poker face.

"You and Elijah are geniuses," I say, unamused. "Bravo, you two. You had me fooled from day one. Now's your chance to deliver the Oscar's award acceptance speech you've been rehearsing since you were twelve."

"It's not like that," Arete says. Her voice is shaking with urgency. "He did what he had to do."

"Did you ever plan on telling me the truth?" I ask.

"Yes," she says, but she's shaking her head *no*. "But then they found the body, and I got scared, and Eli said to keep it quiet until we were safe in case you would betray us. I'm really sorry!"

Her eyes well up with tears. I try my hardest not to feel sorry for her, but I can never stay mad at my friends for long. My life is so unusual that I gave up on trying to make sense of it a long time ago. At least now it's confirmed that I'm not actually at risk of going to jail for the murder of a hitman.

"I want the truth," I say. "And then I'll forgive you. Maybe."

"Technically," she says, "he was telling the truth." (Tell me something I don't know.) "He just knew you'd jump to the conclusion that he framed you." Arete whimpers, likely a bogus sympathy tactic. "Eli checked your ID for your home address, broke into your house, and dumped Galligan in your kitchen."

"What?"

"It was just for an hour!" she says. "You lived, like, five minutes from that alleyway, so it was convenient. And since he had a search warrant when he arrested your roommate, he already knew the layout of your house. So he just carried Galligan over his shoulder and marched right through your front door, so that if anyone saw they'd just think he was carrying his drunk friend home."

"That's..." *What is it? Insane. Stupid. Horrible.* "Bold. Very bold."

"There really was one of your hairs on his shoulder," she says. "Except, Eli didn't leave it there. He plucked it off so there'd be nothing to prove you were there. Then he burned Galligan's personal belongings, used your trash bags and duct tape to wrap him up, and blah blah blah."

"I feel so... violated."

She shrugs. "It could be worse. He thought about washing the body off in your bathtub, but he—"

"Stop! Stop right there. Skip to the part where he's out of my house, please."

"Well, after that, he chopped Galligan up and dumped him in the river. I don't really know the details, sorry."

As impressed as I am by Elijah's strength and... *creativity,* I'm not going to acknowledge that any time soon. "Did he tell you how he burned his stuff?"

"I didn't ask."

I have a theory that it has something to do with the batteries that were missing from my smoke detector. Elijah never explicitly said why he burned my house down. All he gave me was a bunch of word salad, probably knowing whatever conclusion I would jump to would cover his ass. In reality, he destroyed the evidence in the most dramatic way possible. Figures. It was tempting to share this with Arete, but it would only cause problems. I should just be relieved that I got away with someone else's murder. It's time to move on. No matter what I do, my life will always revolve around Mr. & Mrs. Satan. I'm too hooked on this mansion with an open-ended stay, and they're the baggage that comes along with it. I'd better make the best of it.

"Please say something," Arete says. "You're scaring me."

"Something."

Arete presses her lips together and narrows her eyes. I don't deserve to find pleasure in such an unoriginal, smartass remark, but even I'm not easy going enough to accept this "apology" today. But I'm satisfied with her answer (for now,) so I change the subject.

"While we're on unpleasant topics... Exactly how close are you and your uncle?"

"Well, that's random," she says, clearly puzzled but also relieved that I dropped the topic. "Not very. I mean, it's not like he hates me or anything, but he never treated me like family. Why?"

"No reason," I say, looking down into my tea. I'm not good at bluffing, but I try.

Arete gives me puppy dog eyes. "I betrayed my fiancé's trust and told you everything after I promised not to say a single word."

Now I'm in trouble. I can't tell her why I think Antonis is trying to seize the company from her without telling how I found out. She'd pester me until I admit how I know who owns what shares in the company, who's next in line, and why that bothers Antonis. Then she'd be one step closer to realizing she's engaged to her stepbrother. I have to play dumb.

"I overheard your uncle talking on the phone to someone named Mikhail."

"That's my cousin," she says.

"Well, he seems to think Mikhail should have your shares in the company now that your father is gone. He sounded really shady, so I thought I should ask you if that meant anything to you."

She sips her piping hot tea, trying to play it cool. "I'm an only child," she says. "I have no one to pass the company down to. If I'm dead, he'll be the full owner of Konstantinou Enterprises."

I didn't expect her to come to that conclusion so quickly. Does anyone in this family trust each other? Aside from Elijah trusting Antonis too much, of course. I can't expect him to come around on his own, since he's reacting on emotion alone and has once again abandoned all logic. For someone who won't call himself a Konstantinou, he's strongly invested in keeping the family together.

"Did you tell Elijah?" she asks.

It could cause problems later down the road if she catches me in a lie. I opt to pull a Hollywood Perfect and keep my answer as vague as possible.

"Yeah. The second I found out."

"My uncle's a greedy bastard," Arete says. "He owns 49%, and I own 51%. I have more power and no experience, and he hates it. He and Dad spent a lot of time arguing about it, especially when he was drafting his will before he died. My uncle said his kid should have it because I'd be a bad businesswoman, but Dad didn't want to leave me out. I don't really want it, but I don't want to go against my dad's hair-brained wishes either. For some reason, he never entertained the idea of Antonis gaining full control. I think it's because he takes more risks with white collar crime, him being a lawyer and all. I mean, when Dad said that laws are for poor people, he was just kidding. But when Antonis said it, he was dead serious."

"There's got to be some way to keep your uncle from killing you over it," I say. "Should we give the police an anonymous tip or something?"

"No," Arete says. "Even if we had a shred of proof, I have to think of the future of Konstantinou Enterprises."

I dip my finger into my tea—still too hot. "Which is more important? Your life, or your company?"

"Both were equally important to Dad, so..." She loses herself in her thoughts. "I'll push the wedding ahead."

"What?" I ask.

"Elijah is impatient anyway," she says. "I'll name him as a shareholder, bear him that child he wants so damn badly, and leave it to the kid. Hell, I'll build an army of children."

An army of children? Dear god, she really is insane. Either that, or she spiked her tea.

"Stop looking at me like that," she says. "I'm serious. Ish. Not about the kids, that was a joke. Just naming him as a shareholder."

"Have you talked with Elijah about this?" She's making a life-changing (or life-creating, since there's a little truth in every joke) decision about their relationship, and I'm not sure how Elijah would react to this. Sure, it's everything he wants, but being impatient for engagement is a far cry from having a speed wedding just to eliminate Antonis as either a suspect or a threat.

"Uh... No..." she says. "But I will. Tonight at dinner."

"Oh my god, please no," I say, pleading. "I don't want to hear that conversation."

*

"Eli, there's something I want to tell you."

This is it. I use the edge of my fork to poke at the roasted Brussels sprouts on my dinner plate. Brussels sprouts are near the top of my Would Not Eat it if I Had a Choice list, but I'm grateful for anything I can use to pretend I'm not listening.

"What about, Kit Kat?" he asks.

"My uncle," Arete says. She clears her throat, and acts as distinguished as possible. "I'm 110% sure he wants the company from me, and if I die, everything is all his. He's the only one who would profit from my death."

Elijah is shooting me a dirty look. I don't have to look up; I can feel it.

"Think about it," she says. "Who else has anything to gain if I die? Nobody. Who else would hire a hitman? Can you think of anyone else?"

I take a quick peek and see Elijah's head turned away from her, staring off into space with a solemn expression. He won't answer her.

"Please listen to me," she says. "We need to find a way to cock block him from my shares."

That's an... interesting way to put it, but her fiancé doesn't so much as bat an eye at her word choice. It's not because he's out of it; it's because he's used to it.

"How about I just threaten him instead?" Elijah asks.

That's the closest Elijah is going to come to admitting that his uncle is out for his Kit Kat's throat. She takes it.

"Why does this bother you so much?" she asks. "And I can't let you do that."

"Why not?" Elijah asks. "William, tell her she's making a bad decision."

I drop my fork and cover my ears. "Leave me out of this, I'm not here right now."

"Somebody has to take care of the company," Arete says.

"That's not what I mean!" Elijah says. "I can just threaten him to leave your shares alone. He can keep his 49%. Or maybe you could negotiate 50/50."

"What makes you think I'm capable of negotiation?" she says. "I'm not fit to be a CEO, and neither is Mikhail."

"Didn't your father start teaching you everything he knew from when you were a kid."

Elijah phrases it like a question but says it like a fact. I consider his childhood, before his father married his pregnant mistress. Georgios was probably grooming Elijah to take over Konstantinou Enterprises since before he could walk, only to leave him empty-handed in the end. If there's anything I learned lately, it's that blood means nothing to the Konstantinous.

"He did teach me a little," Arete says. "But he eventually just decided I was too stupid, and taught me what to look for in CEOs. Stuff like that. I tried to prove him wrong at first after he died. I even tried to take my part in the action, but my choice wasn't very popular. People made fun of me. My first business decision was to make sure there was a ficus in every office room."

Elijah creases his brow in confusion. "What?"

She shrugs sheepishly. "Well, I heard plants purify the air and it sounded like it might increase productivity level or something, I don't know. It wasn't cheap, but it *was* worth a shot, right?"

He furrows his brow and contorts his mouth. His birthright was given away to an idiot who had no place running anything, let alone a multinational conglomerate.

"That's not really a business decision, hon." He starts sawing off a piece of steak. He wants to get out of here even more badly than I do, I can tell. "A business decision... Is like your decision not to report your uncle because it would be bad for Konstantinou Enterprises. Or when you appointed Goldwater as CEO. It's knowing when to play it safe and when to take risks. I'm not trying to insult your ficus strategy, it's just that there's not any strong science behind it. If you really put your mind to it, there's more you can offer the company than a ficus."

"I wish you weren't so dead set on being a lawyer," she says. "I think you'd make a great CEO."

He nearly chokes on his steak. "Arete..."

"What?" She says. "I mean it."

"Konstantinou Enterprises is a *family* business." He looks down and touches the back of his neck. "I'm not family. Not really."

Arete's eyes are bright. "Sure you are, Eli! The moment you slid that ring on my finger, you became family. You're a Konstantinou."

He looks down and swallows. "I..."

"Yeah?"

"I'll find a way to take care of Antonis for you."

"Thank you," Arete says. "Because the more I think about it, the more it makes sense. He has connections at Penn, so I wouldn't be surprised if that was his fault too. Actually, I'm surprised I didn't get expelled."

"Do you think that was his end plan?" Elijah asks.

"Yes. Because I would have gone back to Oz, and I would have surrendered for sure."

I enter the conversation willingly for the first time. "A second attempt at removing you from the company?"

"I don't want to admit it," Arete says, "but that's all that makes sense. That professor has a lazy reputation, he never grates that quickly."

"So he's really the one responsible for all of this," I say. "Sorry, Elijah."

He grumbles. This is like the lactose intolerance thing, except instead of dairy, it's attempted murder. His worst lies are the ones he tells himself.

Arete looks out the window. "He probably burned your house down in a second attempt to kill me. You should consider telling your landlord to open up a new investigation."

"No!" I say, a little too quickly. Elijah and I exchange worried glances. "You see... I don't want to, um... Expose my landlord to potential danger." That's the dumbest excuse I've ever come up with in my entire life. "We should get more concrete evidence. I'm sure he covered his tracks with the hit man and the fire, or the police would have found something."

"But what about the suspension?" Arete asks. "We'll ask the teacher. Whitney's in his class with me. Will, I know you're not the type to use people, but... Can you pretend Professor Hiscock one of your favorite writers or something?"

"Sure," I say. "This is life or death, I mean. So what's his name?"

"Professor Hiscock."

"I mean his *real* name," I say. "Is it Hitchcock?" As in, *not what you've been calling him just because you had to face the consequences, you spoiled brat.*

Arete smiles. "That is his real name. Hiscock."

I frown. "How do we make this work naturally though?"

"Be direct, I guess." Arete says. "Text her, say Hiscock is your favorite writer, you missed his book signing, you want to meet him."

I hesitate, plagued by a chronic case of girl shyness, and Arete gets impatient. "What are you waiting for, Will? This is life or death! Text her."

"Right," I say. "What do I do when I get there?"

Arete gives a quirky smile. "Just bring up Antonis Konstantinou. If he knows him, he'll react. You're smart."

"Got it." I don't really feel like I've got it, but what else am I supposed to say?

Arete puts her hand on Elijah's shoulder. "Eli, how far are you willing to go?"

"For you, I'll do anything." His words are sweet, but he still has that absent gaze.

"You may need to go farther than you've ever gone before," Arete says.

Elijah gives a curt nod.

No. Arete is trying to hint to Elijah to kill someone, I know it. I go back to pretending not to listen. That isn't something I want to be involved in, not again. I just got out of the last murder by the skin of my teeth; the last thing I want is to be an actual accomplice.

"Good," Arete says. "Because I think we should get married. Now."

"Now?" Elijah and I ask simultaneously.

"ASAP. We can have a speed wedding in Vegas," Arete says. "I'll wear my mother's wedding dress. Elijah, you want this, right?"

Elijah cringes and holds up his hand. "Yeah, but—"

"William, you're our witness. Do you own a decent suit?"

"I don't have a suit. The last time I wore a suit was to my mother's second wedding when I was fourteen, and she was finally marrying my father."

I regret my words, expecting Elijah to say something like, "Good, it should still fit, then." I walked right into that one… and yet, he has nothing to say.

Arete hands me her credit card. "Knock yourself out, don't get something cheap."

I hesitate before taking it. I know rule numero uno is not to take handouts from these people if I ever want a genuine apology, but if I "ruin" Arete's wedding by showing up in jeans and a Six Flags shirt, she'll never forgive me. Sham or not, I know how she gets about these things.

"But, Kit Kat," Elijah says. "This is… exciting, but I thought you wanted a big wedding."

Arete nods. "We can still do that over the summer. We can have a wedding party any time."

Elijah half-smiles. "And you said *I* was the impatient one."

"It's only a piece of paper," she says.

Judging by the look on Elijah's face, he disagrees. But he's almost impossible to read right now. No matter how agreeable he acts, something isn't sitting right with him. I guess it's just that he's a romantic.

Arete snaps her fingers and points at me. "You, go buy your suit."

"Gotcha," I say. I head for the door, but skid to a stop. "Wait, I don't have a car."

"Use mine," Arete says. "It's not like I can use it, I have to retake my driver's test. I'll go find the keys. Elijah, search for a last minute flight to Vegas. Get a private jet if you have to."

"Okay," he says, as if he can afford a private jet if he has to. That'll be coming out of Arete's pocket.

"Wait a minute." I glare at Arete. "You had the wedding thing pre-planned this morning, didn't you? You were just trying to set me up with your friend!"

My phone vibrates.

YOU LIKE HISCOCK'S POETRY?? WOW. No points 4 taste but I can take u 2 meet him. I'll text u back later

Too late.

"Oops," Arete says, deadpan. "You caught me."

*

"Do we have everything ready?" Arete asks when I come through the front door. There are suitcases next to her, and a dress and suit are draped over the couch.

"I didn't pack yet," I say.

Elijah stands up and points at my bag, again using all four fingers and his thumb. "I took care of that for you."

"Why do you point like that?"

At first, I think he's going to ignore me, but he eventually says, "Marines. Some asshole officer told me pointing is too antagonistic."

"Can I see the suit?" Arete asks.

"Sure," I say. "Oh, and here's your card back." I hand her credit card back to her and unzip garment bag.

She gasps. "Oh. My. Goth."

"What?"

"I'll say 'what.'" She picks up the suit and surveys it. "As in, what is this polyester *nightmare*!"

I can hear Elijah snickering in the background.

"Well... I don't want to spend too much money, especially since you're paying for it."

Arete zips up the bag and hands it back to me. "This goes back to the store. *Now*."

"Honey, shouldn't we get on the road?" Elijah says through laughter. Looks like his mood improved since before I left. "We have a flight to catch."

She groans and picks up two suitcases, one in each hand. "I'll remember this," she says, storming out the door.

Elijah smirks. "I always knew she'd be a bridezilla."

It still freaks me out how quickly his mood can change, but honestly, I'm just glad he's talking. It's scary when he just sits there and steams.

Sunday, March 22, 2015

Las Vegas, Nevada

Arete insisted that she and Elijah get married at the same chapel where Britney Spears had her infamous 55 hour wedding. I guess even goths love Britney. The Little White Chapel is true to its name; the sign is bigger than the building. It's just a simple, white chapel for speed weddings. There's a drive through on the side that, according to the sign, is a 24 hour drive up wedding window. The bride wants a "real fake wedding" though, so we go inside.

The building is decorated in a way that I would describe as cheap but cute. Fake white flowers are everywhere. The walls are covered in white wallpaper, and there are six or so pews that seat two people each. I'm their only guest and their witness, so I have the front row to myself. Lucky me. I'm so excited. There's nowhere else in the world I'd rather be than at Arete and Elijah's sham wedding... other than anywhere. I don't feel like a witness to holy matrimony—I feel like I'm witnessing a crime.

Arete's father (or "father") isn't alive to walk her down the aisle, but that's okay; she is escorted down the short isle by an Elvis impersonator as he sings *Love Me Sweet*. And frankly, it would be awkward if he were alive to see his children marry each other.

The two stand by one another, their arms linked together as the officiant speaks. "We are gathered here today at the world famous Little White Wedding Chapel to join together Elijah and Arete," he says. "Elijah, will you take Arete to be your lawfully wedded wife, to love and to cherish, for rich or for poor, in sickness and in health?"

"I do."

"Arete, do you likewise choose Elijah to be your lawfully wedded husband, to love and to cherish, for rich or for poor, in sickness and in health?"

"I do."

(Zzzz.)

"You may now read your vows and exchange rings."

Arete laughs nervously. "Uh, we didn't write any..."

"You didn't?" Elijah asks.

Arete tightens her lips into an awkward smile and shakes her head with wide eyes. Elijah looks down to his left and lifts his brows.

"I guess it's not that important," he says. "It's just a speed wedding. Can we skip to the end? The very end."

Ouch.

Arete nods in agreement and laughs nervously again. "Yeah, that would be ace."

"Very well," says the wedding officiant. "And by the power invested in me in the state of Nevada, I pronounce you two husband and wife. Elijah, you may now kiss your bride."

Elijah puts his hands on the small of Arete's back and pulls her close. First, they accidentally bump noses. Strangely, Elijah isn't into it at first, but when the wedding march plays and they press their lips together, they get lost in their own world.

Last time I checked, the "just married" kiss was supposed to be a quick peck on the lips, but my newly wedded friends didn't get the memo. It's uncomfortable to watch, but I don't want to ruin their wedding the way they're ruining my eyes. Even when Elijah gropes Arete's rear, I don't say anything. I just tap my fingers on the pew and look away. At least their relationship is passionate enough to forget the wedding shade Elijah just dropped, albeit at my expense.

When I look back a minute later, they're still going at it.

"Guys," I say, "this is supposed to be a speed wedding."

Arete breaks away. "Sorry. We just wanted to savor the moment."

I furrow my eyebrows. "You're getting married twice, remember?"

"Fine, Boy Meets World." Elijah says. "Be *boring*, as usual. Kit Kat, I believe we have a 'just married' Cadillac to catch."

Elijah walks his new wife down the aisle, and I shake my head. They planned to have the 'just married' Cadillac drop them back off at Encore at Wynn Las Vegas, the hotel we're staying in. Even though we have separate rooms, I don't want to be anywhere near them when they consummate their (fake) marriage, so I end up being that guy who goes out to a Chinese restaurant and eats alone at a table for six. I should've taken the hush money so I could hire someone to eat with me. While there, I get another text from Whitney.

OK I talked to Hiscock.. I can take u 2 meet him thurs

She must have been embarrassed that she replied so quickly to the last text I sent, because she put off texting me back. My palms are so sweaty that I can hardly hold onto the phone. If Elijah had the balls to marry his stepsister, *surely* I can ask a girl on a date. It can't be that hard, right? My finger shakes as it hovers over the send button. I press it what feels like an hour later.

I was lying i just wanted an excuse to see u. anything youd rather do?

She follows my lead and replies five minutes later.

Have you ever gone to the Philly magic gardens??

I smile.

No

OK how's Thursday??

Thursday is great!
See you there!

Oh, no, William. You did *not* just send a girl two exclamation points in a row... Hopefully she doesn't judge me too much. There's finally going to be someone in my life other than the Konstantinous/Walkers/Whatever they are. That is, there *will* be someone if I don't embarrass myself.

Now, it's my job to call Antonis. I've never dreaded a phone call more in my entire life, but someone has to do it. Arete's anxiety would hold her back from making a legitimate threat, and Elijah "can't lie," leaving me to do the dirty work. What are best mates for?

230503UMAR2015

Omniscient View

Elijah wakes up next to his new wife at exactly zero three zero three uniform. Or, in civilian terms, 5:03 AM UTC-8:00. It's 8:03 AM in Philadelphia, so by his standards, Elijah slept in this morning. Unlike her, he's always been an early riser; or, at least he has been ever since he joined the Marines. Sometimes he's stricken with a bizarre nostalgia for his military days, almost as if he misses that life. But he acknowledges that if he truly wanted to go back, he wouldn't avoid talking about it. Despite their unbreakable bond, he almost never speaks to the friends he made in the service. He always felt like he abandoned them, but anything that reminded him of Iraq had to go. They understood why he wanted to leave; family is important, and his mother, Tansy Papadópoulos, had gone missing. But still, they realized that wasn't the reason for his discharge.

Soldiers don't get discharged for family emergencies. He tried so terribly hard to keep the others from finding out he failed the psych evaluation, but everyone could tell he had PTSD. The nightmares, the hostility, and even the flashbacks weren't life-shattering, but the longer he stayed the worse it would get. Today, he manages to get by. He's reached the point in his life where he's able to let go every now and then thanks to his iron will and a bit of therapy. The dull ache of forgetting is easier to cope with than reliving the memories, but that's what the little white pills are for.

But when years passed without any breakthroughs in the case, Elijah only felt worse about leaving his friends behind. He failed his most important mission, and he'll never forgive himself for it. It's been years since then. To be exact, Tansy had last been seen five years, four months, and ten days ago, voluntarily exiting a hotel alone. He told her to sit tight, he told her he'd be visiting home soon, but she didn't listen. It was his fault. He should have known she wouldn't listen. She never listened, and now it's too late.

With that said, although Elijah will be waking up next to a beautiful woman every day for the rest of his life, old habits die hard. If he wears a button down shirt, the fly of his pants must be perfectly aligned with his belt buckle and the seam of his shirt. He checks his gig line every hour on the hour and feels naked without a belt. He always thinks in terms of the 24-hour clock, and sometimes gets confused by those who don't. He uses knife hands when he points or yells at someone. He tries to fall in step with people walking next to him. He can't bear to put his hands in his pockets. He even refuses to use umbrellas, no matter how brutal the downpour.

Truthfully, the man never adjusted well to unstructured daily life, though his convoluted personal life is to blame for much of his problems. Most notably, his father showed up out of the blue a few years ago, begging for forgiveness and announcing his terminal illness. After reconnecting and then losing his father a second time, Elijah set his sights on new goals. Law school is his savior and Arete is his escape, but no matter how busy he gets, Elijah will *never* be able to get the United States Marines out of his head.

He worries constantly about hiding the simplest things from Arete, all so he can avoid talking about the military. Once, she asked him why he always used his cell phone in his left hand when he was right handed. He implied that he needed his dominant hand free for "high fives" so he wouldn't have to bring up something as basic as saluting. She looked at him like he was an idiot, (or "drongo," as she would say) but didn't bring it up again.

That was a relief, because he was already keeping so many secrets from her and hiding so many parts of his life. He hates hiding things from her more than anything else, knowing she'll eventually figure everything out on her own, and there's nothing he can do to stop it. She'll find out he's her stepbrother, she'll find out why her mother hated him so much, and she'll find out *the truth* behind what happened to her mother. Simone's death was no accident, that much is certain.

Elijah studies his wife's features as she sleeps. She looks a lot like her mother, and he looks like a *clone* of Georgios. What if Arete figures it out based on that alone? How would she react? Would she think they were some sort of cliché, where their parents' love was reincarnated? Would she be so angry that he kept this from her that she'd never speak to him again? Would he be able to play it off as a coincidence?

Not that Elijah was the only one responsible for her blissful ignorance. He knew for a fact nobody told Arete about Georgios' relationships before his mother, especially not about Tansy. Arete would assume he was her half-brother by blood, and, well... He didn't want to imagine how she'd react to that one. William thinks it's borderline incestuous, but never had the guts to confront him about it. What if Arete would feel the same way?

Elijah sits on the armchair across from the bed and reaches into the pocket of the tux jacket that's draped over the back. He fishes out a crumpled up ATM receipt.

"*Arete!*" he says, hushed. When she doesn't stir, he flattens out the receipt and reads what he scrawled on the back, his voice barely louder than a whisper.

"Dear Kit Kat, *Αγαπη μου*. The current world population is roughly 7.349 billion, and 3.639 billion of these people are women. It almost doesn't feel right that I was lucky enough to meet you—the funny, patient, cool girl that I didn't think existed. I promise to always love and take care of you until the day I die, to make you feel safe when you think the world is crumbling down, and to never take you for granted."

He stands, crumples up the receipt, and tosses it into the waste basket, a bit harder than he intended. On his way to the bathroom, he pauses for another word.

"Sorry they kind of suck. It was the best I could do on short notice, and I'm not very creative with words. I'll do a better job for our second wedding."

Elijah steps into the bathroom and looks in the mirror. Every time he thinks about what he did to Simone, he worries that his morality is slipping. He often wonders if he's evil because Simone trusted him, at least a little bit. But then he remembers Simone was also wholly responsible for what happened to his own mother, and he goes back to hating her again. Simone also ruined his childhood, and he only partially forgave her. He had no idea how he felt because his mind kept flipping back and forth in extremes. Everything and every person was either all good or all bad according to his emotions, even when his head didn't agree. If—no, *when* Arete finds out, will she hold it against him forever like he holds things against others? Maybe if he controls *how* she finds out, they'll overcome it.

How would that conversation go? When he gets out of the shower, he closes the bathroom door and looks into the mirror once again. The mirror is foggy enough, and he and Arete both have dark hair. (Except, she was born with a tuft of ginger hair on her head, but she doesn't know he knows that.) His wavy locks are nearly shoulder-length when they're wet. If he uses his imagination, he can pretend he's breaking the news to his wife. Elijah clears his throat.

"Hey, Arete. So, I have something to tell you."

"What is it, dear?" He whispers to himself in his attempt of a squeaky, Australian accent.

"Your mom killed my mom."

"That's totally BS, you..." *What word would Arete use?* "Wanker. You lying wanker. How would you know that?"

"Because she told me so. But I haven't found mom's body yet or anything like that. So I can't really prove it."

He puts his hands on his hips and leans slightly forward the way Arete does when she yells at someone. "How would my mum even *know* your mum?"

"Well, you see..." He scratches the back of his head and avoids eye contact with himself. "You're my stepsister."

"What?" He puts his hand in front of his mouth and gasps girlishly. "You disgusting wanker! I want to divorce you and then remarry you just so I can divorce you again. And then I'm going to hit you with your own car because I forgot to make you sign a prenup. Then I'll find a hot, young Aussie bloke my own age so I don't end up with another fuckwit old fart like you. Everyone would be happier if you were never born."

He's startled by a voice from outside the bathroom. "Elijah? Are you talking to yourself?"

Elijah grabs a towel and wipes off the mirror. "I was on the phone!"

It's technically true; in fact, a telemarketer called him yesterday evening. He opens the door, and sees Arete roll over.

Her face is buried in a pillow, which she squeezes with her arms. "Why are you awake when the sun is dead?" she asks.

Elijah chuckles softly. She has a way with words, and as long as she isn't using them to break up with him, it's always a pleasure. "Good morning, Mrs. Walker."

Arete groans and rolls over, still holding a pillow over her face. She never took his name. "Don't call me that, it sounds so matronly."

"It makes me feel better though," he says.

"About what?"

He crawls onto the bed and whispers in her ear. "Not using a condom last night."

Arete hates being woken up before ten in the morning, and isn't in the mood for jokes or play of any kind. "I'm on birth control."

"I know, I know…" One of the good things about half-asleep Arete is that she is always straightforward, a trait he occasionally takes advantage of. "Would it be so bad if you weren't?"

She slides the pillow down and opens her eyes, just barely and for only a moment. "It hasn't even been twenty-four hours and you already have baby fever?"

"I'm an old geezer, remember?" He kisses the back of her head. "I'm going to go down to the lobby and bring you some breakfast."

"All right."

By the time Arete manages to summon the will to climb out of bed, her not-husband-yet is gone. His question, however, still lingers on her mind. *Would it be so bad if you weren't?*

Now that she's awake enough to fully process it, it surprises her. She almost can't believe that Elijah brought up kids so soon. She knew he wanted them, but even after her joking with William about having an army of children, she only planned on having them long after she had a well-established career. She had considered having them sooner, sure, but Elijah just blurted it out like it was nothing monumental, like they were hosting a party or buying a vacation home. In the span of 24 hours, she realized she isn't suited for the arduous task of motherhood. She hasn't even finished college. Their marriage is a sham. Meanwhile, how long has her boyfriend been dreaming of fatherhood? Five years? Ten?

The only reason she thought it might be a good idea was so she could bear an heir to Konstantinou Enterprises, and that was a horrible reason to bring a child into the world. Even then, she was assuming that Uncle Antonis would be opposed to murdering a pregnant woman or a child. She never bonded with her uncle, so how would she know? He never treated her like family. He treated her like some kind of stranger that just happened into their world by mistake. This whole idea was a stupid, spur of the moment decision, and getting married was a terrible mistake.

Contemplating the idea of having kids was easy with William, but something about telling Elijah would make it too real. She always felt comfortable sharing stupid things with William, partially because he accepts people as they are, but mostly because he's a loser. She doesn't feel the need to impress him like she does Elijah, who's accomplished so much and is constantly working toward something greater. He can surely handle a squad of wailing, defecating infants, but there's no way she has the maturity to raise a child. She can't even keep a plant alive, and now she's gone off and married a man who wants children. Why did she do this to herself?

She pushes the army of children out of her mind; Elijah saved her life a third time by fake-marrying her. A hit man couldn't kill her, a fire couldn't kill her, and suspension didn't send her back to Australia. If Antonis wants the other 51%, that's just too bad. It belongs to her and her not-husband now. She admires her engagement ring, and then slides it back onto her right hand, where it belongs. It was fun to play house for the night, but she can't let anyone know she's married on paper. How would her friends react? Only Antonis needs to know she's married. As far as the rest of the world is concerned, she and Elijah never flew to Vegas, and they never tied the knot. It's not like it's a genuine marriage; it was a potential life or death situation, and Arete is the type to choose life.

The odds of William being awake at this hour are low, but she can't stand waiting another second to find out what

Antonis said about her marriage. It's not that she's excited or apprehensive; she's worried that William doesn't have the nerve to threaten someone properly. Arete calls him, but it goes to voicemail, just as she expected. He's so useless. She should've never kidnapped him.

Elijah comes through the door not long after, toting a tray loaded with food. Muffins are stacked on top of bagels. There are four different kinds of cereals with milk and orange juice cartons at the side. Napkins are shoved in between them, folded around plastic cutlery. She's amazed that he can balance it on one hand. If she were the one carrying that tray, it would all be on the floor.

In one breath, Elijah says, "When I got down there I didn't know what to get you so I panicked and I brought one of everything except the bacon because you're a vegetarian and it looked gross anyway if you hate everything we can just go somewhere else we have time."

Arete looks at the clock; it's 6:22 AM. She laughs. "You didn't need to go through all that trouble."

"Yes I do," he says. "You're my wife."

Arete purses her lips and bows her head, breaking eye contact. *Wife?* She thought she made it clear that this was a *fake*-real marriage. Or did she say real-fake? It doesn't matter. They dine peacefully, not wasting a moment's conversation on the things that ailed them. There was no talk about Uncle Antonis, or the real-fake/fake-real marriage. They were able to forget and cuddle—until Arete's cell phone makes an awful noise.

She reaches for it. "Oh, it's probably William."

"Noo!" Elijah pulls her back toward him. "There's no way that's William, it's not even twelve-hundred hours yet."

Arete doesn't know what that means and she doesn't care. She resists him and answers the phone. "Hey, William!"

"Hey. How's the married life?" William yawns.

Elijah leans in, clinging to his wife again as he shouts in the receiver. "Never been better!"

"All's well," Arete says. "So, how did it go with Antonis?"

"The man's terrified," William says. Good; that's exactly how she wants him. "I brought up how I knew about his plans to have Mikhail take over your shares of the company, and I told him if he wanted a future at KE, he had to back off. And that it was all over now, because you left it to your badass US Marine husband when you die."

"That's all it took?" Arete says.

"W-well, um, not exactly." William doesn't respond for a couple of seconds. He knows he fucked up. "I mean... I *might* have mentioned that Elijah was the one who killed his hitman, and said that he'd have the same fate if anything happened to you."

"William!"

Elijah overhears. "Dammit, Pool Noodle! What if he was recording that or something?"

What was it his therapist said about anger management again? Think before you speak, use "I" statements, and talk about why you're upset... ah, but alas. He's so angry he *can't* think at the moment, so he isn't allowed to speak. He resorts to deep-breathing exercises. In... out. In... out.

"I'm not very intimidating, I didn't have much of a choice," William says. "He actually laughed at me at one point and called me a πορδοβούλωμα. I don't even know what that means. Besides, you're being paranoid. It did the trick, didn't it? If he turns over what I said, he has to admit he hired a hitman. That's even worse than killing one."

Elijah groans and pinches the bridge of his nose in frustration. It's not that he doesn't believe the poor kid. Πορδοβούλωμα literally translates into "fart plug." Antonis called him a Πινέζα (thumbtack) just a few days ago. Both are rude Greek slang for short people. Antonis must not have been taking him seriously, which is why William would resort to pushing it farther than he asked him to. Elijah wants to smack himself for thinking that was a good idea. Why did Elijah think it was a good idea again? Ah, that's right. Because he can't deliver empty threats to his uncle without weaving an intricate bundle of lies that would trip him for the rest of his life. William was the only option, and an option that backfired. This whole plan is stupid. Antonis is clearly innocent, anyway.

Now he'll have to call up his uncle and do some major damage control, lest he wind up in prison. He's also worried

Uncle Antonis will never forgive him now. Perhaps it's for the best; Antonis hated Simone and likewise rejected Arete—and did Elijah not try his best to always make her feel safe? No matter how insistent Elijah was of his Uncle's innocence, neither his wife nor his best friend trusted him. Whether Elijah likes it or not, his dearest uncle, who always stood by him, even when his father did not, will no longer be in his life.

"I guess you couldn't help it," Elijah says.

It's the only thing he can think to say after William ratted him out for murder. And then it clicks. The kid hasn't been as jumpy about it lately... He knows. William figured out he wasn't framed when Elijah's judgement was clouded by his emotions and he slipped up by admitting the police found no evidence. That would've been at Arete's birthday party, which was days ago. How long has he known? Elijah never made the mistake of underestimating him before; how did it get this out of control? Well, at least the capture bonding strategy is working out well. Except, Elijah is more attached to his pool noodle than vice versa. He hadn't been counting on that, but it hardly matters now as long as William doesn't squeal... or get them caught.

"He got the message," William says. "I promise. He said he'll back off, and asked if you had any other demands."

Arete smiles. "Nah, mate. I just want to enjoy my new life."

Did she really say the words "new life?" Elijah dares to feel a little better, and maybe even distract himself from the new mess. He was worried that their marriage wasn't important to Arete, who considers it fake. But, if she thinks their relationship is somehow different now, she's getting there. Slowly, slowly getting there. And if she can have a new life, maybe Elijah can too. Maybe he can forget the United States Marines—every now and then, at least.

Thursday, March 26, 2015
William Brown Quiñones
Philadelphia, Pennsylvania

Elijah is doing homework, and Arete is busy planning their engagement party. It's about two weeks away, and she's buzzing to plan it perfectly in a short amount of time. To further assert that her marriage is to be kept a secret, she's sure to send Antonis an invitation to their "engagement" party. I flinch when she shows me what she wrote at the bottom.

If you don't come, I'll set your house on fire.

If only she knew. When she wasn't looking, I made a new invitation for Antonis and threw her version out. But today isn't about Arete's drama or Elijah's whining. Today is about Whitney and me.

The most awkward part isn't that I'm waiting out in the rain in front of Philadelphia's Magic Gardens waiting for my date because I have no car to pick her up in; it's that I have no idea what my date looks like. I think back to Arete's vague description of her; brunette in the little black dress. There had to be at least twenty brunettes at that party, and every time I try to guess which one, their faces blur together. I should have told Arete the truth and asked her to show me a picture; but they were all cute, so I figured it wasn't worth the risk of her thinking I'm a desperate weirdo with a bad memory.

What else do I know about the girl I'm texting? Whitney already has a nursing job lined up for when she graduates UPenn this year, but she's going to miss the field hockey team she plays on so much that she almost doesn't care if she passes her finals. She loves reading, but dislikes difficult books because she'd rather relax. She used to play the guitar until she got frustrated, but she'd like to pick it up again someday. Her ancestry is largely Italian, and she has a natural tan. Most importantly, she hates Facebook, Twitter, and any other social media site I could use to find a picture of her. She has an Instagram, but she only posts photos of things like food and her corgi.

How will I recognize her when she shows up? I could shout "Whitney!" at every brunette who comes by. I could pretend to be texting on my phone, and wait for her to come to me. I decide to go with the latter plan, and I feel a tap on my shoulder; I jump and turn around.

A familiar woman with wavy, chestnut hair crouches down under her umbrella and greets me. "I'm sorry! I didn't mean to scare you."

I blush. I can't believe someone this adorable is talking to me willingly. Her big, brown eyes are complemented perfectly by her arched brows. Her nose is slightly broad, and covered in light freckles that spread to her cheeks. Her full lips are curved into the most beautiful smile I have ever seen. I notice her ears sticking out a bit through her hair, but it's a cute feature on a girl.

She offers me her free hand and engages me in a friendly handshake. "Nice to see you again."

"Whitney?" I blurt out. I'm so stupid.

She's caught off guard. "Who else would it be?"

"Oh, I remember now!" I say. "You're the one who cracked that joke about Elijah's pretty boy hair!"

Her jaw drops for a second, but she recovers with a laugh. "You've been texting me all this time and you didn't know who I was?"

I feel the heat rising to my cheeks, and I talk more quickly than I ever knew I could. "No! I mean, I remember you. It's just that Arete only gave me your name, and I met a lot of people that night, and—"

"It's cool. It's actually pretty refreshing."

"How?" I ask.

"It means I was right about what kind of man you are."

I tug at my shirt collar. It's 47° F, so why am I suddenly so hot? "What kind of man is that?"

Her smile is soft and heartwarming. "Deep. Friendly. Patient."

That's a relief; I was afraid she'd find it annoying that I had no idea who she was, but she is impressed that my attraction is based on her personality rather than her appearance. Though, I'm not as honorable as she thinks. I'm no less shallow than any other man, to be honest. I was going off Arete's insistence that "she's sexy, she's sweet, and you're going to love her." That was high esteem for someone she was barely talking to. I've never heard a straight woman call another woman "sexy" before, but it was Arete, so I didn't question it. She's weird.

I remember Whitney as being quiet at the party, but I don't feel awkward around her. She's comfortable to be around, and she looks the part. She wears slouchy pants paired with a light blue sweater. She pulls the look off well, appearing classy rather than sloppy. Meanwhile, I'm nicknamed after a 90's classic for a reason. What does she see in me?

"I can see where you got deep and friendly," I say, "but where did patient come from?"

"You're friends with Elijah."

The two of us share a laugh. I consider asking her how well she knows Elijah, but today is my break from all things Walker. He dropped me off here when he was on his way to buy Arete a wedding gift, and that's the most I'm willing to think of him today.

"Let's go in," I say. "How much do tickets cost?"

"It's the first date," she says. "I think we should go Dutch."

"Are you sure?" I ask.

"Yes."

I would prefer the opportunity to be a gentleman and pay her way, but I don't argue with her. I'm glad to be on a date someone as lovely as her at all. The only thing I would change about her is, perhaps, the fact that she's at least three or four inches taller than me. Ah, who am I kidding? I just wish

I wasn't so short. If she'd at least let me pay her admission fee, I'd feel 10% less emasculated right now.

I've never been to Philadelphia's Magic Gardens before, though I've unknowingly passed it. I expected a garden filled with exotic plant life when I heard the name, but I'm pleasantly surprised by a work of art instead. I marvel at the mosaic tiles that cover the building head to toe, each arranged in interesting patterns and murals that are unlike anything I've ever seen before. If it wasn't arranged in such a pleasing manner, I'd assume it was all random. There's also an art exhibit, and almost none of it is properly secured or protected. I'm anxious I'll break something and have to pay for it. There are also a lot of sexual drawings that I didn't expect to see in a family friendly attraction. Whitney thinks it's hilarious.

When Whitney and I walk through the gardens, I discover what they mean by magic. It's like stepping into another world. Upon stepping outside, I'm drawn to unique additions such as the glass bottles and bicycle wheels that line the walls.

We were warned to walk carefully, as the tiles get wet in rainy weather. I don't listen, and find myself on the ground, grasping my arm in pain.

Whitney gasps. "Are you okay?"

"No!" Wait, did I really just say no? How old am I, four?

She crouches over and takes my arm; I grimace. As long as I don't start crying, I can go back to pretending I'm masculine.

"Don't worry," she says. "I come from a long line of nurses."

"You're a nurse?"

"I will be when I graduate in May," she says, taking a closer look at my arm. She's speaking in a soft, soothing voice. A nurse voice. "We need to get you to the urgent care center as soon as possible, but you're going to be okay."

"Are you sure?" I ask, thoroughly embarrassing myself. I'm a baby when it comes to pain.

"Positive." She smiles. "Take deep breaths and don't worry. I broke my arm once too, and I was out playing field hockey six weeks later."

"It's broken?" I gape at my arm.

She tries and fails to stifle a laugh, and helps me come to a stand. "I've seen worse."

"I can't believe I ended up with only my left hand again," I mumble to myself.

"What?"

"Nothing." I look at my arm again. Why am I such a loser? "Sorry I was such a shitty date."

"It's okay." She runs her fingers over my cheek. "We'll do something... safer on the next date."

"Next date?"

Whitney catches me off guard by giving me a quick peck on the cheek, but then pulls away, looks down, and laughs akwardly again. She has a cute laugh.

"Sorry," she says. "I'm really shy, I just feel comfortable about you for some reason."

I blink once before just staring. She's apologizing to *me*? "No... You don't have to apologize. I'd... I'd like to do it again sometime?"

Now we're *both* blushing, but she's adorable. I'm sure I look more like a flushed gourd.

"Come on," she says. "I'll drive you to the urgent care center."

*

My date with Whitney is over, but our day together isn't. To my surprise, she stays with me in the waiting room, even though she knows it will suck away her evening. It's nice to have someone to talk to, though some of the things she has to say surprises me.

"Arete and I used to be pretty close, actually. Like, BFF close. Our mothers knew each other in college, and when the Konstantinous came here in the summer, we used to hang out."

"Really? I thought you met at UPenn. Like, random roommate match up or something."

Whitney scoffs. "Of course you would. She basically stopped talking to me the second she started dating Elijah."

"Why?"

"I don't know," she says. "Arete got along with everyone so well, and she had tons of friends. Hell, she was the most popular bubble-goth around. But then Elijah Fucking Walker comes along, and she climbs straight up his butt hole and builds a nest there or something."

That's not a pretty picture. For such a quiet girl, she has a lot to say and a very colorful way of saying it. I like it. I'd even go so far as to say meeting her is worth every bad thing that Arete and Elijah ever put me through. And none of it would have happened had I not written *Night in the Fire*, because Whitney was the one who recommended it to Arete in the first place. For the first time, writing that book feels like a good decision instead of a life-ruining, career-ending-before-it-began one.

"I know what you mean," I say. "I have a love-hate relationship with Elijah. He's cool sometimes, but he can be obsessive. And he crashes harder than any grown man I've ever met."

Also, he pretended to frame me for murder, kidnapped me, burned my house down, and married his stepsister. Still gross.

Whitney doesn't know what I was alluding to, but she nods in agreement to be polite.

"I overheard him singing *The Sound of Silence* to himself last time they had a fight," I say. "He was locked in his room with the lights off."

She snorts. "I'm not surprised."

*

I come home at around eleven o'clock, dreading whatever Elijah will say when he sees that my arm is broken. God knows he'll make fun of me, and I'm not in the mood. Unfortunately, Hollywood Perfect catches me sneaking through the hallways.

"Hey, it's late. Where were you?"

"With Whitney," I say, nervous.

Much to my dismay, Elijah turns the light on. He gasps. I am not kidding, he actually gasps.

"Pool Noodle, what did she *do* to you?" Elijah approaches me and surveys the damage. "Why didn't you call?"

I squint. I can't tell if he's serious or not, mainly because it's so unusual for him. When we first met, he held a knife to my throat. It's hard to believe he would throw the fit of a doting mother over a small fracture.

"No cell phones in the hospital, remember?" I don't actually know if that's true or not, but it makes an okay excuse. I sigh. "And it wasn't Whitney's fault, I just slipped on tile."

"Female on male domestic violence is nothing to be ashamed of. We all know how violent field hockey players are."

I roll my eyes. "Okay, *now* you're just making fun of me." His words also indicate that the Whitney vs. Elijah war is mutual. Great. That's just what I need.

Elijah shrugs. "Maybe a little. But, seriously, are you all right?"

"Yeah," I say. "Whitney did first aid and drove me to the urgent care center, and it'll be healed in nine or ten weeks."

"Oh, I forgot," he says. "Whitney is a witch doctor."

Elijah frowns at the mention of Whitney's name. I'm not sure if each saw the other as competition for Arete's attention, or if Elijah just hates Whitney for hating him. I don't actually want to know because I'm too busy feeling guilty. I gossiped about him with Whitney; would he have done the same to me? No. He wouldn't.

"Wait a minute," he says. "I thought you said you were in the hospital?"

"Same difference," I say to avoid getting caught in my phone lie from earlier. I can't tell if he's buying it or not. "Whitney invited me on a make-up date in the morning, so I'm just going to go to bed now."

I expect him to snark about how the first one didn't count, but he says, "Okay. You need your rest anyway."

"Right."

"Good night, kid." Elijah turns off the light and returns to his room. I don't give him enough credit.

Saturday, March 28, 2015

The only thing worse than Whitney vs. Elijah is Arete's awkward dance around her, like she's afraid to be her friend again after she left the dorm they shared together on the rare occasion Arete wasn't sharing a bed with Elijah. So I came up with a brilliant (at least for me) plan that will repair their friendship. I tipped Arete off on our make-up date. Whitney picked me up and drove me to a "surprise," which turned out to be a "safe" coffee shop. Now that we're here, all I have to do is wait.

Arete (somehow) gets out of the house and over here in a record 28 minutes after I lie and tell her Whitney is thinking about leaving. She marches in, not even looking for us in the crowd, and approaches the counter to order a latte.

I poke Whitney and point in Arete's direction. Whitney looks surprised.

"Can you call her over here?" she asks. "I just kind of feel bad that... well... you know."

"Sure," I say. "Hey, Arete!"

Arete whips around and gasps. "What are you two doing here?" she asks on her way to our table.

"Whitney twirls a strand of her wavy, chestnut hair and laughs. "Just on a date. What about you? I thought you hated hipster-y places like this."

"I felt like trying something new," Arete says. "Mind if I sit with you as I wait for my coffee."

"No, that's fine."

It's amazing how easily Arete managed to convince her BFF, who she's known her entire life, that she just bumped into us. Even I believed it for a moment, and I was the one who orchestrated the whole thing.

Arete seats herself, and I can tell she's just as nervous as Whitney. Neither of them bother to hide it. But it isn't long until they're swept away in conversation, like no time passed at all. They're an extension of each other.

"Did you see those lipsticks I pinned last night?" Arete says.

"No," Whitney says, "I haven't been on in a while."

"Oh. My. Goth," Arete says. "Okay, it starts out some weird color like green or blue, but then they change color depending on your personal body chemistry or something sciencey like that."

"That sounds neat," Whitney says. "What's it called?"

"I don't remember, want me to check?"

Whitney waves her hand dismissively. "Nah, I'll just look at your makeup board later. Say, does that detox tea you posted on Insta really work?"

"I didn't try it," Arete says. "But they paid me $10,000 to hold up the box and say I did. Want it?"

"I'll pass," Whitney says. "Congrats on hitting 1 mil by the way."

"Thanks!"

Pins? Boards? Lipsticks? Oh my goth? Sciencey? Detox tea? I give up. I'll never be able to keep up with their girl talk. I need to get into this conversation somehow. Arete was supposed to be the third wheel, not me.

After they lose momentum talking about makeup, Whitney says "Congrats on your engagement, by the way. I'm sorry I didn't say that sooner." She looks down and purses her lips as she waits for Arete's response.

"It's okay," Arete says. "I did kind of break my promise to you. I didn't mean to, but the longer I spent with him, the guiltier I felt about abandoning you. And I thought you wouldn't want to speak to me again."

"You kind of did, yeah," she says. "But after seeing you two together, I understand. Part of me wants to scold you for getting engaged to him so fast, but you look so perfect together."

"You really think so?"

Whitney smiles. "Yeah. I mean, if you want to know if a relationship will last, communication is key. And you said it yourself when you first started dating, he's a sharer."

Arete rolls her eyes. "Only every other detail of his day."

"I mean, the age difference is kind of..."

"Squicky?" Arete says.

They both laugh.

"I try not to think about it," Arete says. "But when I do, yeah… he could be, like, my uncle or something. Or maybe an older brother."

I choke on my drink.

Whitney puts her arm around me. "Are you okay?" she asks.

No. no, I am not even remotely okay. Even after I recover from the coffee that went up my nose, I continue to fake-cough until I figure out what to say.

"I am now."

She smiles again. God, I love her smile. I don't even care how cliché that is, I am mesmerized by her smile, and I'll say it again. I let her know by smiling back.

"I want to smack you two for being so cute," Arete says. "I take it all is well?"

Whitney blushes. "Well, are we?" she asks me.

"R-really well." I say. As embarrassing as this is, I'm glad to finally be able to talk at all. I was starting to think I'd have to sit here and meditate as they persist to talk about girly things like—

"Oh my *god*," Arete says, "is that Zach Effron?"

Whitney cranes her neck and they look over my shoulder. I duck.

"Never mind," Arete says. "False alarm."

Speaking of false alarms, guess who's left out again.

Whitney groans. "Great, now 'Status Quo' is stuck in my head."

Arete shushes her. "Don't you remember our pact? We're not supposed to admit to watching that."

"It's just William," Whitney says. "You said it yourself, he's not judgmental."

And now they're talking about me like I'm not here; my life is shit. Arete soon launches into an unrelated, but very defensive rant about how much better it is to date an older man because older men (AKA, not necessarily Elijah, but definitely Elijah) are more responsible, have more money, and care more about commitment than the cute, aesthetic, goth boys she wasted her youth on. With the exception of the cute, aesthetic, goth boys detail, I feel personally attacked as a 25-year-old loser who's just trying his best. I keep my mouth shut and bear it because Arete is clearly just being defensive about her choice to date Elijah, but it still stings a little when Whitney nods and says she understands. It may be our first make-up date, but I really need to step up my game.

After two long hours of listening to them talk about confusing girl stuff, the frat parties Arete missed, and people I've never met, I give up and send Arete a text.

> Hey i don't want to be a dick but im on a Date so can u just... leave??

Arete responds after a few more minutes of BFF-only chitchat.

Um, RUDE.

"Oh, look at the time!" Arete says, putting her phone away. "I really hate to leave but I promised Elijah I'd go out with him today and I'm already late. I am the worst fiancée ever."

"No, you're not," Whitney says. "He seems patient, he'll understand."

Elijah.

Patient.

Ha.

Ha.

Ha.

"But I feel like a bad BFF too for abandoning you *again*," Arete says.

"We've been talking for almost two hours now," Whitney says. "We *really* got carried away."

"Catch up later?" Arete asks.

"Sure thing," Whitney says. "See you at yoga!"

With that, Arete rushes out the door as if she really *is* late. The difference between her genuine personality and her performance is *seamless*. Remind me to never trust her again.

But now I finally have Whitney to myself, and we can have a normal date. Well, as normal as a make-up date can be.

I'm so lucky she's into socially inept, scrawny nerds. Arete and Elijah could frame me for murder (for real this time) and lock me in a basement for the rest of my life and I still wouldn't regret it; otherwise, I would have never met Whitney.

"So what do we do now?" she asks.

"Uh… I'm okay with just sitting here talking," I say.

"Okay. I'm kind of tired, though."

"Oh."

Well, at least I tried.

Friday, April 10, 2015

Manayunk, Pennsylvania

The magazine Elijah worked for has its headquarters located in a residential area of Manayunk. When I arrived at a shotgun house, I thought I had the wrong address until someone came out to greet me. It's apparently a common mistake.

The woman who's interviewing me right now is named Stacy Montgomery. She isn't the most polite individual I've ever met in my life and she gives the impression that she isn't all that into her job—at least, not as much as she's into herself. I can't put my finger on why. Maybe it's how she looks at herself every time we pass a reflective surface, and she chews her gum with her mouth open. She's also kind of creepy, to be honest. She's as thin as a skeleton, her hair is shaggy and white, and she tries to mask the stench of her cigarette habit with an overabundance of vanilla perfume. I'm able to put that aside to look like a shining star employee. For someone with such "spotty" work history, I'm not bad at convincing people that I'm the best man to hold down a stable job.

"How much do you know about CE Pulp?"

Rattling off company history is the part of a job interview I do best, so I relish the opportunity. "CE Pulp, AKA Common Era Pulp is a modern pulp magazine that was founded in 1997. It brought back the feel of the pulp magazines that died in the fifties, but with readable stories and prices adjusted for inflation. Due to financial circumstances, CE Pulp is no longer circulated, but is still accessible online and on e-readers."

"Well, you've obviously put a lot of research into our magazine." She smiles.

No, please, stop doing that. Your smile is terrifying, like... like...

That's when it hits me: she's the coworker Elijah was talking about. She's The Crypt Keeper!

I shiver. "Y-yeah."

"Who referred you?"

"Elijah Walker." I hold my breath.

"I don't know who that is," she says.

"Uh, I mean, Elijah Papadoppasomething."

"Ah, that Greek boy," she says. "He worked here about fifteen years ago... My, my, how time flies. Couldn't have been older than seventeen. He was a jumpy one."

"Elijah was... jumpy? Really?"

"Oh, yes. Every time I passed by, I saw him jump. Very skittish. He left when he turned eighteen, said he was joining the Navy or something." Stacy laughs a hearty, smoker's laugh. "I didn't think he'd last very long out there, but if he's still alive I guess that means he got discharged. How is he doing?"

Stacy has no idea she's Elijah's kryptonite, the Achilles' heel of Hollywood Perfect—both her and his retainer. I'm not sure what to say, but I manage to shoot something out.

"He's doing pretty well."

"I see," she says, but she doesn't believe me. "Anyway, I'd love to hire you on the spot, but I see you have a... disability. Can you type like that?"

I look at my arm, wrapped tightly in a cast. "I can in nine or ten weeks."

"Well, the job will still be here in three months," she says. "On your resume, you listed a few short stories and a book you published. If you have any new ones, you're welcome to send them in."

"Thank you," I say. "I do."

I don't actually, but by the time I'm able to work, I surely will.

After some idle chitchat that couldn't have ended sooner, we do the obligatory just-finished-a-job-interview handshake and part ways. It's a good thing I keep hand sanitizer in my pocket.

Saturday, April 11, 2015
Philadelphia, Pennsylvania

I'm not at all surprised that Arete is throwing a goth-themed engagement party. I watched her plan it, after all. But I'm utterly floored when she allows Elijah to add a few country elements at the last minute, and not because he likes them. Elijah's mother was a shameless fan of country music, unlike Arete who despises everything about it. Clashing decor won't bring Tansy Papadópo-something back, but Arete allows him to display a small number of his mother's old things, like cowboy hats and cacti. He doesn't exactly have an eye for design.

He was apparently planning this, because he paid to have a saguaro cactus shipped from Arizona. Dropping $2,500 on his mother's favorite species of cactus was almost as extravagant as it was weird, but at least he had the sense not to buy a fully grown saguaro. They can reach over 70 feet in height and weigh several tons, but his is only around six or seven feet tall. He wanted everyone to appreciate it, so he placed it on top of a chair so all of the guests could see it above the tables and "embrace the marvelous beauty of nature." Nerd.

Both Arete and I think it's an artistic sin, and that's saying something because I have no taste, but we don't dare protest. For all we know, he considers the cactus to be symbolic of his mother, and would snap if we told him to send it back to Arizona. I can envision him guilt tripping us over that for the rest of our lives.

That's no cactus sitting in that chair. That's my mother, whose consciousness is being channeled through wherever in the world she's hidden. This could be the closest you ever come to meeting my mother, and you want to send her back to the desert? Is your heart gilded in lead?

Actually, that's probably what it really is. It's his mother sitting in a chair watching. From what I hear, most of her stuff is sitting in a storage unit in case she comes back, but couldn't he have just brought a photo and lit a candle? Maybe Arete could cast one of her crazy goth spells and summon his mother from wherever she's hiding. Although, I privately think she's dead. I would never tell him that though. He said it himself, most missing persons are found fairly quickly. Tansy is either dead, or she really doesn't want to be found.

Guests start to arrive just after noon. I think it's a little early for an engagement party, especially since alcohol is being served, but Arete insisted that we should have a party outside during the day. She also didn't want to serve everyone dinner three hours into the party or make them wait, so she decided lunch time was best for everyone.

As for the seating arrangement, I'm seated next to Arete, Elijah, Tommy, and Keyon. As grateful as I am that Arete let me stay in my comfort zone, I'm crammed between a married couple and an "engaged" couple, which is on the awkward side. Then again, I spent the past few months as the third wheel. Being the fifth wheel until Whitney gets back from the bathroom can't be so different. With Tommy and Keyon running late and Whitney still in the restroom, Elijah, Arete, and I reminisce on things I thought I'd never be able to talk about without screaming internally.

"When you were drunk that one night, you insisted that we come up with nicknames for each other," I say to Arete. "But the weird part is, you never actually came up with nicknames yourself."

"I vaguely remember that," she says. "And you never came up with names for us either."

After a long pause during which I let my eyes wander, Elijah says, "You did."

"No I didn't," I say.

Elijah grins. "You just haven't told us what they were."

"No!" I'm not a good liar, and I don't even deserve points for trying.

"Come on," Arete says.

"I call you Boy Meets World and Pool Noodle," Elijah says. "It's hard to imagine your names being worse, or any more embarrassing than things you've already admitted. I mean, you already said you want to screw me."

"I did *not* say that." I sigh. "Mr. and Mrs. Satan. Bonnie and Clyde once, but that didn't stick."

Arete frowns. "Eh. Kind of boring, but I can live with that. You're a boring dude."

Ouch.

"Oh, so you don't have a special name for me?" Elijah says.

No amount of teasing will make me confess. "Nope."

"Liar. All the shit I've said to you, and the Snark Queen can't even shoot out one name? Besides, you hesitate for a split second half of the time you say my name."

I take a deep breath. Elijah is one perceptive bastard. He won't stop until I finally give in, and I'm too nervous to come up with a new one that's believable. "In my head, I call you Hollywood Perfect. Hollywood for short."

Elijah laughs so hard he cries; Arete blushes and giggles. When I laugh too, I realize that they're the truest friends I've ever had. We're a family—America's most dysfunctional family, but still a family. But I still can't survive the embarrassment without explaining how he got his name.

"Hollywood Perfect, you terrified me when we first met, and I was just trying to figure out what your 'fiancée' saw in you. Figured it must be the cheekbones."

Arete pinches Elijah's left cheek. "Sounds about right."

"You can call me Hollywood Perfect any time you want, Boy Meets World."

"I'll just go with Hollywood." I wipe a tear out of my eye. "So people won't think that we're in some sort of weird three-way relationship."

"And you don't have a name for me?" Arete asks.

"Nah," I say. "I go easier on girls."

Arete kicks her feet like a bored child and samples her wine, but immediately spits it out without swallowing. "Ew! This is plonk!"

"Good enough for me." Elijah takes her glass and drinks the wine she just spat out. Disgusting. "I plan on getting drunk this evening."

"Actually drunk?" Arete asks. "Like, not just buzzed? What kind of drunk are you?"

Elijah sets the glass down, and fills it up to the halfway mark. "Assuming I'm in a good mood, I get kind of hyper. Childish. I think everyone is my best friend."

Arete smiles even wider. "I think I'm marrying, slash married to the best man in the universe."

"Why, thank you, miss, slash missus."

"I'm looking forward to this one," I say. "Have all you want, I'm designated driver." Seeing Hollywood Perfect drunk sounds more fascinating than all Seven Wonders of the World combined. If not that, it will at least be amusing. His tolerance is incredibly high though, so he'll probably have to drink a whole bottle just to feel something. This is going to be an *awesome* day, I can feel it.

Tommy and Keyon seat themselves. "Sorry we're fashionably late," Tommy says.

"It's my fault," Keyon says. "You know how meticulous I get about parties and my appearance. I'm not as relaxed as Tommy."

By relaxed, Keyon means that Tommy is a slob. I barely know Keyon, as I've only seen him in passing for the most part. He's more stereotypically gay than his husband, complete with an acute sense of style and the so-called "gay lisp." I don't know much about fashion, but I notice the pastel pink suit is just the right shade for his cool, dark skin tone. I should expect no less from the man who decorated Elijah's old apartment by himself. Tommy, however, has the vibe of a typical Seth Rogen character. Opposites attract, I guess. I wouldn't look any better myself if Arete didn't force me to wear an Armani suit she picked out.

The "polyester nightmare" I wore to her sham wedding ended up in the trash, which reminded me again that Arete and Elijah aren't as perfect together as they think. I caught Elijah digging it out of the trash later; when I asked him about it, he complained about how wasteful rich people could be, and donated the "perfectly good suit" to the Suiting Warriors Foundation. I'll never understand why he's so insistent that he keep even the tiniest secrets from her. I will never ever *ever* do that to Whitney, I promise myself.

I look at my watch. "How long is she going to be in the bathroom?"

"You mean Whitney?" Arete asks, as if she doesn't already know. "Be patient, it's only been a few minutes. She's probably touching up her makeup."

A few minutes my ass. It has to have been at least an hour, maybe two. I check my watch; it's only been thirteen minutes.

Elijah leans over and whispers in my ear. "All you ever talk about anymore is Whitney."

"All you ever talk about is Arete," I snap.

Elijah doesn't get angry; he just shrugs. "Touché."

I spend the next two minutes making frequent glances toward the bathroom, waiting for her to come out. I can't help myself. When Whitney finally emerges, I wave so it will be slightly less creepy that I'm staring at her as she walks. It's hard not to. Her white sundress flatters her figure perfectly, and I love it when she wears her hair down. Would it be douchey for me to ask her to do it more often?

Whitney sits next to me, and Tommy and Keyon introduce themselves to her. I think Whitney changed something about her makeup while she was in the bathroom, but I can't quite place it.

Now that we we're all together, we have a chance to get to know each other better. As far as I know, this is Whitney's first time really getting to know Elijah, and she tolerates him for Arete's sake. She's also a little clammed up with Tommy and Keyon around, having never even heard of them before. I wish I had thought to warn her that there would be other people sitting at our table, but I'm new at this whole 'socialization' thing. Whitney is so comfortable around me that I forget how shy she is. Because of her, I have to overcome my fear of ordering food.

I stay at the table and keep Whitney in her comfort zone while everyone else is up and about. Medical school is time-consuming, so the two of us don't get to spend as much time together as we'd like. That doesn't stop Elijah from breaking away to interrupt us. Apparently, no amount of alcohol makes him ready to meet Arete's family. He secretly wishes they had stayed in Australia.

"Care to dance with me, Pool Noodle?" Elijah holds out his hand.

"I don't dance."

He looks over his shoulder. "We have to dance, and we have to do it now!"

"I *can't* dance."

"Everyone can dance when they're drunk," he says.

"I'm not drunk. You are."

Elijah grabs my arm anyway and drags me away from my girlfriend.

"You have to learn if you ever want to impress a woman," he says. "Don't you want to impress Whitney?"

Drunk men aren't the best tutors, but he isn't going to stop asking until I agree. Both of us suck for different reasons; I have two left feet and a cast on my right arm, and Elijah's world is blurring together.

"We're getting kind of close to the beams, and that huge cactus," I say. "Maybe we should move to the— Hollywood, no!"

Elijah loses footing and falls backward in what feels like slow motion. I try to catch him, and if I had two available hands, I might have succeeded. Instead, he hits the back of the chair, toppling the saguaro cactus over. I extend my right hand, but there's nothing I can do.

Antonis, who is seated behind the cactus, whips around and cries out in fear. The old man can't get out of his seat in time to escape the 600 pound cactus. Within seconds, it collides into his face, knocks him over, and crushes him.

Elijah rushes to his side and pushes the cactus off of him using a nearby chair, but it's in vain. By the time he manages to move the cactus, hundreds of needles have pierced Antonis' skin and his bones have been crushed. Elijah looks away and buries his face in his palms. Antonis Konstantinou is officially roadkill.

The collective screams and gasps of the people around me crowd my ears, but I'm too stunned to make a single sound myself. I can't process that this is happening right now. Good thing kids were banned from the guest list.

First an icicle, and now a cactus? Accident or not, Elijah is responsible for some increasingly creative deaths. Or is this one on karma? I feel better calling it karma, because I'm no less guilty than Elijah. I mean, I dropped my friend on a cactus. I'm such a bad dancer that I dropped my friend on a cactus. I watch Antonis' wife kneel by his side and wail, and feel like a jerk for getting lost in thought, wondering if Elijah could find a way to kill a man with a rubber chicken. I find it hard to feel sorry for Antonis after all he's done, but there are people who loved him. I look away and search the crowd for Arete, wondering what her reaction will be.

On the one hand, Antonis tried to have her murdered so he could steal her inheritance. On the other hand, he was still her uncle. And it's also safe to say that her engagement party will go down in history for all the wrong reasons. Elijah runs in an inefficient stagger to comfort Arete; I'm too far away to hear what they're saying, but whatever it spurs Arete to shove past him and run to the restroom. Whitney catches up with her. Elijah nonverbally admits defeat and leans against the bar.

When it really hits me what's going on, being six feet away from a body isn't enough distance for my taste, so I join Elijah. And honestly, what kind of friend would I be if I didn't?

"Are you okay, man?" I ask.

"No," he says. "Arete is *never* going to forgive me for this one."

"I'm sure she'll realize it was an accident."

Elijah laughs, not out of humor but as a social defense. "No, she's going to hate me forever." He calls the bartender's attention. "I'd like a bottle of zinfandel."

The bartender tears her eyes away from the misfortune and uncorks a fresh bottle of wine. I try to warn

Elijah that drinking like an animal was what got him into this mess, but when the bartender takes a glass off the shelf, Elijah says, "No, I meant the whole bottle. I need to dull the pain."

I'm not sure if he's talking about the emotional pain, or the cactus needles sticking out of his back. I shudder. The bartender doesn't question his poor life choices; she uncorks a zinfandel and passes it to him. "Anything else?"

"Yeah," Elijah says. "While I'm sitting on this stool, how about a noose?"

"Water!" I say. "He'll take water."

Elijah clenches his eyes shut and takes a long gulp of wine. Depressing. By the time some on-duty cops arrive ten minutes later, he's finished off the entire bottle and is lying on the bar while I pick cactus needles out of his back. I'm about halfway done when I'm forced to turn him over to the police. He resists arrest at first, telling them he wants another bottle before he gets taken away, but they don't humor him.

*

The city jail isn't where I want to be on a Saturday night, but we don't have much of a choice. Without hesitation, Arete marches to the front desk and digs through her purse. I brace myself before joining her because just being here gives me hives. All of the law-breaking I've been involved in over the past couple of months swirls around in my head, and I've always been paranoid that policemen are mind readers. I'm still waiting to be reprimanded for the pencil I stole off my teacher's desk in third grade.

"I'm here to pick up my fiancé," Arete says. Her eyes are puffy and her black eye makeup is running down her cheeks. The rest of it is on her knuckles. "His name is Elijah. Elijah Walker; I think he used to work at this station."

"Yes, we all know Elijah," says the stressed secretary. "And the entire station is talking about it, believe me."

"Cut the crap," Arete says, handing her a credit card. "We need to take him home. Now."

"Okay. That will be $25,000."

Arete's jaw drops. "$25,000? That is a *ridiculous* bail for a cactus!"

"Miss Konstantinou, you're not bailing out a cactus, you're bailing out a grown ass man."

"You *know* what I meant." Arete puts her hands on her hips and leans in. "Under what grounds is $25,000 an appropriate bail?"

"You're lucky we're letting him out. He's still being charged with involuntary manslaughter... You didn't know?" The secretary returns Arete's credit card and calls for them to bring out Elijah. "Your pet idiot will be out in a second."

"No, he did not tell me *anything*!" Arete shouts, jerking her card out of the woman's hand. "He just said he was in jail and to bring my credit card. And you have *no right* to call him an idiot!"

"Hey. Don't take it out on me." The secretary shrugs. "No one here thinks the charges will hold up, but he has a bitter widow who won't make it easy. Your fiancé knowingly placed the cactus on an unstable chair and... 'danced' into it. We love him, you know we do, but it was irresponsible."

Arete's face contorts. I never want to see her like that again, so I try to change the subject. "So what happened to that cactus anyway?"

Arete scowls. "*William,*" she says in a tone I thought only Kristi could pull off. "Now is *not* the time."

"You're not going to put Jose to sleep, are you?"

She glares at me. "You named it?"

I was trying to make her feel better, but I made a mistake by assuming the usual jokes would help alleviate the situation. I was never much for common sense. Or women. Or socialization period.

I hear a familiar, slurring voice behind me. "It's still in evidence."

I turn around and see Elijah staggering over, disheveled. His *TRESemmé oh la la!* hair looks like the coat of a sewage-dwelling rodent, and only one small corner his dress shirt is tucked in. He left his jacket behind; I found it on the bar counter and left it in the car. As for his missing left shoe, that's a mystery.

"Well, former officer," the secretary says, taking a small box of confiscated items out of the desk drawer. It contains the expected items like his wallet, knife, and phone, but also his silk tie, belt, dental floss, mouth wash, and a single shoestring. "You're very lucky to have a rich, white girl who's willing to drop all that money on you. God knows I wouldn't." Elijah reaches out for his belongings, but I'm glad when she passes them to me instead. Honestly, the way he was talking at the bar, I've been thinking about checking him into a mental hospital.

"Yeah." Elijah scratches his head. "She's pretty special." He turns to face her. "Thanks, baby!" He holds out his arms and sloppily attempts to hug Arete. His beloved wife/fiancée/stepsister responds by slapping him on the face.

"You. Are. DRUNK!"

"Oww... That stings," Elijah slurs, rubbing his cheek. I think it's pretty awful that a woman can slap a man who isn't in the condition to defend himself and get away with it in a police station of all places. But he did just kill her uncle at their engagement party, so I kind of get it.

"You owe William a thanks, too," she says. "If he hadn't sworn off alcohol forever, *no one* would be here to pick you up. You would be spending the night in jail!"

Elijah nods slowly. "With the people I arrested..."

"Yes!" Arete makes air quotes. "With the people you arrested!"

"So, what now?" I asked the officer who escorted him out of his holding cell. She was stout, but strong-looking woman who wore her hair in a short afro. She introduces herself as Chauntal.

"You can keep him for the weekend, but he needs to be at the courthouse first thing Monday morning for his official arraignment. You had better get him cleaned up... If that's possible." Chauntal shakes her head and put her fingertips to her forehead out of secondhand embarrassment. Elijah is no longer officer Walker, the local hero who saved a boy's life and rescued two people from a house fire. He's *that* guy, the drunkard who accidentally killed his in-law with a cactus. Public opinion is so fickle.

I look over my shoulder and watch as Arete rips her fiancé a new asshole—figuratively, of course, though I'm sure she'd kill him if she were anywhere else in the world. He knows it, too. Misery is written across his face; I have a feeling he won't be able to rely on her for a while.

"Okay. I'll go with him."

The officer sighs. "I've never seen him drunk before. Buzzed, but not flat out drunk. How many did he have?"

"He was drinking all night, but after the whole dancing cactus fiasco, he downed an entire 25 ounce bottle of wine in less than five minutes."

Dancing cactus fiasco? Is that really the best I can do? What kind of writer am I supposed to be again?

"That's... Impressive," she says. "How is he still alive?"

I glance at Elijah. He's hanging on Arete like a child and begging for her forgiveness and unconditional love, but she doesn't want to look at him. "No idea," I say. "He has the tolerance of an elephant."

She nods; this isn't surprising to her.

"So..." I say, "What happens to Elijah if he's convicted of involuntary manslaughter?"

"It's a first degree misdemeanor," Chauntal says. "Five years is the absolute highest, but I don't think he'll get that long. He served in the military and was with us for four or five years. Not to mention that kid whose life he saved. They'll go easy on him."

"Does it matter that he was drunk?" I ask.

"In this state? No."

"I'm just so confused about this," I say. "How is tipping a cactus over involuntary manslaughter?"

"I know it sounds stupid, but that cactus shouldn't have been placed there. He placed a seven-foot-tall cactus weighing several hundred pounds on an unstable platform right next to an old man's seat. The prosecution is going to argue reckless behavior if they have any sense at all."

"What's his best bet?"

"Honestly?" Chauntal says. "He'd better suck up to his rich girlfriend and get one hell of a lawyer. Stick to arguing his good character and community standing as often as possible, instead of doing some sort of ridiculous *Drop Dead Diva* ploy."

"I'll be sure to tell him that."

"And I hope he listens for once," she says. It makes me wonder what other messes they've had to clean up for him.

Monday, April 13, 2015

There's nothing visually spectacular about the courtroom if you ask me, but I doubt courtrooms are designed to be beautiful and inviting. They're designed so that the judge can be suspended above everyone else, enabling them to destroy people with their condescending gaze. Today's judge is Jihyun Park. What she lacks in height, she makes up for with a stolid tone and a grouchy poker face. When I first saw her out the corner of my eye, I thought she was Sally Field, leaving me a little disappointed.

I came with Elijah because I knew Arete wouldn't be here to support him, but I'm pretty embarrassed that he showed up buzzed. This is going to be a disaster.

Judge Park stares at the empty seat next to Elijah. "Mr. Walker, where is your lawyer?"

Elijah stands up. "I will be represented by Elijah Walker today."

The judge leans over on her podium. Her glasses slide down the bridge of her nose. "You can't represent yourself."

"Your Honor, the law states that I can do pro se legal representation."

"What I meant to say is, *you* can't represent yourself," she says. "You've only completed one semester of law school, you were *disgraceful* in mock trial, you're not half as charming as you think you are, and you will *not* win."

She tries too hard to act stern, which makes me think she's masking sympathy. I don't suppose judges are allowed to have feelings, though it appears she's already familiar with Elijah but doesn't want to let on that she's biased. She at least knows about his apparently disgraceful mock trial performance, so either his circle of acquaintances runs deep, or it was so bad that people were talking about it at the water cooler.

"I have made my decision," Elijah says. "I will be defending myself."

She frowns and shuffles some papers around. "Very well."

Elijah Walker is, without a doubt, the dumbest smart person I have ever met in my entire life. He can pretend to be a confident law whiz all he wants, but I know his claim of "I have Philadelphia on my side" is his way of saying "I spent all of my personal assets on a 14 karat engagement ring, but marrying Arete made me too rich on paper to be appointed a lawyer, and I don't want to ask my so-called 'fiancée' for money." His only shot now is a plea deal, and if he's lucky he might get six months in jail and community service.

"Elijah Walker, you have been charged with involuntary manslaughter," she says. "Do you waive the formal reading of the information and how do you wish to plea?"

"I plead not guilty, your honor."

"And do you want to waive the formal reading of the information," she repeats.

He hesitates. "The..."

"Do you want me to read the charges against you out loud?" she asks, enunciating each word slowly.

"Uh... no. That isn't necessary."

The judge shakes her head. "I have some questions about a few inconsistencies." She shuffles papers around. "First, I'm going to ask you why you threw an engagement party to begin with."

Elijah's anxiety peaks. "Because I got engaged."

"Yes," the judge says. "But records show, despite what you've been telling everyone, you are already married to Arete Konstantinou."

"That was a speed wedding," Elijah says. "No one takes those seriously. We were drunk, we had fun."

I was concerned he would shoot himself in the foot by keeping up with that ridiculous lie detector game in court, and it looks like I had a good reason to be. He's just carefully constructing more lies by omission. But the judge jumped in with both feet, and even the best liar would have a hard time keeping this from going to trial without help. Unfortunately, Elijah isn't entirely comfortable with his wording and the judge sees right through it.

"It's still relevant," Judge Park says. "Need I remind you that you are under oath?"

"It was... convenient for us to get married," he says. "For money reasons."

"Money reasons?" She scoffs at the ridiculous wording. "And what are these 'money reasons?'"

"You see. It's that her engagement ring cost most of my inheritance," he says. "And she knew that my inheritance was all I was living off of because I'm in school."

"I see," Judge Park says. "And can you explain why you brought a cactus to an engagement party?"

"Well. Your honor, I..." Elijah pauses. "I want a lawyer."

"Well, I suppose there's no point in asking about your income. Now that you've married into the richest family in Philadelphia, affording one should be no problem for you." The judge strikes the sounding block with her gavel. "I will grant you continuance for one week to find a lawyer. We will resume next Monday. Mr. Walker, I implore you. Get a *real* lawyer."

"What happens if my wife says no?" Elijah asks. "Is there any way I can get one appointed to me?"

"A word of advice," she says. "*Beg.*"

*

I sit in the dining room with Arete and discuss the trial.

"So you're telling me," she says, "that he tried to represent *himself* because he was too ashamed to ask me for money?"

"Yep."

She puts her elbows on the table, buries her face in her hands, and groans. "I am going to *kill* him!"

While I wouldn't blame her at this point, after everything I've seen in the past couple of months, I'm worried she's serious.

"Who *does* that?" she asks. "I thought he was smart! Please tell me he's changed his mind!"

"He has," I say, "but only after the judge questioned his honesty. They found out about your secret Las Vegas speed wedding." She goes unusually quiet, which concerns me. "Are you okay?"

"No," she says. "I married an idiot."

At the worst moment possible, Elijah walks into the room with a stack of envelopes and papers. "I brought in the mail."

"Anything else you brought?" Arete asks. "Like an apology?"

Elijah sets the stack of mail on the table. "Yes." He bows down on one knee and takes Arete's hand. "Kit Kat, love of my life, please forgive me for ruining our engagement party, killing your uncle, and appearing on the front page of The Philly Pop Sunday."

"WHAT?" She snatches her hand away.

Elijah pushes a stack of junk mail and bills aside and shows her the local tabloid paper. The headline reads "*LOCAL HERO ARRESTED AT ENGAGEMENT PARTY FOR KILLING MAN WITH GIANT CACTUS.*"

Arete turns her head. "I can't even look at you right now."

"The picture isn't that bad," he says, holding it in front of her face. "My hair looks great, and you can't tell that I was drunk."

"You are being taken away in *handcuffs*!" Arete says.

I take the tabloid and read the article aloud.

"It feels like only yesterday that Elijah Walker was Philadelphia's favorite Marine. After taking a bullet for an innocent nine-year-old boy and later rescuing two people from a burning building, he seemed cemented as a local hero. As of March 15th, he has been engaged to Arete Konstantinou, the woman whose life he saved from the roaring house fire.

"This heartwarming love story took a tragic turn of events on April 11th at the couple's engagement party, when he tripped and knocked over a giant cactus, which then crushed his fiancée's uncle. Witnesses say Walker tried to save the man from his prickly fate, but it was too late. Walker has since been dubbed The Cactus Guy by the media.

"'The f█cking idiot was drunk dancing with his weird friend, and he knocked over this ten-thousand pound cactus,' states an anonymous witness. 'I know it was an accident and I almost feel bad for him, but it was just so irresponsible. Whose idea was it to bring a real cactus?'

"We don't have a quote from Walker himself, but he has taken to Twitter to describe his ordeal. 'worrst nit of mh lifef imm ani diot,' he tweeted to his remaining 4,096 followers, presumably after his fiancée bailed him out of jail. He is now over 1,300 followers poorer, but we have high hopes that he'll make a comeback soon and give us his side of the story. █

"I can't believe it," I say.

Arete snorts. "I know, right?"

I set the paper on the table. "You used to have over five-thousand twitter followers? I only have twelve, and I don't even know if they're real people."

Whether a local hero dating Insta-girl Battybabyx or a drunken idiot, I strongly doubt that he would be anywhere near this popular if he wasn't so hot.

Elijah checks his phone. "Cool, I have 17,133 now from notoriety points. I was never this popular back when people actually liked me. I think if I win over the media, I can win this case."

"We have a few days until the arraignment continues," I say. "You could go to the local news and give them your story."

"That's a good idea." Arete says. "So good, in fact, that I'm going to speed divorce you in Reno if you don't do it. I'm tired of people asking me if I'm still engaged to 'the cactus guy.' People keep harassing me in my Instagram comments and I can't take it anymore!"

"I'll help." Elijah swipes the screen of his smart phone and starts typing.

"What are you doing?" she asks.

"I'm tweeting. How does this sound: *Please stop harassing my fiancée. None of this is her fault, and I'll answer your questions soon.*"

"Whatever," Arete says. "You can't make anything worse than it already is."

Elijah leans over next to Arete and holds the phone in front of their faces. I see a flash.

"Delete that!" Arete says. "Delete that picture right now!"

"I'm trying—"

"Then stop!" she says. "Just stop trying. Social media isn't good enough. They made you a *meme*!"

"I know," he says. "It doesn't really bother me; it's a just punishment. Besides, some of them are pretty funny. Like this one."

He scrolls through his gallery and shows her a still from Lord of the Rings, the scene in which Boromir says, "One does not simply walk into Mordor." Elijah's face is photoshopped over his, and it's captioned, "One does not simply walk into a cactus."

By saying, "It doesn't really bother me," I think he's hiding from Arete the fact that he enjoys it in a strange, masochistic way. Otherwise he wouldn't have derogatory memes of himself saved to his phone. Also, he was signing autographs when we were approached in a convenience store. He may have her fooled, but not me. He's getting some sort of high off this notoriety.

Arete rolls her eyes. "Florence Cho owes me a favor, maybe she can fit you in last minute before your makeup arraignment."

"Florence Cho?" he asks. "From that garbage talk show?"

Arete ignores him and scrolls through her contact list as she leaves the room.

Friday, April 17, 2015

It's rainy in Philadelphia, with a temperature of 61°
Fahrenheit. Not many people like a rainy day, but I suppose it's
fitting for a funeral. The Konstantinous are members of the
Greek Orthodox Church, which is something that I didn't know
existed until today. The funeral is being held at the St. George
Greek Orthodox Cathedral, where Antonis worshiped every
Sunday. It's hard to imagine Antonis as a churchgoer, but you
learn all sorts of things about a man at his funeral.

After the drama my "polyester nightmare" caused, I
didn't resist Arete's urgent pleas that I go shopping with her
again and pick out a suit *again*. That's how I ended up in some
designer brand today. As if this funeral wasn't awkward
enough already, I have to wear a costume. I envy the black veil
that hangs off the front of Arete's hat. Maybe if I had one of
those, I could hide the fact that I don't care. At all.

Arete is the reverse, putting on her best effort to
pretend she's not that torn up over it. Her acting talents have
their limits. If she didn't care, she wouldn't have bought
another black dress just for this funeral. She would have found
something in the back of one of her several walk-in closets full
of almost nothing but black, or worn one of the few red
dresses she owns.

Elijah decided it would be better if he stayed at home;
his highly transparent excuse was a fictional ear infection. Not
that the high and mighty Elijah would lie, of course, so he

asked me to do it for him. I suggested that a better excuse would be that he has to stay behind and pack for New York, since we're flying there tonight. He insisted on going with the ear infection story because Arete wanted our appearance on the Florence Cho Show tomorrow evening to be a surprise. Otherwise, Antonis' widow might prepare for it and cause a scene. That sounded reasonable, but I can't help but wonder if he has some other reason for wanting to project his absence as shameful.

I hold the umbrella over our heads as Arete leads me to the cathedral. When we make it to the top of the steps, I let her inside before closing the umbrella, splashing rain droplets all over myself. After hanging it on the rack, I realize I already lost track of Arete. I look around. The few people I see, I recognize from the engagement party, and now I'm paying for the fact that I ignored them all. Because of that, I'm stuck in a foreign church, wearing a strange suit, and surrounded by mourning strangers.

We arrive a bit early, much to my displeasure. To be fair, Arete regrets her decision the moment she spots a tall woman with flawless skin and the body of a supermodel. Arete groans.

"Who's that?" I ask.

"That's Tonia Pratt, Antonis' eldest daughter. She's about a year younger than me, and every time I see her I want to chunder."

"Chunder?"

She rolls her eyes. "Vomit. It means vomit."

"Oh. Well, I think you're prettier than her."

My compliment has no effect on Arete. "Tell that to the fact that she got married first. To a rugby player."

"Why does that matter?" I ask. "You're married now too."

"Yeah, I got speed married in Vegas so I wouldn't be murdered." She has a point, but I wasn't going to bring that up.

"*But* your husband is more attractive than hers," I say.

"What, you mean that guy with a face like a busted arsehole?" Arete asks, pointing at the man standing next to her. "That's her second cousin on her mother's side. She's married to the bloke over there in the corner." She moves her pointed finger and settles on a man with sandy blond hair. He's trying to drink out of a water fountain, but keeps getting the water on his nose. "Elijah may be way hotter, but her husband isn't bad looking. And newspapers aren't calling *him* 'the cactus guy.' Oh, and he's independently rich."

"That doesn't mean she's better than you," I say. "The media will find someone else to make fun of soon, I'm sure. Maybe Lady Gaga and Madonna will fight again, or a Kardashian could do... anything at all."

Tonia spots Arete and waves. Arete waves back with false cheer, and Tonia saunters over.

"Oh, great," Arete says. "She saw me."

"Hello, Arete!" Tonia hugs her, but Arete barely wraps her arms around her. Tonia pulls back and grins. "Long time no see!"

Ew. She's forcing a fake British accent, and she's clearly trying too hard. She's a stereotypical mean girl, really, right down to the blond hair and... Are those real? Damn, this is a funeral; how much cleavage do you need? She's not a Barbie doll white chick, though; she's white-passing Hispanic, like me, except I'm not trying to look white. And she's tall. Really, *really* tall. Taller than Arete.

"Are you her new fiancé?" Tonia offers me her hand, but I don't take it.

"No," Arete says before I can answer. "You'd know that if you came to my engagement party."

"Sorry," she says. "I've been living in London, and then I had that photoshoot in LA. Oh, guess what—I might be the next Covergirl! Isn't that exciting?"

"Yeah," Arete says, monotone. "That's exciting."

"I've never been happier! For my career, I mean. Not my father." I haven't been to many funerals in my lifetime, but something about this conversation gives me the impression that Tonia is sociopath. She's smiling with her mouth but not her eyes, as she has been through most of this conversation. The only times she looks happy are the times when Arete looks vulnerable. "So, what have you been up to?" she asks Arete. "How's your acting career?"

"Oh, it's going great," Arete says.

"Really? I heard you were suspended."

Arete pouts. "So, what are you doing, other than getting your arse photographed in fugly clothes and calling yourself an artist?"

"I started singing," Tonia says, ignoring her cousin's obvious shade. "It was only a month ago, but my coach says I'm a natural. You should join me. It would look great on your resume. Maybe if you work hard enough, you'll get a small role in a musical someday."

I'm getting tired of listening to Tonia brag. I say a short prayer for Arete to end it soon.

"I can already sing," Arete says.

"Really?" Tonia asks.

"Of course. I'm g-great at singing."

"Oh really?" Tonia says. "I've never heard you sing before. Want to sing with me tonight? I'm singing my father's favorite song as he's being buried. You could be the backup vocalist."

"I can't right now, sorry. I have... an ear infection." Arete fake coughs.

"That sucks," Tonia says with false disappointment. "We might not know the same songs though, since you still haven't grown out of your goth phase. I can't stop singing along to Taylor Swift lately, for some reason. What about you?"

"You're right, there's no way we'd have anything in common," Arete says. "I sing songs like... *Manic Depression* by Emilie Autumn... and *Toccata and Fugue in D Minor*."

I whisper in her ear. "None of those songs have lyrics, Mrs. Elijah Walker."

Arete whispers back. "Shut up! She always sees right through me."

What Arete won't admit to was singing along to *Shake it Off* in the Lyft on the way here. Arete can't exactly carry a tune, but she had enough fun to momentarily forget her troubles. That's what counts in times like these.

"Well, let me know how that works for you," Tonia says. "I hope your 'ear infection' clears up."

"Thanks."

"Tell Cactus Guy I said hi," Tonia says as she whips around and trots off.

Arete inhales sharply and clenches her fists.

"It'll be okay," I say. "People like her always get what's coming to them."

Arete grabs my hand and starts marching toward the door. "We're leaving."

I grab her arm to stall her escape. "Wait! That's what she wants."

Arete stops and turns around. "Don't you get it? Everyone here thinks I'm a bloody moron!"

She's wrong. There is one person here who doesn't think she's a bloody moron; it's not me though. A young man with shaggy hair and nerdy glasses is coming to Arete's side. The keys attached to his belt loop jingle as he walks, and I noticed an Avenged Sevenfold key chain; whoever he is, he didn't look like he fit in with the other attendees.

"Not everybody," he says with sincerity. He puts his hand on her shoulder.

"Thanks, Mikhail," Arete says. She looks down and rubs her eyes raw. Her eye makeup is all over her hand again. "But I see the way everyone looks at me."

"My sister's a bitch," Mikhail says. "She always has been. If it makes you feel any better, her marriage is falling apart and the Covergirl story she keeps telling everyone is faker than her boobs."

Arete is too choked up to laugh, but she makes an odd noise that comes close. "Should've known... But at least *she's* not married to 'the Cactus Guy.'"

Mikhail shrugs and sticks his hands in his pockets. "I was there, I know it was an accident." He lowers his voice. "Well, that and karma." He's trying to hide his frustration, not with Arete or Elijah, but with the situation. He's doing a strangely good job at it considering the circumstances. He can't be much older than eighteen.

Arete hugs him. "Condolences. I'm very sorry."

"It's not like we were that close." Mikhail sighs and prepares to vent. "It hasn't even fully processed in my mind yet. It's just... our last conversation, I was telling him off for trying to get me to quit the band and convince you to 'hand over KE.' I told him I hated him. Those were my last words to him, I told my father I *hated* him, and now I'm stuck with KE after all. I'm not ready for that power, but it looks like I don't have a choice now."

"I'm sorry," Arete says. "I don't want it either, but it looks like we have to appoint a new CEO for a while."

"We'll talk about that later. I'll testify on Elijah's behalf," Mikhail says. "When's the trial?"

"He hasn't even had his arraignment yet," Arete says. "And wouldn't that make your mum mad?"

Mikhail looks over his shoulder at his sobbing mother. She looks a lot like Tonia, making it easy to piece the family tree together. Antonis married a Mexican woman and had at least two kids whom I have just now met. It's hard to believe Mikhail and Tonia are related at all.

Holy shit. I can't believe it took this long for it to hit me, but Elijah is related to these people. Mikhail has Elijah's strong jawline and cleft chin. Tonia has Elijah's aquiline nose and full, defined lips. How is it that no one is seeing it? Is it just because they aren't looking for it? Shouldn't Antonis' widow know? Arete and Tonia are around the same age. It's a pretty tight time window, but if she met him even once, surely she'd remember him. He has a different name now, but the family resemblance is so strong that it shouldn't matter. That's a mystery for another day, though. Today is about watching other people grieve and pretending to care.

"She's no better than Tonia," Mikhail says. "She hated Dad, she's mad about the will. Dad left the house to me, so I could honestly kick her out if I wanted to."

"But what about everyone else?" she asks.

Mikhail is silent.

"Well?"

Mikhail adjusts his glasses. "They don't blame him. But they still call him the cactus guy behind your back."

"I *knew* it." Arete covers her eyes. "I have to change my name, shop at Hollister, dye my hair some mousy color, and move back to Oz!"

"Please don't do that," Mikhail says. "You're my only normal relative. You just need a vacation."

"I'm going to be sick."

He pats her on the back. "You'll be okay."

"Mikhail," I say, "I think she's actually sick."

"I've got to go to the dunny!" Arete yells as she runs to the restroom, as quickly as she can in heels.

Mikhail and I exchange awkward glances. "Nice to meet you?" I say like it's a question.

"You too." He puts his hands in his pockets and stares in Arete's general direction. "So... Thanks for coming."

"You're welcome."

"She should be okay," Mikhail says, immediately steering the conversation clear away from his father. "If I had her problems, I'd stress-barf too. Like, I was there when it all happened. I know it was an accident, but everyone acts like it was her fault somehow. Not even his, but *hers*."

"Her fault?"

"Yeah," he says. "Like he's a plague she brought in on them. Thankfully, my family is as small as it is unbearable."

I pull my vibrating phone out of my pocket. It's a text from Whitney.

Sorry I can't be there. We'll hang later, ok?

"Girlfriend?" Mikhail asks.

"Yep," I say. My smile must have given it away. "Arete introduced us." I look back in Arete's direction. "She says she wants to go back home. I mean the house in Philly. Should we?"

"She went to the wake yesterday," Mikhail says. "I don't blame her for not wanting to stay and get stared at by all these people who don't even know her. It'll mostly be business partners from here on out; not many people are left on our side of the family. Really, I'm the only friend she has here."

"Really?" I ask.

"Yeah. Sure, she's a sociable girl, albeit a bit of a basket case. Making casual friends is one thing, but here, she's alone. I don't want to say this in front of her, but she's right. Everyone thinks of her as the cactus guy's fiancée, and strangers keep asking me if she's still engaged to him."

"Ouch..." I want to say that this is a *prickly* situation, but telling bad puns to someone at their father's funeral isn't the greatest idea.

Mikhail nods. "I've been telling them that they *needle* to back off." He forcibly frowns at his joke, probably ashamed of smiling at a funeral. "Not everyone gets it."

"Oh my god, I was going to say that it was a *prickly* situation!"

He high-fives me. "It's nice to meet someone who's not talking to me like they have to walk on eggshells."

"And it's nice to meet someone rational."

Mikhail's mother comes up behind him and grabs his arm, scaring him. "God, Mom, what the hell?"

"I need to talk to you," she says. "Now."

"Whatever," Mikhail says. As he's being dragged away by the hem of his collar, he waves at me. "You can go on and take Arete home. I'll *cact-us* with you later!"

I wave goodbye. "Have a *spine* day!"

"Good one!"

Saturday, April 18, 2015
New York City, New York

I don't know how Arete did it, but she managed to get Elijah an appearance on the Florence Cho Show in a matter of days. Arete went with him for feigned moral support, but I decided to stay in the germ-saturated, two-bed hotel room and watch them embarrass themselves on live television instead. I disinfect the remote and press the power button. I almost forgot how much I hated germs.

I was never a big fan of Florence Cho; she's headstrong, which is fine, but she has the tendency to start tabloid-worthy trouble off screen. Still, Elijah Walker was barely a somebody before gaining international infamy, so I'm both amazed and grateful that she's giving him the opportunity to defend himself publicly. At the same time, he wouldn't be on there to begin with if she wasn't there to leech off of his recent news presence. Odd stories attract a lot of attention, especially when you combine death, alcohol, and cacti. If comment sections are any indication, most of the world just wants to make fun of him, while the rest want to sleep with him *and* make fun of him. I haven't seen a single comment in his defense.

Arete handed me a ticket for a seat in the third row, (Someone bailed when they heard about the last-minute guest change) but I turned it down so I wouldn't have to deal with the crowd. The show is filmed on a large, circular platform with contemporary couches. Florence's chair looks like a throne in comparison, which suits her overbearing personality. The wall behind the studio has fake, potted palm trees lined up along the windows, which supposedly overlook the night skyline of New York City. The windows are actually an illusion. I know this for sure now, because it's only 5:59 PM.

The second six o'clock strikes, Florence struts onto the stage in her stilettos and waves to the audience like a beauty queen. She sits down upon her throne and crosses her ankles, first rattling on about trivial things nobody cares about. Come on, woman. No one is here to listen to you ramble about your new perfume line.

After her overlong introduction, she welcomes Elijah to the show. The costume department apparently wasn't satisfied with what Elijah was wearing when he left the hotel room. His usual business casual isn't sensational enough for TV. He comes out looking like the cover of a romance novel.

Hollywood Perfect, where the hell is your shirt? An open vest is not a shirt. Does that even count as a vest?

When the audience cheers and whistles, I realize he won't have to say anything at all to win over the straight girls. I envy him until I remember why he's there. This isn't positive attention; this is the punishment of a woman scorned.

Florence, in her usual shameless banter, teases the audience by asking Elijah if he was ever an underwear model. The top left corner of the screen displays an appropriate hashtag (#WalkerOnFlorence) in hopes that viewers will trend it. I hate to admit it, but Florence Cho is about to save him years of jail time and increase her falling ratings by exploiting his abs and notoriety.

"So, tell us, are you still off the market?" Florence laughs playfully and leans forward, showing off her bust. I admit it's hard not to stare, and I hate myself for it. She's dressed to kill, as usual.

"Completely off the market," Elijah says. "Arete and I never fight. Ever since the fire, we've been inseparable."

I choke on my Sierra Mist. Arete and I had a bet on whether or not he would detach himself from his internal lie detector for this performance. The loser has to share the second bed with Hollywood Perfect. That's me. I'm the loser. Damn you, Arete, for cutting him off from his allowance and making him pay the airfare and room fees. Can't you just cut him one break? Is it not enough for the man to humiliate himself on national television for you? You can't even pay his way, and you drag me along anyway? Fuck you. I'd rather sleep on the floor.

I had already shared the bed with him voluntarily last night and it was the most awkward experience of my short life. He sleeps in the yearner position and I was kept up all night wondering if he'd roll over and put his arms around me in his sleep like he does Arete. That never happened, but it kept me confined to the very edge of the bed to give him space. I don't want to go through that again.

"It's wonderful to hear you're still close with your fiancée," Florence says. "To what do you owe your sudden popularity?"

"I'm an internet meme. I wouldn't exactly call that popularity. Well, not until you stuck me in this outfit, anyway." The audience laughs, claps, and whistles. "I went from local hero to 'Cactus Guy meme' for a reason. I saved a few lives only to kill one of my in-laws with a cactus. It's embarrassing to even show my face in public."

No. No, Elijah. *Arete* is the one who hangs her head in shame and only leaves the house to go to class. We went to the bookstore Wednesday, and you let someone pose for a photo with you. *You* love this. *You* think it's hilarious because you hate yourself, and *she* thinks it's horrible because she loves you. Stop lying; it's hurting my brain.

"I see you're not beating around the bush with this topic," Florence says. "Is that you saying you take responsibility?"

"I take full responsibility for my actions. I was drinking like a frat boy at my own engagement party because I was nervous about meeting her family. I'm lucky Arete forgave me."

It's both impressive and scary how easily Elijah can manipulate the public. I didn't expect him to do this well.

"But you did try to save her uncle, right?"

"Please call him Antonis." Elijah bows his head for a brief moment. "He was a real man with a name and dreams."

Gag.

"Antonis," Florence says. "I apologize."

"Yes, I did try to save Antonis. But I just wasn't good enough. I was afraid of getting cactus needles stuck in my hands, so I didn't catch the cactus as it fell, or immediately try to roll it off of him. I moved it indirectly with a chair. By then... it was too late."

A single tear comes from his guy cry, and it's a crocodile tear. Leave it to Hollywood Perfect to make crying look masculine. Granted, this is all fake. Arete told me when he cries, he sobs like a thirteen-year-old girl whose crush kissed her best friend at her birthday party.

Elijah doesn't wipe his crocodile tear away. "I was a coward. I deserve no credit."

"A lot of people would disagree," Florence says.

"I ran through fire. I've taken bullets. I even disarmed a bomb once. But in the end, I couldn't handle a little cactus? It wasn't like I didn't already have some needles already stuck in my back."

I wince. Bad memories.

"Little cactus?" Florence says. "I read somewhere that it was ten feet tall and weighed fifteen-hundred pounds."

Elijah raises his eyebrows quizzically, like he's hearing this for the first time. "No. It was seven feet tall and only weighed about six-hundred pounds."

"Only!" Florence says. "I don't know many people who can lift a six-hundred pound cactus."

"I couldn't, I only rolled it off." Elijah fails to suppress a nervous laugh, which he covers up with a quip. "But I sure as hell managed to knock it over, didn't I?"

"True, true," Florence says, laughing along to set the tone. "You're a strapping man."

He only knocked it over because he was dumb enough to put it on top of a chair. For his own good, he doesn't mention that part.

"So, tell me." Florence uncrosses her legs and leans back in her throne. "You mention that Arete has forgiven you, but what about her family? Do you think you'll be welcomed in?"

"I am in no position to ask for their forgiveness." Elijah turns the false suffering up a notch. "Since I'm an orphan, I was hoping to finally have a family of my own. But it looks like that will never happen now."

He puts his fingertips to his forehead and acts like he's trying not to cry, but he's just contorting his face as much as possible to keep himself from laughing. Drama queen. Whatever works, though; the audience is eating up the byronic hero act.

"An orphan?" Florence asked. "I don't believe this was ever released to the press. Can you give us more?"

Orphan my ass. He was thirty when his dad died, and he doesn't even know what happened to his mom. With a family like theirs, I wouldn't blame her if she ran away. I'm tempted to run because of all the drama the Konstantinous have brought into my life. That, and I'm still not completely over the fact that he burned my house down.

Elijah slumps over. "My father abandoned me, and my mother was ostracized by the family for her borderline personality disorder and for giving birth to me, her only child, out of wedlock. While I was serving in the military, she went missing shortly after she was discharged from the hospital. She was never found. That's why I became a police officer after I left the service. I thought that maybe if I became a detective, I could find her. But the case went cold. I failed to solve the mystery. I... *I failed my mother*."

Cue the collective utterances of pity from the audience. As far as I know, that was the first honest thing he's said since he got here. Still, he has the drama turned up way too high. I don't know why people are buying into it.

"I'm so sorry," Florence says. "You must have been carrying this weight on your shoulders for a long time. What does it feel like to talk about it?"

"It's nice to get this off my chest... But it's not a topic I want to linger on."

Florence smiles and reassures him he doesn't have to talk about it, which proves to me beyond a doubt she's acting. This is a *talk* show, of course she expects him to talk about it. She'll get it out of him somehow.

After Florence announces a commercial break, I decide to get on Elijah's laptop (which I'm surprised he lets me use liberally, considering his secretive nature) and check Twitter.

Sure enough, he has not one, but two hashtags trending. The first is the forced hashtag, #WalkerOnFlorence. The latter is #CactusGuysAbs, a backhanded compliment in itself that links to thousands more backhanded compliments.

One of the top tweets is from Arete, whose comment is too chipper and gag-inducing to be from her. The last time I saw her, it looked like she was going to choke him. As a matter of fact, I'm convinced Florence Cho borrowed her cell phone without asking.

"#CactusGuysAbs all mine, ladies and gents!! #WalkerOnFlorence"
—@ARKonstantinou

It's rare for me to scroll down Twitter through commercials, but this is my friend we're talking about. Or should I say "tweeting about?" It's like knowing a celebrity.

"Are you ready to hear the Cactus Guy's side of the story? Only on the Florence Cho Show, tonight at 6 #WalkerOnFlorence"
—@FlorenceCho

I decide to join the fun and submit an attention-seeking tweet of my own. Why not?

"And I'm the pool noodle who couldn't keep my dance partner from falling into a cactus #WalkerOnFlorence PS u can buy my book on Kindle"

—@NathanFaustBooks

I was never good at clever tweets, but Arete retweets me, opening me up to exposure I would have never gotten otherwise. The Konstantinous are good friends to have; exhausting, but helpful. My question of what talk show hosts and guests do during commercial breaks is answered when Elijah retweets me and replies.

"@NathanFaustBooks You're still my best mate forever, my favorite pool noodle, but f u for staying in the hotel"

—@ElijahJWalker

Just like that, my follower count slowly increases. My book is getting more exposure all because I got tweeted by someone who just changed his Twitter name to "Elijah theCactusGuy." Owning up to it and turning it in his favor isn't a bad strategy; it got him a couple thousand more followers already. It's a good thing he doesn't take himself too seriously.

When the commercials are over and the show is live, I'm surprised to see Arete being introduced. I shouldn't be; she's a natural on stage. She doesn't strut like Florence or brood like Elijah. When cameras are focused, she's a charming princess with effortless poise. The costume department toned down her goth look, putting her in a cute, lacy dress. It shows off her long legs, but without compromising her youthful, innocent appearance. Arete without raccoon eyes is almost as freakish as Elijah without a lie detector.

She and Elijah sit next to each other on the loveseat, looking like the picture perfect couple they wish they were.

"Thank you for coming here, Miss Konstantinou," Florence says.

"It's my pleasure. And please, call me Arete."

Florence weaves her fingers together. "Arete. How are you coping through all of this?"

"I've been better," she says. "The worst part about losing my uncle to this horrific accident was that he was the last piece of my father I had left."

Florence appears sympathetic. Key word: appears. "What happened to your father?"

"He and my mother both died not long ago," Arete says. "I'm lucky to have Eli to pull me through all of this."

"So you don't blame him at all?"

"Not even a little bit," Arete says. "Eli is exaggerating. My mother's side doesn't hate him at all, they just think he's a dumb pretty boy." Arete's charisma draws light laughter from the audience. "Say, for the sake of argument, Eli was dancing somewhere else and tripped. Nobody would've gotten hurt, and nobody would care. It's like that. There's no crime here, no guilty mindset, just a mistake. Even my cousin, Antonis' oldest son, realizes it was nothing but an unfortunate accident. But it's very stressful for him to run his piece of the company."

It's so painfully obvious to me that this was scripted. This sorry excuse for a script just keeps getting sloppier and sloppier. The fact that the audience is connecting with them is a stronger testament to Arete's acting ability than anything the Florence Cho Show has written for them to say. I don't understand what the Florence Cho Show has to offer that a livestream doesn't, except mainstream views.

"You mean Konstantinou Enterprises?" Florence asked. She sits up and crosses her legs again. "How is that going?"

"I'm not going to lie," Arete says. "It's rough. Mikhail is only nineteen, so we're going to try to appoint another CEO to run his shares. After seeing what a bad job we're doing, I think I understand why Uncle Antonis wanted to take the company from me so ba—"

Arete slaps her hand over her mouth as if she made a gruesome mistake. Florence's jaw drops, and she nearly jumps out of her seat in excitement. People were going to be talking about this interview for years.

"He was trying to take the company away from you?" Florence asks.

"Oh, curse my mouth! Please forget I said that," Arete says, her voice the perfect blend of innocent and pleading. "Uncle Antonis wasn't always so horrible. He always told the best jokes."

Arete will stop at nothing to clean up Elijah's reputation, even if it means dragging her uncle's name through the mud. This isn't the Arete I know. This Arete is ruthless and cunning, and would make an excellent CEO. If she wasn't such a good actress, I'd tell her to just quit now and take over.

"Did Antonis ever do anything to hurt you?" Florence asks her in a tone that reminds me of a therapist.

Arete fakes her tears the way only a top tier actress could and leans on Elijah's shoulder. He puts his arm around her to look like he's comforting her.

"We've all made mistakes," Elijah says. "Antonis was only human. The truth is, he was a great asset to the company, which he co-founded."

"What's in store for KE now?" Florence asks. "With the recent deaths of the original founders only one year apart, what will become of all the investors, employees, and consumers?" The sudden change in topic all but proves she knows their story is a complete façade. I wonder if she knows just how much they're lying. They're lying about their lies.

Arete sits up and rubs her eyes, regaining the composure that she never truly lost. "Mikhail is young, but capable of great things. I didn't originally want the company, but as the only child of Georgios Konstantinou, it is my responsibility to carry on my father's vision. Right now I'm still in college, but someday I'm going to shatter the glass ceiling and take a more active role in KE!"

Sure she is.

"You go, girl!" Florence claps, spurring the rest of the audience to clap as well. "And who will run the business in the mean time?"

"My husband will."

The camera cuts to the audience reaction; eyes widen, mouths drop, and there are a few gasps even. I wonder if any of these people were paid.

"Your husband?" Florence asks with a smile. Yes. She's *definitely* in on their game. Afterward, another hashtag is displayed at the upper right corner of the screen. *#Arelijah*.

Arete and Elijah both stand up, holding hands, and speak in unison. "We would like to announce our marriage!"

Florence spurs everyone to cheer and give the newlyweds a round of applause as the two sit down.

"We're all *dying* to know the story," Florence says.

"Should you go?" Elijah asks, looking into Arete's eyes with this dreamy expression.

"No, you should," Arete says.

Elijah faces the audience, but doesn't let go of Arete's hand. "We had only been together for a short time, but I knew she was the one. On March 8th, Arete and I flew to Melbourne. She thought we were just there for a concert, but once we got there, I had dinner reservations for her and we spent the night on a small yacht. It took all of my savings, but I wanted everything to be perfect for her. I proposed to her on deck, under the stars. She immediately said yes."

It's a good thing I didn't attend because I laugh so hard that I start snorting. The audience, however, is so touched that I think their hearts are going to fly out of their chests. A few people are actually *crying*. There's no way Elijah is going to jail.

"We didn't announce the engagement until her birthday party," Elijah continues, "but we had a dilemma. Arete wanted a big wedding with all her friends and family, but we also didn't want to wait another second. We flew to Nevada, where we eloped in the city of angels."

"Beautiful," Florence says. "It's like your love was written in the stars by angels."

Arete blushes. How do you fake-blush? I'm never trusting this woman again. Never.

"Thank you," Elijah says. "Everyone deserves to be as happy as we are together." He must hate the idea of other people having love.

"I don't mean to be a Debbie downer," Florence says, "but what happens to KE if you're found guilty? An involuntary manslaughter sentence could keep you in prison for up to five years."

"If I'm found guilty?" Elijah pretends to think deeply. "My wife doesn't have enough time to manage her shares on her own, and Mikhail can't handle the stress of 100% at such a young age, so Konstantinou Enterprises will have to downsize. A lot of Americans will lose their jobs, and then there are the nonprofit organizations we won't be able to support anymore..."

Arete interrupts gently. "Now isn't the time to be modest, hon. I'm sure I told you this before and forgot about it, but KE is one of the largest employers in America, with millions of workers." She faces the audience. "I can sell, but if I do that, I can't guarantee your jobs won't be moved to China. Some of the 1% don't understand how much power they hold, or how much responsibility they have to the public. The wrong CEO could devastate the economy, but my husband and I will do everything we can to protect it. Because *we* stand for the American Dream."

Judging by the audience's peaking anxiety, everyone believes the entire nation depends on Elijah's freedom. Something about it bothers me. Arete and Elijah already won the case, do they have to drive a final nail into the coffin by holding millions of US jobs at ransom?

"Terrible," Florence shakes her head and purses her glossy lips. "There's no justice in the justice system. Jailed on a technicality... and from what you were saying earlier, he sounds more than qualified."

"Of course," Arete says. "He's at the same law school getting the same degree Uncle Antonis did. When he met Elijah for the first time after the fire, he offered him a summer internship on the spot."

"I'm still a bit nervous though," Elijah says.

Arete looks into Elijah's eyes. "Don't be. You know what he said to me after I introduced you? He said 'He reminds me of your late father, my brother, and that's who this business needs right now.'"

Shoot me in the face. This is disgusting; the worst part is, that sounds like something Antonis would actually say. Not to mention there's nobody on this earth more like Georgios than Elijah. #Arelijah is so Freudian it should be illegal to think about.

"He really said that?" Elijah looks down for a moment. "That makes me feel worse."

"But you're not guilty," Arete gazes into his eyes. "It was an accident. I know it, you know it, and my ancestors in heaven know it." Arete gestures toward the audience. "Now say it to them. Say it!"

"I'm not guilty," Elijah says to the audience with pleading eyes, "I know what I did was stupid, but convicting me won't undo my mistakes. It will only keep me from making up for them. Please forgive me so I can fulfill my duties to my new family. My only family."

This is the worst script I have ever heard. Nobody is going to buy this shit. That line just killed his chances. We're all screwed.

Florence smiles and faces the audience. "So, what do you say? Should we forgive the Cactus Guy?"

There's a collective of cheering and yes's, not quite drowned out by a passionate standing ovation. I have to admit I was wrong. Elijah went from unloved "orphan," to local hero, to the cactus guy, to national hero and sex icon. Great. I couldn't be more proud. Yet, I have a hard time passing judgment on my friends. I'm too impressed, and not to mention relieved.

Their methods are unorthodox and manipulative, but Arete and Elijah are uniting as a team to stand up for each other. Even when they're fighting, they're still wholly devoted to each other, and it's beautiful in its own dark, twisted way. Elijah has the opportunity to reclaim his birthright and carry on his father's legacy. Arete garnered national attention that will help take her acting career to the top. I'm a real writer who's selling more than one copy per year. If we all played by the rules, none of us would be where we are today. The three of us would be in jail, with the people Elijah arrested.

The show continues on until 7pm, although they've already won. I don't know enough about Elijah's past to tell what things are true and what things aren't, but most of it is probably lies. Most of the questions Florence asks from that point on are about their relationship, including a fictionalized version of the day they met. At first I thought it was a terrible idea and they should've quit while they were ahead, but it looks like they're doing a good thing by turning this into a love story. By talking about his past and his marriage, he's becoming more than just the cactus guy. He's an approachable guy who loves his wife and will never give up on his dream: making the world a better place. It's making America love him, but as for me... well, I just want this to end so I can have the old Elijah back.

*

My friends don't arrive back at the hotel until around midnight. Elijah is okay enough, but Arete is still in a foul mood. Not foul as in angry. Just blank. Maybe she's tired; it was a long night, and they ended up holding an unplanned question and answers session. They also signed a few autographs and had a photo opportunity. I'd been stalking them on twitter all night, waiting for them to come home.

I try to lighten the mood with a cheery, "Good job, you two."

Arete rolls her eyes and bends over her suitcase. She rummages through her belongings until she finds her pajamas, and retreats to the bathroom to change. Elijah pretends he doesn't notice her snub and greets me like I exist.

"Thanks. How's that book coming along? It'd be a good idea to release it as soon as possible. You should self-publish a short story anthology or something, before our fifteen minutes of fame is up."

"That's good advice," I say, mostly to make him feel better. The truth is, I don't have enough stories for a decent anthology. "So they didn't let you keep the Fabio outfit?"

Elijah half laughs. It's a sad laugh, but the only genuine one he's had all night. "No. I felt so awkward in that thing. I begged them to give me a shirt, but I wasn't in the position to argue. At least my performance worked. Everyone loved me."

He glances in Arete's general direction. "Except maybe my wife," he whispers.

I see. He was able to lie because he told himself this was just a performance.

"What's going on?" I ask. "You two fought so hard for each other earlier, I expected you to come back in a good mood."

"We were. For a while." He digs through his suitcase. "She felt pressured to exaggerate her faith in me, and I think she's burned out now. And she still doesn't feel like this is really a marriage. She's acting like she feels trapped with me by a piece of paper that says I'm entitled to half of everything, and I can't tell what's real."

All I can manage is "Oh."

He finds a flask in his bag and takes a long, pained gulp. There's no right thing for me to say or safe question to ask, but there are so many things I want to know about the show. *Does she feel like she did the right thing? Do you feel like you did the right thing? How much of it was fake? Are you really going to start modeling underwear?*

Elijah looks down. "I hope you don't mind sharing a bed with hashtag Cactus Guy's abs for a second night," he says, answering my unasked question about whether or not he knew about the bet. "I don't think the missus is going to forgive me for a few years."

"Why not?" I ask.

Arete exits the bathroom and leans on the door frame. She looks at us like we're ticking clocks, and her most boring class just began exactly 11 minutes and 23 seconds ago. "Are you going to tell him?"

"Tell me what?" I ask.

Elijah faces the wall. "Antonis was giving us shifty, dirty looks all day."

I step around him so I can see his face. "What do you mean?"

"Boy Meets World..." Elijah looks away from me again. "I did it on purpose."

"You *what*?"

"Yeah." Arete crosses her arms and leans her side against the wall, unfazed. "Eli murdered my uncle at our engagement party, in broad daylight, in front of a bunch of cops."

Elijah whips around. "I did it to protect us!"

"There were dozens of police officers there," Arete says. "You're a paranoid bastard and you just won't admit it."

"So let me get this straight," I say. "You killed a man with an icicle, and now a cactus? What's next?"

"I'm resourceful," he says. "You know what they say. The bolder the move, the less anyone questions it."

"That's a Pretty Little Liars quote," Arete says, humorless. "And it was about asking the police for a ride home so they wouldn't be caught drinking underage, not committing *premeditated murder* in front of twenty-three off-duty cops at your engagement party."

"Details, details."

"Can we put this behind us?" I ask, surprised that I don't care. Before I met them, I would call the police over something like this. Now it's just routine.

Elijah approaches Arete and takes her wrist. "Please."

When he kisses her hand, her mouth twitches to a smile for a fraction of a second before she forces the corners back down. He takes this micro expression as permission to embrace her.

"Reunions don't work when there's a third wheel," I say. I don't want to choke on their passion and barf. It's bad enough that they're stepsiblings who are still mourning the murder of their uncle.

"You got over this fast," Arete says. "I don't get it. You're usually so... idealistic."

I shrug. "I never cared to begin with. Did you really come to New York to threaten America's economy and introduce victim blaming though?"

Arete smirked. "Well, I'm not here to fuck spiders." It's another Australiaism, I assume. Her face falls. "Eli... I have a confession to make."

"Yes, love?"

She presses the palm of her right hand to his chest. "I'm glad my uncle is dead," she says, her eyes pointed toward the ground. "That's the real reason I was mad at you. Because you made me face that feeling. I felt like I betrayed my family."

Elijah massages her bare shoulder with his thumb. "That's all?"

"Yes."

They're lost in their own world, so I clear my throat to get their attention. "So, should I get lost for a bit, or are you two going to use the elevator?"

Arete glares at me. "Seriously?"

"Well, I can't tell you to get a room," I say. "You already have a room."

Arete digs through her purse, crumples up two hundred dollar bills, and throws the wad of cash at me. "Since he chose *Comfort Inn*, this should be plenty."

Elijah mouths the word *sorry*, but I know he can't help it. Hey, at least I don't have to share a bed with #CactusGuysAbs again. It's kind of anticlimactic and therefore disappointing, but that's not the point. Thank you, #Arelijah.

Monday, April 20, 2015
Philadelphia, Pennsylvania

Hollywood Perfect bursts through the front door grinning like someone who just won the lottery—or someone who got away with murder. They must have hired one hell of a lawyer, because it didn't even make it to court. I'm almost surprised, but Arete has been smug since we got back from New York. It makes sense, since she's the one who won it for him. I also have a sneaking suspicion that a certain judge was given a large donation. We could celebrate tonight, but we all agree a quiet night in would be better. We sit in the sunroom on pillows gathered around a wicker coffee table. I take notes for a novella I'm working on, Arete is "studying," and Elijah is just enjoying the sunshine—and the fact that he'll be free to feel it for the next five years.

"Arelijah" now bears a decent resemblance to their talk show appearance, but they still bicker behind the scenes. I tend to be on the receiving end of their rants. Elijah has decided that I am his best friend and confidant, and Arete decided I'm the backup Whitney, so each of them come straight to me to whine about the other.

"Don't tell her this," Elijah said, "but ever since the wedding, she's been *so* moody. Is this some kind of post-marital stress, or is she still secretly mad at me for the whole cactus thing?"

"Don't tell him this," Arete said, "but I wish he'd stop overcompensating for his low self-esteem by treating me like a porcelain doll. It was cute at first, but I'm twenty-two. I can open doors by myself."

"Don't tell her this," Elijah said, "but sometimes I wish my wife had a mute button. Why is it so damn important for my shoes to match my briefcase? Why? I'm going to class, not a photoshoot."

"Don't tell him this," Arete said, "but part of me wishes I never said I do. His American dream obsession is annoying, and he talks like we're legitimately married. He never asks what I want, he just assumes we're on the same page. He thinks 'no' means 'ask me later.'"

Playing both sides is difficult, but I manage. Arete has Whitney to go crying to, so she serves as a buffer for me while fully knowing it. Just another reason to love Whitney. Elijah, on the other hand, is convinced that he has no one else, so it's all on me. If I was better at giving advice, I could use their trust to my advantage to diffuse their disputes. It would have been useful earlier this morning, when Elijah presented me with this piece of ignorance:

"Don't tell her this," he said, "but I secretly wish she'd drop out of school and become a housewife. She's not cut out for college. I mean, come on, her GPA is a 1.34. I'll take care of everything at KE. I mean, let's just be honest, she's not the business type."

I tried to explain to him that Arete wants to be an actress, and that she doesn't think she's ready for a motherhood role. This went in one ear and out the other.

"Well, I'd never actually *tell* her to drop out," he said. "But she can become an actress anytime, and I'd rather have kids before I'm thirty-five. Besides, there's actually a pretty decent margin of error with kids as long as you love them. She shouldn't worry about it, she'd be a natural."

He then proceeded to ramble about the American dream Arete vented to me about. All of his children will have Greek first names, as per the family tradition, but Arete can choose whatever middle name she wants. When his firstborn starts Kindergarten, he's going to adopt a golden retriever puppy so that they can grow up together. Having a puppy will make it easier for this child to adjust to school life and getting less attention when baby #2 comes along. Once baby #2 is done nursing, he will adopt a deaf-mute child and name him Croesus after a Lydian-Greek myth where his deaf-mute son speaks to save his life or something. I stopped paying attention at that point. No wonder Arete regrets the speed wedding.

Sometimes it's hard to tell when one of them has the other's best interest at heart, or when they're just being selfish. The power dynamic is set in stone, however. Elijah owes Arete a serious debt for keeping him out of prison, so he always lets her get her way in the end. Sometimes I wish they'd actually fight about it, just once, and leave me in peace. I don't get to have a life of my own. #Arelijah is my life. And now I'm sitting with them in a sunroom, wondering what I did wrong to end up here, the permanent third wheel to a couple of socialites. So far, there have been no attempts on Arete's life since the death of her uncle. I no longer have the need for Elijah's protection with him out of the way. The police don't care about Hoyt Galligan. I wonder if he would object to me leaving, but cast the idea aside when I realize I don't want to leave. I like it here with my friends—and he does owe me for burning my house down, so I'm not really imposing. I think I'll stay here, at least until my career takes off.

Arete turns the page of her textbook, which I doubt she actually read. Without looking up, she says, "I think I should host a social event."

"No more parties," I say. "Bad things always happen at your parties."

"And whose fault is that?" Arete gestures toward Elijah.

"Not mine," Elijah says. "It's always someone else's fault."

"I noticed." Arete shoves her nose back into her textbook. "I'm not talking about a 'Cactus Guy's not going to jail' party. I'm talking about a 'we just selected a new CEO' party. Nothing big, just a small, company party."

"It doesn't look like anything I say will change your mind," I say, trying not to think of all the things that could happen. Elijah could commit homicide by misadventure again, or my parents could show up. Not that they know where I am or who I'm living with, but if I learned anything this year, it's that nightmares can come true.

Elijah sips his coffee. "So who's the new CEO?"

Arete grins. "You, silly!"

Elijah gags and spits out black coffee in shock.

Arete laughs. "Gotcha!"

Elijah wipes coffee off his face and looks at the huge stain on his shirt. "That was *not* cool."

"You'd better get used to hearing it, seeing as how we announced it on live television."

I wipe some of Elijah's coffee-spit off the corner of my notebook. *Germs.* "I still don't get why you did that," I say.

"Easy," Arete says. "Elijah and I came up with a plan that targeted three types of jurors, in case the case went to trial. One. It's hard to have sympathy for the newly rich idiot who squashed his fiancée's uncle with a cactus, but the newly rich idiot who's an orphan with a tragic past? Priceless.

"Two. Sex appeal. We made him look like a remorseful, brooding lover who wants to make up for his horrible mistake, and will move Hell and earth to fix everything. And you saw that outfit. We built a fan girl mob right off of his abs and a mostly-real love story.

"And three. We covered our bases for the people that would hate him anyway by making it about their wallets. Everyone knows someone who works at a Konstantinou Enterprises subsidiary. If they think Elijah is the last hope for an at-risk, multibillion-dollar empire that employs half of America, jail time doesn't seem like the best idea."

I frown. When did Arete Rene Konstantinou of all people grow a brain? "So in other words, that TV appearance was like a jury trial to you two? Arete, are you sure you don't want to be an executive?"

"I'm sure." Arete closes her book and gently sets it back on the table. "I'm going to be an actress."

She must not have watched a recording of her guest appearance on the Florence Cho Show, because then she'd know that she already *is* an actress.

She zones out and phases into her own little world. "I can see it now... Tonia will be my irrelevant cousin. Sweet victory."

"So we have this party for me, or for the *real* CEO?" Elijah asks.

"For both of you," Arete says. "Goldwater will act as CEO until his retirement, probably. And as for you, I think it's best for KE if you *are* involved."

"What do you mean?" Elijah asks.

"You know what I mean," Arete says. "If people think the Konstantinous are a bunch of liars, nobody will use our services or buy our products, and you'll be The Cactus Guy again. I'm not saying you can't finish school, but Elijah, we need you."

"Kit Kat," Elijah says. "First of all, I'll *always* be The Cactus Guy. And I'm okay with that. Second, the most I've ever done at KE was work at one of your mall restaurants when I was sixteen. My job was to try to get people to sample gyros, and to exaggerate my Greek accent to make them sound more authentic and less greasy."

"I have officially appointed you the new face of Konstantinou Enterprises," Arete says.

"The face?" Elijah says. "So in other words, it's the same thing I was doing before, except without the accent."

"See? You were born for the job."

"I can't argue with that," Elijah says. "So, any ideas on where we're having this party?" he asks, changing the subject. I'm glad. It was getting a little too close to family territory, and she still doesn't know the truth about who she married.

Arete shrugs.

"Why not have it in your back yard?" I ask. "It's big enough, and the deck is pretty nice."

"The detached deck with the fire pit?" Arete asks. "Are you blind?"

"I've got to agree," Elijah says. "It's a cheaply-made waste of expensive materials, and it looks so out of place. Why is that eyesore even there?"

I don't take offense to their comments; I've been told I have bad taste my entire life. I'm not surprised either, since Elijah's whined to me previously about all the changes that were made to the house while he was away. It's weird because he usually doesn't mind change, but he's highly sensitive about all the changes Simone made to his father's dream house. I get the impression it wasn't there when he was a child.

Arete confirms this when she says, "Actually, it's pretty weird. My mum *insisted* that a deck be built there immediately. She had lots of different workers rotate shifts, and it was done in, like, 2 days. We weren't even going to use it any time soon, winter was on the way."

Elijah hesitates. "How... When it was built? What year?"

Arete taps a pencil on her textbook as she thinks. "I was sixteen, so..." She starts counting on her fingers.

"2009," Elijah whispers to himself.

"Are you okay?"

After an awkward silence where Arete and I exchange glances, Elijah bursts out into rapid speech. "Well, best two out of three, we all think it's hideous. Let's have it removed. Now. Right now. I mean, why wait? It's horrible. It's not even the same color of wood as the gazebo, it's cheap as hell, and it creaks when we step on it. So let's just dig it up. Now."

Arete and I exchange glances again. "Okay," she says to him. "I'll call th—"

He stands up. "Where do you keep your tools?"

"The attic, but—"

Without a second's hesitation, he runs off to do it himself, leaving Arete to gape in confusion without the clingy goodbye kiss she's accustomed to.

Thursday, April 23, 2015

The rain beats down on Elijah's back as he hunches over in the mud, clearing away the last pieces of the deck. It's been raining like that for a while now, huge droplets smacking down the tulips and drumming on the roof like bullets. Any construction worker would stay home, but Elijah's been working tirelessly for days. Help or no help, he will spend his last breath digging under the deck's remains if he has to.

I'm not helping; Philly's rain smells like smog, rainclouds are gloomy, a chicken could lift heavier than me, and nothing good can come out of this. It's not the best day to write in the sun room, but it gives me a good view of the deck's remains. I feel obligated to peek out the window every ten minutes or so to make sure he isn't dying of hypothermia or something. Arete is more worried than I am, mostly because he's leaving her in the dark. Instead of pestering her with daydreams of love and babies, he's barely speaking to her at all. He barely eats enough to stay alive, only sleeps so he can have more energy to work the next morning, and has been putting the bare minimum into his grooming. Her only consolation is that he still leaves to go to class, so he hasn't completely abandoned his future for whatever he's trying to achieve with this madness.

Arete is at UPenn taking her final exam when I hear a scream and jolt out of my seat. If Elijah could get through the attack of a hit man and fall backwards into a cactus without much more than a grimace, what could possibly make him *scream*? With that in mind, I grab my umbrella and rush to check on him.

When I come outside, the first thing I see is Elijah, crouched on the ground with a ghost-like expression. He's drenched and muddy, his clothes and hair clinging to him like a wetsuit. He doesn't respond when I call out to him, so I round the corner to see what he's looking at.

The harsh rains are unearthing something filthy and ivory. I take a closer look, standing at the edge of the construction site. I watch curiously as the rain reveals more and more, and don't understand why Elijah is so transfixed. After a while, the ivory is washed clean and more of the shape is revealed. I had to take anatomy twice, but I'm convinced that's a bone. As a matter of fact, I'm "89% B+, Big Improvement!" sure that's a femur. And by the look on Elijah's face, I bet he knows whose it is.

I crouch by his side and hold an umbrella over our heads. "Hollywood?"

"Six years," he says.

"What?"

"I've been trying to solve my mother's murder for six years."

"Murder?" I ask.

I can't get him to say anything else. He sits at the foot of the grave staring at the bones like he can change the past if he concentrates hard enough.

*

Detective Charlotte Pfeiffer finds Elijah sitting in the exact same position I saw him in earlier, and she manages to coax him into the house. It becomes apparent that, although Elijah had been a cop for several years, the two of them haven't met before. The department must have chosen her strategically, knowing they will never be able to be impartial to their old friend. It makes me regret calling the police, but I didn't know how else I could get him to move. I tried tugging, coaxing, and telling him I was going to order pizza.

I pass up the sitting area and invite Det. Pfeiffer to the living room so she can question us, mostly because Elijah is covered in mud and it's easier to clean leather than velvet. She asked my permission rather than his, since he's still despondent and Arete isn't home to protect me from the most terrifying detective on earth. She's a young woman and probably hasn't had this job for long, but she maintains a straight face at all times and has a bad case of bitchy resting face. She would be cute enough if she didn't have such thick, angry eyebrows. Her dark brown hair is tied back in a bun, and I notice the slightest tinge of yellow roots. Blond detectives don't have more fun, I guess. She must dye her eyebrows too. God, why do I keep thinking about her eyebrows? I just... I can't stop staring at them. They're just so *bold*. And her heavy-lidded, hazel eyes—I have to pinch myself to make sure I didn't drop dead from her glare. She's more intimidating than Elijah ever was, and all she's doing is sitting there.

Meanwhile, as I let myself be distracted by a pair of intimidating brows, Elijah sits on the couch, soaking wet, only speaking when spoken to—sometimes not even then. When Arete comes home from school, she finds us by following the trail of mud that he tracked through the house.

"What's wrong?" Arete asks, trying to keep the panic down. "I saw the cop cars."

Elijah ignores her.

The detective clicks her pen. "Mr. Walker, what makes you so sure that the remains belong to your mother?"

"Remains?" Arete asks.

Elijah doesn't react to his wife. He keeps his head pointed toward his lap. "This is the first place Mom would go. I don't know why I didn't think of it sooner."

Arete sits next to him and speaks gently. "Baby, what are you talking about?" She wipes her fiancé's soaked hair out of his eyes and slicks it back with loving care, but Elijah still doesn't seem to see her. She presses her fingertips to his forehead. "Honey?" she says. "You're so cold."

When he continues to tune her out and stare at the wall, Arete turns to Det. Pfeiffer. "I'm going to come back with some towels and a blanket. Please refrain from further questioning my husband until I'm back."

"Of course," Pfeiffer says. "Don't keep me waiting too long."

Arete huffs. "I'll take as long as I damn well please."

She leaves the room after giving a blatant order to the most terrifying woman on the planet. How does she not feel the Det. Pfeiffer chill? Why doesn't it affect her? No, no! She's looking at me again, pointing those eyebrows at me! Arete, why didn't you say "refrain from questioning my friend?" You've left me exposed, you traitor! And Elijah, or should I say E*liar*, did you not promise to protect me? Those eyebrows are more piercing than any bullet, Hollywood.

"Can you go over what happened one more time?" Det. Pfeiffer asks.

I want to say *no*, but she's using some sort of compulsion that makes me blurt it all out in one, fearful breath. "I was upstairs and I heard Elijah scream so I went outside and it was raining and I saw something sticking out of the mud and it was a femur and he acted like he was expecting something like that but I wasn't so I called you and then I puked in the vase I have no clue what's going on so please stop asking me."

I take a deep breath. She doesn't respond, so I collapse into my lap, avoiding eyebrow contact. The silence is awful, I have to fill it. "I've been living here since my house burned down but I don't really know these people that well I'm their charity case so whatever they did I don't know about it so please don't look at me like that I don't think I can stand it anymore."

"For someone who claims not to know them, you're awfully worried about them," she says.

Am I sweating or is it my imagination? "Do I really have to answer these questions?"

"No," she says. "I just find this situation curious."

When is Arete going to get back? I can't take it anymore. Det. Pfeiffer keeps looking at me, and it's hard to tell what she's thinking. Oh my god, what if she digs into my past with these two, and it turns out Elijah didn't clean the body well, and there were actually *two* of my hairs on the hitman, and she arrests me for murder? My life is over. It's over.

"Are you okay?" Det. Pfeiffer asks.

I jump. Is that supposed to be her smile? That is the grumpiest smile I have ever seen in my entire life. She needs to get those bitch brows waxed off her face and draw new ones on. If she doesn't say anything to me between now and the time Arete gets back, I'm going to confess to the murders of Hoyt Galligan, Antonis Konstantinou, Tansy Papadópo- whatever, and all of Arete's potential bio-dads—every last one of them. I am guilty; her eyebrows tell me so. Is this how she breaks people? Eyebrow hypnotism?

Arete returns with an armful of fluffy towels, temporarily breaking Pfeiffer's hex by crossing in front of us on her way to the couch. She sits next to Elijah, drapes a blanket around his shoulders, and plants a kiss on his cheek. He doesn't smile or thank her, but she's pleased when he pulls the blanket around himself.

"Mr. Walker," Pfeiffer says, "Why do you believe the remains are your moth—"

Arete fires a quick glare at Pfeiffer, silencing her. It looks kind of like this:

Amazing. Truly amazing.

Elijah, if he sees anything at all, doesn't catch this look in her eyes before she turns around and pats his forehead with a towel.

"You said I could question him after you got back," Pfeiffer says.

Arete lays her hands on his shoulders like she's protecting him. "Can't you see he's in shock?"

Pfeiffer cracks a smug "smile" and says, "Perhaps you'll answer a few questions then, so I can leave. Mrs. Walker, have you ever met Tansy Popa-p-p..." She holds the paper closer to her face and squints. "*Pah·pah·doh·poo·lou*... your mother-in-law?"

"*No*, I have *not!*" Arete says. "And it's Παπαδόπουλου!"

"That's how I said it?"

Arete rubs Elijah's back and towel dries his hair. "Ψυχή μου, it can't be your mom. I'm sure she's out there, you just have to keep looking."

Elijah stands up, letting the blanket fall on the couch. "I'll be right back."

He leaves a distraught Arete behind as he leaves the room. I can hear his feet as he drags them up the stairs.

Pfeiffer studies Arete's demeanor and adjusts her tone accordingly. "I'm very sorry about this," says Nice Detective Pfeiffer. "I'm not interrogating you. I'm just as confused as you are, and that's why I have to ask questions. All I want is your cooperation so I can figure out who was buried under that deck and why."

Arete crosses her arms. "Are you sure they're human remains?"

"They're definitely human, Mrs. Walker."

Defeated, Arete slumps over. "He's probably mistaken then. He's been strange lately, he must be confused."

"Can you elaborate on that?"

"It started a few days ago," Arete says. "I told him that my parents had a deck built suddenly in November 2009, and how it was a weird time to build a deck, and how it looks out of place. And after that he flipped out and immediately started ripping it apart. He was obsessed."

Arete is broken down, and may give Nice Detective Pfeiffer too much. But there's no way I can stop her without tipping Pfeiffer off or making her suspicious.

The detective scribbles something on her clipboard. "How obsessed?"

"He still went to class, but he barely talked to me. All of his free time was spent on that deck. He worked to exhaustion, I was terrified."

"Any idea why your husband didn't call the police instead?"

"No."

"Is there any other suspicious behavior?" Det. Pfeiffer asks.

Arete takes a deep breath and wraps her arms around her torso, like she's trying to hold herself together. "I don't mean shifty or suspicious. He's... completely out of it. I just don't see how his mum could have been here. He and I just met a few months ago. This is too coincidental to be true."

Pfeiffer opens her mouth, most likely to ask another annoying question, when Elijah returns with a familiar manila folder from his safe. I can see the wrinkles from where it's been pushed to the holding limit, but he took most of the papers out before coming down.

"It's not a coincidence," he says.

"What's that" Arete asks?

Elijah ignores her and hands Det. Pfeiffer the manila folder. She thanks him and thumbs through the documents; they stick together at parts because of his wet handprints.

"What are you saying, Mr. Walker?" Det. Pfeiffer asks.

Elijah is about to sit down next to his wife, but hesitates and goes for the armchair next to me. He has a hard time finding words.

"Sorry," Elijah says to no one in particular. "I had to go upstairs and get those. Before we got into this, I wanted to make sure you knew that Arete and I aren't a familial match."

Arete has the weapy eyes of a lonely kitten. She's finally figured it out, and at the worst possible time. She rubs the inner corners of her eyes, trying not to cry. I cover my ears and bend over. This isn't happening. This is a bad dream. That's all. There's no way he's that inconsiderate. How hard would it have been to tell Arete directly at any point? Figuring something like that out on your own, no matter how small the leap, is like *being* on your own.

"Πλάκα κάνεις;" she asks Elijah. When he doesn't respond, she continues to plead. "Σε παρακαλώ. Αυτό πρέπει να είναι ψέματα. Είσαι φως μου. Σ' αγαπώ, μου λείπεις, σε χρειάζομαι στη ζωή μου. Σε παρακαλώ, πες μου πως λες ψέματα. Ότι όλο αυτό είναι κόλπο για να ξεγελάσεις αστυνομία. Θα μου πεις αλήθεια αργότερα, σωστά, αγάπη μου;"

He still doesn't say anything, but he hides his face in his hands, like he can make himself disappear. Or maybe he wants everyone else to disappear so he can be alone. It's hard to tell at this point.

As Pfeiffer reads, her poker face drops straight to the floor. "So…" She clears her throat. "You married your stepsister?"

"Ωρίμασε πια, Elijah!" Arete yells at Elijah, suddenly furious. "Πρέπει να μου μιλάς! Καλώς ή κακώς, εγώ είμαι η σύζυγος σου! Ο κόσμος μου καταρρέει και εσύ δεν κάνεις τίποτα για να βοηθήσεις!" Frustrated with his silence, she turns back to Pfeiffer. "Can I go now?"

"I'm not finished yet," Det. Pfeiffer says. "Did you know about this?"

"Obviously not, *ηλίθιε*!" Arete snaps.

I hear papers shuffling, and then Det. Pfeiffer speaks. "Georgios Konstantinou is your father?"

"Yes," Elijah and Arete say simultaneously.

"You have *got* to be kidding me!" Arete says. "That's not possible!"

Pfeiffer shuffles through the papers. "If you and your husband aren't a familial match, that means you're not related to Georgios Konstantinou. He must have fraudulently signed your birth certificate."

All the tears Arete was holding in burst through like a floodgate. It's nothing like the times she's cried before. Her wailing could blow the house over and flatten the whole Main Line.

Pfeiffer continues to sort through the folder's remaining contents. "There's a report here from an OB-GYN, proving that your mother was already pregnant when she married Georgios. A few family photos... Yes. Strong resemblance." Pfeiffer turns a photo over and reads the back before holding it out for Arete to see. "Do you recognize this woman?"

"No," she says through sobs.

"This is Tansy, the woman who—"

I jump when Arete screams, "Γαμήσου!" and leaves the room with the grace of a hurricane. I hear her stomp up the stairs. I follow behind her, but she rushes up the steps, dashes through the hallway, and slams her bedroom door behind her. The best thing a friend could do right now would be to comfort her, but it's hard to do that when you're one of the people responsible. To hell with Elijah's privacy; I should've told Arete the truth as soon as I found out.

I return to the living room to find that Det. Pfeiffer is undeterred by Arete's dramatic exit. The weeping stepsister clearly knows nothing and is of no use to her investigation.

"Mr. Walker," she says, "why would Tansy return to this house?"

"Because she loved my dad," Elijah says without hesitation. "Even when he cheated on her, married a teenager, and shipped her off to the psych ward, she never stopped loving him. She always asked me about him on the phone, even though she knew my dad and I never talked. I was staying with my maternal grandparents, and they hated me as much as they hated my mom and dad."

"Did Tansy tell you she was coming here to visit your father?"

"No."

Det. Pfeiffer writes something. "And who was Arete's father?"

"I don't know for sure," he says. "Her mom was gang raped. So it could be one of seven men. It was seven, right?"

Nice performance, asshole.

"I'll have to check the police report," Pfeiffer says. "So that means both... um, all *three* of your parents... you two's three parents..." She groans and I barely hear her muttering, *"This is just so fucked up"* under her breath. She regains composure, but not without a grunt. "They're deceased now, correct?"

Elijah takes a deep breath. "The Konstantinou family... *is cursed.*"

"Cursed?" the detective asks, perhaps finally starting to understand what Arete meant when she implied he was crazy.

Det. Pfieffer shakes her head, deciding not to address it. It's a wise decision. "Why did you marry her?"

He sits in a hunched over position with his head bowed down, but opens himself up a little now that Arete is gone. "I know this looks bad, but I really do love her. That's why I didn't tell her the whole truth." He sits up, only to lean back and stare at the ceiling. "She'd never date me if she knew that side of the story, and the whole story would've just been too overwhelming for her. Case in point."

Pfeiffer's pen moves so swiftly across the paper; she must have figured something out, and that's terrifying.

"Did you have any ulterior motives to marrying your sister?" Pfeiffer asks.

"Who cares?" Elijah asks, irritated. "They're dead, we're not related, nothing matters!"

"Just answer the question."

Elijah glares at her. "Am I being detained, you frigid, anti-love bitch?"

Pfeiffer huffs. "No. You are not being detained."

As an ex-detective and seasoned lawyer who won an entire case with help, Elijah knows his rights. He wasn't detained, so he doesn't have to stay. It's not at all suspicious to refuse further questioning after digging up a body. Nope. And to make himself even *less* suspicious, he stops to passionately bark, "And she's not my sister!" on his way out of the room.

Now it's my turn to be questioned, and I regret not leaving with Arete. Actually, I regret calling the police to begin with. But I haven't lost sight of what I *don't* regret. I don't regret walking into that alleyway on February 24, 2015. I don't regret getting kidnapped, mislead, or used by my friends. They had their reasons, and it doesn't matter because I'm happy here. But I *will* regret it if whatever trouble Hollywood Perfect has gotten himself into burns him, all the while knowing I could've done something to save him. Do I hate him right now? Yes. But it's my duty to protect my family, and this will blow over eventually. We're best mates forever.

"How long have you known them?" she asks.

I'm afraid to look her in the eyebrows. So I don't.

"February," I say. I try to think of the same story I gave Tommy, in case they question his old roommates. Unlike Elijah, I'm not above telling a lie and admitting to myself that it was a lie. I can do what he can't. "February of this year. We became fast friends, and Elijah let me stay with him after my house exploded."

"Are you three close?"

"Yeah, I guess," I say. After seeing Arete cry, I kind of want to strangle Elijah half to death, but I decide to leave that part out. The feeling will pass... eventually.

"How would you judge Elijah's mental state? He's... *unhinged* at best."

"He is," I say. "He hasn't slept in days. He left the house to go to class, but other than that, he'd been obsessed with the deck. He barely talked with me, but I stayed close to check on him. I think deep down he knew all along."

"Knew what?" she asks.

"That his mom was dead."

"What tipped him off that *a body* was buried there?" she asks. "You can't be sure it's his mother."

I refuse to tell her anything she doesn't already know, especially not with that ignorant comment. "Arete said it was built in 2009 when it was almost winter, and... Oh, I don't know. That's when his mother went missing, and something just clicked in his head. He's smart, that's all."

She starts packing everything back into her briefcase, including that clipboard. I catch a few words on the paper, like 'stepsister' and 'deck.' 'Suicide' is crossed out; 'murder' is written next to it, underlined twice. Aside from a few stray notes, the rest of the page is filled with doodles, scribbles, and the words "HOLY SHITBALLS!!" underlined twice.

"That's true," she says, "but until recently, he was aiming low. He joined the Marine Corps when he could've started a lucrative career. He earned a doctorate in forensic psychology while he was there, but never went up in rank above a corporal. He was a low-ranking police officer too, if I recall. He said he wanted to be a detective, but when the chance was offered to him, he quit his job. That's when I transferred here from Pottstown."

What is she doing? I understand why she would stop questioning me—I'm useless—but why is she telling me all of this? Wait, is that a *wedding ring* on her finger? Who would marry those eyebrows? *Okay, William. Focus.* I could ask something along the lines of what's wrong with forensic psychology, but any attempt to derail her would work against me. Can I kick her out even though it's not my house?

"I'm confused," I say. "Are you still questioning me?"

She "smiles;" I'm assuming it's a smile because of her tone of voice. "No. Just a chat... I find it funny, is all. They say he was pretty vocal about wanting to be a detective, despite being the worst patrol officer on the force, only to turn down the promotion. I'm guessing he has a low self-esteem?"

"Of course not," I say. "The man is just following his dream to be a lawyer; he wanted to be a lawyer his whole life, you know. Being a detective was what he wanted at that phase in his life. That's why he majored in..." *Shit. What was it again?* "...in *forensic criminology*, but when the job fell into his lap, he realized his inheritance would cover his tuition, and he could finally afford to satisfy his lifelong dream of being a lawyer. He was limited by funds, not self-esteem."

I'm so proud of myself for pulling all of that out of my ass. My bullshit game is strong today.

"Are you sure about that, Mr. Brown? He may have been lazy, but he was qualified for work that paid much higher than monitoring traffic and patrolling the streets. I just transferred here, but the department still talks about him. They almost didn't hire him because he was too smart. He scored a 162 on the MENSA IQ test."

"162? Holy shit!" Oops. Is it okay to swear in front of the police? "Sorry, I knew he was smart, just not THAT smart."

"You look surprised. The force often rejects people for being too smart, and Walker knew this, so he lowballed his test performance on the entrance exam."

"Why do they reject smart people?" That actually explains a lot.

"Because they tend to have low job satisfaction and leave," she says. "They thought Walker was too much of an underachiever to go that route, especially after they found out he was hiding a doctorate in psychology so he didn't look overqualified. But then along comes UPenn to prove everyone wrong."

I hope she can't tell I didn't know any of that just by looking at me.

"N-no," I say. "He just wanted to attend his father's alma mater. That's all."

His father went to UPenn, but it was his *uncle* that went to Penn Law; I decide to leave that part out. #CactusGuysAbs isn't where I want this conversation to go. Memes lead you down a dark path.

"Really?" she says. "I assumed he held a lot of resentment toward his father."

"He does," I say. "I mean, his dad was a pathological liar, so..."

"But that didn't stop him from keeping all those secrets from you about Arete and their family. Doesn't that bother you?"

I'm screwed if she figures out that I already knew all of that stuff, so I shrug as a part of my act. "Nah. He means well, and he's funny sometimes."

"You see the best in everyone," she says. "You don't judge, and I like that. It's a rare quality to find in a man nowadays."

"Thanks," I say, uncomfortable. Why do people always talk about me like I'm an all-loving marshmallow harvested from the asshole of the purest unicorn? Well, it is useful sometimes, but right now she's just using it to butter me up so I'll spill information.

She stands up. "He went through great lengths to marry his stepsister, gain access to the house, and then he solved his mother's disappearance in a matter of months. Why couldn't he have done that as a detective? It's such a waste of talent."

"I dunno."

"You know, never in my life have I met a genius who wasn't troubled." She frowns. "His father died of ALS, his stepmother died in an accident, and if he's right, we finally know that Tansy Papadópoulos was murdered. This is as happy an ending as it will ever get for those two. I'm afraid it's all downhill from here."

"Accident?" I ask. I don't know how much Pfeiffer's brushed up on Konstantinou history, but since it's such a high-profile household, it's worth a shot to ask how. I don't have the balls to ask Arete. "Sorry, this is my first time hearing how Simone died. What happened, exactly?"

"The heel of one of her plastic stripper shoes snapped off, and she fell down the stairs. Just another reason to wear flats, if you ask me."

"That sounds... painful," I say.

An icicle, a cactus, and now a stripper shoe? This has *Elijah* written all over it.

"I have to be going soon," Pfeiffer says, "but Walker dodged my last question. You don't think he had any ulterior motives to marrying his stepsister, do you?"

"No," I say. "He really loves her. They love each other."

At that moment, I indistinctly hear Arete and Elijah screaming at each other upstairs. The detective looks in their general direction, and I can see her skepticism.

"I swear, they're usually not like this," I say.

She frowns. "You know, these sort of things... They rarely end well."

"I know."

"If there's anything you—"

We overhear Arete yelling. "Why don't you go to your room from when you were twelve then? It's rightfully yours, so why don't you just stay there! Go!"

The detective hands me her business card. "You have troublesome friends, Mr. Brown. Be sure to call if you think of anything, and dial 911 in case of an emergency."

"I will. Thank you." Her advice to dial 911 unnerves me, but it was probably meant to. If she really thought I was in danger, she wouldn't be leaving me alone in a house full of psychopaths... right?

"Your broken arm..." she says. "I'd hate to ask, but do you feel threatened here?"

"Oh, no. I slipped on wet tile."

"Just checking. Have a nice day, Mr. Brown."

"Thanks. You too."

On her way out, I realize what I just did; I wasn't engaging in a friendly chat. She knew getting me to talk would be a breeze. I was the easy target. I curse myself; so much for protecting my "family." If we're unlucky, she'll go the extra mile and come back the next day, and every day after that until she finds out about Hoyt Galligan and Antonis Konstantinou. I'm not even sure if Elijah is safe from being tried for murder since the case never made it to court. Why did I tell her so much? And to think I called *Arete* an idiot. At least she refused to be questioned.

*

I'm not sure exactly where Elijah's bedroom was when he was twelve, so I take a chance on the always-locked door across from Arete's childhood bedroom. It's still locked, but I know Elijah is in there. I can feel the negative energy and guy cry.

"I know you're in there, man. And you're really pissing me off!"

He doesn't respond.

"I can't *believe* you let her find out this way! You're a complete and total *ass!*"

Elijah opens the door and slips out. "Can you tell me off out of her earshot, at least? It looks far away but she's right down the hall."

As much as I hate to admit it, he has a point. He shuts the door behind him and we walk to the study. The room is practically soundproof, as any good study should be, but I don't know what to say once we get there. By now, my anger has dimmed, but not subsided.

"If you told me, why couldn't you tell her?" I ask.

Elijah looks out the window. "I know you were digging through my safe. You don't have to pretend you didn't see my file on Simone."

"Simone?" I ask. "I thought it was a file on Arete!"

"No." Elijah turns toward me with the most genuine quizzical look I've ever seen. "Why would I need a file on my wife when I can just ask her anything I want? You know why we agreed not to tell her."

"Well, what's your excuse now?" I ask. "What big, dark, scary secret are you going to hide this time, and what excuse are you going to use to shut me up?"

He picks at paint chips on the windowsill. "William..."

"What is it?" I brace myself. Elijah doesn't call me William. He has *never* called me by my real name, not one single time.

Regretting his openness, Elijah ignores me and fidgets with a pen button. My heart pounds faster and harder with every click until I finally reach my breaking point.

"Come on," I say. "Spit it out. No more bullshit, no more half-truths, no more games. Why did you have a file on your stepmother?"

Elijah takes a deep breath and looks me in the eye. "Simone was a serial killer."

"A what?"

I think back to all the mugshots and police files Elijah had on Simone's rapists. I remember scanning through them and wondering why the murders I had witnessed were so different from the ones he kept files on. Now I know why.

"So..." I clear my throat, trying my best to remember the timeline. "You're saying Simone was a serial killer, and she started with your mother?"

He nods. "Yeah, but—"

"That's insane."

"William," he says, "this can't get out. Arete *can't* know about this. All that stuff with me sneaking around to hide the fact that we were connected—that was child's play. This is something that could really push her toward the edge. *She cannot know.*"

"It's better if she hears it from you."

"That's Simone's business," Elijah says, as if she's alive to experience humiliation. "Not mine. Honestly, she covered her tracks so well that I can't prove she killed anyone at all. I haven't found a shred of proof, just dead ends. I thought if I figured out what she did with them, that it would lead me to my mother's body. But Simone took it all to the grave with her."

"But you're serious about this whole serial killer thing?" I ask.

"Circumstantial evidence doesn't mean anything in the court of law, but I'm 99.8% sure she was a revenge killer. The puzzle may be missing some pieces, but it all fits together perfectly. Simone was a sharp woman—she scared me, actually."

Pfeiffer was right. Elijah could have made a great career as a detective. Great deductive reasoning, meticulous record-keeping, dedication, eye for detail, and the ability to step back and see what's not working. I'm surprised they *let him* walk away. I'd be throwing FBI offers at him.

"So basically," I say, "you're telling me there's no point in telling Arete because nobody will ever know?"

"Exactly," he says. "So please refrain from burdening Arete with questions no one will ever be able to answer—"

I hold out my hand for him to stop, and backtrack to my conversation with detective Pfeiffer. "One more question, before I abandon you indefinitely... Was Simone's death really an accident?"

"Ye—No..." Elijah tightens the left corner of his mouth and looks around the room. "It was a *half*cident."

"God dammit, Elijah! There's no such thing as a halfcident!" I massage my temples. "You're crazy. You are fucking *crazy*."

"I know," he says. "I dropped everything to find my mother, only to find out that Simone pushed her off the balcony. She admitted it to my face. I was so angry. I wasn't thinking. I just snapped."

"So your first instinct was to kill her?" I stand up and walk to the door. "I am *so* done with you."

"Wait!" he says. "You're not going to tell Arete, are you?"

Before leaving, I look over my shoulder and glare at the mess who's standing behind me. "You mean that she married a serial killer who murdered her mother, who was also a serial killer? No. You're right. She's been through enough. We've *all* been through enough."

Sunday, March 2, 2014

Omniscient View

Melbourne, Australia

Elijah was walking down the halls of Melbourne Private Hospital on his way to see his father. The weather was pleasant that afternoon, and he wished he could take his father's hospital bed and wheel it outside. It wasn't that Georgios never left the hospital and went home, it was just that he never got to sit outside with Elijah. He could only see his father during his scheduled hospital stays, which were unnecessary to his health—he could hire one who was just as competent at home, or go somewhere more relaxing. They served only as their alibi.

Unfortunately, there was no such thing as a perfect crime; Elijah caught sight of Simone as he was coming around the corner. No matter how well they got along, one law of his universe would never change: deep down under, of all the deadly creatures in Australia, from crocodiles to venomous snakes, nothing terrified him more than his beloved stepmonster. He tried to slide back around the corner and slip into another room, but it was too late.

"Elijah Walker? What the ever-loving *fuck* are you doing here?"

"V-visiting Dad..."

Simone narrowed her eyes and scoffed. "You're calling him 'Dad' now? When did this start?"

"Recently," he said.

He tried to show peace by carrying on as if nothing had happened, but ever persistent, Simone blocked his path.

"What is it you want? Money?" she asked. "You know, demanding a raise is the number-one cause of death for blackmailers."

On the defensive, he sized her up. There were seven years between them, so that made her thirty-seven years old. She aged well; she looked a lot like she did twenty years ago, when she married Georgios as a teenager, except for some fine lines that were ironed out by a proficient plastic surgeon. Her workout routine did her a lot of favors. None of this was a surprise to him, of course; it wasn't his first run-in with Simone since then. But something about her had changed in the short time since they last met in person; it was the way she stood her ground. Some weight she carried on her shoulders a few months ago was gone. She was powerful. And from what Elijah knew about Simone, her outfit and jewelry combined had to be worth more than one year's rent on his apartment. She wasn't as intimidating as she was when he was twelve, but by then he towered over her by eight inches—five if you accounted for her pink pumps.

"How am I a blackmailer?" he asked. "I thought it was a gift."

"Fine," she said in a way that indicated she was anything less than *fine*. "Perhaps blackmail isn't the right word."

"It's not even close," Elijah said. "Paying my rent was your idea, Mrs. Martyr. And why does it bother you so much that I'm calling him Dad again?"

Simone looked both ways, checking for eavesdroppers. "Because it makes the past few years *extremely awkward*!"

He considered just walking right past her, since it would be just as bad for her if Georgios knew she'd been talking to him for years, but he dreaded the idea of meeting his baby stepsister. There was no escape in sight, but maybe he could attempt to start their conversation off on a better foot. It was his fault, after all. They had an agreement that he should stay away from Arete, and he was pushing the envelope just by being in the same city as her—especially since he wasn't sure what she looked like. (If only he knew it was as easy as looking her name up on Instagram.)

He offered Simone his hand. "Officer Elijah Walker, at your service."

Despite her usually domineering personality, her handshake was timid that day. Simone tried to look stern, but her mouth twisted into a quirky smile. To that day she still couldn't comprehend that Elijah became a police officer of all things; it simply didn't suit him. He was as bright as he was broke. When they first met, he wanted to be an astronaut, and if anyone had the brainpower it was him. Admittedly, he was about ten when they first met. But a *cop*? At no point in his life did he have respect for authority. Maybe he exceeded the maximum height for astronauts and gave up on NASA altogether. The little shit always was a quitter.

"I'd love to chat," she said, "but I don't have time for this. I know you're not here to visit me, so what do you want?"

Of course Simone would see it that way. She was the sort of woman who never did anything without an ulterior motive. Though, Elijah himself was less than trustworthy. They kept enough secrets from each other to inspire a soap opera, and they had a sort of mutual trust in which each thought that there was only one liar among them. In Simone's case, she knew she was a filthy liar, though not without reason, but saw Elijah as too blunt to bother misleading her. In Elijah's case, he knew lying was Simone's native language, but believed himself an honest man. And so it bears no surprise that he would always call her the "Simonster," be it hateful or affectionate.

"I'm not here to cause problems," Elijah said. "I'm just visiting Dad. Look, we'll talk later, Simonster. I promise."

"No, it's going to be *now*. Arete's in there." She extended her elbow. "Walk with me."

Elijah huffed and allowed her to link arms with him as they walked down the halls. Well, *he* walked. Simone strutted like she was walking a purebred dog, and their arm linking was actually Simone squeezing his bicep like a titanium nutcracker.

"Care to explain what's going on here?" she said, looking straight ahead.

"Look, I'm sorry. *Dad* reached out to *me*, not the other way around. He's been buying me plane tickets so I can get to know him again before he… passes."

"And how long has this been going on?" she asks, accusatory.

"Just since March." He left out that it was March 2012.

She sent a contemptuous, sidelong glance in his direction. "And you thought I wouldn't find out?"

"It's not like I broke the agreement," he said. "Listen, I'm sorry for what I did to Arete. I've told you that over and over again. But that was eighteen years ago. I was just an angry, impulsive preteen. I've been paying for it every day, and that man in there is the only family I have left. Please. He wants me there… And I'm using unpaid vacation days for this."

Simone pursed her lips and looked away. She felt guilty about something, that much he could tell. That was her default when she talked to him—or, more rather, it was how she behaved on the rare occasion he talked about himself. Maybe that guilt was for ruining what was left of his childhood. What else could it be?

"I don't know what to do," Elijah said. "You don't want me to go, but you don't want to talk to me either."

"If we're not talking, then what do you call this?"

Elijah scoffs. "An interrogation. Can't we just sit in the lobby and talk this out?"

"No," Simone said. "Arete might see you on her way out. My house."

"Your house? Isn't that worse?"

"The cabin," Simone said. "Nobody will be there. I'll take you."

"But—"

"You can see Georgios tomorrow. Maybe. Now that I caught your clumsy arse, you may as well just waltz in our house when Arete's not home. I'll distract her. Really, you should have told me about this a long time ago. Things would've gone a lot more smoothly if I were the one in charge."

Simone was infuriating, but Elijah didn't have much of a choice. It was the best he was going to get out of her, so he reluctantly agreed. Hospitals were sad, anyway. Behind Simone's icy tone lay an offer for a nice change of scenery.

*

Georgios and his replacement family spent most of their time in Melbourne, but apparently also had a seldom-used cabin bordering the Sherwood Forest, since camping wasn't their style. That was where Simone decided to take him. It was, however, the most awkward road trip Elijah ever had to endure, and he was on the verge of joyful tears when she pulled into the driveway. There were few things worse than being stuck in a car with someone who was mad at you. Among those things was being stuck in the car with his infuriated stepmother whom he, for some inconceivable reason, trusted more than his father.

Unlike the house he grew up in, the Konstantinous' suburban vacation home was modern to the extreme. It didn't resemble a cabin at all. Elijah hated everything about it, from the fact that the front of the house was made up almost entirely of windows, to the boxy design.

"What? Don't like it?" Simone asked.

"No," Elijah said. "Does Dad?"

Simone flushed. There were few things worse than hearing someone her own age call her husband "Dad." Among those few things was hearing her husband being called "Dad" by "Officer Walker," whom she, for some inconceivable reason, trusted more than her husband. He was only doing it to tease her, she knew that, but it was worse than any hangover and had similar symptoms.

The two of them walked to the front door, and Elijah took in his surroundings. The other houses were similar in the fact that they were small, modern, and didn't resemble cabins. That one was by far the ugliest on the street.

"Is your other house this awful?" Elijah asked. "Because if you don't mind, I'd rather visit Dad there in the future."

She grunted. "I haven't even said yes yet."

He appreciated her word usage. "So where's your house?"

Simone thought for a moment. "P. Sherman, 42 Wallaby Way, Sydney."

He knew she was quoting *Finding Nemo*, but he decided to play dumb. "Cool, can't wait to visit. Does Dad still have visitation rights for every other weekend, or is it different now that we're all grown up?"

"Don't make me regret bringing you here," she said as she dug the keys out of her purse. "Hold my bag."

"Okay." The unexpected weight of the purse jerked Elijah's arm as he received it. "Geez, Mom, I have barbells lighter than this."

"Don't call me your mum," she said, her face even redder than before. She was having trouble getting her key into the hole. It would be easier if her hands weren't shaking. Why were they shaking?

"I didn't call you Mum," he said. "I called you *Mom*."

Simone opened the door. "Do you always blow stars and stripes out your arse, or is it only when you're visiting a better country?"

"Ouch," Elijah said as they entered the house.

"Don't pretend you're hurt," Simone said, leading him through the house. "We all know America is horrible."

Simone had favored neutral tones when she decorated and chose sleek, minimalist furniture. It made the place look more roomy. The only decoration in the living room was a vase of fake flowers that was set on the coffee table, which was a few inches askew from where she last left it. There was always some subtle sign that her daughter liked to sneak over there with her friends to party; that day's was an askew coffee table and a corn chip. Simone decided to ignore it, since Arete wasn't a problem child. It was better for her to get it out of her system then as opposed to moving to Hollywood and having a public nervous breakdown. She was terrified fame would do to Arete what it did to Britney Spears or Amanda Bynes, and she was secretly trying to minimize the damage before it began.

"*Actually*, I enlisted to die for America," Elijah said in protest.

Simone was probably right, of course, but that didn't mean he was going to admit it. To insult his country was to insult its military, and to insult the military was to insult the people who chose that life.

Her face softened and her guilt returned. "You never told me that."

"You never asked," Elijah said. "Marine Corps, seven years, honorable discharge, snore. Where are we going?"

She took it he didn't like talking about the Marines, and assumed he was deployed to a war zone. She wasn't used to him clamming up like that on the rare occasion she invited him to talk, and it was such a shame it happened then. She was particularly curious about what got a healthy, young man like Elijah discharged, but afraid to ask, she stuck to business. She was quite good at that.

"Down the hall, up the stairs and toward the back," she said. "There's a cute, little tea table upstairs, and I'd rather chat there. Where *no one can see us*. You're insufferable."

"If it's so private, why are there so many windows on the front of the house?"

"Because…" Simone shook her head. "Because shut up, or I'll shove my Jimmy Choos straight up your arse. Nobody saw us go in, there are no windows on the side, the back windows on the first story are covered by a privacy fence, and the tea table is a few feet from the landing. AKA, in the center of the house. No windows. The neighbors aren't home, and yes, I know this for a fact. We're good."

She sashayed through the house like it was a runway, and Elijah followed her upstairs, wondering if she held secret meetings in that house or something of that nature. She knew how to hide in this house a little too well, and the whole street was suspiciously quiet. All else aside, once they settled themselves at the tea table, they both had the same thought: *this is going to be exhausting.*

Normally, Simone would act cheerful and offer her guest herbal tea and dainty snacks, but today was different. She had business to discuss, and the sooner she was done, the sooner she could relax. If she hurried, she might even be able to kick him out in time to watch *The Real Housewives of Melbourne*. It was a new show, but she was convinced she saw Jackie Gillies at the bookstore. Maybe if she watched it a few more times, she'd be able to figure it out.

"So, what is it you want to talk about?" Elijah said.

"Nothing, technically."

As a matter of fact, she'd rather be sitting at home with Georgios while she still had the chance, but she had to face the skeletons in her closet instead. As if it wasn't hard enough that her husband was terminally ill.

"Look," he said, "neither of us really want to be here right now, not under these circumstances."

Simone grunted; she almost covered her mouth in embarrassment for making such an embarrassing noise in front of him. "Exactly. So just cut straight to the point."

"I want you to change the terms of our truce," Elijah said.

"Make your case."

"I never set out to hurt my stepsister," Elijah said, pleading. "And I've stayed out of her life for the past eighteen years, just like we agreed. But I'll do anything; I'll pretend I'm an old business partner, hell, I'll impersonate a doctor, but *please* don't make me leave my father. Not again. This is my last chance to ever know him. I forgave you a long time ago, so why can't you forgive me?"

"Our relationship has always been... odd," she said. "I enjoy our chats, but we can't be friends. Not really."

Elijah usually found it amusing that she refused to admit she gave a single fuck about him, but it got in the way of forming a genuine truce. "Why not? We're not that different."

"We just can't." Simone frowned. "Under any other circumstances, we *could* have been friends. Like Dexter and Sirko in season seven."

"All I want is to see my dad," Elijah said. "It's not like I'm stealing him from you. Hell, you spent more years with him than I did."

Simone closed her eyes, unable to look at him. It wasn't about what he did to her, (aka, nothing) or what he did to Arete. It was about what she took from him, and the fear of her already emotionally unstable daughter disowning her forever. Arete would have a hard time handling the whole secret brother thing, and then Simone would have to explain why it was a secret to begin with. If it got out that she "accidentally on purpose" pushed Tansy off the balcony, she'd lose both of them; and lately she talked to her stepson more often than she did to her own daughter. It was bad enough her husband was dying. Maybe it was time to take the first baby step to letting go of all of the bad blood, before she ended up alone.

"Fine," she said. "You may see him."

"Thank you."

"But you can't come in contact with my daughter, and you can't come to Georgios' funeral. It's too risky. And don't tell him I talk to you, either. *EVER*. Is this settled?"

"Sure," Elijah said. "I promise. Oh, and season seven sucked."

"We're all entitled to our opinions." She sighed and looked at the floor. "Georgios was right."

"Right about what?"

"That you weren't a bad kid. That you'd end up being a fine, young man." Tears started to well up in Simone's eyes, but she held them back. "Hell, you're twice the man my husband is. You're a war veteran, you're a police officer, you're kind... Kind of a douche bag, at least."

Elijah smirked, more bemused than flattered. It was fun to watch Simone deal with an inner struggle and he was elated to get his way for once, but a compliment from *Simone*? That was bizarre and unheard of. She hated men, and was generally vocal about putting Elijah toward the top of that list. Last time he checked, he was at number nine, right between her father and Justin Bieber.

The two of them stood up and exited toward the stairs so their meeting could come to a close. Simone stopped just before the stairs. Her legs were a little wobbly.

"I don't know how all this happened," she said. "You've been through so much, and a lot of it's my fault... You're losing your father and I didn't help. It's bad enough your mum died—" She shuts her mouth immediately and swallows.

"Died?" Elijah repeated.

She stammered. "Yes..."

Died. It's bad enough your mum *died.* She said *died.*

Elijah was dizzy. There was no reason for her to bother to bring it up to begin with...

Unless...

"She's still on the missing person's list," he said. "Has been for almost five years now..."

A tear rolled down Simone's cheek and she backed up. "Sorry. It's just that it's been so long I assumed she was dead. Your dad told me all about it years ago. And I just always felt like it was kind of my fault. Not directly, of course, just in a way. Since I ruined her life and all. Not that your father didn't help."

Elijah knew what he heard and he wasn't going to back down from Simone. Not this time. "No, you didn't just 'assume.' Who killed her?"

"I didn't mean to say—"

"Was it Dad?" he asked.

"No!"

"How did you know my mom is dead?"

"It was an accident!" She backed up and held her open palms in front of her. "We were fighting, and I pushed her—"

In a blind rage, Elijah shoved Simone as hard as he could. At the time, it was more "animal instinct" than "eye for an eye, tooth for a tooth," and the poetry did not register with him.

The back of Simone's head hit the wall and she lost her footing. Time stood still as she fell. Strands of red hair stuck to her painted lips, which remained parted after her words. Her eyes held no scorn; they were big like a Keane painting and glistened like Monet's *Water Lilies*. She reached out her hand and whispered. *"Please."*

Would Simone save Elijah if he fell?

Did Simone save Tansy when she fell?

Elijah reached for his beloved stepmonster, his dear friend and bitter rival, and caught her hand. It was ice cold, but soft like rose petals. And when she beamed in gratitude, so happy to be forgiven, he loosened his grip. Her hand slipped from his like a silk glove. The betrayal wiped away her smile, but she didn't scream when she tumbled down the marble staircase. The only noise that came from her was the crack when her head hit the sharp edge of a step.

As Elijah descended, Simone reached for her cell phone, which had slid across the room. She attempted to get up, but the best she could do was flip herself over onto her back. With a smile, Elijah stooped over her and looked into her eyes.

"You were wrong," he said. "I'm not a fine, young man."

"You're not." Although her chest heaved, she remained obstinate to the end. "You're... just like your mother."

"No." Elijah leaned over, inches away from her face, and whispered. "I'm *worse* than my mother."

He stood up and started up the stairs, until he heard a whimper. Elijah approached her, watching as she choked out her final words. The life faded from Simone's eyes as she stopped moving, her pretty face slumped over in a puddle of her own blood.

After realizing she was beyond resuscitation, he closed her eyes. It wasn't as easy to hate her when she was lying on cold tile, her precious head cracked open by his own doing. Simone lived her life craving two things: beauty and ultraviolence. She would be delighted to hear she died with both. But guilt is immortal. Blood feuds go on until there's nobody left to bleed. Elijah knew this well, and thus had to make tragedy look like an accident—*Simone's* accident.

Monday, April 27, 2015
William Brown Quiñones
Philadelphia, Pennsylvania

Whitney, who stayed the night with Arete for moral support, got up early to make us all French toast. I'm normally revolted by the idea of being woken up before noon, but I still got like fifteen hours of sleep, so I'm good. She excluded our dear "friend(?)" Elijah, who is uninvited, as he has been for four days. We didn't actively ban him; we just never asked him to come. Living in the same house as my girlfriend is a little awkward in a way, but Arete needs the company. She needs a friend that knows her well. Luckily, neither of them have figured out that I knew all along, and Elijah hasn't ratted me out. To be more dedicated to the role of confused friend, I ask the same vague question I asked yesterday and the day before that.

"Did you ask Elijah to explain yet?"

Arete finally gives me an answer to the question I *wanted* to ask. "No, but I'd be lying if I said I was shocked."

"What do you mean?"

Arete looks up at the family portrait, a large oil painting. Georgios stands next to Simone, who is holding a three-year-old Arete in her arms. They're decked out in formal wear suited more for a dinner party than a family photo, and standing as stiff as an old Victorian photo.

"Look at him," she says. "I look *nothing* like him at all. The parts of me that my mum doesn't have can't be traced to his side either. No one else has gray eyes or a tiny nose. Just me."

"Do you who your bio-dad is?" I ask.

Whitney presses the heel of her pumps into my toes from under the table, and I wince. It's kind of hot how she takes charge, though.

"I have a theory," Arete says.

She stares at her plate, red-nosed and weepy-eyed. There's no point in asking her if she's okay. A single glance is all it takes to confirm that she isn't, and won't be for a long time.

We dine in silence, until Whitney can't stand it anymore. "I hate to say it, but maybe you should send him off for a while. It can't be easy for you to relax with him upstairs."

Arete doesn't respond.

"She has a point," I say. "Our only proof that he's not dead is the food missing from the fridge."

"So you haven't talked to him then?" Whitney asks.

"A little bit," I say. "He's not much for conversation right now. I knocked on his door Thursday night because I felt kind of shitty for yelling at him." (As far as Arete knows, I only yelled at him for misleading her; I left out the stuff about him killing her killer mom.)

Arete shifts uncomfortably in her seat. "How was he?"

"I think his exact words were something along the lines of…" I try my best to imitate Elijah, Greek-Philly clusterfuck accent and all. "I have fallen into an infinitely deep abyss of despair, and my heart has been withered, dried out, and crushed into sand. Leave me to die, Boy Meets World."

Whitney faces me, wrinkles her nose, and discreetly mouths, "*Seriously?*"

I nod in confirmation.

"Of course," Arete says through sobs. "And I'm not allowed to be mad at him, because his mother died. I'm a cold bitch for not being there for him, even though he hurt me, because his mother died."

"You're not a bitch," Whitney says. "He's a bitch."

I understand why Whitney's acting the way she is. Ever since Arete started dating Elijah, she and Whitney grew apart as she fell deeper under his spell. Her world revolved around him, which isn't unheard of for new couples, and Whitney is still too sore to realize what Arete needs to hear right now. Whitney's afraid if they get back together, she'll be the invisible fourth wheel again, except the fourth wheel actually makes the wagon work again. Wait. That doesn't make… forget it. Doesn't matter. It's up to me to give Arete decent advice that makes things work out for all four of us in the end.

I put my hand on Arete's shoulder to comfort her. "Elijah will be fine. He's just afraid he's going to lose you too, and he thinks if he hides up there long enough, you'll eventually come by to check on him. He never wanted to hurt you, and he hates himself for letting you find out this way."

"Are these words from his mouth?" Arete asks.

"Yes, he said it just last night. But I didn't stick around long."

I don't feel guilty for lying; it puts her at ease to know that Elijah still cares for her. It's not hard to intuit how he feels. In reality, I've only exchanged a few words from him since he told me to go away last week. Our longest conversation was Saturday, and it involved me knocking on his door to tell him I was ordering Chinese and ask if he wanted anything; I left his order in front of the door. The day after that I knocked on his door to ask if he was alive, and he responded by knocking back.

And yet, as the days pass, I feel more and more guilty. I knew all these things and also hid them from Arete. I'm doing all the things that I condemn Elijah for—you know, other than murdering three people and marrying my stepsister. Still gross.

"I can't do it," Arete says. "I can't see him right now. Do me a favor?"

"Sure."

"Stay with him for a while," she says. "Whitney and I are having a spa day, and we won't be back until late. Maybe you can convince him to get some fresh air."

I suppress a groan. I'll have to stomach his wailing after all. "Okay. I'll try."

Whitney holds up her index finger. "Actually, I *did* hear him leave late last night. Like, really late, past three AM."

"Really?"

Whitney shoves a huge piece of French toast in her mouth and nods. By corking her mouth shut, she's stopping herself from saying something that will offend Arete. The quiet ones always have the loudest minds.

"Well, once we're all done, I guess I'll go visit the tumor upstairs."

I said that like I have a choice. When a woman asks me to do something, there is no choice. I can't help it. I'm too weak.

*

Elijah Walker is the last person I want to kiss and make up with, but I promised Arete I would comfort Elijah in her stead, and I promised Whitney I would knock some sense into him. Whitney can be a tough woman to manage, but at least she didn't kick me out of the entire right wing of the house and exile me to the room I occupied in the nineties. Then again, he brought it upon himself by not telling her the truth sooner.

I wait until they leave that afternoon, and then head to the door across from Arete's childhood bedroom, the one that was always locked. Nobody told me that's where his room was. It was just easy to figure out through process of elimination, and the fact that noises were suddenly coming from that mysterious room. It's adjacent to mine, after all. There's no response when I knock on the door, but I hear what sounds like a chair being pushed back and something being dropped on a hard surface. I guess I scared him.

"It's just me, douchebag. I'm here to check on you."

I wait for a response, but there isn't one. I don't know why that makes me so nervous, since he's obviously alive in there.

I tap on the door again and soften my voice. "I'm not going away, Hollywood. Open up."

I hear Elijah rustling around in his room and listen impatiently. Chair legs screech and what sounds like a drawer opens. There's a clack, like he's dropped something, and the sound of a drawer shutting. I have a bad feeling, so I jiggle the doorknob; it's locked, as always.

"Hollywood?" I ask.

He groans, and finally drags his feet to answer the door. When it swings open, the first thing I notice is how guilty he looks. That, and he hasn't shaved. I don't realize he's so heavily intoxicated until he gives me a bear hug, hurting my broken arm.

"I knew you wou-wouldn't hate me foreverrr!" He lifts me off the ground and squeezes me like a stuffed animal. His shoulder crushes my windpipe, and he reeks of rum. We're off to such a great start.

"You're choking me," I say. He's so happy to see me that I almost forgot I hate his guts.

"Sorrry, Pool Noodle," he says, putting me back down. He tries to jump onto the bed, but falls halfway off. "I'm okay!" he shouts when his knees hit the floor. His voice is muffled by a fuzzy, white blanket. Peeking out from underneath, I notice Star Wars bed sheets. His shirt is filthy and he's wearing boxer shorts, but at least he took a shower. Now that I think of it, he's wearing the same shirt Arete exiled him in.

How's your banishment going?" I ask.

"G-greaaat. Never been bet-better."

Ah, sarcasm. Even Elijah isn't above sarcasm. Now that I've seen the inside, I realize it's not a horrible room to lock yourself into; especially since he has his own bathroom. The unfortunate tradeoff is that a man who stands at over six feet tall has to curl up and sleep on a twin size racecar bed.

The bay window is cushioned on the sill to form a reading nook, which is accompanied by a modular bookshelf that wraps around the corner wall. As a child, it seems he enjoyed light reads, such as *The Origin of Species* and *Animal Farm*. Most of the books are about foreign languages, which I assume was his specialty, though he does have a lot of novels. The only titles I recognize are *Where the Sidewalk Ends, Gulliver's Travels,* and *The Old Man and the Sea*... wait, why does he have a copy of *Grey's Anatomy*? What kind of parent lets their kid read *A Clockwork Orange*? What kind of *kid* has the periodic table of elements hanging on his wall? He's written something on the wall under it in crayon...

Polonium oxygen phosphorous.

I reference the chart. *Po O P*. It spells out *poop*. He wrote poop on the wall and got away with it. Clearly nobody watched him as a kid. No wonder he grew up to be such an arsenic sulfur.

The TV facing his racecar bed is nicer than anything I've ever owned in the nineties, but it's unplugged and askew. He was probably one of those kids who got everything he wanted, especially judging by all the video games lined up on his shelf... and the ones lying on the floor. This is the messiest I have ever seen Elijah's anything. As for the screeching chair I heard earlier, it's stationed at a desk that would have been contemporary in the 90s. The computer is a Windows 3.1 relic, and it's playing annoying 32-bit game music.

"I'd in...invite you to play Ss-super Nintendo," Elijah slurs after he climbs on top of his bed. "But the... but my second controller is dead. But the computer still workss, so I've been playing Quest for Glory... The four-f-... Shadows o-of Darkness. But I-i-it re... it reminds me o-of Arete for some reason..."

I nod, unamused. Is he going to ramble like this all day? A bottle of champagne is open on the nightstand; it's the bottle that was supposed to be popped open at the Konstantinou Enterprises CEO appointment party, which was canceled due to "extenuating circumstances." Now it's eleven o'clock in the morning, and he's throwing himself a pity party to make up for it.

"Hollywood," I say, deadpan. "You're an alcoholic."

He hiccups. "Are you saying I shou-shoul... should follow your lead and be *boooring*?"

"If by boring, you mean eternally sober, then yes."

He laughs, but I don't remember telling a joke.

"Th-this was... was my bedroom... when I was t-twelve," he says, as if I didn't already know. "It looks almost *exaaactly* l-like it did in the na-nnineties, but I moved some of the... the stuff around. See that corner... over..." He points at the corner opposite the bed, where a rack of dumbbells stands. "That was where my TV... but where the... I played Super Mario World."

"Cool story."

The delirious, unshaven wreck rolls over onto his back, his legs hanging off the bed, and groans. "And now, this room is my prison."

"That… is a bit of a leap."

"Nooo it isn't," he says. "Fr-frog… is a leap."

The Pac Man wall clock ticks and tocks, serving as a reminder that every second I let him speak is a second wasted. He's regressing to his childhood, and there's no easy way to achieve both Whitney's and Arete's idea of what I should be doing with Elijah. I can't give him a reality check and comfort him at the same time. Maybe if I can lure him back into the adult world and motivate him, he'll be in better shape.

"So… Are you going to go to class?"

"It's w-reading week, no class till finals, blah-blah, nobody cares… Wh—…what about Arete?" He looks like he could cry just saying her name.

"Oh, I keep forgetting Penn Law has a different calendar," I say. "She's doing fine. She hasn't missed a single class and I saw her open a textbook once."

Cue Elijah's gross sobbing. "H-how many times did I walk over to-top of her… and didn't even know it?"

"Walk over her how?" I ask. "You can be a little pushy, but you've always given her the freedom to make her own choices."

"Not m-my wife." He sniffs. "My mom."

Oh. Duh. For the past three months, Elijah had been sitting on that deck to cuddle with Arete by the fire pit, all the while unaware that his mother's bones were buried beneath his feet. That must weigh heavy on his soul. How could it not?

"Do you think Simone did it on purpose?" I ask.

Elijah shakes his head. "I think she... she did it... o-on halfcident."

I sigh. "That is *not* a word, for the eightieth time."

"Yeah it is!" He smiles with pride. "I made it up... I... I have some of the... I have some good advice for you."

"I somehow doubt that."

Elijah takes a deep breath. "Listen c-careefully." He purses his lips for a moment and narrows his eyes. "Never. Trust. A woman."

"Seriously?" I say. "That's it?"

He sits up and points at the ceiling. "That's all a man needs t-to know in life... in... in order to soar ab-bove the clouds."

"I think you should stick to quotes," I say.

"Fine. Here's one for ya, ki—" He hiccups. "Kiddo..."

"I'm waiting."

"I know just-st the one," he says. "If you can't... handle m-me at my worst... then you sssure as hell don't deserve me at... at my best."

"Marilyn Monroe?" I say. "You just told me not to trust a woman."

"Y-heah, I ju-I just gave you a good example of why."

"Shut. Up." I put my hands on his shoulders and shake him a bit. "You are the least trustworthy person who has ever lived under this roof. The word 'lie' is in your name. It's time to wake up. *Snap out of it.*"

"I t-trusted Ssssimone," he says. "For years and y-ears I trusted that monts-ner. And I... look what hap-happened... because of the whole time, my mom... Hey, d-don't look at me... like that... Okay, I'll tell you exact... exactly what happened."

My mother's method of finding things out didn't work on him, but a disapproving stare does? He desperately wants my approval, but he's going to have a hard time getting it. He looks disgusting. In fact, he looks so disgusting that I feel bad for him.

"Mom... sh-she was released from the... the loony bin in Nov-nov... Novemb... 2009," he says. "Juuust in time for m-me to get out of the Iraq... I guess she came back... here instead of going to the hotel... I bought her a hotel... a-a-a room, I mean. I paid over the phone. I know, I know it l-*looks* like a suicide, but it... like Detective Bitchface told me. Y-you don't... you don't try to cover up a suicide." He hiccups. "I think Simone pushed her off... off the balcony. M-mmaybe in the heat of the moment..." He rubs his face. "I didn't... I sh-should have g—let her talk... S-simone. I should have lisssten..."

"Why would your mom come here though?" I ask. "I mean, you got her a room and everything."

"My best guess... She wanted Dad. Sh-she wanted him back. But she... Simone... she was... My mom was clingy, like me."

The word *clingy* hasn't occurred to me before, but now that he mentions it, it's so clear, unlike every other word that's tumbled out of his mouth today. For as long as I've known him, he's had a meltdown every time he gets rejected. He wouldn't even *let* me say no to Paddy Whacks. If Arete leaves him, he'll probably kill himself.

"So you think she still loved him after all that time?"

"I don't think... I *know*." He hiccups. "She nnnever sto-stopped loving him. When he left... when he fu-fuc... maarried Simone, Mom attempted suicide. To g-get his attention. Instead of helping her, he just... sent her off. Her at-atattempts to keep people were j-just so extreme that it ended—" He hiccups. "—up d-driving them away. It'ss ironic. She just wanted... a family. Just her and Dad... and m-me. No mistress, n-no bastard child, no shhhotgun weddings... Boy Meets World... I think it's my fault."

"Your fault?" I ask.

"On the phone..." he says. "Sh-she kept asking me about Dad and I wa... I wasn't thinking b-because I was annoyed... I let it sl-slip... implied Arete waswasn't my blood s-sister. She knew too much. My mom."

"Why would Simone kill her over that though?" I ask. "That sounds kind of drastic."

Elijah shakes his head. "Before I... I pushed her... that's what we were arguing about." He sniffs. "I wan... I wanted Simone to let me talk to Dad... and she said okay, but... only if I continued to hide fr-from Arete..."

"Why?" I ask. "What did you *do* to her?"

"I p-pushed her down the stairs, weren't you listening?" He puts the bottle to his lips; the height at which he tips the bottle to drink shows that it's at least halfway empty.

"I mean when you were twelve," I say.

I was hoping for a comprehensible answer, but he instead shuts his eyes and mumbles something incoherent about Simone. I can't understand it, but he sounds miserable. I don't pressure him to tell me. It's not hard to guess why Simone would hate Elijah. Pick a reason. But there has to be something more to it.

"Why were you talking to Simone in the first place?" I ask. "I mean, you hated each other."

"We ha-ad a truce," he says. "But then sh-she implied my mom was dead... and I'm not as st-st... stupid as everyone knows I am."

"Knows?"

"Thhhinks," he says. "I meant thinks, b-... but none of it matters now. Sheee... she's dead. All this time... and I kne- knew it and I still searched. Like it wassn't wea-real. The-the only person I lied to... wa-was me." He's about to down the rest of the champagne when I snatch it away. "Hey! G-give it..."

I give him a firm "no," pull the curtains back, and draw the blinds. He covers his eyes and groans, but it's for his own good. All the lights are off, and it looks like he has himself locked away in a dungeon.

Elijah grabs the nearest pillow and holds it over his eyes. "Why are you do-doing this to meee?" he says, his voice muffled. "I thought we were frieeends!"

"Shut up. When's the last time you left your room?"

"Uh... I we—I went jogging at... zero dark thirty."

"To clear your head?"

"No. I just like *literally* wun-running away from my problem, and then coming straaight back for my... f-for more abuse."

I like the not-so-subtle implication that Arete is his problem. He slowly peels the pillow away from his eyes and squints. That's when it occurs to me that he hasn't seen the sun in days.

"You've been asking... que—a lot... of questions," he says. "Can I aask..."

"Sure," I say. "Fire away."

"Does Arete... Does ssshe we-regret it... marrying me?"

I open my mouth but don't know what to say. Arete never explicitly said she wants a divorce, but deep down, Elijah and I both know the truth. Arete would have never married him if she knew he would keep such a huge secret from her, and what she just found out is only the beginning. I can feel it.

"No," I say.

"She hates me," he says so matter-of-factly that it's almost comical. Hopefully he won't remember this.

He sits up and looks out the window. In the light, I can see the dark circles that lined the bottom of his eyes, the five o'clock shadow, and the frown lines. He aged twenty years in two days. It's hard not to feel sorry for him, even after all he's done. And he *did* just dig up his mother's corpse.

"She loves you, don't doubt that," I say. "She just needs time to adjust." It's not very reassuring, but it's the best I can do.

He gives me a firm squeeze. "And wh-what am I supposed to do n-n... in the mean time?"

"I don't know." I return his hug and pat him on the back. "Arete and Whitney are going to be gone all day. So can I convince you to come out of this cave for a few hours?"

Elijah drags himself out of bed and rubs his eyes. It's a miracle he can stand. "When y-... when you came, I f-feared this day would come. I just did...d-didn't think it would be sso soon."

"Just relax, drama queen," I say. "Arete and Whitney are going to class and then stopping at a spa or the mall. I wasn't really listening. We won't run into them, I promise."

"So... j-just you... and me? A-a day without the hoes?"

"They're not hoes."

"Oh, right," he says. "Sorry. I for-forgot you, you were ssstill in your honeymoon phase. Before ya know it, she'll hate you too!"

I scoff. "No offense, but I've never lied to Whitney."

"I-I've nevvver lied to Arete!" He staggers out the door, and I follow.

"Hollywood, I love you, but a lie by omission is still a lie," I say. "Are there any *more* dark secrets you're hiding?"

"Yeahhh," he says.

I stop dead in my tracks. "Wait, what? How can you say that so casually?"

"I jus—I plead the fifth."

I give him my best look of disapproval; it worked last time. "You can't plead the fifth. You're not on trial."

Elijah is, without a doubt, the most frustrating man on earth. What did Arete ever see in him? For that matter, what do *I* see in him, other than a foul mix of pity and loathing coupled with wasted potential?

"Tha-that's because I'm a good plannerr," he says. He's still depressed, but he looks proud of himself.

I just stare.

"I started this whoole thing m-months before act-tu- ...talking to her. It took forever to get a subst-su-substantial DNA without bw-breaking and entering her dorm. I waited for an... just thhe right opportunity, and t-took some blood from a Band-Aid... she threw i-in... in the trash."

I grimace. "Eww..."

"H-hey, don't judge! My dad lied, he lied a lot, and I didn-I didn't want to wi-risk bonking my sister." He shakes his head. "I can't even be-*begin* to tell you how *happy* I was... when I confirmed she was just my *step*sister."

Still gross.

I also have my doubts he got enough blood from one singular bandage to do a blood test, but it's not worth the effort to try to get an intelligible truth out of him when he's sloppy drunk. I can't tell if he's misleading me on purpose or if he's just like any other drunk, thinking he sounds like a Ted Talk guest when in reality he's a brainfogged fool. I'm thinking it's the latter. Would knowing more about him collecting his stepsister's blood bring me any peace? Probably not, so I drop it.

"So you basically sat there yearning from afar while you waited for a lab to double-check if it was okay for you to ask her out on a date?"

"Yep," he says.

I can feel all of the brainpower I've managed to accumulate over the years leaking out of my orifices. Nothing about this is normal. "You sound like a stalker."

He snort-laughs. "I am."

"At least you admit it..."

Elijah staggers over to the toilet and gags himself with his index and middle finger. He hasn't had a haircut in a while, so I hold his hair back while he vomits. I know it's kind of a girl thing, but he probably won't remember this anyway. When he's done, he collapses on the bathroom floor, leaving me to wipe the vomit off his face and clean the bathroom. I'm not strong enough to drag him to bed, so I settle with throwing a blanket over him and sliding a pillow under his head. He mutters his appreciation, and sleeps there for about three hours.

Once he's woken up, I help my drunk friend down the stairs and outside. Elijah sits on the steps in front of the door, squinting his eyes at the sunlight while his Hollywood perfect hair ruffles in the breeze. He's posed like *The Thinker*. I'm half-minded to leave him there because watching a man's mood swing and listening to birds chirping for hours isn't my idea of a good evening. But if he's left unattended, he'll probably trip and crack his head open. Is this what it feels like to be a parent?

After a while of saying and doing nothing, I decide it would be a good idea to get him to talk about something other than Arete or something connected to her. It's not easy to find a topic, because the only things I knew about him all go back to either the Marines or something I only know because Arete told me; even when he does talk about himself, he never reveals anything without careful consideration.

"So, Hollywood," I say. "I heard you can speak sign language. What's the story behind that?"

Elijah chuckles. "That... came out of nowhere." He puts his hand down to mirror the other. *The Thinker* pose is successfully eliminated. "I started learning it in middle school. There was this kid at lunch who always sat alone and never talked to anyone. I felt bad for him, so I decided... I introduced myself. At first I thought he was ignoring me, but then I realized he was a deaf mute.

"So I checked out some books. From the library, because nineties. And I learned the ASL to introduce myself. His name was Ruben. From then on, he taught me sign language daily until I mastered it. He was me bes... my best friend."

"Did he leave?" I ask. "Maybe you can get back in touch."

"No," Elijah says. "When the Simonster kicked me out, I had to leave him behind. We didn't have the Facebook or... or texting back then, and my grandparents threw away his letters. I looked him up a few years ago. Turns out a drunk driver hit him. Ruben couldn't hear a car coming."

I wish I never asked. If his life sucked that badly, no wonder he's obsessed with the past... and with his stepsister, I mean fiancée, I mean *wife*. I realize it's my job to help him, not because Arete and Whitney ganged up on me, and not because it's the best way to keep the peace between the four of us, but because Elijah has no one else.

"You know what," I say. "Let's go fishing."

Elijah perks his head up. "Fishing! I forgot all about that!" He looks in the general direction of his bedroom and mumbles. "I thought I took care of everything before I died..."

"What? That's a little dramatic," I say. "Arete wasn't going to lock you in there forever."

I'm about to explain to him that he needs to be more careful about what he says when we go out in public, but then I remind myself that he had been in the drunkest state I had ever seen him in when I first found him. I shouldn't expect any taxing mental effort out of him for the next hour or so. Nothing he says will make sense; I just have to be supportive and wait.

Elijah stands up and starts to walk off. "I'll go get a glass of water," he says, ignoring my comment.

"*Wooder*," I whisper.

Elijah pauses and turns around. "What was that?"

I get up to follow him. "Nothing."

Elijah gets his glass of "wooder," drops it, and watches it shatter on the kitchen tile. The poor bastard can't even get his own glass of water, and I'm supposed to think he'll be good to go fishing in an hour? I consider helping him when he reaches for another glass, but I hate those dishes anyway. What's the point in having couches with cup holders if the drinking glasses are square?

Even the Konstantinou Manor has a junk drawer in the kitchen. That's where Elijah says I'll find the note, and once I do I read it out loud for his benefit.

> "*Dear Kit Kat,*
> *I'm going fishing with Boy Meets World,*
> *Love, Elijah*"

I don't know if he heard me over the glasses breaking in the background, but I turn around to find a mess of broken glass lying on the floor. I look up. Elijah is sitting on the countertop next to the sink, his back against the wall, drinking from a plastic *Teenage Mutant Ninja Turtles* cup, circa 1989.

"You broke *all of them?*"

"They had it coming." Elijah pauses to think. "It doesn't leave us with many options. We could go fishing for compliments, but, uh, that's weird." He hiccups. "We could try to fish something out of a gas well, but that stinks. Literally." He snickers at first, but it falls flat. "I guess we have no choice but to actually go fishing."

"Okay," I say. "So where's your fishing equipment."

Elijah drops the cup in the sink and almost falls in trying to retrieve it. "I don't think we have any. I've never been fishing, it was just some excuse I came up with because I wasn't thinking straight. I don't even know how. What about you?"

"Nope... I guess we have to go buy some fishing equipment then. But I only have about twenty bucks, so..."

"Other than the money I set aside for my tuition, I have $12.19."

My jaw drops. "Holy shit, Hollywood, how did you blow your entire inheritance in a year?"

"It's actually been... a liiittle over a year now," he says. "Well, iff you w-really want to know... I started out with one mil. I set aside three years of Penn Law, which is about

$165,900. So that's put away in savings. The year's rent I dropped on that apartment was $35,268 plus tax."

"You don't have to answer, that was rhetorical—"

"Then there's the standard bills, of course," he says. "Like the storage unit I was renting for my dead mom's things in case she returned, the web hosting for findtansy.com, and so on."

"Elijah, we need to talk about your definition of standard—"

"And the second I got my inheritance, I blew about $10,000," he says. "Then I paid $45,867.26 on the Benz."

"How do you remember the price tag?"

"It's hard to forget a price like that. Anyway, then there was the steep price of dating a spoiled, wi-rich girl. The first ring cost $4,239.98, but it turns out that was too cheap for her tastes. And then there was that trip to Australia, let's see... the tickets... There were the plane tickets, and the cancellation fee since I had to move up the flight. Well over $4,200. The one week yacht rental was about the same. The concert tickets were over about $300—fucking scalpers—and the dinner was $140, and—"

"How do you spend that much on a dinner for two?"

"We bought wine, and I'm including the tip. Anyway,—"

"Please, stop."

"—the car wen-rental was almost $260, since I had it booked for a week and they wouldn't refund me. And then there were all those little things... according to my bank statement, my failed proposal cost $13,380.35."

I'm starting to understand why he sulked in his room for days after she said no. "Didn't you put any of it in savings?"

"Other than for Penn? No. I told you, I'm bad with money. I actually spent almost 4,000 money on just general dates and gifts over the past three months. Oh, and the second engagement ring cost $600,000."

I whistle. It's not surprising, just sad.

"And then there was your electric bill."

I squint. "What?"

"Well, when I broke into your house I saw all those late bills stacked on the kitchen table. I mean, I couldn't start an electrical fire in your house if—"

"Stop."

"Fine," he says. "But a tip, if I may: a house that size doesn't need two refrigerators. Mini fridges can be real energy hogs, just like a full-size fridge. Anyway, I blew *a lot* since I got my inheritance last year, and that leaves me with $12.19."

"What would you have done if she said no?"

"I don't know... cry and ask her again? Did I wish you a good morning yet? I don't think I did. Good morning." He hugs me again, spilling cold water all over my shirt and the backseat of my pants. I'm screaming internally, but I pat him on the back.

My voice is strained as I pry myself away from him. "Doesn't Arete give you an allowance or something?"

"What, like a sugar baby? No. We have a joint account, and she puts seven percent of her monthly income in it. She doesn't use it, I don't think, but she can track my purchases."

"Only seven percent?" I ask. "Why?"

"Because she's good with money, and knows I'm not. That's a misleading number, though. Remember, she's a CEO. Well, president is a better word, but Dad had been calling himself a CEO since Konstantinou Enterprises was a lemonade stand. Figuratively speaking, I mean."

"Never mind all that," I say. "Why don't you just take money out of the joint account?"

"I have been. Mostly on legal fees and alcohol. If I buy all the fishing equipment we need, she might figure out we didn't really go last time, and if I take money out she'll wonder what I'm hiding."

"Oh."

Awkward. Elijah is a more talkative drunk than I gave him credit for. I now know more about his finances than I ever needed to, or even wanted to. Over the past few months, he's gotten so attached to me that it's actually kind of scary. When my friendship with Elijah was first beginning, I would have never guessed he'd be this open.

"What about a game?" he asks.

"What?"

"A fishing game." He sets his now empty cup on the counter. "I don't have anything like that on the Super Nintendo, but maybe we could find something."

"I have an N64. But it's, well... unavailable."

"Did I set it on fire? I'll replace it."

"No," I say. "It's..." I take a deep breath. "It's at my smother's house."

"Awww. Boy Meets World has a smother? How cute."

"Shut up. I haven't seen my family since Christmas for a reason."

He scowls. "You haven't spoken to your parents since Christmas?"

"Yeah? So?"

"How could you?" Elijah asks in a crybaby voice. "I would give up *everything* for a five minute goodbye to my parents, and here you have a full set of parents that you don't even talk to?"

I roll my eyes; I'm not in the mood to be guilted into seeing my parents. "First of all, the entirety of your assets is twelve dollars and a Benz. And nobody even lives in the same town. I'd have to drive all over Pennsylvania to visit my family."

"I had to cross an ocean to visit my dad. Every weekend for two years until he *died*."

And with that, we end up at my mother's house two hours later.

*

I stand at the front door of a narrow townhouse in Allentown, taking all the time I need to brace myself. If I knock gently enough, maybe Mom won't hear me and we can leave. Elijah takes care of that for me, pounding on the door like he knows them. I had hoped he would sober up in the passenger's seat, but no such luck. I couldn't get him to eat more than three saltine crackers, and we had to make two stops so he could puke at the side of the road, but at least he can walk and talk now. He's getting there.

Living in Philadelphia's Main Line spoiled me, and now I realize the row house I grew up in is, well... ugly. Compared to the Konstantinou Manor, my parents' house is a dilapidated hell. My father filled up the crack in the front door with tile caulk, but the shutters still look like they could fall off if a breeze blew too hard. I didn't realize how poor I was because I never wanted anything money could buy.

I hear the knob turn, and the door creaks open. Before now, I didn't notice it creaked. It's a garish noise. My mother's face peeks out.

"William?" she asks.

"Y-yeah."

She blinks. "W-what made you decide to drop by?"

She acts like she hasn't seen me in years or something. It's only been... One, two, three, four... five months? Has it really been five months since I've spoken to my mother? I barely noticed the passage of time, but Mom is looking at me like she doesn't recognize me.

"Uh, not much. I just…" How do you say 'I'm only here to get my Nintendo 64 and leave' in a way that isn't offensive?

"What happened to your arm?" Mom touches my arm, just under my shoulder; I flinch in pain.

"It comes off in a few weeks," I say. I refuse to confess I broke my arm by slipping on wet tile on a first date. That's a new achievement in loserdom, even for me.

"And who is this young man you brought with you?" she asks.

I gesture toward Elijah. "Young man? Mom, please. He turns thirty-two in a month."

"You haven't told your parents about me yet?" Elijah asks, feigning surprise. "We've been living together since February."

Well, looks like I'm paying for the age comment. It took him all of sixteen seconds to rat me out. I haven't seen my mom's eyes open this wide since I crashed her car into a fire hydrant.

"Oh! That…" She purses her lips for a moment. "That explains a lot."

"Pleased to meet you, ma'am." Elijah holds out his hand. "My name is Elijah Walker."

"Sofía Quiñones Garcia." Mom shakes his hand, more giddy than I ever thought possible.

"You're so cute and tiny!" Elijah says. "I could just pick you up and stick you in my pocket." He turns to me. "I love her already."

He didn't mean it sexually—otherwise, I would kneecap him. It's a common reaction since she's 4' 11" and aged fairly well, but most people aren't so, well... vocal. She always loved attention, though.

"Oh, would you like to stay for dinner?" she asks him, flattered. "I'm making pozole."

I kick Elijah's leg as hard as I can while being discreet, but that doesn't keep him from saying, "We'd love to!"

Mom pulls the door wide open and ushers us inside. She always cared about making a good impression, and this is the first time I've brought a friend home since I was a teenager. I hope to god she doesn't treat him the way she treated my first roommate out of high school. By that, I mean doting on him and thanking him for being my friend, while secretly hating me for leaving her. She has good intentions, but it makes me look and feel pathetic.

Elijah enters ahead of me and takes a look around, seeing the pink wallpaper peeling off the walls, those old, oak stairs in front of the door, and that TV we've had since 2003. If only Mom knew where he lived, she'd be as embarrassed as I am to show him around. It's not dirty per se, but it's cluttered and it's been a while since they've vacuumed. Most of our furnishings came from thrift shops and yard sales.

But Elijah isn't judging; he finds it charming. He doesn't ask to see the whole house; he just kind of ends up at the mantle of our (fake) fireplace, staring at old family photos. He looks fondly at one and picks it off the mantle; I have to walk around him to see which one he's looking at. It's me on my 2nd birthday with chocolate cake all over my mouth, hands, onesie, and somehow my feet. It's almost like he didn't realize I was a toddler once.

Elijah puts the picture back and turns to my mother. "¿Hablas español?"

My mother nods, impressed. "Sí, es mi lengua materna."

"Por favor Discúlpeme," he says. "Estoy un poco sorprendido: no sabía que era latina."

Seriously? Elijah speaks more Spanish than I do? Oh, no. That means Elijah is going to have a conversation with my mom in front of my face, and I'm not going to have a clue what they're talking about. Maybe I should just stand there and watch, so he'll think I understand and he won't say anything stupid.

"No estoy sorprendida," Mom says. "Lo esconde de todos."

"¿Tiene algo que ver con su tez?" Elijah asks.

"Sí, exactamente." Mom crosses her arms. "Solía usar Quiñones, pero comenzó a usar el apellido de su padre porque la gente lo acusó de mentir sobre su origen."

Elijah lifts his eyebrows and frowns. "Lo siento, no quise molestar."

"No, no." Mom smiles and waves her hand dismissively. "William debería ser honesto respecto a sus orígenes."

Elijah returns her smile and puts his arm around my shoulder. "No hace ninguna diferencia para mí. El siempre será mi Pool Noodle."

Oh, come on. They're talking about *me*? Elijah thinks I know what he's saying, but my mother of all people should know better than to talk about me right in front of my face. This is exactly why I never speak to her.

"Gracias," Mom says. "Me alegro de que finalmente haya encontrado un novio guapo, encantador y de mente abierta. Estaba empezando a preocuparme de que nunca traería a un hombre a casa."

Elijah removes his arm and steps to the side, glancing at me for a moment with widened eyes. I take that awkward glance as my queue to intercept whatever's going on.

"Yeah," I say. "So we're... we have this... special needs dog... and he needs an insulin shot twice a day."

Mom lowers her voice and covers her mouth. "No sabe hablar español."

I can at least translate that; she just ratted me out. She and Elijah laugh hysterically, and that can only mean one thing.

"Mom, are you saying embarrassing stuff about me?" I ask.

They laugh even louder, which means the same thing in every language: yes.

"Hold on," Mom says. She walks around toward the front door and shouts up the stairs. "Sherry! Your brother popped in for a surprise visit!"

Great. As if it isn't bad enough that I have to spend the day rotting at my parents' house, Sherry is in town. The old stairs creak as she steps down, making her grand entrance.

"Hey, asshole!" she shouts. "It's been forever, why don't you ever call?"

Um, because I hate you? "I figured you'd be busy and all, since you're a successful marine biologist."

"You say successful like it's a bad word," she says. After greeting me with one of those awkward, one armed hugs, she faces Elijah. "And who is *this*?"

"My... roommate," I say.

Mom leans over and whispers in Sherry's ear. "Finalmente encontró un novio. ¿No es guapo?"

Seriously, Mom? Spanish again? Sherry's eyes widen and her jaw drops. Is there some sort of secret club that I'm not a part of? What's going on?

Elijah shakes Sherry's hand. "Nice to meet you."

"Nice to meet you too," Sherry says. "How long are you staying?"

I butt in. "Not long! We're just staying for dinner... when is dinner?"

"The pozole's already on the stove," Mom says. "It'll be done by five. Your dad just got off work and he's taking a nap, so try to be quiet."

Great. Dad. I'm so excited for Elijah to meet my dad. At least when he comes down, I can use him as a buffer—he's the only person under this roof who speaks less Spanish than I do, and since he's as white as a ghost, no one expects him to learn it.

Sherry pokes me. "So how long have you two been, well... you know..."

"A few months," I say. "Why do you care?"

"Uh—" she chokes. "It's just, you never come around. And I'm surprised."

"What about you? Why are you just randomly in Allentown?" I don't know if I said that to be polite, or to be rude. Maybe it's a little bit of both.

Sherry gives me her classic 'ur sooo dumb' eye-roll. "I come in every week. Reading is only an hour away."

"Reading? I thought you lived in Baltimore."

Elijah laughs. "I thought I was going to meet your family, but it looks like *you* haven't even met them yet."

Again, I ignore him. "Sherry, why are you looking at me like that?"

"Like what?"

I lower my voice so Mom can't hear; after all, she's excluding me by speaking Spanish, so this is the best I can do. "Like I'm an entirely new person just because Elijah convinced me to stop by."

Sherry scoffs. "Oh come on, don't act like..." she glances at Elijah.

Our awkward non-conversation continues along that vein until my lethargic father comes downstairs and my mother drags us all to the kitchen while she finishes dinner up. It's just as bad as the rest of the house. The floral wallpaper is peeling off the walls, water stains are on the ceiling, and a reddish-brown sauce has been spilled on the stove. Don't they consider how many germs are multiplying on the countertop?

I sit at the long corner of the table, closest to the door. Elijah sits in the seat adjacent to me, with his back facing the wall as always. When Sherry sits next him, he scoots closer to me. I take it he doesn't like Sherry, which is fine; I don't either. Dad sits next to her and she whispers something in his ear. Unlike her and Mom, Dad isn't shocked at all. They must just be surprised that I'm actually capable of making friends, because they prod at him like he's at an interview and I'm the job.

Mom looks over her shoulder as she digs through the cabinets. She's so short that she has to sit on the countertops to reach them. "How long have you known my son?"

"Since February 24th," Elijah says. "I remember exactly."

"But," Sherry says, "you've been living together for like three months, so that means..."

"Yeah, I know, we were practically strangers," Elijah says. "But he didn't have anywhere to go after his house burned down, so I took him in."

Oh, please. Now he's making me sound like a charity case. Thank you, Saint Elijah, for delivering me from poverty by burning my house down and not-actually framing me for murder. And, of course, cue my overbearing mother.

"YOUR HOUSE BURNED DOWN?"

Thanks a lot, Elijah. Thank you so much. After today, I will *never* come here *ever* again.

After I pull a story out of my ass about how I didn't want to worry her, Dad says, "So how serious are you two?"

"Dad!" Sherry says. "Don't be so blunt!"

"You mean William and me?" Elijah asks. "Your son is my best friend. I'd be dead now if it wasn't for him."

Sherry twists her mouth a bit. "That... was a little dramatic."

"Is this really why you've been so distant all these years?" Mom smiles. "William, of all the things you could be, I couldn't care less about you being gay."

"Gay? Wait—"

"You don't have to hide it, brother," Sherry says. "There's nothing wrong with being a twink. What you do with your butthole is between you and your boyfriend."

"He's not my boyfriend, and I'm *not* gay!"

Dad snorts. "Tell that to your Backstreet Boys poster."

"Arthur!" Mom says. "If he's not ready, he's not ready. He'll come out on his own time."

Elijah is doing everything in his power not to laugh, and I'm doing everything I can to not cry. I'm not secure in my masculinity or sexuality like he is, and he knows it. I may just have to punch a wall to feel like a man again.

"*Mi pequeñito*," Mom says. She smooths my hair. "I understand what you're trying to do. You were testing the waters to see what we'd think about Elijah. Son, I love you no matter if you're straight or gay. You're a smart, handsome young man, and you've finally found someone who appreciates you."

This is the worst day of my life.

"For fuck's sake, Mom, he's MARRIED!" I glare at Elijah, who has apparently taken his wedding band off. "Why are you doing this to me?"

I consider telling them about Whitney, but I don't want to introduce her to my parents this early—or ever. It would be undue torture for someone as shy as she is, and I can't subject her to all that unwanted attention. Thankfully, Elijah has an Achilles heel that I can exploit.

"Fine," I say. "Elijah, if we're gay lovers, say it out loud."

He smirks. "It."

"You've got to be fucking kidding me, HIS FINGERS ARE CROSSED IN FULL VIEW, WHY AREN'T YOU LOOKING!"

He uncrosses them before anyone sees. He has the reflexes of a god and is employing new tactics; I cannot win this battle. I surrender. I admit defeat. I am gay. From now until I leave this property, I am gay.

Mom pats me on the back and returns to the stove. My father feels so awkward that he's reading at the table—most likely to avoid being sucked into an argument. I sit in silence as Sherry shamelessly flirts with my boyfriend.

"So, are you a fitness model?" she asks him with a wink. One of my least favorite things about her is that she's a fag hag.

"Stop!" I say. "You're embarrassing me!"

"Don't worry, Pool Noodle," Elijah says. "She's not my type. I'm committed, remember?"

I groan and lie my head on the table. Maybe if I pretend I'm not here, this will go faster. I can hear Mom tsk-tsking at Sherry for trying to steal my boyfriend. Elijah brushes my hair out of my face, and I swat him away. I guess living with Keyon and Tommy taught him everything he needed to know about gayting. But, hey, at least my parents are proud of me for once. It could be worse. He could be talking about what I've *really* been up to for the past few months. Or how he's a serial killer, and worse still, a *meme*. Thank god they're all media-hating technophobes. The beard Elijah is sporting doesn't make him much harder to recognize.

"What do you do, though?" Dad asks him, likely to change the topic.

"I attend Penn Law," Elijah says.

"You're going to be a lawyer?" Mom asks, offended. She never liked lawyers. I always thought it was because she blames them for her last employer screwing her over. Long, boring story, but it's why I grew up a poor Chicano stereotype. But if she doesn't want one in the family, it's got to be something else.

"What's wrong?" Elijah asks.

"You'll waste your life away." Mom points at him with the mixing spoon. "What about *familia*?" Ah, there it is. *La familia*.

Dad reaches out his hand. "Honey, let's not get upset now."

"I want to give your son a good life," Elijah says. Dad is waving his hands and mouthing the word *stop*, but Elijah continues anyway. "How can I support my family without money?"

"*Money, money, money.*" Mom shakes her head. "What good is it when Daddy is gone all day and locked in his office all night? How can you support them like *that*?"

"Well, they'll have two dads and us," Dad says to placate her. "He just wants to provide a good life for them."

"Arthur!" Mom snaps.

"So if Elijah is the dad," Sherry says, "Then William must be the mom."

"We're not adopting kids!" I say.

"There will be kids, don't you worry, Sofía." Elijah grins. "I want at least three kids. One will be a deaf-mute named Croesus, because kids who have special needs are less likely to get adopted. And I want a daughter named Cosima, and a son named Alesandro. And, of course, I'd like to bring them over here often so they can grow up bilingual. Well, except Croesus, of course. Don't worry, ASL isn't that hard. It should be a piece of cake for you, since you speak English so well. Do you want me to start teaching you now?" He extends a straight, open palm from his forehead and out, kind of like a salute. "That's how you say 'hello.'"

Mom grimaces and signs, "Hello."

Elijah turns to my sister. "How do you feel about donating your eggs?"

Sherry's jaw drops and Mom drags me by the shirt collar into the living room. Somehow, this is more embarrassing than what Elijah is doing to me. After briskly kicking a box out of the way, Mom pulls the door shut behind her. That door had been propped open so long I'd forgotten there was a door to the kitchen. The family room is suddenly making me feel claustrophobic.

"We need to talk."

I groan.

"Call it a mother's intuition, but there is something off about that man."

"I thought you liked him," I say.

"I was caught up in the moment," she says. "Didn't you hear him in there? He's controlling, manipulative, and *clearly* drunk. Ever since he got here, he's been cheesier than chili, and it's all superficial."

"You don't put cheese in your chili."

She responds with the Mom Glare. The one that makes me give up everything. I can't talk my way out of this one... Wait, why do I care? Misplaced loyalty gives me an excuse to *never* come here again, and they'll never try to contact me. I set aside my dignity.

"He's just trying too hard because he wants you to like him. He had a glass of champagne before we left because he was nervous."

She scoffs. "More like a *bottle* of champagne. And you trust this man? He's a liar, I can tell."

"You pronounced 'lawyer' wrong."

Mom ignores my comment and puts her arms around me. "*Mi renacuajo,* I'm sorry. But he's hiding something from you."

I don't hug her back. "Elijah would never hide anything from me," I somehow say with a straight face. "And he's not controlling, just passionate."

Mom pulls away. "Listen to your old mother. When you reject them, the most passionate lovers are the most dangerous. I'm begging you, *please* get rid of this man and go be gay with someone decent."

Elijah is only dangerous when you hurt someone he loves, but I can't tell her that. There's too much to explain, and nothing good will come from me making excuses for his behavior. He really is a douche bag. I should've never let him talk me into coming here.

"Listen to me for once!" I say.

"Your arm," she says. "Did he do that?"

"No!" I say. "I slipped on wet floor tile."

"You always lie when you love someone," she says. "Not that it's ever sinful to love someone, but that doesn't mean you should let yourself get pushed around."

This isn't going in the direction I thought it would. "It's never sinful to love someone" is a line she's tossed around before, and I thought I'd get the chance to use it against her for once. This isn't going the direction I thought it would. She'll never trust my judgment, but maybe there's something I can add to make her warm up to him—anything to keep her from calling me up at gross hours in the morning to ask me if I've dumped him yet, or begging me to move back in with her. Elijah's wife didn't make him sign a prenup, and that's the next best thing to having money. "He's rich, you know. And not one of those lazy rich people, he's a really hard worker. We could have a great life together."

"I don't care," she says, "you are breaking up with this man."

"Stop telling me what to do!"

Mom is almost as taken aback by my comment as I am. I rarely say no to her, and something awful usually happens when I do. The whole reason I left was so I could have a life and choose my own mistakes. Moving to "big, dangerous" Philadelphia in spite of her begging was hard enough, and remains the foremost reason I never come around. Now I've implicitly said, "Fuck you, Mom, I do what I want now" by choosing a fake relationship over her. I don't know why, but her comments hurt even though it's not real. Maybe it's because I've spent so much time around Arete and Elijah that they've become my family. Not a "replacement" for my *familia*, but still an actual family. And Elijah and I do share a pretty nice bromance when he's not teasing me or having a meltdown, so I'm forgiving of his flaws.

Her expression of shock turns into a somber frown. "Fine. Stubborn as always. But be warned, if you stay with this man you *will* get hurt. He's bad news."

I swallow hard. "Duly noted."

*

I must have checked my watch at least thirty times, which is depressing since dinner barely lasted fifteen minutes, and Elijah didn't even take his usual ten-hour bathroom break after the meal. Dinner was so awkward that it makes me think fondly of all my Waffle House memories. Mom gave Elijah dirty looks every time he talked about the domestic life we share together, Sherry was strangely quiet, and Dad talked to him like they'd been friends for years. The second my "boyfriend" put his fork down, I retreated upstairs to my bedroom and packed up my Nintendo 64, quadruple-checking to make sure I had *absolutely every part*. To my dismay, Dad insists on carrying it, leaving me free to hold hands with Hollywood Perfect on our way to the car. It's not as humiliating with just Dad here since he's more easygoing, but my cheeks are burning.

I half-expect Elijah to kiss me, but he just waves goodbye to my dad and hops into the driver's side of his Benz. I contemplate telling him to move to the passenger's side, but it's been about six hours since his last drink and he's finally had something to eat. He should be fine, and I don't feel like driving.

He slides his wedding band back on as soon as we're out of sight; I'd be pleased that he's still dedicated to Arete, but I'm disgusted that he took this prank so far. I don't talk to him all the way home. It's not that I don't want to talk to him or that I don't have anything to say. It's that I don't know where to start. He doesn't talk to me either until I pull into the driveway.

He picks up the N64 from the backseat. "Newer televisions aren't compatible with composite cables, so we'll have to hook it up in my room."

I don't respond because that wasn't an apology. Instead, I imply my agreement by leading the way to his 90s-time capsule prison. He slows down to match my pace.

Setting everything up is a challenge thanks to my cast, but I reject Elijah's offer to help by ignoring him. I insert the game cartridge for The Legend of Zelda: Ocarina of Time and prepare to go fishing. Hyrule has been waiting to be saved since 1999; they can wait another fifteen years for me to defeat Ganondorf.

"You know, part of going fishing is talking," Elijah says when I (or should I say Link) makes it to the fishing hole.

I snap. "Then tell me why you did that!"

"I'm sorry..." he says. "I did it because... I'm jealous. Here you have your parents, and they're happily married, and you have an annoying older sister... I'd kill to have my parents back, and you never even talk to yours. It pissed me off."

"So you decided to humiliate me?"

"If it makes you feel better, I didn't plan it that way," he says. "Your mother just assumed I was your boyfriend, and I didn't know what to say. And I was so jealous, I played along."

I scoff and return my attention to the game. My mother jumping to the conclusion that I'm gay only makes it worse. My only consolation is that he isn't blaming his actions on the champagne.

"Look, I really am sorry," he says.

I suck in the corner of my mouth and huff. "I know."

"I have a confession to make..." he says. "Part of the reason I got so carried away was because I liked being part of your family. No homo, but I almost wish it was real because I really liked playing house, and I don't have any family."

"My mom hated you," I say.

"Yeah," he says. "None of my other girlfriends' moms liked me either."

"I'm not your girlfriend."

He smirks. "Admit it, you loved it."

"No, I didn't!"

He pinches my cheek. "So cute."

I swat at him and my cheeks flush.

"You should really ease up on your family," Elijah says. "I can tell why you don't talk to them, but they love you a lot. You never know when you'll lose someone."

"You'll lose Arete if you keep avoiding her." As soon as the words slip my tongue, I regret them. I don't want to talk about Arete right now. Not yet, anyway.

My mental clock ticks a good nine seconds before he responds.

"I've already lost her."

"Then go find her," I say. "If you want a family, start one. Go make Alesandro and Cosima, go adopt Croesus, and go get super-married. Whatever order you want."

"Are you going to help me out with this?" he asks.

I roll my eyes. "Fine. I'll talk to Whitney."

"Why Whitney?"

"Look, Arete *hates* you," I say. "And as long as Whitney is rooting for your marriage to freeze under Cocytus, it's not going to work out. Luckily for you, Whitney tells Arete *everything*, even if it's supposed to be a secret."

"How is that lucky?" he asks. "Whitney hates me too, and no offense, but I hate her back."

"That's been your mistake this whole time," I say. "You hate Whitney because she hates you, when you should have been sucking up to her. You're lucky that she's my girlfriend, and if I influence her opinion in your favor, she'll pass that along to Arete, thinking it was her idea to do so. After that, all you have to do is continue to ignore Arete, leave the house and pretend you have a life, and she'll eventually come back to you when she sees you out flourishing without her. Girl science."

"Wow..." he says, wide-eyed. "You're awesome."

I scoff. "Thanks for finally noticing."

"How do you know these things and I don't?" he asks, amazed.

"I have a sister."

"So do I," he says.

I give him the stink eye, and he laughs. Can't he just go back to denying it? Or is he just doing this because today is Make William Uncomfortable Day?

He stops laughing abruptly and becomes frustrated. "Wait a minute. How am I supposed to flourish when all I have is $12.19?" he asks.

"Flourish with her money," I say. "She didn't make you sign a prenup, so she might stay with you based on convenience."

"I don't know," he says. "That might just piss her off. I don't want her to stay with me just because she doesn't want to pay alimony."

I pause to think. "She's always on Instagram. Go to Starbucks, fish an empty cup out of the trash, and pose with it. Like you just topped off the greatest jog of your life with overpriced coffee."

"That's... weirdly plausible." His train of thought drifts and his eyes widen. "Oh, that reminds me, I never thanked you for helping me save Arete."

"What are you talking about?" I ask, wondering how this is remotely related. Something in his brain must be wired incorrectly. Every thought he has is misconnected to the Arete region of his brain.

"That night with Galligan. I thought I could take him on no problem. I underestimated him and got cocky. When he disarmed me, I thought it was all over. But then you slid into that alleyway screaming and distracted him. It bought me enough time to arm myself and finish him off. If it wasn't for that, we could have both died. So, thank you."

"I didn't even know I did that," I say. "You're welcome, though."

Elijah's relief slowly fades into anxiety. "Do you really think I have a shot?"

I hand him the controller. "Yeah. Do you know the controls?"

"No," he says, probably aware that I'm only pretending I think he meant catching a fish. I don't think I can pretend he has a good chance of getting Arete back what with the whole paper incest thing, but I'll try my best.

"I've never played this game," Elijah says.

I try to show him by example, but my cast keeps getting in the way. "Cast your line with B. And then you can wiggle the lure around with the control stick, like this. Then, when the fish bites, hold down A and pull the stick back to reel it in."

Elijah does as I instruct, and several minutes pass.

"So," he says, "How long does this take?"

"Too long. But not as long as real life."

Fishing gets a little easier after that. I mean, not the actual *fishing* part, but the talking part. We slide back into casual conversation, talking about normal things other than #Arelijah.

"So, what's your full name?" he asks in a teasing voice.

I groan. "William Donatello Julio Romeo Arthur Brown Quiñones."

He whistles. "And I thought Ηλίας Ιάκωβος Παπαδόπουλος was bad."

"I thought you were born Konstantinou?"

"My parents were never married. It was Papadópoulos, but then Mom changed it to Konstantinou when we came to America so I could have a more prestigious name, and I started going by the westernized version of Ηλίας so Americans would have an easier time pronouncing it. Then my grandparents changed it back when I got kicked out, and then later I came back to America and changed my name to Elijah James Walker for obvious reasons."

By obvious reasons, he must mean hiding his true identity from his family. Maybe Mom was right about him. But to think, she shamed *me* for "pretending to be White." Meanwhile, Elijah picked his Whitey McBritishboy name out of nowhere because he thought it sounded cool and American. Still, this conversation is getting too close to the dreaded Family Drama Zone, so I change the subject.

"So what's your doctorate in?" I ask.

"Doctorate?" He cracks up. "Where did you get that from? I graduated with a GPA of 2.67 because I was busy with the military and rarely did my homework. I only got into Penn Law because of my perfect SAT and LSAT scores and a few business connections, aka, MENSA and a letter from my dead uncle."

"Pfeiffer... She told me you had some kind of doctorate, and an IQ of 162."

He raises his brows. "I have a *bachelor's* degree in forensic psychology, if that's what you mean."

"Shit. She was trying to gauge how well I knew you, and I played along like a dumbass."

"Don't worry," he says. "She's not trying to peg anything on you. She was just picking on you because you're easy to crack. If anything, she's assumed that you're useless to her investigation."

"How do you know that?"

"I was a cop." he says.

I don't bother to point out that he was a traffic cop throughout most of it. It took me a while to figure out, but now I realize that his dismissive reminders that he was a cop are part of an effort to downplay his intelligence. "But is the IQ part true?"

"162?" he says. "Maybe. I haven't taken an IQ test since I was nine, and 162 is the highest a kid can score. But I doubt it's much higher than that, so don't assume I'm a mega genius or something. But that's not important. How did you react when she told you?"

"Shocked as hell. Because I was."

He rubs the back of his neck. "I'm kind of offended? But whatever, that's good. She'll probably leave you alone, unlike me."

"Why?" I ask. This is the first I've heard from him about Pfeiffer. "What does she think about you?"

He gently taps the control stick and sets the bait. "She's harassing me because she thinks I'm a murderous danger to society who could snap at any moment."

"Oh... really?" Again, we're going too close to Arete territory. "While I'm asking, what was your rank again?"

"Sergeant."

"Is that higher than corporal?"

His jaw drops. "Did she really demote me? That's low, even for her."

"If it's any consolation," I say, "I bet you were a great sergeant."

"I don't know, I think everyone would've been better off if I was killed in action."

Arete-talk has been narrowly dodged, and yet again, this isn't the direction I wanted this conversation to go either.

Luckily, his thought pattern is interrupted by the controller vibrating. "Hey, I think I caught one!" he says.

"Reel it in!"

And, as luck would have it, the fish gets away immediately, and the fishing hole guy gives his irritating failure message. "Wah ha haah! Did you set the hook by pressing (A) and (control stick) down?"

I expect Elijah to throw the controller across the room and curse at the TV like I always have, but he just looks confused. "Set the hook? What?"

"How are you not pissed off right now?" I ask.

"I'm not really that invested." He frowns. "I admit... I don't work hard enough on anger management, and I apologize for that."

"I never said—"

"You didn't have to," he says. "If you're surprised I can handle losing a fight with a virtual fish, that means you see me as an angry person. And I hate myself when I'm angry. More than usual, I mean."

I don't know what to say to that other than a simple "It's okay." We take turns fishing in silence for a good twenty minutes before I respond.

"I don't hate you," I say. "It's true you blow up a lot, but you're usually over it in like five minutes. And things that would drive other people insane, you just get mildly annoyed. I mean, when you're bad, you're awful, but when you're good, you're great. You make friends fast and you're really loyal to

Arete, even when she doesn't want you. Hell, you're loyal to her even when *you* think you don't want *her*. You're a great person."

"Thanks." He's surprised, but flattered. "Well, I guess there are only three things that still piss me off beyond redemption. Traffic, banks, and..." He takes a deep breath and releases it slowly, like a sigh. He saddens. "And family matters... I just can't let it go."

"If you can't forgive Arete, how can she forgive you?"

He abruptly stops fishing and stares off into space.

"Hollywood?" I say.

He drops the controller, turns to me, and grasps my shoulders. "Pool Noodle, you beautiful person!" he says, his face lighting up. "You just saved my marriage with your Mexican wisdom!"

I furrow my brows and raise my upper lip, unsure if I should be confused, offended, or patient. "Is me being biracial really that amusing?"

"I'm sorry," he says. "Just... thank you."

I crack up. "Oh, whatever, I can't stay mad at you."

We bro-hug it out and continue fishing. We don't catch anything over eight pounds—no reward for me—but he's calmed down and that's all I wanted.

*

As soon as Whitney and Arete arrive home, along with at least twelve shopping bags, Elijah climbs under the covers and pretends to be asleep. I guess he still needs time, but I can report a successful mission. Whitney turns down my offer to help bring the bags in; unlike Arete, she rejects chivalry, believing gender roles need to die. I don't complain because if she believed in gender roles, she wouldn't be with me anyway. Arete is refreshed by "retail therapy," but exhausted. She goes to bed without asking any questions about Elijah; she's better off for it. I think I succeeded in helping him, but I don't know what to tell her. Sure, he feels assured he *can* earn Arete's affections back. The question is whether or not he's interested in carrying on right now. He loves her, and she loves him, but they did so much to hurt each other that it could go either way. Or maybe I'm deluding myself because deep down I hope that, while he's out "flourishing," he realizes he doesn't need her after all.

But I can't let my whole life revolve around #Arelijah. I put my pitiable, injured brain on the back burner and lead Whitney to the Gazebo.

"Why did you take me out here?" she asks. "I know you hate the cold, and it's half past ten."

"I wanted to be able to talk to you without worrying about being overheard," I say. The remains of the deck are Elijah repellant, and he's the last person I want to overhear this conversation. I mentally rehearsed what I was going to say to her, but it's not the script Elijah is hoping for.

Whitney and I sit on the gazebo bench overlooking the koi pond rather than the bench on the left. That one overlooks piles of wood and mud, all wrapped up in yellow tape. The bones are gone, but sorrow is still there, rearing its lonely head.

She leans her head on my shoulder. "What's this all about?"

"Elijah lied—well, he *hid* so many things from his wife that it destroyed their marriage before it really had a chance. And I don't want our relationship to be like that, so I want to tell you the truth about everything I can. I can't spill his secrets because I promised I wouldn't, but the things that had something to do with me, I think you should know."

"I understand."

"Well, uh... Things went okay today. He's hiding in his room again, but we went out and he got a good perspective on life and stuff."

She sits up. "You're beating around the bush."

Of course I am. This is the last thing I want to talk about, but I saw what lying did to Elijah and Arete. There's no way I'm going to let that happen to Whitney and me.

"I didn't really meet Arete when she stopped by the gas station," I say. "I mean, I did, but that's not really how it goes."

She raises her eyebrow. Yes, just one. No, wait—the other one is raised by at least a millimeter. Or are her eyebrows just uneven? I never noticed before.

"Focus," she says.

"Right. First of all, I lied, she wasn't buying a soda. She bought condoms."

"Oh my *god*, she told me she was a virgin until—"

"She was, she was," I say. "She didn't get to use them."

"Why are you telling me this?"

"They were interrupted," I say. "I mean, they rented a sleaze motel, but I guess they changed their mind on impulse and decided to do it in public. In an alley. But I heard a scream, and ran over, and there was a man attacking Arete."

"Holy *shit biscuits*! Why didn't she say anything?"

"It was Hoyt Galligan. That hit man on the news, who turned up dead not long ago."

Whitney nods. "I read about that... But..."

"Elijah killed him in her defense," I say. I decide to leave out the part about the icicle; this already sounds fake. "But instead of just calling the police, he covered up the murder. I don't know why. He was drunk."

Whitney's jaw drops. "Is this a joke?"

"I wish. That's when I walked in, unlucky as usual. Arete, who was really, *really* drunk, by the way, recognized me from my author portrait. So Arete decided to keep me from running off with sex toy handcuffs so I wouldn't tell the police, and then Elijah took us back to a sleaze motel where I watched *Law & Order* and waited for him to dispose of the body, and then we went to Waffle House, where we bonded over hash browns. Then my house burned down and, well, you know the rest."

Whitney blinks her eyes in confusion. Not to be cheesy, but she has beautiful, dark doe eyes. If she wasn't using them to squint at me right now, I'd be in heaven.

"And… You're serious about this?" she asks.

"Elijah ended up letting me go, and made it sound like he framed me for the man's murder. I know he just conned me into jumping to that conclusion in case I was a snitch, but I'm still kind of mad about it."

Still squinting, she pushes out her palms. "Wait, wait, back up. You're telling me that two drunk people kidnapped you with a sex toy, took you to Waffle House, and you became *friends*?"

"W-well, Arete was more drunk than Elijah. He can control himself… Or, at least, he *used* to be able to control himself. Now he's disgusting."

Her squint gives way to a frown. "All this time, I thought she wasn't talking to me because she was in Stupid-Happy Boyfriend Land. But she was hiding *this*?"

"Don't you believe me?" I ask.

"Of course I do," she says. "It explains everything… Why she started avoiding me, why she crawled up Elijah's butthole so fast, why she acted like she was hiding something…" Whitney looks down at her hands in her lap. "But you said Galligan was a hit man, right? Someone ordered a hit on her?"

"Antonis hired him," I say. "He wanted full control of KE. But Elijah took care of him too when he found out. But I wasn't really involved in that, I'm just a shitty dancer. But anyway, he worked really hard to save Arete's life, and that's why she won't call it quits. His commitment to her is... unparalleled. Screwed up, but unparalleled."

Whitney is dazed, and her mouth hangs open. Elijah was found not guilty of the murder of Antonis, so she couldn't get him arrested even if she wanted to, but maybe I went too far.

"I'm sorry I hid this from you," I say. "And lied about it, over and over again—"

"Okay, hold up!" She gestures for me to stop. "He murdered her uncle, who was actually his uncle, by tripping into a cactus, risked jail time, got himself publicly humiliated and dubbed 'Cactus Guy,' all on purpose so he could protect Arete?"

"Yep," I say. "Except, I'm 112% sure he loves being a meme."

She closes her eyes and shakes her head. "I know my brain is kind of hopping around right now, and I should probably be worried, but this is just... weird. I'm sorry."

"It's okay," I say. "It's hard to concentrate on the serious stuff when every word sounds like bullshit."

She scrunches up her nose. "But that means he killed his own uncle..."

"I know," I say. "And I'm sure you grew up with a different view of Antonis, and so did Arete... But I promise Elijah did the right thing. Arete could be dead by now if he hadn't."

Whitney's tone levels out and she calms down some. "Well, if you and Arete feel safe with Elijah around, I guess I do too. This is all hard to swallow, but I won't tell them you told me."

"You don't have to if it hurts to hold it in," I say, secretly relieved.

"No," she says. "And I'll keep his secret too. If he really did all that for her, he must really love her, even if it's kind of nasty. And all this time I assumed he was just using her as a tool to solve his mother's murder, or he had some step-Oedipus complex."

"Do me a favor and don't *ever* say that again."

She laughs, and I crack a smile. Her candid comments are disgusting sometimes, but there's never a dull moment.

"I was pissed at him for letting her find out this way," I say, "but I forgave him after today."

The squinting stare is back again.

"Whitney?"

"You knew the whole time?" she shouts.

I jump. I expected Whitney to be angry, but not about this. What do I say, what do I say... "I knew Arete would react this way unless she heard it from Elijah."

"No!" She leaves our seat, and I notice a flash of fury in her eyes as she walks to the other of the gazebo—the side overlooking the crime scene. At this hour, all you can see is the slivers of wood, barely illuminated by the light from the dining room. I take the risk and stand by her side.

"Please try to understand," I say, too anxious to use a decent soothing voice. "I begged him to tell her over and over again, but he insisted she was better off if she didn't know who her real father was."

"Who was he then?" Whitney asks without looking at me. "Arete told me she doesn't want to know right now."

Great, now I have to tell. "Nobody knows. Simone was gang raped."

Whitney whips around. "Mrs. Konstantinou was...?" She couldn't say the word, not that I blame her.

"Please," I say, openly desperate. "This isn't the kind of thing you just tell someone."

Tears are starting to well up in Whitney's eyes when she throws her arms around me. "I'm sorry."

"It's okay," I say as I hold her. "It's a lot to take in."

"I won't tell her any of this," Whitney says. "You're right. This is something she *can't* know. It'll destroy her."

I wipe the tears off of her cheeks with my thumb. "Here's the story we'll use. If Arete asks who her dad is, we'll just say we don't know, Elijah doesn't know, and then we change the subject. It's true, and there's no point in making her feel like she ruined her mom's life just by existing."

"You're right," she says. "Thank you for including me in this. I thought she was shutting me out because I hated Elijah. Now I know Arete wasn't rejecting me, she was just protecting someone who protected her. It hurts, but I feel better knowing."

"You're important to Arete," I say. "Don't doubt that."

"I won't," Whitney says. "You know what? I think I'm going to talk to her about Elijah."

"Really?"

"Yep. I mean, don't tell them this, but I saw them together on Florence Cho, and they were so happy. At first, I thought they were just acting, but then they came back happy. I think they can be like that again."

Whitney's a little deluded, but hey. Two birds, one stone. I helped Elijah *and* came clean to Whitney in one conversation. I can call this day a success.

Thursday, July 17ᵗʰ, 2014
Omniscient View
Camden, New Jersey

Elijah felt his phone vibrating in his back pocket, but ignored it. It was probably someone from the station trying to suck him into an unwanted shift, or Natalie Park trying to suck him into an unwanted relationship. She didn't care a bit about him until he started showing up in the news, but saving a kid's life didn't exactly make up for murdering Simone. It made him feel worse because he was being hailed as a hero. He would never be anyone's hero. He was nothing more than the local news' favorite fluff story.

Elijah retreated from Philadelphia and crossed the bridge to Camden, New Jersey, just so he could be somewhere nobody recognized him. He couldn't wait until his fifteen minutes of fame were over. He was a patrol officer, not a knight in shining armor. If only that bullet was a fraction of an inch farther to the right. Then he wouldn't be alive to deal with undeserved admiration. Every wave and smile was a reminder that he sacrificed himself for ten-year-old Danny Wheeler, and that both of them survived. That wasn't supposed to happen.

Taking his descent into madness out of the equation, it was one of the best days he had in a while. Maybe it was just the nostalgia of Adventure Aquarium, but something about being in a glass tunnel with sharks swimming over his head was relaxing. In his childhood, Georgios would spend every Friday afternoon with him, and their favorite place was Adventure Aquarium. It was almost hard for Elijah to believe he turned thirty-one a month ago. Time flies when you're having fun, or so they always said. In Elijah's case, it was more accurate to say time flies when you're not traumatized.

When his six-year-old Samsung vibrated a third time, he gave up.

"Hey, Uncle Antonis."

His uncle almost never called him, mainly because they were both busy people, but also out of guilt and paranoia. His wife Maria, though sworn to silence, never thought well of Elijah, Georgios wouldn't have approved, and Simone would have slaughtered him. Of course, Simone wasn't a problem anymore. The two engaged in awkward small talk for a while before Antonis finally brought up the courage to address his reason for calling.

"Georgios passed away," he said.

"When?"

"This morning, at around five."

Elijah knew it was coming, but he didn't expect it to hurt this badly. He listened with half an ear as Antonis continued talking about hospitals and funeral arrangements. Elijah didn't believe it yet.

"The funeral is this Saturday," Antonis said. "I bought you a plane ticket."

"Simone said I wasn't allowed to come," Elijah said.

"You didn't hear?"

Elijah tried to zone out by watching a hammerhead shark as it swam, moving its head side to side as its tail gracefully followed. He envied the shark; guiltless and ignorant to all the ugliness of the world. Woe was Elijah Walker, local hero and international murderer.

"Hear what?"

Antonis hesitated. "She's dead... She fell down the stairs. Karma, I guess."

"Oh, that's a shame," Elijah said, with too much haste and irreverence to sound ignorant. Luckily, Antonis didn't care enough to question it. He had hated Simone from the beginning and never budged.

"Nobody else knows who you are."

"I met a few relatives when I was a kid though, when they first got married," he said. "What if they remember me?"

"That was twenty years ago. Listen, I know you have genius goggles, but us little people don't have memories as vivid as yours. They're not going to remember you, let alone recognize you. Hell, Simone dedicated herself to erasing you, and she did a damn good job. She may have been a bitch, but she was one tough cookie, you can count on that."

"What about the Konstantinous?"

"Well, your great grandmother is gone. All my kids were born in the nineties. I never showed them any pictures."

Elijah was too nervous to drop the subject. "Yeah, but you always said I look like a carbon copy of dad when he was younger."

"Not a single living person remembers your dad when he was young. Literally nobody."

Elijah decided against pointing out that his uncle misused the word *literally*, even though it was a pet peeve of his. "If I wear sunglasses to hide Mom's eyes and hunch over a quad cane, I may as well *be* my father."

"What you're being is paranoid," Antonis said. "Georgios was almost 70, there's hardly a resemblance now. You changed your last name, so we can pass you off as a distant cousin if anyone asks. I'll smuggle you in if you're that worried about the Simonster judging you from beyond the grave. No one will notice."

Saturday, July 19th, 2014

Melbourne, Victoria

Elijah was settled in a back pew in the far corner of the church. His strategy was that, if anyone noticed him at all, they would be too lazy to walk several dozen yards just to ask a stranger how they were holding up. He took someone from them, and he would have a hard time making peace with that. Was Simone the most horrible person he had ever met in his life? Not quite, but definitely up there in the ranks. Still, "halfcident" or not, he should have taken responsibility for pushing her. His punishment for that was that he couldn't properly mourn his father. If he had played nice, Simone might have considered letting him in for five minutes. If he had turned himself in, they may have escorted him to the funeral with an ankle bracelet if he was on good behavior. The life he was living was a prison anyway. Now, he couldn't approach his father at all.

My stepmother was trash, he told himself. *She was a homewrecker who married an old man with a son who was only seven years younger than her, got him to sign a birth certificate for a child he knew wasn't his, created a huge conspiracy to hide it, exiled her stepson's mother, kicked her stepson out of the house to fend for himself with his neglectful grandparents, and then murdered his mom. She slept soundly at night as if all her actions were justified because she was raped and had a hard childhood. Murder was karma.*

He cursed himself. When he thought of Simone's sins, he had to confess to his father's, funeral or not.

My father was trash. He knowingly dated a sixteen-year-old, married her at seventeen, sacrificed his entire family for her and a daughter that wasn't even his, and probably knew his wife murdered his ex-girlfriend, the mother of his only son. He was a sex offender who should have died in jail. ALS was karma.

You mustn't speak ill of the dead. He hushed his thoughts and observed his surroundings. Stained glass windows, imagery of saints painted on the walls, and stained, wooden arches all contributed to a holy atmosphere that was unbearable for a sinner. The saints' faces were expressionless, but in Elijah's imagination, even the Monastics were judging him. Elijah never believed in God, but from the corner of his eye he could swear he saw Saint Simone on the wall, condemning him to Hell. There isn't an exclusive list of people who can become a Greek Orthodox saint. All you have to do is die, and believers could pray to you like the Virgin Mary. Naturally, there was no way to guarantee his prayers would make it down to Hell.

His father lied in an ornate, open casket, but Elijah couldn't see inside from the angle he was sitting; he wasn't sure if he wanted to. It may as well have been Georgios' church. Unlike his *heathen* of a son, Georgios was a regular church-goer and donated regularly; he said "if the house God gave me can be so beautiful, then the least I can do is make sure that God's house is moreso." The reality is the money was only a small fraction of his fortune, and Georgios was trying to buy his way out of purgatory ahead of time in case no one bailed him out. He elected to ignore the parable of the poor widow described in Luke, as well as any other part of the bible that gave him grief for the way he wanted to live his life.

If anyone desired to rescue him from Hell, it would be the young woman standing next to his casket. All Elijah could make out from that distance was her pale skin and the long, black hair that fell to the small of her back. She was dressed in all black of course, as per tradition, but her makeup was dark too. From what Elijah's heard of her, it must have been Arete. Who else would tolerate hugging strangers as they came to her in a single file line? A lot of them were probably only there to fill a social obligation. But she was in a daze, as if she didn't know where she was. Mascara had dried in a line from her eyes to the base of her jawbone. She was the only person there who was suffering the same loss Elijah was. Well, similar. Georgios was Elijah's father but didn't act like one, whereas he wasn't Arete's father but acted like he was. It was close enough to give them shared experiences of the same man. If only he could speak to her, perhaps they could lighten each other's load. But, of course, he ruined that comfort for himself.

Antonis approached him from the side, knowing that quietly approaching his skittish, ex-military nephew from behind would end badly for all parties involved. "How are you holding up?"

"Not well," Elijah said. "Is that Arete?"

Antonis nodded. "Do you want to meet her?" he asked, more quietly than usual.

"My stepsister?" He paused to think. "She doesn't know I exist. It's better that way. It's how Dad wanted it."

Antonis gave his nephew a sympathetic pat on the back, buying his excuse. "She's giving the first eulogy inside the columbarium, and then after I speak we're going to the mausoleum to lay him to rest."

Elijah didn't know what to say, so he just nodded.

"I'll take you through the back door," Antonis said. "You can stand in the back hallway. No one in the audience will be able to see you from that angle."

"Okay," Elijah said, relieved his uncle wasn't pushing his boundaries. There was no way he'd be able to explain himself... at least, there was no way to explain himself without getting caught.

After being guided by his uncle, Elijah hid in the hallway and waited for Arete to take the floor. When she arrived, it was his first time seeing her up close. Facially, her resemblance to Simone was striking, but she didn't remind him of her mother. Simone was an anal-retentive redhead who suppressed her stereotypical Irish rage and always tried her best to act like sunshine walking the earth. Something about Arete was real.

She was almost as lifeless as her "father" as she stood at the podium to deliver his eulogy. She gingerly pulled the microphone to her level and tapped it with her fingernail. The dull tap echoed off the marble walls and caught the wandering attention of the other mourners. The podium shielded her from onlookers who would otherwise notice she was fidgeting.

When Arete was done blowing her nose, she brushed her hair out of her face and straightened her hat. "My father..." She cleared her throat, but still sounded congested. "My father, Georgios Konstantinou, left behind such a great legacy that I don't even know where to start. I didn't prepare anything. I just thought I could stand up here and, well... *talk*. And all this beautiful prose would flow out. But I can't. It doesn't work that way."

Arete shifted uncomfortably and tugged on the hem of her dress. She was expected to continue the eulogy; She wasn't ready, not by a long shot, but she couldn't just excuse herself. "My father accomplished so much before I was even born, and I'll never be able to live up to his legacy. I'm not worthy of Konstantinou Enterprises. I'm going to his alma mater, the University of Pennsylvania, and I'm going to study theater. Yes, you wankers, *theater*. And I have my father's blessing so *shut up* and *stop asking me about it*!"

She backed away from the podium and her lip quivered. Before she could break out into messy sobs in front of everyone, she deserted them. Arete briskly fled the columbarium, brushing up against Elijah on her way out.

Without thinking, he reached out for her. His fingertips met with a sort of electricity that brought a rush of blood to his cheeks. She didn't feel it, nor did she notice his touch or presence. But for Elijah, time stood still, his arm outreached in her direction as she escaped. The moment replayed in his head on loop until somebody pushed Elijah's hand down.

It was Antonis, who was in her pursuit as well. "Leave her alone for now," he said, mostly to himself. "She'll be all right."

Elijah stared out the open door. "She's cute." His eyes widened and he faced Antonis directly. "That is *not* what I meant to say."

Antonis didn't judge; he only chuckled. "You'd be cute together."

Elijah wished he could blanch the redness from his face. Was there no way to redeem his pride? "I should have said I liked her speech. It was refreshing. She was honest..."

Honest was code for *absolutely nothing like the deceptive vultures that raised her*.

"She always is," Antonis said. "And you two should date. It would be nice to have you back in the family, and KE might have a chance after all."

"Eww," Elijah said automatically. He didn't actually see Arete as a stepsister, or remotely related to him in any way. Even when he was a child, Arete was just a piece of Simone and only Simone. From the age of ten, he knew the real father was one of seven rapists, and handled that information by acting like she had asexually reproduced so he wouldn't have to feel sorry for her. As a grown adult with no living person standing in the way, he was now denying himself the chance to meet her out of sheer helplessness.

"Don't even pretend you think it's gross," Antonis said. "I know you ship Boone and Shannon on *LOST*."

Oh, dear. The old man knew what shipping meant. It was shaping up to be a dark conversation indeed.

"You don't even like her that much," Elijah said.

"How is that relevant?"

Elijah ignored that comment, not sure where he was going with that conversation or if it had a point. "Aren't I a little old for her though? I held her when she was a baby."

"Nonsense. There were, what, thirty years between Simone and your father?"

Elijah frowned. He was very well aware of this fact, and spent his whole life trying not to think about it. If anything, Antonis had just given him another reason to back off. Elijah missed his father dearly, but he didn't want to be anything like him. Not to mention, Antonis always disapproved of their relationship, so it was a blatantly transparent excuse on his part.

"You've only got ten years over Arete," Antonis said. "It's not like you could be her father."

"Can we stop talking about this? It's weird. How did my dad even *get* Simone?" Elijah said, his grudge toward his father coming dangerously close to the surface. "They got married after being together for, what, three months?"

"About half a year, I think," Antonis said. "Maybe longer, but it doesn't matter. Tragedy brings people closer together. She was gang raped, he stood by her side. She was about to be ostracized by her family, and Georgios gave her a way out. They thought it was romantic."

Elijah grunted.

"Sorry," Antonis said. "I should've known you were still touchy... You're not still jealous of her, are you?"

"Arete? Of course I am," Elijah said. "I wish I could go to Penn too. Study law, like you. I can't believe she publicly rejected everything I ever wanted."

"You have the talent," Antonis said. "You'd be an asset to the company, CEO or not... As for Penn Law, I've got the connections and you've got the resume. With a couple of phone calls, I can get you enrolled for this semester."

"Thanks, but I can't afford it."

"Well, surely you didn't think your father left you with nothing but that knife? Do you have it with you?"

"I always have it with me," Elijah said.

He pulled the knife out of his pocket and ran his fingers along the handle until he felt a small, barely visible indentation. When he pulled it, the butt of the knife opened to reveal a secret compartment. He dumped the contents into the palm of his hand, and was rewarded with a rolled-up piece of paper and a small key.

Antonis smiled. "I'm surprised you didn't find it sooner. You were always such a whiz kid."

Elijah unrolled the paper to find an address. "What is this?"

"That's everything you need to open your safe deposit box," Antonis said. "He trusted it in my name so Simone wouldn't find out. Now it's time to pass it on to you."

Elijah's face was glowing so bright that he almost felt guilty. You weren't supposed to be happy at a funeral, but for the first time in nearly twenty years, he felt like his father regarded him as a son. He gave him that knife while Simone was still alive so it was probably just whatever pocket change he could stow away without Simone noticing. He expected 30 grand at most, but it was a start. "Is it enough for me to go to Penn Law?" he asked, hopeful.

"It's enough for you to go to Penn Law *and* buy enough goats for the dowry of twelve Indian princesses."

Elijah faked a laugh to satisfy his uncle's ego, even though he always thought his jokes were as fresh and thrilling as mold growing in a petri dish.

"Okay," Antonis said, "I'll say it in Greek."

"Why Greek?"

"To make sure you haven't forgotten your roots." Antonis winked. It was creepy.

"Αυτός σου έδωσε ένα εκατομμύριο δολάρια."

"He gave me poison footprints?"

Antonis sighed. "Poison is δηλητήριο, and footprints is χνάρια. I said ένα εκατομμύριο δολάρια. Which is..."

"One million moons?"

"Moons is φεγγάρια. Well, don't feel too bad. I know it's your native language, but you've been in America for a long time..." Antonis caught a slight glint in Elijah's eyes. "You know exactly what I said, don't you? Watch out, you're not too old for a noogie."

"I'm too tall for one, though." Elijah grinned. "I'm just waiting for you to say you were kidding. One million dollars... That's a lot of money."

"You know what? You have the money now, and you're a pro at the language. How about you come with me to Greece next summer?"

"Ευχαριστώ!" Elijah was so emotional that he threw his arms around his uncle; the self-proclaimed orphan couldn't even wrap his brain around the fact that he was wealthy again, let alone that his uncle was going to hang out with him in public. He was a Konstantinou. Ηλίας Κωνσταντίνου. *Elijah Konstantinou.* He liked the sound of that.

Antonis hugged him tightly. "Σ' αγαπώ, Ηλία."

Elijah was so touched that he almost cried. "Κι εγώ σ' αγαπώ, θείε Αντώνη."

Saturday, May 2, 2015
Philadelphia, Pennsylvania

"Do you ever wonder what the Pope is like in bed?" Arete asks.

I look behind me, but no one is standing there. Arete is seriously asking me this question. Do I ever wonder what the Pope is like in bed? Really? Does anyone? Would anyone? Would Whitney be subjected to this question if she weren't in the restroom?

"Yeah," I say. After all, this is Arete's yacht, and I don't know how you're supposed to treat the host on their yacht. Hell, I didn't know there was a boat dock on the Delaware River; the thought had just never occurred to me before. This is all a mystery to me, so I'll just follow her lead. She may be dumber than a box of rocks, but she's the poshest person on this boat until Elijah gets here. He would know how you're supposed to act on a yacht.

He'd at least have the charisma needed to ask if we can listen to something other than The Cure without offending her. It's 73 degrees. It's sunny. It's a perfect day. Why are we listening to this depressing 80s music? With my luck she'd say "Sure thing, mate!" and then put on something worse, like Siouxsie and the Banshees.

"I bet his favorite position is missionary," Arete says. "Not because of the name, but because it's a great view of the tits."

"You would know, right?" I say sarcastically.

"Well, that's what Elijah is always telling me," she says with a smirk before taking a long sip of her lemonade, which the bartender dyed black. Gag me; I should hold my tongue. She's not even drunk. It's a virgin lemonade. This is just how she is, and I hate it.

"Where is he, anyway?" I ask.

"Off being a super Gemini," she says. "You know his rising, Sun, Moon, Mars, and north node are all in Gemini?"

"I don't know what that means," I say. "He told me astrology is all a bunch of bull shit anyway because the universe is expanding, but astrology stays the same."

Arete nods slowly. "What a Gemini thing to say."

"Miss me?" Whitney says when she comes out to the deck. Her beloved pet corgi, Sammy, darts out behind her and happily runs around the deck.

Before I can open my mouth to answer, Arete asks, "Do you ever wonder what the Pope is like in bed?"

"No," Whitney says. "But I bet his favorite position is missionary."

Dear God, if you are real, please get Elijah here as soon as possible. I don't know if I can bear another second of third-wheeling. Amen.

I try to take Whitney's hand to remind her I exist, but reflexively pull back when the most menacing growl comes out of that tiny dog.

"Sammy!" Whitney says. "Sit!"

Dear God, if you are real, I would like to revise my prayer. Please give me some alone time with my girlfriend, jealous dog not included. Amen.

*

Elijah shows up about an hour later, carrying a shopping bag. His first move is to kiss Arete like he hasn't seen her in years, but I'm accustomed to that. He opens the bag and tosses me a t-shirt.

"Happy early birthday," he says.

"Oh, thank you!" I say prematurely before unfolding it. It's a graphic tee with a duel-gun-wielding taco wearing a sombrero, captioned *Hostile Tacover.* "What is this?"

"It's a shirt that captures your true soul," Elijah says, like he's enlightening me on some profound truth and doesn't understand why it's not clear to me. "Arete wants a group photo, so I got everyone a shirt that captured their true soul. Even the dog." He searches the bag and withdraws a baby bib with a picture of a cartoon unicorn that's captioned *miracle.*

Whitney laughs. "You've never even met Sammy."

"All dogs are miracles," he says.

I'm filled to the brim with jealousy when Whitney agrees and holds Sammy still so Elijah can tuck the bib into his collar. It's not because Sammy already prefers Elijah over me after knowing him for two seconds, or even because Elijah's winning my girlfriend over—I pressed for that so we could have peace at long last, after all. I'm jealous because Elijah views this dog he never met as a "miracle," meanwhile I'm reduced to an angry taco wearing a sombrero. Also, I really don't want to be the ugly friend in a group photo next to all these hot people. I'm not photogenic. I don't take selfies. My smile looks dorky. I'm an introvert. I don't want this.

Elijah reaches into the bag and pulls out another t-shirt, which he tosses to Arete. She unfurls it and beams in gratitude. "Aw, you really do understand me!"

"Of course I do!" Elijah says. "Kit Kat, how could I not understand the woman I love?"

Arete holds the shirt up so Whitney can see it, and I dash over to her side to get a better view. She immediately takes my hand, possibly to compete with #Arelijah PDA. What was I doing standing next to Elijah anyway? Whitney is my girlfriend, not him.

Arete's shirt is captioned *Dead Inside, Bread Inside*, and has a cutesy graphic of a piece of bread with x's for eyes and a bite taken out of the top. He understands her perfectly. Meanwhile, he sees me as an angry taco.

Elijah digs through the bag. "Whitney, this one's for you."

She lets go of my hand and accepts the gift. "Thank you!" She holds up the shirt. She laughs and reads it out loud. "I'm not a bitch, I'm just shy and a bitch." Meanwhile, I'm still an angry taco. She slides the t-shirt on over her tank top. Goodbye, cleavage. "Oh my god, this is so me," she says.

"Arete helped, actually," Elijah says. "I texted her a photo first."

"Aww, I told you to take credit, you drongo!" Arete says.

Elijah shrugs. "The pressure got to me."

"Well, thank you both," Whitney says. "Where's your shirt, Elijah?"

"I'm already wearing it." Elijah removes his jacket, revealing his "true soul:" a parody of the USDA beef grade, which is labeled *A Grade TRASH*, in comic sans. That's how he sees himself. I take off the shirt I'm wearing and toss it onto a chair, wondering how Elijah always manages to get his way. Goodbye, Spongebob. Hello, angry taco.

Arete slides her shirt over her swim top. "I kind of don't see it," she says. "The one you picked for William, I mean."

"Well, you see," Elijah says in a tone that suggests he thinks he's a hotshot, "he's Mexican and they didn't have a smart-ass taco, so I settled for the mean one."

"Oh, come on!" I say.

Not explicitly telling Elijah that my race is a secret was a mistake. I should've known he wouldn't see why it was such a big deal to me. He handled it pretty well, and he probably just assumes everyone else will too. And how would he understand? He looks like he was sculpted by an Ancient Grecian, and he has that beautiful olive skin tone. People may occasionally argue about whether or not Greeks are white, but at least no one will ever question that he's Mediterranean. I brace myself for all Hell to break loose.

"You're Mexican?" Arete looks me over. "Ah. That's why you got mad when I put caviar in the tacos."

"No it isn't," I say. "That's a crime against humanity. I thought you were a vegetarian anyway."

"I eat eggs chickens lay too," Arete says. "What's it matter if they were laid by a fish?"

I frown. I don't even know where to start with this one, and we're not off to a bad start considering the direction this could've gone. Of course Arete wouldn't care about my skin tone; what was I thinking? She's too self-absorbed to doubt my race. In fact, I matter so little to her, she probably won't even commit this conversation to her long term memory.

"I feel kinda dumb," Whitney says. (How anyone can feel dumb when Arete's around is beyond me.) "I didn't know you were Mexican. That's pretty dope."

"You're not dumb," I say, relieved. I thought there was no way she'd understand. "I try pretty hard to hide it."

"Why?" she asks. "Mexico has a beautiful culture."

"Well," I say. "It's just that I'm too White to pass as Mexican."

"Why would that matter?" Whitney asks.

"That's insane and wrong," Elijah says. "It's like I told Arete. Your skin tone doesn't invalidate the culture you were raised in."

"At least she can speak Greek," I say. "I wasn't born in Mexico and I can't even speak Spanish. Two years in high school and every day at home wasn't enough to get through my thick skull."

"You can do anything," Elijah says. "You are a Mexi*can*, not a Mexi*cannot*."

"You need to stop looking at memes," I say. "But thanks for the words of encouragement, I guess."

"If it means that much to you, I'll teach you Spanish," Elijah says.

"Oh, that sounds fun!" Whitney says. "Can you teach me too?"

"Of course!"

"Fine," I say. "I guess. But I'm warning you, I'm hopeless."

Seemingly out of nowhere, Arete starts crying. It's the ugly sort of crying with a grimace, a long wail, and a fat stream of tears.

Whitney tepidly steps forward, but Elijah beats her to the punch and immediately swoops in to comfort Arete, leaving Whitney frustrated. I hold her hand in spite of Sammy's protests, mostly because I'm afraid she and Elijah will start fighting over this if she doesn't calm down. I'll take my chances with the jealous dog.

"Kit Kat, what's wrong?" he asks.

Arete rubs her eyes, smudging her raccoon makeup. "I'm not Greek, my dad isn't my dad, and I don't even know what I am! I don't know anything anymore!"

Elijah gently shushes her. "You were raised in a Greek house with a Greek culture by a Greek man." He holds her closer and smooths out her hair. "Why should the circumstances around your conception change that?"

"But it's not in my blood," Arete says.

"Fuck blood," Elijah says. "It's in your name and it's in your upbringing."

"You called me a whitey before," Arete says. "Why should I trust what you're saying now over your first impression?"

I recall our Waffle House conversation back in February—he did say that, didn't he? I remember how weird and unfounded it seemed back then; now it makes more sense.

"Forget that," Elijah said. "I was just jealous that Dad chose you over me. I was being immature, and I'm sorry. You're Greek and I love you."

He talks like it's all in the past, but I get the impression that Elijah still harbors some resentment against their father. He never explained what happened, but their marriage didn't change the fact that he was shipped back to Athens about 20 years ago. All of this is lost on Arete, who slowly calms down.

"I love you too." Arete leans her head on his chest. "I'm sorry I'm ruining everyone's day."

"What?" Elijah asks. He turns to me. "William, is Arete ruining anything?"

"No," I say because it's the only answer.

He looks Whitney in the eye. "Whitney, is Arete ruining anything?"

"Only her makeup," she says.

Laughter breaks through Arete's sobbing. What the actual fuck? There was an answer other than "no?" A risky answer, no less? And Whitney thought of it before I did? That's it, this is the girl I'm going to marry someday. She's perfect.

"See?" Elijah kisses Arete on the forehead. "Everything is fine... Hey, you know that thing we talked about last night?"

Arete nods *yes* in response.

"Whitney," Elijah says, "our house is big and that makes it feel emptier when one of us is out. Arete was really happy when you were staying with us."

"What are you saying?" Whitney asks.

"I want you to move in," Arete says. "I mean, you don't have to..."

Whoa, wait. No one consulted me about this.

"I'd love to!" Whitney says.

Oh, no. No. I wanted to take things slow. This isn't taking things slow. This is like super-gluing a jet pack to a turtle. I'm not ready to live in the same house as my girlfriend. I haven't even made it to second base yet.

"Yay!" Arete says, her good mood now fully restored. "We'll have so much fun."

"It'll be like a huge sleepover."

Whitney looks at me. "What do you think?"

I give up. "I can't wait," I say.

She smiles. "That's great!"

Maybe this won't be so bad. Princess Arete summons me to her room to do menial tasks every now and then like help her find the mate to her shoe, or her often-disappearing keys that usually turn up in her coat pocket. Sometimes she calls me over just to listen to her rant about something that no one cares about, like the time another Instagram star commented something rude on one of her photos, and she couldn't reply or delete the comment because she was pretending it didn't hurt her feelings. Maybe having Whitney around will take the load off.

"Let's take the picture now," Elijah says. "While the lighting is still good."

"What about Arete's makeup?" Whitney asks.

"Meh," Arete says. "William, can you tell the bartender to come over here and take the photo?"

I roll my eyes. "Yeah."

So much for Whitney taking the load off. I fetch the bartender, a well-dressed Black woman whose name I don't know, and Elijah herds everyone together at the nose of the yacht. Sammy eagerly follows Whitney, his paws pitter pattering across the deck.

"Taco, you're on the edge of the frame," the bartender says. It takes a few seconds too long before I realize she means me. I step in a little closer, and Whitney puts her arm around me. Sammy paws at her legs.

She laughs. "You want upsies?"

Sammy barks, and Whitney lets go of me and picks up her miracle dog. Fine. You win this time, Sammy. But mark my words: I'll live at least twice as long as you, and I'll win in the end. I'm pretty cute in an ugly way. I'll get her attention somehow, and you'll be the one awkwardly standing there waiting for love.

"I'll take the picture on three," the bartender says. "One..."

I settle for leaning in closer.

"Two..."

Elijah spontaneously picks Arete up and she shrieks in laughter.

"Three!"

05/02/2015 07

Sunday, May 3, 2015

Arete rushes down the stairs. "Okay, so I've been looking through the Alfreda Angelo's Disney collection, and I can't decide between the Rapunzel dress or Sleeping Beauty."

"How would I know?" I ask.

"William?" Arete stops dead in her tracks. "I didn't even know you were there... I'm talking to Whitney."

"I'd have to see them on you," Whitney says, "but I think Rapunzel's dress is perfect for you."

"Wait, Whitney," I say, "how do you know what dresses she's talking about?"

Please tell me Whitney doesn't look at wedding dresses in her spare time. I'm not ready for this. I can't afford this. Why do women compete when it comes to getting married?

Whitney raises an eyebrow, (yes, just one, this time I'm sure of it. Now *that* is talent.) less than amused. "You *really* think this is our first time talking about something as important as a dress?"

Oh.

"I thought she already had a dress though," I say.

Arete rolls her eyes. "I can't get married in the same dress twice. And don't you *dare* tell Eli what you overheard."

"Why would I?"

Overheard? She didn't know I was here and she's acting like I was eavesdropping on a wedding that, until the other day, wasn't even going to happen. Whitney offered her blessing and convinced Arete to go through with the wedding, thus officially putting an end to the Whitney vs. Elijah feud. I'm proud of my efforts.

"*Do* ask him this though," Arete says.

I groan.

"It's simple. I just want to know what he thinks about getting married on the beach in Athens. I know my dad... *our* dad was born there."

Still gross.

"Dude, he doesn't care *where*," I say. "He's just glad you're actually marrying him *anywhere*."

Arete's phone rings. "This better be the florist... Hello?" Arete grimaces. "Tonia! Nice to hear from you." Arete scoffs. "Sure. Send 'em over." ... "1432 Hartwell Lane, Philly. Thanks."

She hangs up the phone and exhales sharply.

"What happened?" Whitney asks.

"Tonia happened." Arete points her finger at her open mouth and makes a fake gagging noise. "She said she found all these pictures of Uncle Antonis, Dad, and me in his crap, and she's sending some in the mail so I can display them at the wedding since, and I quote 'he can't be there.' Wanker."

"Are you sure that's a dig?" I ask.

"Of course it's a dig," Whitney says. "This is Tonia we're talking about."

"It is a pretty weird way to say 'fuck you for marrying the guy who killed my dad,'" Arete says.

Whitney shrugs. "She's probably just jealous that you're skinny without having to puke everything you eat."

"You should write that on the invitation," I say.

Arete laughs. "I'll keep it in mind for the next time. I really don't want her at my wedding."

Arete sorts through the stacks of unmailed invitations on the table until she finds the one she's looking for. She rips it in half and throws it at the garbage can, missing by a few feet. I think it's safe to say that Tonia is officially uninvited from her big, fat Greek wedding. The real mystery is why she was ever invited to begin with.

Saturday, May 16, 2015

I'm working on the worst short story I've ever written in my entire life when Arete comes in my room. The distraction is welcome until she tells me why she's here.

"Can you help me sort through these pictures Tonia sent?"

I know I was only exposed to Tonia for five minutes and Arete has had to deal with her her whole life, but I would rather be dangled over a lake of piranhas than see that phony for another five minutes. Arete sloppily spreads all the pictures out onto my bed, and I'm relieved to see that it's not Tonia's "photography." I believe Arete's exact words were, "She takes Polaroids of her naked arse, photoshops them, and posts them all over Tumblr."

"I thought you weren't going to bother with those," I say.

"I wasn't," she says, "but I had second thoughts."

It takes me a while to recognize him, but most of the photographs are of Antonis at various ages, ranging from his childhood in Greece to this past year.

"You're not really going to display these, are you?" I ask.

I wish she had gone to Elijah, but he's busy settling into his shiny, new executive's office at KE, and she might explode waiting for his return. As for Whitney, she finished nursing school with a 4.0 and she's already landed a job at the hospital. She graduates Monday. It looks like Arete and I are alone in the failure boat.

"No, of course not," she says. "But I might keep some of them for an album. I know this wasn't a nice gesture, but I do like some of these pictures. Like this one."

She taps one of the photographs with her fingernail; I'm a little distracted by her nail polish—black with a white cross, like a coffin. Once I look, I see a candid photo of Georgios and Antonis together at the beach, building a massive sand castle with tweenage Arete. They all look so happy.

"I had such a lovely childhood," Arete says. She frowns. "He wasn't always a monster."

"Adulthood sucks for everyone," I say as I pick up another photograph. It's of Antonis at a funeral, talking to Arete next to the casket. I try to hide it from her, but she snatches it out of my hand.

"That *bitch*," Arete says. "Funeral pictures? Really? I had a legitimate excuse to bail, I barfed. I thought I might be... sick."

"What's wrong?"

"Nuh uh." Arete picks up one of the photographs and holds it closer to her face. "No way..."

I take the photograph and look. There's a candid photo of Tonia and Mikhail chatting toward the back of the church.

Elijah is sitting in a pew behind them. "He came to Antonis' funeral?"

"No," Arete says. "That's my dad's funeral, you drongo!"

"That's not possible," I say. "That's got to be your uncle's funeral. We never went past the lobby, so how would you be able to tell?"

"No, my dad's funeral was in Australia. I recognize the saints painted on the walls."

Shit.

"Maybe it's a cousin. I mean, it's kind of grainy."

She squints. "No, I think it's Eli..."

"Nah," I say. "Can't be."

She jerks the photograph out of my hand. "I'm like 5,000% sure this is my fiancé."

"Photoshop. You're cousin's a photographer."

"Glamour model. She's a glamour model." Arete takes a deep breath. "He's been there the whole time."

"We can't be so sure, it's such a small picture."

Arete throws the picture and springs off the bed. "Dammit, William, I know what I saw!"

"They could still be fake," I insist. "Maybe she's just trying to get rid of Elijah because—"

"Stop gaslighting me!" Arete turns away from me. "He didn't just 'bump into me' at Penn like it was fate, William! This changes *everything*!"

"Not really," I say. "I mean, he still loves you, and you love him, right?"

"He's been hiding this from me from the *second* he met me. He couldn't even tell me this small detail!"

"You're blowing this way out of proportion," I say. "I mean, do you really expect him not to go to his father's funeral?"

Wrong answer. Arete scoffs and leaves the room. Great. It's Civil War II all over again in the Konstantinou Manor.

*

When Elijah makes it home from his first busy day as the face of KE, Arete is waiting for him by the front door. He doesn't even get to set his briefcase down before she starts grilling him. I'm sitting in a nearby chair and half-assedly "reading" a book as a thinly veiled excuse to be close by. Arete thinks I'm here for moral support, but really, I'm the umpire. Somebody has to be here to call 911 if she starts choking him.

Arete jams her index finger into his chest. "WHEN DID YOU FIRST MEET ME?"

"Uh..." Elijah rubs the back of his neck. "The day you were born."

Arete puts her hands on her hips. "That is *not* what I meant and you know it!"

"Fine." He looks at his feet. "I saw you for the first time in almost twenty years at our father's funeral. I tried to talk to you after your speech, but you ran past me, so I didn't think you noticed me. And the longer we were together, it seemed increasingly less significant to bring it up."

Arete says nothing at first, fuming in silence until he asks her if she's okay and reaches out to touch her shoulder. She responds by slapping him across the face. Elijah doesn't so much as flinch. He looks her in the eye, perhaps trying to catch some remorse, but finds none.

"Did you follow me?" she asks.

Elijah doesn't reply.

"Did you follow me to Penn?" Arete asks again, louder this time.

"Yes."

"Were you *stalking* me?"

"No—" Elijah closes his eyes. "Yes. Yes, I was stalking you." He looks to me, hoping I'll come to his aid, but I'm not siding with him on this detail. He knows how creepy I think it is that he hunted down his stepsister.

Arete twists her mouth into the sourest expression ever to be seen on a human face. It's kind of cute in an ugly way, which makes Elijah laugh. This only throws her into a deeper rage.

"Look," Elijah says. "I didn't go to Penn to stalk you. Uncle Antonis passed me my inheritance that day, and later he told me I could be an executive at KE, but only if I proved I wasn't 'still a lazy little shit.' His exact words. I chose law instead of business because it was a better backup career if he changed his mind."

"I can't believe you're talking about this like it's no big deal!"

"THAT'S BECAUSE IT FUCKING *ISN'T*, ARETE!" Elijah surprises himself by shouting. Both Arete and I jump. "I'm sorry," he whispers.

"No, you're not," Arete says.

"I swear, I had the biggest crush on you from that moment on, I couldn't just talk to you normally, I got nervous every time I tried."

Arete huffed. "This is the *last time* you lie to me by omission."

"I swear, I won't do it again."

"I'll believe that when I see it," she says. "Were you the one who sent me the dead flowers?"

He doesn't say anything.

Arete nods. "That's what I thought. And you expect me to think dead flowers are romantic? Or an animal's heart?"

He looks guilty. "No..."

"And the photograph of my ex-boyfriend cheating on me?"

"You needed to see that!" He turns defensive. "I also sent you the bracelet. And you wore it the next day."

Arete grows angrier. "It's always hot or cold with you, isn't it? I can't believe I thought it was two different people. Get the Hell out of my house!"

"Wait, please!" Elijah puts his hand on Arete's shoulder, but she brushes it away.

"Too late! The wedding is *off*!"

Elijah's lips part, but he doesn't say anything.

"You heard me," Arete says. "We're done."

As Arete stomps off toward the ballroom, Elijah shouts, "I never loved anyone before you... You can't leave me!"

He's about to chase after her, but I grab his arm. "You'll only make it worse."

"Can it get worse?" he asks.

"Yeah," I say. "She could fire you and start throwing your stuff out on the lawn in garbage bags."

Elijah nods, despondent. "Will you check on her for me? I... I don't want her to hurt herself because of me. Don't tell her I told you this, but she's a cutter."

"A cutter? Oh, shit," I say. That explains why he always sends me after her when they have a fight. I just thought he was trying to prove to himself that he wasn't jealous, but now I see his goal may have been to keep her from finding alone time when she could cut herself. "Yeah I'll go find her. You should probably leave though. She needs some distance to think."

"All right," he says, grumpy. "I'm going to go crash with my gay friends in their gay world and turn green with jealousy just looking at their perfect, happy, gay marriage."

He swallows hard, holding steadfast to denial even as I try to push him out the door. I find myself disillusioned with Elijah to some extent. When Elijah mentioned his stalking, I thought along the lines of well-meaning observation because he never gave me any indication otherwise. Threatening gifts like dead flowers and animal hearts never even crossed my mind. This is beyond the point of damage control, especially if he's comparing his marriage with opposites like Tommy and Keyon. Tommy admitted to me that they actually fight frequently because of their differences, and that they just don't do it in front of others. After Elijah left, they no longer had to play nice, and Tommy finds himself on the couch pretty often without his buffer.

I refuse to delude Elijah into thinking that he didn't fuck up, but I assure him I'll try my best to salvage what I can. Everyone is better off if Elijah has some shred of hope. There's no telling what he might do if he loses everything. Arete cutting herself is a big problem, but looking back on Elijah's frequent suicide jokes makes me anxious. Before setting off to find Arete, I text Tommy and ask him to look out for Elijah.

*

I find Arete brooding in the kitchen drinking golden champagne. Her eye makeup is smudged across her face like the Winter Soldier, and her nose is Rudolph red. She's been blowing her snot onto the rough napkins that are crumpled up on the countertop next to her wedding ring, which is depressing, but at least she's not cutting herself. At least, not right now. I check the clock on the stove; if it's right, I only have one hour before Whitney comes by for a visit. My game plan involves preparing for that oncoming storm by calming Arete down before Whitney says something insensitive and sets out to behead Elijah in a fit of renewed hatred and overprotectiveness.

Whitney is supposed to move in after graduation on the 18th. That's two days from now. I have to get rid of the champagne and get Arete out of the house. Then I'll steal her cell phone, turn off all chimes and vibrations, and check it throughout the day to delete whatever stupid drunk texts Elijah will send her. I'll keep her busy until ten o'clock, when Whitney goes to bed like clockwork. I won't sleep tonight so that way I can make sure I'm awake to distract Whitney when she gets up. And then she'll say "William, I thought you hated surprises," and I'll say, "Not anymore." If I'm lucky, I can convince her to stay somewhere else with me that night. If I'm *really* lucky, I'll get past second base for the first time in my sorry life. And after that, well... I'll just have to hope it blows over by then.

I approach Arete like she's a skittish horse. "Hey, Arete. Are you okay... ish?"

"No," she says, rubbing her eyes.

"I hope you didn't drink too much of that, because it's not really going to help. I told Elijah to go away, so we can go sit down and talk in the living room if you want."

"This is apple cider," she says.

"Oh. Why are you drinking it out of a champagne glass?" Sometimes I could have sworn I had the attention span of a gnat. My "family" is falling apart, and here I am picking apart details.

"I'm playing pretend," Arete says. "Like I used to when I was a teenager and couldn't drink."

"I'm so sorry," I blurted. "I told you that you were over-reacting, but I didn't know the half of what you've been through with him in the past. You know, you don't have to make a decision today. You and Elijah can take a break for as long as you need until you're ready to either forgive him or move on. He won't understand, but I will."

"Thank you. But I can't just take a break," Arete says. "Everything is different now."

"No, it isn't," I say. "You're still young. Take some time to yourself, finish college, meet some new people. After you get out on your own for a while, it's easier to think."

"It's too late for any of that now, William! I'm pregnant!"

My jaw drops. "Like... *Pregnant*-pregnant?"

"*Yes.*"

"You're *actually* going to have a baby?"

"Yes!"

"And you're sure it's Elijah's?"

She glares at me, not that I blame her. Judging by the apple cider, abortion isn't an option. Inconvenient #Arelijah spawn is on the way.

"How long?" I ask.

"Just short of nine weeks."

"No, I mean, how long have you known?"

"Deep down, I've always known," she says. "But I couldn't bring myself to admit it. I didn't take a test until Thursday night."

"What about Elijah?" I ask. "It's his baby too."

"Elijah? No way. I didn't even tell *Whitney*. He'll never know."

"You can't just hide it from him," I say.

"No, mate. I'm taking this baby, and I'm moving away. Far, far away. To France."

"Why France?"

"French is the only foreign language I speak some of. Other than Greek, but that's literally his native language. I figure it might slow him down if he has to learn a new language and save up for a plane ticket, since he's broke now."

"I wouldn't count on that," I say. "Last week he was watching *Amélie* without subtitles."

"He can speak *three* languages?" she asks.

He can actually speak five that I know of including American Sign Language and Spanish, but I can't stray off topic.

"Please don't do this to him," I say. "I know he's a jerk, but he would love being a dad. You know he'd be a great dad."

She scoffs. "Jerk is an understatement, he's a bloody sociopath! You should hear some of the things he says when nobody else is around!" She imitates his voice. "*I did this for us, Arete. I don't care who else has to suffer as long as we have each other.*"

"No offense, but your Greek-Philly accent sucks."

She crosses her arms. "You know what? He wants this house so badly, he can keep it. It's cheaper to stay married and ignore him. I'm going back to Australia."

"He'll follow you, you know he will."

"I'll figure it out."

"He killed two people over you. Do you really think he wouldn't go through Hell for his child? Arete, I'm begging you, don't go down this path."

"Not even two fucking minutes ago you called him out and now suddenly you're defending him? Even after the things he's done to *you*?"

"I think he's changed," I say. "You can get through this."

She glares at me. "A baby isn't going to fix things, William. I thought you were on my side?"

Not anymore, bitch. I'm not on anyone's side. This kid is doomed. I should be driving her to the abortion clinic, but Elijah would literally murder me over his unborn child. He's not anti-choice, but it's what he wants more than anything else, so I know I'd be toast. All I can do is pray she has a miscarriage.

"I am," I say. "I just think that keeping a child from a man who's dreamed of family his whole life is a little on the cruel side. He doesn't have anyone."

"If you love him so much, why don't *you* marry him?"

The first thing that comes to mind is that's bigamy. The second is, if I'm going to marry anyone, it will be Whitney. If I say either out loud, I'll never live it down. Luckily, I don't have to, because she keeps talking.

"That man is like a clogged sink disposal."

I raise my eyebrows. "Huh?"

"Every time I think I've seen it all, he spits out more gunk."

"I always thought he was more like an onion," I say.

"Because the more you get to know him, the more layers you expose?"

I shrug. "No. Because when you cut him, it makes me cry."

Arete glares. "You can go cry for the Devil all you want. I'm going to go do his laundry so he doesn't have an excuse to hang around longer after he gets back. He is going to get his things, pack, and leave. And no, I am *not* going to tell him. And don't you tell him either."

"I won't tell him anything," I say. "I promise."

*

"Hey, Hollywood, I need to tell you something important. Call me back the second you get this."

I hang up, frustrated with the fact that he hasn't been returning my calls. He's either rejecting them, or he turned his phone off, because all my calls are going straight to voicemail. I call Tommy, who says Elijah never showed up or even called them.

Hey, I had my fingers mentally crossed when I made that promise. Arete isn't keeping her pregnancy a secret because she's trying to protect her child; she wants to hurt Elijah. Sure, he's problematic to say the least, but nothing he ever did warranted being estranged from his child. The man often bored me with talk of how badly he wanted children, and how he wouldn't make any of the mistakes his father made. If nothing else, he's devoted, and he'd do anything for his child. Meanwhile, Arete doesn't even want the kid. Elijah should at least have every other weekend, if not full custody. I can't see Arete wanting anything to do with this kid. She'll just resent it for ruining her acting career.

Finally, after spending all night wearing down the tires on Arete's Lamborghini, searching for Elijah at all his usual haunts, I get a call from him at around midnight.

"Hollywood, where have you been? I've been trying to call you for hours!"

"Sorry, my phone was off," he says, depressed. "I drove to the beach."

"Seriously?"

"Yeah," he says. "Ocean City."

I meant that rhetorically; I can hear the sound of waves crashing in the background. He must be along the water.

"How are you doing?" I ask.

"I saw a Kit Kat bar in a vending machine and I cried."

"Oh." I wish I knew what to say to that, because it sparks the most awkward silence I've ever had to endure.

"I'll be back tomorrow to get my crap," he says. "I'm thinking about moving to Portland. I mean, I've never been there, but I'm clearly not wanted here."

"That's not true," I say. "Look, there's something I need to tell you."

He scoffs. "Whatever it is she said, it won't make a difference."

I hold my breath; he's right. He does deserve to know that he has a child on the way, but this isn't how he should find out. I shouldn't give up so quickly. If I'm the one to tell him, he'll have a violent reaction, their relationship will be over and I'll be forced to choose between Elijah and Whitney.

And that's assuming Whitney forgives me for betraying her best friend. If I convince Arete to tell him, they may have a chance at talking things out.

"Never mind then," I say. "Just... don't drown yourself in the ocean, okay?"

He fake laughs. "Drowning would be one hell of a way to die... Did I leave my coat there on the rack?"

"Yeah," I say. "If you want, I can bring it to you."

"No, no! That's okay. I'm just rambling because I'm lonely. Will you stay on the line with me?"

I want to decline and go to bed—not to sleep, but to hide—but I can't bring myself to do that to him. He's been rejected enough times throughout his life, and I can't trust him to take care of himself. Sure, he burned my house down and interrupted my once peaceful life, but I think he's just misunderstood. We aren't actually that different; I just hold myself together better.

"Sure. What are friends for?"

"Thanks, Boy Meets World... We'll still be best mates forever, no matter how this ends, right?"

"Of course we will. We came up with nicknames, remember?"

"You promise?"

"I promise," I say. "We're team Hollywood Noodle."

"Good. Because I think you're the only person who's ever been able to tolerate me for who I really am. Most people would be coddling me and telling me that Arete still loved me, but you've always been honest with me, even though I don't deserve it."

Guilt burns an ulcer into my stomach. How can I just *not* tell him? What kind of sorry excuse for a best mate am I?

Sunday, May 17, 2015

"I can't keep this secret anymore!" My fingers are trembling and my legs are like gelatin. What I'm about to say will change everything forever. My breathing is heavy, but holding it in hurts more. I have to tell him. "Arete is *pregnant!*"

The mailman shuts the curbside mailbox and looks over his shoulder to see me panting. He raises his eyebrows and rubs the back of his neck.

"What, is she your girlfriend?" he says with a thick, Brooklyn accent. "Well, congrats to the happy couple, I guess."

I sigh. "Never mind. I just needed to tell someone and get it off my chest."

He shakes his head and returns to his mail truck. He gives me a final, judgmental stare before driving off.

This encounter wasn't the therapeutic release I needed. I take out my phone and scroll through my contacts. With *Hollywood Perfect* selected, my finger hovers over the call button, and it takes a full six minutes for me to work up the courage to tap the phone icon. With every ring, another droplet of sweat drips from my brow. It's not that I'm nervous. It's just that it's hot out here. 62° F. Whew...

Elijah sounds angry when he answers, which makes me more hesitant to come clean right from the start. How do I do this? Ah, I know. I can introduce it slowly, acting like I think he already knows. It's a great strategy, and I already have the perfect sentence: *So who gets custody of your child?*

"So who gets custody of..."

"Custody of...?" he asks, impatient.

"Custody of me." I'm a failure.

"You're old enough to live with whoever you want," Elijah says. "But don't choose Arete."

"Why not?"

"I need you with me, and there are giant spiders in Australia. Anyway, I'm stopping to get gas. I'll be there in about an hour." He blows the horn. "IF THIS FUCKING SUV DOESN'T HIT ME!" There's more honking. "ΆΙ ΣΤΟ ΔΙΆΟΛΟ ΚΑΙ ΑΚΌΜΑ ΠΑΡΑΠΈΡΑ!"

"So... What about Arete's..." Come on, just say it, William. *What about Arete's pregnancy?* "Are you two really separating? I mean. Come on."

Elijah scoffs. "I thought about it last night, and I realized that I actually hate her. I seriously *despise* that selfish bitch. Her very *existence* has fucked me over. I hope she steps on a land mine."

The phone shakes in my sweaty hands. "So. Ouch. Really? Not even a chance?"

"I don't need her to be happy," he says with conviction.

"That's not what you said last night. You know, when I stayed on the phone with you for *four hours*."

"Well, I changed my mind. Again. Hey, want to go to Greece with me this summer? I was supposed to go with Antonis, but, well, I kind of murdered him. You know, so I could keep a woman I hate."

"Of course I do," I say. "But what about the..." *What about the baby?* "...plane tickets?"

"Arete didn't make me sign a prenup," he says. "Dumbass probably doesn't know what one is. If things go as I plan it, I'm going to have the house and as much of KE as I can get my hands on. Yeah, so I'm not *entirely* sure what I'm doing, but here's what I'll do if we divorce: she can have all that Melbourne trash. And I'm going to go for our dad's Lamborghini and the Manet. And the Xbox. And for no other reason than to piss her off, I'll take Simone's yacht, since she was legally *my* mom too. Fuck, I probably knew her better than Arete did."

I nod. "It must be rough, divorcing your sister."

"Stepsister," he snaps. "She is my *step*sister."

Still gross.

"All right, I just found a gas station," he says. "See ya soon, Boy Meets World."

"See ya, Hollywood." I hang up the phone and whisper. "By the way, your wife is pregnant and I'm the worst friend ever..."

After I recover from my awkward phone conversation, I join Arete, who is sitting in the living room. I don't know what to say to her, so I keep it brief and stick to the facts.

"I just got off the phone with Elijah," I say, closing the front door behind me. "He'll be here in an hour."

Arete nods to let me know she heard me and takes a deep breath. She sits on the corner of the couch, squeezing a throw pillow in her lap. She's gothed up to the nines today, wearing a dress I recall Elijah once saying was his "favorite." I don't understand why she's putting in extra effort for a man she plans on divorcing. Can't they just get a marriage counselor who isn't me?

"You don't have to do this," I tell her. "I understand. You're pregnant, you're scared, you're hormonal—"

"I've made up my mind," she says. "I *almost* feel bad for him, but he can't stay. He's kept too many secrets from me, and I know he has to be hiding more. I can't double-marry a man I don't know. He's probably planning something right now. He's always had a plan."

I don't want to admit it, but she has a point. He'll probably never tell her that he "halfcidentally" killed her mother, or that he found out her mother was a serial killer. If that comes out, she would sooner burn him alive than forgive him. They bring out the worst in each other without trying, and it's a relationship that has to end. If it doesn't end, the world probably will. Something about her tone worries me though. Not only does her voice shake slightly as she jitters, but it's like she's both paranoid and passionless at the same time. I didn't even know that was possible.

"You sound kind of indifferent," I say. "And a little unstable. Not to be an ass, but did you take your anxiety medicine?"

"Yeah," she says. "I took a double dose of Xanax thinking that would help more but it made me drowsy. So I mathed and took a double dose of caffeine pills to cancel it out. And that gave me the jitters and a headache, so I took some Ibuprofen. But then I started to feel sick at the stomach, so I had some Dramamine. That didn't work, so I took Mylanta."

Great.

"Maybe you should just take a breather," I say. "You're not in the right mindset for something like this."

"I am dead inside and I have no feelings, now will you just go away?"

My way of saying 'no' is to not budge. I don't care what she says, I have a bad feeling about this. I've refereed them enough times to know better than to leave them alone to their massive breakdowns.

"So what are you planning on doing?" I ask.

"I dunno," she says.

"What, so you're just going to wing it?"

"I've always been good at improv."

"But the decision you make today affects your whole life. For fuck's sake, Arete, you're pregnant."

"And that's why I have to do this," she says. "He's planning something. Now go away."

"I know this is upsetting," I say, "but is there something you're not telling me?"

Arete scoffs.

"If I have to referee this, I want to know what's going on," I say. "I've been third-wheeling with you two all year. What changed since yesterday?"

"Everything I ever knew," she says. I see the hint of a fire beneath her eyes, a pure rage that she's suppressing. Other than that, she's still impassive, and that's how she stays.

I spend nearly an hour trying to engage her in conversation, talking about everything from what we're having for dinner tonight, to which version of the Full Metal Alchemist anime is better. But she doesn't respond, not even to tell me to shut up.

After a while, I see a shadow from the driveway and look out the window. Elijah's car is sitting there. Why didn't he call me? Maybe he just now pulled in. I ask Arete to hang on, not telling her he's here, and go outside to greet him. When I tap on his window, he looks half asleep. I'm not sure how long he's been there, just that he was supposed to be here an hour ago.

He rolls down the window and fake-smiles. "I'm here."

Rum is on his breath; I notice an opened bottle sitting in the passenger's seat. A few shots are missing.

"Hollywood! Were you drunk driving?"

"Just rolling the dice," he says.

"I thought you didn't do that!" I say. "You could've killed yourself!"

"I could've died when I crossed the street without looking both ways, but it looks like I'm not a lucky guy."

"Elijah, shut up. This isn't funny."

"You should probably leave," Elijah says. "This is between me and Arete."

"Arete asked me to stay," I lie.

"You don't have to play the mediator," Elijah says. "Things will go the same way regardless of whether you're here or not."

"How so?"

"Go spend the day with Whitney," he says. "Don't waste your time on us."

"Why?"

I expect him to deflect this question too, but he says, "Love isn't enough to keep two people together forever. I thought I learned that lesson when I was a kid, but then I had that first date with Arete… we went ice-skating at some Valentine Sweetheart thing, and there were little snowflakes dotting her eyelashes. Her smile made me forget every lesson I ever learned, and I let my guard down. Nothing has been the same since then." He sighs and bends forward, resting his elbows on his lap and on face in his palms. "I'm sorry," he says.

"No, it's okay," I say. I wait for him to go on, but he doesn't have anything else to say. I pull on the handle of his car door, but it's locked. "Arete's waiting for you."

"Oh, I'm sure she is," he says. There's a distinct edge in his voice. "Tell her I'm not here yet and give me some time."

I hesitate, but say, "Okay."

"I'm serious about what I said though," Elijah says. "Go spend time with Whitney while you still can."

I turn to leave. "I hear you."

"Wait," he says. "Are you really staying? I can't talk you out of it? I'm using my best persuasive tactics here."

"And they're not working," I say.

"What about this?" He pulls his sunglasses down the bridge of his nose and flashes me a gleaming smile. Then he winks without looking creepy. It's so majestic.

"Nope, still not enough."

Stern again, he says, "Just go away."

"I'm not going anywhere."

He swallows. "Be brave, kid. I can't protect you forever."

"I'm pretty sure you're contractually required to do that unless I rat on you, remember?"

"Fuck that contract," he says. "You're free."

"What are you talking about?" I ask. "I'm here because I want to be."

"No," Elijah says. "You're here because I kidnapped you, misled you, and burned your house down. And now I'm letting you go."

He rolls the window up, leaving me with his confusing words. I can't imagine a world where we aren't friends. This is far from the drunkest he's ever been, but this is the least sense he's ever made. They had good reasons for everything they put me through, and they've done a lot to make up for it.

Who would pass up living in a mansion with a small movie theater in it? Everything I could ever need is here.

I return and find Arete still sitting in the exact same position she has been for the past few hours. She hasn't calmed down at all. Her back is straight, she's clenching the throw pillow on her lap, and her eyes are still fixed on the wall, tracing the patterns in a way that reminds me of *The Yellow Wallpaper*. She's not holding the pillow like a comfort object. She's squeezing it in her arms like a stress ball.

I sit on the couch and face her, crossing in front of her so she knows it's me—though I suppose it's a waste of time since I don't have a stompy walk like Elijah does. She would recognize her husband's footsteps. Still, she flinches when I sit next to her.

"Arete?" I say. "Elijah isn't here yet. Give him a little more time."

"William, are you on my side?" she asks, implicitly accusing me of being a traitor.

"Of course," I say. "I'm on both of your sides. We're all best mates forever, remember?"

She doesn't respond, but she squeezes the pillow tighter. It's like she doesn't have a personality anymore, only fear and instinct.

Since Arete is (to be blunt) creeping me out, I wait in the foyer for Elijah. I stare out the window as I wait for him to come out of his car. When he finally does come in, about twenty minutes later, he doesn't announce his presence. The first thing he does when he comes in is to grab his coat off the rack next to the door. He puts it on, groping the outside of his pocket afterward. For some reason, this sticks out to me. I lead him to the living room in silence; the scary look on his face deters me from conversation. His jaw is tight, his hands are twitching, and his eyes are filled with contempt. He's walking at a steady pace, so I scurry off and sit next to Arete before he makes it there. I'm like a child trying to decide between Mommy and Daddy, except my parents are both indignant psychopaths.

But Elijah's countenance changes when he sees Arete sitting there. Somehow oblivious to the fact that she's glaring at him, his lips part, his muscles relax, and his eyes soften.

She stays seated, but establishes eye contact. Both of them probably rehearsed what they were going to say, but neither can bring themselves to say it. I hold my breath, waiting for one of them to start.

"Y-you..." Elijah says. "I don't know what to..."

"I want a divorce," Arete says, blunt.

Elijah and I exchange glances. I don't know what he expects to see in me, but he looks down when all I can give him is a sympathetic nod.

"I don't," he says.

"That's just too bad," Arete says. "I don't love you anymore, and I'm not sure I ever really did."

Despite her word choices, she wasn't putting any extra effort into being cruel. She just didn't have to be that honest.

"So that's it then?" Elijah says. He tries to add something else, but he trembles.

Arete plucks at a loose thread on the throw pillow. "That's all we need to say. We can't be together."

Elijah's lips narrow. "I don't want to do this, but I guess there's no other way." He hesitates for only a second before stuffing his hand in his right coat pocket; his face falls when he grabs whatever is inside. He slowly withdraws his hand, pulling out a toy gun. He taps the trigger twice, and chuckles when water squirts out. "Clever. You even loaded it for me."

He isn't surprised when he looks at Arete and sees that she has his gun. That's why Arete was hugging a throw pillow in her lap. That's why Elijah wanted his coat last night. I'm such a fool.

Arete leans back on the couch and dangles a gun from her finger. "Oh, is this what you're missing?" she says in her best taunting voice, like a true actress playing the Strong Female Character. "Men's pockets are huge. I'd never be able hide a gun from you like this."

Elijah smiles like he's pleased. "Oh, Kit Kat... How did you know?" he says with genuine affection.

Arete stands up and tosses the pillow aside. "Don't you 'Kit Kat' me now, you wanker. In the short time I've known you, not *once* have you ever told me you owned a gun. Hell, you even had the nerve to tell me that you'd never touch a gun again after what happened in Iraq." The mention of Iraq makes Elijah twitch. I can't tell if Arete noticed it or not. "I was doing your laundry, and I found *this* when I was searching for the wash instructions."

"Things change," he says. "But I'm impressed. I really am."

Arete narrows her eyes. "Why did you buy a gun?"

All he says is, "I couldn't cope with losing everything." His vague words linger in the air like a thick cloud of smog poisoning the already sour atmosphere.

"So it's true, then?" she says. "You... you were planning to kill me?"

Say no. Say no. Say no.

Elijah has a lump in his throat. He takes a deep breath, contemplating his next move. An eternity passes before he exhales and says, "Yes. I considered it."

I scoot to the far end of the couch. I don't know what's worse; the fact that he came here with the intention of murdering his wife and my friend, probably with the delusion that I would support him because we're "best mates forever," or the fact that he's still connected to the lie detector when he's *facing the barrel of his own gun*.

Arete scoffs. "Why haven't you done it already? Killed me, I mean. You had plenty of opportunities, why something this sloppy?"

He smiles with only the right corner of his mouth and gives a nonchalant shrug. "You're holding my gun. What am I going to do? Nothing up my sleeve."

She scoots back in a defensive posture and glares. She doesn't believe him, not that I can blame her. She's actually holding it wrong, but that doesn't make me any less nervous. Actually, that makes it worse. So, who do I side with? The sanest one, of course—me.

I butt in. "SO, can we, like… *not* kill each other? It's a nice thought."

Arete's hands shake, but she maintains her aim.

Elijah, confident that Arete won't shoot, doesn't move a muscle. "You've never held a gun before, have you?" he asks, bewildered, like he's realizing this himself as he speaks. There's a subtle hint of concern in his voice.

Arete tightens her grip, but her self-esteem is waning.

"You're holding it wrong," Elijah says. "You could hurt yourself. You're supposed to grip it with both hands or the recoil—"

"*What are you doing?*" I ask in a hushed voice.

While Arete is busy trying to figure out how to properly hold a gun with two hands, he mouths the words, "I'm making it up as I go along."

"T-terminar!" I say. "Tú… soy hablas el estúpido!"

Arete gives me the stink eye. "What?"

"Uh…" Elijah puts his finger and thumb under his chin. "I think he meant 'stop, you're saying stupid things?' But the literal translation is 'to end, you am speak the stupid,' so I'm not sure…"

Arete huffs. "Well, he has a point then." She still has her gun aimed at Elijah, but her hands are wrapped around each other and her thumbs are crossed.

Elijah raises his brows and shakes his head. "Kit Kat, honey, if you fire like that, the slide could..." He pauses. "Never mind, I'll just show you."

Arete's hands shake harder as Elijah holds his squirt gun for demonstration. She holds her ground as seriously as she would if she were facing an AK-47. Now that I've figured out what he's trying to do, I realize this may be the only smart move he's made today; if Arete fires the gun holding it the wrong way, her target will be unpredictable, and he won't be able to dodge if he can't tell where she's pointing. She could also hurt herself by mistake, or worse, me. I wonder how many bullets Elijah loaded in the chamber. Not too many, I hope.

"You need to wrap your hands around it like this." Elijah turns slightly to the side so she can see how he's holding it, which makes Arete's hands shake furiously. "That's not it," he says. "You need to... hold on, I'll show you."

He walks at a normal pace, but his approach startles her, causing her to fall. I squeeze my eyes shut as she aims for his chest and pulls the trigger... but nothing happens.

"You have the thumb safety on," Elijah says.

Arete turns gun over, searching for the thumb safety. My only comfort is that she probably doesn't know what a thumb safety is, a dream that is crushed when she finds it almost immediately.

"WHY ARE YOU HELPING HER?" I ask.

Elijah gives the same carefree shrug he did earlier; I jump off the couch and turn to run away, like he *should* be doing, but Arete points the gun at me and cries for me to stop.

"Don't even *think* about it!" Arete shouts. She doesn't look like herself. It's like her heart just died in her chest, and she's forgotten who I am. Does she recognize herself at all? "Hands in the air, don't move!" she yells. "If you call the police, you know Elijah will rat me out. I'll go down with him, and that is *not* going to happen!"

Having a gun aimed at me for the first time in my play-it-safe life makes me doubt that I know her as well as I thought. Is this what "nervous breakdown" Arete looks like? I mean, I've seen "nervous breakdown" Elijah before—at least once a week—but this is new. I hold my left hand in the air and step back, hoping she won't be picky about the fact that I have one arm in a cast.

I look to Elijah, who has backed up several feet. He drops his squirt gun, puts his hands in the air, and returns my frown. Maybe he was trying to get close enough to her to retrieve the gun, since he knew he had it locked. But that's a risky move, since she could have unlocked it previously. Besides, he lost his chance for that by giving her the answer. I guess I'll never know what his plan was since Arete's going to kill both of us now.

Arete points the gun back at Elijah. "I want answers, and *nobody* is leaving this room until I get them."

"Please," I say. "Nothing good will come of this. Shooting your husband won't solve anything."

Arete scoffs. "I think it'll fix a few loose ends."

"Like what?" Elijah asks.

"I filled in a few blanks on my own," she says. "You're the only son of the man I thought was my father. But, for some reason, he chose me and my mother over you. With them gone, there was nothing to keep you from coming back. You used your inheritance to fund your plan to marry me so you could take back what was yours. Am I right?"

He gives a curt nod. "All those things are true."

"What I *don't* understand is how Uncle Antonis fits into this," she says. "Why did he pretend he didn't know you?"

"He was in on it."

Arete adjusts the gun in her hands, her right thumb crossed behind the slide (still wrong) while maintaining her aim at Elijah. "That doesn't make any sense," she says. "I want the *whole* truth, not technicalities."

"Very well," he says. "It was his idea, in a way. He thought we'd make a cute couple, and at first I thought it was too taboo, but it didn't stop me from having a huge crush on you. But none of that means I don't care about you."

Arete glares, skeptical. "That doesn't explain why he pretended he didn't know who you were."

"He did it because I asked him to," he says. "I wouldn't say he and I were close, but he did want me to follow in my father's footsteps."

"Bullshit. Why would he try to kill me and steal my shares?"

"He didn't hire the hit man to kill you," Elijah says. "You guys came up with that one on your own. I hired him."

I jump back and trip on my own feet. Arete loses composure and almost drops the gun.

"So you could kill me and he could give you 49%?" she asks.

"No," he says. "So I could rescue you."

Arete's mouth hangs open.

Knowing how he operates, I ask, "Can you say that in a complete sentence?"

Elijah laughs. "Sure thing, Boy Meets World. I hired Hoyt Galligan to kill Arete so I could save her life."

I rub my eyes. "You have *got* to be kidding me."

"Why would you do something that *stupid*?" Arete asks.

"You didn't trust me," Elijah says. "I needed you to fall in love with me, but it wasn't going fast enough." Elijah gives me an irritable side glance. "But then *somebody* had to show up and complicate things."

I groan. "Oh my *god*, I am *so* sorry I ruined your plans to be a hero and get laid!"

"Shut up, William!" Arete turns her head back to Elijah. "And you are SICK!"

Elijah ignores her and faces me. "While I'm confessing to things, I burned your house down for the same reason."

"WHAT?" Arete and I say in unison.

"I thought you were destroying the evidence!" I say, though I can't be any angrier about it than I already have been. I'm mad the asshole burned down my house period; I couldn't care less *why* he did it.

"Yeah, also true," Elijah says. "Kind of a 'two birds, one stone' deal. Well, three birds. Burn the evidence, get the girl... and keep an eye on you. Sorry, Pool Noodle. I just didn't trust you yet."

Arete's voice shakes as she holds back her tears. "What are you *doing*? You should be apologizing to *me*, not *him*!"

"Why would I apologize to you?" Elijah asks. "You weren't supposed to find out. And, let's be honest, you kind of deserved it."

Arete pulls the trigger, causing a loud, resonant blast. I duck behind the couch, not that it would help because I'm behind Arete, but Elijah doesn't move. I peek around the corner.

"You missed," he says, uninterested.

"I didn't mean to," she says.

"I know." Elijah lowers his hands to the level of his neck, but doesn't reach out. He takes cautious steps toward her, but she backs up in fear. "You have a clean shot," he says.

"And you know what I think? I think you're too scared to fire again."

I pull out my phone again, but Arete hears the keypad beeping when I type in 9. She points the gun back at me. "Don't think I won't shoot—"

Before she can finish her sentence, Elijah shouts in a panic. "I murdered Antonis because he found out about the hit man, not to protect you."

I slide my phone toward Arete. Instead of taking it, she swings her arm around, pointing the gun back at Elijah. He exhales in relief.

"You said he was in on it!" Arete says, livid.

"Sort of," Elijah says. "His plans didn't involve killing anyone though, so when Boy Meets World told him about the hit man, he confronted me. That's not to say he wasn't trying to take the company—he was using Mikhail to tip the balance so he could have an additional 2% of KE, making him the 51% owner. He was in a rush when he found out we were getting married, because he knew I wouldn't cave as easily as you would. I mean, he expected having me in the office, but not so soon. You were more of a... minor inconvenience to him. So you were never in any danger."

Arete twists her mouth in frustration.

Elijah forces a smile, but it comes off as awkward. "But hey, if we stay together, we can buy out Mikhail. He can do his band, and we can endorse him. Win, win."

Arete sobs, and tears start to well up in her eyes. "You are the *Devil*! We have *nothing* together!"

"That's not true," Elijah says. He approaches Arete, his arms still held up in surrender, until she's backed up against the wall. "I'm not going to hurt you."

She whimpers, but doesn't fire. He lays his hand on the barrel, but he doesn't seize it from her. Instead, he gently pushes her hand down. She doesn't drop the gun, but it hangs limp at her side. As she hyperventilates, he hushes her and wipes her tears away with his thumb.

"We have *everything* together," he says. "I know my methods were a little... unorthodox. But I never did anything to hurt you, Kit Kat. I love you."

"Never hurt me?" She pushes him away and sidesteps several feet out of his reach. Her hands still shaking, she resumes her aim at his chest. "You used me, lied to me—"

"I *NEVER* LIED TO YOU!" Elijah shouts. "NAME *ONE TIME* I LIED TO YOU!"

His sudden eruption makes her scream, and enormous tears roll down her cheeks. "You never lied, but you were never completely honest with me," she says to sate him without removing his blame.

"That's *your* fault," he says. "If you wanted me to share more, you should've asked and listened. It's not like you tried to get to know me anyway. All you ever wanted was sex and a security blanket. You are the most *cold-hearted, selfish*—"

Arete pulls the trigger. Being the brave man I am, I cover my ears, close my eyes, and crouch down. Elijah doesn't scream, but I hear a low grunt under the gunfire. My instinct is to rush toward him like an idiot, just like I ran into that dark alleyway on February 24th. He's grimacing and putting pressure on his thigh, but I have a feeling she wasn't aiming for his thigh.

"Are you okay?" Elijah asks.

"Me?" I say. "*You're* the one bleeding out all over the floor. How are you not screaming?"

He laughs. "This isn't the first time I've gotten shot, and it probably won't be the last."

Arete ignores my presence at his side, aims the gun, and yells at Elijah. "You want me to get to know you? Fine!" She smiles with her mouth, but her eyes are wide open. "Why did my parents hide you from me? What is it about you that's so *awful* that they *erased* you?"

He scoots up against the wall to support himself and closes his eyes. "They thought I was a danger to you."

"Why?"

"Because that's what I wanted them to think," he says. "I was playing them. The truth is, I loved you to pieces. We played together every day. You were my favorite person in the world, no matter where you came from. I knew we weren't related, but I didn't care. When I held you for the first time and looked in your eyes, I decided I wanted to be the best older brother I could be. I've always loved you, every day of your life."

Elijah is bleeding on the tile, Arete is hyperventilating, and there's a good chance I won't see tomorrow... but now more than ever, I can't help but think: *still gross*. Downright nasty, as a matter of fact. It's inconceivable that I ever wanted them to be together. But the only person whose opinion matters is the one who's holding the firearm.

Arete is holding the gun the same way as before, but her finger twitches away from the trigger. She stares at the hole she put in his leg, watching his hot, sticky blood climb through the fibers of his jeans.

"I was trying to get rid of Simone," Elijah says, snapping her out of the trance. "My mom tried to kill herself because she couldn't bear to see Dad with a younger woman. Dad wouldn't let me visit her in the psych ward for some reason. And he was always at work. And Simone, well, she and I fought like siblings. We were close in age and competing for the same man's favoritism. Don't get me wrong, I didn't hate her. But I thought, if Simone was out of the picture, Mom might get better and we could be a family again. I knew getting rid of Simone would mean getting rid of you, but I didn't think losing my mom was worth the risk."

Arete's wrist quivers. "What did you do?"

"It was stupid." He looks down and presses his fingertips to his forehead. "I had just turned twelve... I thought if Simone thought I would hurt you, she'd take you and go back to Australia."

"*What did you do*?" Arete is near tears.

"I... That recurring dream you have..." He swallows. "It's my fault. I choked you. I acted like I was going to kill you, but pulled away for a second so you could scream and wake Simone up. She did, but the second he saw those marks on your neck, Dad chose you two over me and sent me off to live with my grandparents in Athens. Then they erased me from your life."

Arete's mouth twists, but it's to cover up the sadness in her eyes. She doesn't want to feel sorry for him. She probably sees it as another reason to hate him if anything, but with each new bit of information, her paranoia is being eased. Or maybe she's just sobering up.

"I miss things the way they were," Elijah says without the slightest hint of rage in his voice. He looks up at her, using his eyes to plead. "I just want to pretend it none of it ever happened. We can move forward, have a family."

"How can we move forward when you're still living in the past?" Arete sniffs. "I am *not* a time machine that will bring your parents back. You think you love me, but you don't!"

"I do love you," Elijah says. "I'm *obsessed* with you. That dorky look on your face when you get lost in thought, how you're still afraid of thunderstorms, your quirky smile, how innocent you look when you sleep, the baby chick noise you make when you sneeze, the way—"

"Stop!" Arete sobs. "You're a lunatic!"

"All I ever wanted was a family." Elijah's eyes glisten with a peculiar mixture of hope and sorrow. He blinks away the first and only tear he's shed through this whole ordeal. "Arete, we don't have to fight over this. You know I had good intentions."

I wouldn't bank on that last bit. I mean, I'm a little confused, but this is what I've got down so far: He hired a hitman to kill his stepsister, to kill the hitman, to impress his stepsister, to take his stepsister's inheritance, which is actually *his* inheritance, which his father kept from him, which is somehow his stepsister's fault. Got it. Can I go home now?

No, I can't, because Elijah burned down my house to impress his stepsister, then bought a gun to *kill* his stepsister, then changed his mind and left it in his coat pocket, then changed it again decided to kill her, who then decided to kill him, and now... I give up. I don't know what's going on right now. I just want to know why they BOTH decided to carry on with whatever plan they had even though I stayed here, like I'm some ride-or-die friend who would help either of them cover up a murder. Again. The whole point of me being here was to prevent something like this. I regret my persistence. Elijah was right; I should've just borrowed Arete's Lamborghini and taken Whitney out on a date. This isn't how I want to die.

"Why should I forgive you?" Arete says. "You were going to *kill* me!"

Elijah's smile is inappropriately wide and delirious. "And I suppose *you're* going to kill *me*?"

Arete glares. "Maybe."

"You don't even eat meat." Elijah says. "You cried once because Dad killed a spider instead of letting it outside. Do you remember that?"

Her eyes widen. "H-how did you know that? I was a teenager."

"Dad reached out to me in the final years of his life," he says, mild this time. "That was one of the last things he said to me. I think his exact words were 'that girl is too gentle for you, and that's why I can't let you see her again.' And I guess he was right. I've done some callous things to you without even trying."

She acts confused. "You were talking about me?"

"Dad talked about you a lot. He was proud of you. You were the only one of us who turned out right."

Arete lowers the gun for just a moment. I'm not sure if Elijah's plan is working or not, because she raises it up higher than before. I think she's trying to point it toward his head, but it's hard to tell because her hands are shaking.

Elijah looks up at me. "Will you help me up?"

"I don't think you should stand," I say.

He reaches for my hand anyway, and I do my best to help him come to a stand. He nicknamed me 'Pool Noodle' for a reason, of course, so it's no surprise that he's still getting most of his support from the wall. Taking his hand, I try to hold him back, but he isn't interested. Still holding his bullet wound, he grimaces and staggers toward Arete, who adjusts her aim accordingly.

"Don't even think about touching me," she says.

Before Elijah can meet her, he stops in his tracks and involuntarily bends over. "You shot me and I still love you. Isn't that enough?"

She pauses for a moment. "No."

He searches her eyes for warmth, but finds none. They stare at each other, not saying a word. I consider breaking the silence with an interjection before someone gets hurt. Elijah deserves to know that he's going to be a father, but there's no telling how Arete would react. She's a dangerous mix of paranoid and violent, and she's holding Elijah's gun in an unstable position with trembling hands. I can't count on Elijah either; his mood keeps swinging like a pendulum. My phone is all the way across the room, and if I make a sudden movement to retrieve it, I'll be a dead man. I consider making a speech about friendship like in an anime, but she'd probably just shoot me so I'd shut up.

"Then what more do you want?" Elijah asks her. "Just tell me, whatever it is, I'll give it to you."

"I…" Arete hesitates. "I want you to leave."

"I can't do that."

"You can't, or you won't?" she asks.

"We're perfect together," he says. "I know I started off with ulterior motives, but by the time I got to know you, I was doing all of this for *us.* All we have to do is pretend it never happened. We can forget about the Konstantinous and start our own family—the Walkers. I'll make sure you have your dream wedding. You won't have to worry about KE; I'll take care of that, so you can be an actress. And you know I want kids more than anything, but I'll wait as long as I have to if you're not ready. It'll be hard, but I mean that."

Arete steals a glance at her own abdomen and furrows her brow. "Shut up!"

"It's a big house, but we'll have Pool Noodle and Whitney here," he says. "We'll be one big, happy foster family."

"I said *shut up!*"

"Would you rather move to Australia?" he asks. "I love you more than I hate Australia."

"Stop saying you love me!"

"I could never live without you," Elijah says. "Συγγνώμη, αγάπη μου. Αν με συγχωρέσεις, μπορούμε να αρχίσουμε μια καινούρια ζωή μακριά από όλα αυτά. Θα είμαι ειλικρινής μαζί σου, ψυχή μου. Θα σου λέω τα πάντα."

I have no idea what he just said, but it sounded beautiful and sincere. Whatever it was, it wasn't what she wanted to hear. Mistrusting and infuriated, Arete scrutinizes his every movement as he tries to straighten his posture. I provide some help, but he manages well on his own, considering. He gives me a courteous smile to thank me for my efforts, and stops using me as a crutch. My hand travels to my shoulder, brushing the area he abandoned.

Elijah's demeanor is peaceful, but Arete doesn't expect him to release his leg wound and step toward her so suddenly. Arete staggers, stepping on my phone and sliding backward. Her hands slip as she falls, pulling the trigger.

I clench my eyes shut, falling backward and landing on my rear. Somehow, this gunshot feels louder than the last, not just in volume but in force as well. It's so close to me. It's almost like I...

But no. Other than a cracked tailbone (and a broken arm), I don't feel any pain. I'm okay. I dare to open my eyes.

Elijah is lying on his back. He tries to lift himself up, but can only manage a few inches. His chest heaves as he coughs, blood rising to the surface of his mouth, coating his teeth and lips bright red. I see that there's a new bullet wound, this time in his chest. Frozen in place, I cover my mouth.

Arete's hand falls, and the second her gun hits the floor, I take the opportunity to jolt across the room to retrieve the offending phone so I can dial 911. Arete shrieks, finally realizing what she's done. The madwoman frantically bows down over her husband's body, her knees at either side of him, and her hands over his chest. She uses her bodyweight to put pressure on his wound, trying in vain to stop the bleeding. Her teardrops fall on his face.

"Oh, what have I done?" Arete says through sobs.

Inexplicably, Elijah laughs. "You shot me in the chest." Blood erupts from his cough.

Arete's lips quiver. "I didn't mean to."

"I know." Elijah strokes her cheek with his thumb and gazes at her fondly. "It's okay."

"I didn't mean to!" Arete says again. She's crying so hard that her words are barely coherent. "I didn't mean to, I didn't mean to shoot at all, you just scared me, and I slipped—"

Elijah shushes her. "It'll be okay, baby."

A Quick Thanks

Hey! Thank you for reading my book. If you enjoyed it, please take the time to submit a review and tell your friends. Harry Potter spread through word of mouth, and I can't underrate how much it means to writers when you share our work. People like to say that the written word is dead and no one reads anymore, but we know better. Book 2 is in progress, and will have far more illustrations and a larger budget. In the meantime, did you know you can find the lead antagonists on social media? Arete is on Instagram as @battybabyx, and Elijah is on twitter as @ElijahJWalker.

twitter.com/ElijahJWalker | instagram.com/BattyBaby

Discussion Questions

These questions are designed to spark deep analysis and discussion for individuals or groups, ie., solo readers, book clubs, booktube. There are no right or wrong answers to these questions. Have fun.

1. Why do you think William so easily became preoccupied with the lives of his captors?

2. Elijah made some puzzling choices in the last chapter. What do you think he was trying to do and to what end goal? Were William and Arete's respective understandings of the situation correct? If not, what do you think they get wrong?

3. Is Elijah truly in love with Arete, or is he obsessed with her? Can he be both at the same time, or does one preclude the other?

4. Growing up, William was occasionally criticized by other Latinxs for being "too white," and he took it to heart. Do you think he would be closer with his family if he didn't feel ostracized by his own community, and how does his life of self-isolation factor into the story's development?

5. Arete and Elijah are mutually codependent, with Arete controlling finances and expecting Elijah to make and approve decisions for her, both big and small. Judging by their pasts and what you know of their parents, why do you think each of them are okay with this arrangement? Can a relationship like this be sustainable?

6.   Do you think William is intentionally lying to the reader about his sexuality, or do you think he's in denial of being bisexual? Why? Along that vein, do you think William is unaware of his feelings for Elijah, or is he hiding them from the reader? Do you trust William as a narrator?

7.   Despite being heterosexual, Elijah has a lot of gay and bisexual guyfriends. What do you think he gets out of these friendships that he can't get out of straight men, or even women of any sexual orientation?

8.   When it comes to the antagonists, Arete and Elijah, do you sympathize with one more than the other? If so, why?

9.   If you were in William's shoes, what would you have done differently?

10.   If you took all of the red flags from #Arelijah, tied them together, and braided them into a noose, would they get the point?

11.   The Schukyill and Delaware Rivers together provide Philadelphia with 230 million gallons of drinking water daily. Is that enough water to quench William's tragic thirst?

Tentative Description for Book Two

Rewinding to the 90's, sixteen-year-old Simone Wagner escapes her abusive family in Australia by graduating high school early and attending an American university. It was supposed to be a fresh start, but she soon finds out that the cost of finding freedom too soon is being scared and vulnerable. Things quickly go from bad to worse as she struggles to live an adult's life, so she resorts to a sugar daddy for security while secretly crushing on her college friend Lola DiPietro. Soon, keeping up the façade of being eighteen and struggling with her sexual orientation becomes the least of her troubles when she encounters a much bigger threat.

Nine-year-old child genius Elijah is still adjusting to his life in America. His biggest comfort in leaving Greece was believing his parents moving in together was the end of an on again, off again relationship and the beginning of a secure family unit. However, that dream falls apart almost as soon as it begins because of his father's wandering eye and his mother's instability.

www.ingramcontent.com/pod-product-compliance
Lightning Source LLC
Chambersburg PA
CBHW071728110726

47908CB00006B/1534